Silver Well

by

Alexandria May Ausman

Book cover illustration by Alexandria May Ausman
Editor: Jon M. Ausman

Library of Congress Control Number: 2025905274

ISBN: 978-1-963335-40-8 (ebook)
ISBN: 978-1-963335-39-2 (paperback)

Published By:
Ausman & Cousins LLC
1700 North Monroe Street
Suite 11, Box 284
Tallahassee, Florida 32303-0501

For author interviews: ausman@embarqmail.com

Shadow King Jon M. Ausman
2024 to Present

Das Kaiser Haus Series

The Collar King Series

The Most Brutal Man in Europe Series

Claus's Revelations (Chapters 1 to 8)
Priceless Changes (Chapters 9 to 17)
Silver Well (Chapters 18 to 25)
Book Four (coming soon)

The Psycho Series

Cemetery Kid (Chapters 1 to 20)
Stop Calling Me Psycho (Chapters 21 to 33)
Motor-Psycho (Chapters 34 to 44)
Delusion of the Collar and the Key (Chapters 45 to 53)
Brutality's Prisoner (Chapters 54 to 64)
Aesthetic Akathisia (Chapters 65 to 74)
Metallic Burden (Chapters 75 to 83)

27 Masters Series

Anita the Benevolent (Chapters 1 to 7)
The Beast and the Witch (Chapters 8 to 16)
High Priestess of Schizophrenia (Chapters 17 to 24)
The Professional Dominatrix (Coming soon)

Stand Alone Books

The Grannybat's Weird Tales & Gothic Stories Volume 1

Book 3 Characters: Silver Well

Agnette Krauss: the mother of Christian Axel, daughter of Gregor and Ingrid

Albertus: a former Torture Master who serves Valintin

Amanda: a Haus Torture Mistress

Anna Altergott: a Haus FemDom

Annette: a deceased Haus black collar

Attila, Doctor: the Haus physician

Audry Baus: a Haus FemDom, spouse of Fritz

Birgit: a black collar maid, lover of Xavier, sister of Viviana

Blum: spouse of Almut

Bora: a Russian Guard

Byron Schmidt: a Haus Dominant, a Voting Council member, son of Xavier and Birgit

Cary: the Shadow King, 1973 to 2024

Christian: the anger and lust shard

Christian Axel Schmidt: a Haus Dominant, the Priceless, son of Xavier

Claus Albrecht: an Elder of the Haus

Cora Reinhardt: a Haus Fur Queen

Dämonen: the Demon sharing the shard Maximillian

Der Goldene Hund: the Voice or the Boss shard; the Conscious shard

Der Makellos: Leo's German Shepherd named 'the

unblemished'

Die Brutale: three shards melded together; Mad Max, Max, and Christian

Edelle: a Dungeon Mistress

Eric: a Haus Dominant, co-founder of FBL

Felicity: the Mother Lamb, a shard

Florian Schmidt: the first Priceless, deceased

Freidrick Schmidt: a Haus Voter, son of Bernt

Fritz Finck: a Haus Dominant

Geraldine: a lamb that prepares Christian Axel's meals

Gisla: a Haus Femdom

Gretta Albrecht: a Haus FemDom, the Silk Queen

Grisla: a Russian Guard

Heidi: the deceased Mortar Queen

Henri: the deceased Mortar Prince

Hubertus: a former Torture Master who serves Magnus

Ingrid Reinhardt: spouse of Xavier, ally of Claus, sister of Keifer

Isoff: a Russian Guard

Ivan: retired captain of the Russian Guard

Jacob Wagner: a Haus Dominant

Jager: Jacob Wagner's partner

Jason: a Black collar Torture Master

Johannes: a Dungeon Master

Jonas Weiss: an Elder of the Haus. Spouse of Christian Axel

Jon M. Ausman: current Keyholder, Shadow King 2024 to

present

Justus Schmidt: son of Bernt and Ingrid, half-brother to Christian Axel

Karstin Baus: a Haus FemDom

Kay: a Haus Dominant, co-founder of FBL

Kilian Altergott: a Haus Fur King

Leo Albrecht: an Elder of the Haus, cousin of Claus

Lucus: a Haus Dominant, a royal

Mad Max: the sadistic shard of Maximillian, aka the Heart and Judgment

Mad Maxx: husband of Meine Liebe; a Haus Dominant

Mad Maxx: the masochistic shard, also the Brain and Guilt

Mad Maxximillian die Brutal: the most brutal man in Europe

Magnus: a Haus Dominant, member of the Wolf Pack

Maksim: a Russian Guard

Malfred Krauss: a Haus Elder

Marc: a deceased Black collar

Matilda: spouse of Ruslan

Matz: a Haus Dominant, a pimp and manager

Max: the Soul shard

Maximillian: the seductive shard, the Libido

Maxximillian: the shard controlling the wheel

Meine Liebe: submissive and spouse of Mad Maxx

Milo: a deceased Haus black collar Torture Master

Mott: a Haus silver collar

Nele: a fifth floor Black Collar attendant

Nicholas: a black collar head waiter, married to Karstin

Noah: a Dungeon Master, son of Bladrick Reinhardt

Peter Schmidt: a Dominant of Der Kaiser Haus; uncle of Christian Axel, son of Bernt

Petrov: a Russian Guard

Rachel Krauss: an American, known as Meine Liebe, designated wife of Christian Axel

Reece Altergott: a deceased clinical psychiatrist

Rolf Schmidt: a Haus voter, son of Derbeck

Roselina: a Haus black collar, spouse of Cary, Dark Bonded to Rolf

Rudolph: a Haus Stable Master

Ruslan: Captain of the Russian Guard

Samuel: spouse of Rudolph

Sasha: a Russian Guard

Sigrid: a Haus FemDom, candidate to be Christian Axel's Regent

Taube: a Ram, Taube in German is "Dove"

Valitin: a Haus dominant, a member of the Wolf Pack

Vivianna: a Haus FemDom, sister of Birgit

Xavier Schmidt: deceased Fur King, father of Justus, Byron and Christian, brother of Derbeck and Bernt, known as the "Child Killer"

Preface

The Mortar King, Christian Axel, has evaded multiple assassination attempts whether by the Stasi, yard dogs, torture, or disease. Facing a deadline five months away where he will be imprisoned in the "Mortar Palace" for life, Christian seeks love. He also prepares the groundwork to protect his allies and the few true friends he has.

As King, Christian Axel, has made a few people royal after the death of his Mortar Queen Heidi. Rather than be loyal, some of these new royals make a power play to usurp the Mortar Throne for their own children.

The is the story of Christian Axel acting to cement his position as King and Master of the Haus among those who are grateful and ungrateful. To do so he has to put in place a Vampire, a retired Captain of the Russian Guard, and the badly wounded but ever determined Silk Queen.

There is a person who lives within the walls of the Haus both unseen and unheard by the residents and those who serve them. Is this person a benefactor for Christian Axel, a deadly opponent, or more mentally challenged than Christian.

Language in italics is a conversation between the adult male Master Mad Maxx and his female submissive Meine Liebe. The editor is related to both.

Chapter 18: Regency Inn

Noah followed behind me without any sound but that of his ragged breathing. No doubt he was thrilled. He must have been thinking he was about to be viewing treasure that he could only imagine in his wildest dreams.

However, that joy was about to be crushed. Just as it had been for me not that long before. The Palace was the exact opposite of the many rumors und speculations spread by the Haus residents. The stories they told each other had become pure myth over the centuries since the founders first invented the Mortar Throne.

I could tell his initial eager steps were becoming slowed with confusion as we grew closer to the dungeon staircase. It wasn't the secret that the Mortar King's court was located somewhere within the foundations of the Haus. I assumed he was wondering if this were the truth. Then why did I seemed to be leading him out toward the way to escape the dark cells below. When we reached the end of the stoney hallway that spilled into the final stretch before the steps, I turned around to face him.

With the sparkle of mischief in my gaze I said, "Hold on there, stud. We need to wait until we are certain no one will become the accidental witness to things I wish to exclusively show you. Now, you go out there in that empty space. I want you to make sure that there isn't any stray Dungeon Masters, Mistresses nor slaves about to wander into this area. Do not fail me, Noah. If you are shoddy in fulfilling this command I give to you. Then I assure you the results will prove deadly. For both of us. This you understand, ja?"

Noah's expression became frightened as he nodded and replied, "I do, your Majesty. What signal do I use if I find that your conditions for complete stealth have been met?"

I chuckled low and responded, "Just glance my direction and nod. Then watch my hand signals. I will need your help in retrieving something with quickness. We won't have even a second to fool around with misunderstandings. Plus speaking to each other may draw unwanted attention. Now, go. Hurry up. We are wasting time I don't have, dammit." I motioned him to do as I said, and he took off in the rapid stride to obey.

I leaned back into the hallway wall. I was careful to hide out of sight within the pitch blackness of the dimly lit corridor. Noah's huge frame could be viewed easily from my vantage there in the shadows. He walked nonchalantly from one path entry to the next. At the mouth of each, he would pause. The Head Master pretended to be stretching while he stood there straining his ears. I knew that he was carefully listening for the sounds of approaching footsteps.

Appearing to hear nothing of interest, he turned his attentions to the narrow stone staircase. I watched him take the place on the bottom step and gaze up them with extreme interest. This behavior made me think that he was sure someone was coming down.

However, he broke from this examination of the final entry point and looked toward my direction. Without a sound he nodded his head toward me.

I took a deep breath and braced my resolve to see this necessary action finished to completion. I was aware doing this was dangerous as hell, and not just because I was being accompanied by the unexpected accomplice. If I were spotted or if Noah turned out to be the stool pigeon, my fate as the Mortar King would seem the mercy in comparison to the punishment I would endure for it.

I rushed toward him and gestured him to follow in silence. He left his first step perch with speed. When I halted abruptly in front of the ancient wooden door located under the dungeon staircase, the surprise was evident in his expression. I put my finger to my lips with the motion of the 'shhhing,' then pointed at the toe of my left boot.

Noah's eyebrows lifted to demonstrate shock at this strange silent message I was giving to him. With the glance of irritation I swung the leg that I wished him to show attention to and pushed it toward him.

The Head Master caught my foot mid-air and watched me again point with urgency toward the toe of my boot. He leaned down and examined the tip, trying to understand what it was I wished him to do with it.

Suddenly, his eyes lit up with excitement. He'd noticed, at last, the irregularity in the sole. Without another moment's hesitation he pulled down the tough leather and removed the item I'd stored within that hidden compartment.

I gestured him to release me, then for him to use the key to unlock the Palace door. Noah moved quickly to obey. While he worked the lock, I took the moment to glance around. I wished to be damned sure we were not being spied on by the Dungeon dwellers nor any wall DJs. It made me feel a bit better to be unable to identify anyone lurking about in the halls.

The old rusty hinges wailed in protest as Noah forced it open. He moved aside and I pushed into the cracked space while motioning him to follow. I let out my breath thankful that we'd managed to get inside without incident.

It was so dark we could barely see our hands before our faces. I touched Noah to get his attention. He appeared to understand that I was trying to inform him that door needed to be locked behind us. I didn't want anyone to notice the Palace was entertaining visitors, ja?

While the Head Master saw to it that our tracks were covered, I slowly limped down the dank hallway. I could hear Noah using careful steps doing his best to follow without straying too far from my lead.

That trip through the blackness wasn't the long one. The narrow corridor quickly emptied into the vastness of the torturous coronation hall. Even in the dim light I could make out the outlines of the oil lamps used by the staff that attended the Palace every week.

I hurriedly grabbed one of them and granted us the mercy of light within a few moments after. Noah's illuminated image indicated he was more than a little befuddled by the sights that were shown before his eyes.

A small chuckle escaped me upon seeing his confusion, then I said in the whisper, "What's the madder, lover? You look like you've seen the ghost."

Noah shook his head and with the frown and replied, "Forgive me, Mad Maxx, but I wish to ask you. Why would the Founders hide the Mortar Palace under the dungeon staircase. I've passed that door for years and always thought it was the locked broom closet or storage area for the black collar maids. Everyone that lives in the Dungeon has passed it a thousand times. As far as I can recall no one ever thought it was of any importance, nor asked questions about what's in there."

I nodded and said with the humored tone, "You already answered your own question, Noah. There is never the better hiding spot than the one in plain sight, ja?"

He smiled slightly and replied, "Ah, you are right as usual, Mad Maxx. That does make sense, but now I wonder something else."

I had to stifle the giggle as I said, "What could you possibly be confounded by now? Perhaps you wish to know how long it is going to take to reach my Palace from this dark hell hole. Especially since it is supposed to be the fantastical place among the clouds of Heaven. That is lit by the golden rays of precious gems of rare purity."

Noah shook his head slowly and his frown returned as he replied, "Nein. I'm not ignorant enough to think that we can travel to your Palace quickly, Mad Maxx. I realize this is the false front intended to fool anyone that may accidently enter. It must be the long journey through empty halls behind that silver gate over there. I assume they added many security measures to ensure those that come this far will believe there's nothing worthy of further investigation. What has peaked my interest is the reasons the Founders would desecrate the graves of their loved ones as they have done." That response wasn't one I was expecting to hear.

I burrowed my frow as I asked, "What is this you're saying? Why would you think you're standing in the catacomb tombs of the ancients?"

He nodded and cast his eyes toward the gated hallway as he replied, "This must be. I can smell the old death and decay of their graves. Wait, are you saying this isn't the place the dead have been stored?"

I shook my head and took on the expression of seriousness as I said, "Noah, this is the Mortar Palace reception area. Come with me and I will take you on that tour I promised you of my fine castle. You know, the one that is allegedly decorated with silver and rare stones. If you wish I can even get you the first dance with one of my most beloved court members. my King's men and King's women are always eager to do whatever they can to get ahead in my favor." I burst into maniacal laughter while Noah's expression took on that of total terror.

He trembled slightly as he pointed at the silver gate and said in the whisper, "I think you are trying to tell me that I made too hasty the decision to wish to know the secrets that lay behind that enclosure, ja? It's too late to unknow the known. I say to you, Mad Maxx, no matter what horror you are about to reveal to me, your most unworthy servant. I won't stray from my loyalty to my Lord and Master. I beg of you to lead me down the dark path of knowledge and you shall see me feast upon it without complaint of its bitter taste." He took to his knees at my feet, then bowed his head in reverence.

I got my demonic humor noises under control as I replied, "Rise then dearest Head Master and follow your King. There is good reason entering the Palace of the Foundation Monarch is forbidden to all but the most vile of this Haus. You are about to find yourself burdened with the nightmare that will never end. Not for me and now never ever again for you either." Without another word I motioned him to stand.

He followed while I limped to the gate. Silence was between us while he used my contraband key to unlock the last barrier to that horrible cell called the Mortar Palace. We walked in single file slowly down the dank, dark, foul smelling hallway. I could hear Noah making audible gaging noises behind me. I didn't know what was causing him to feel the need to retch. The smell of rot doesn't bother me in the least. It may have at some point in my younger years but by that time the scent of decimation, well it was like the long lost brother to me. Yikes!

At last, we arrived at the cell that was nothing more than the room carved into the mortar foundation of the Haus. He stood there with his eyes wide in pure disgust upon the vision before him. The silver bars that covered the entire length of my cell glistened in the weak light of my lantern. I quickly moved it to the best position to help him open the metal lock of the door.

Noah made the noise of near vomiting as he exclaimed in the desperate wail, "Nein, this cannot be it, Mad Maxx. Oh my God, why would they do this to the King of the Haus? If this is a joke, consider me fooled. End this cruel game you're playing with me. Please, I beg of you, stop it." He fell to his knees in front of the cell door and began to sob violently.

I shook my head then calmly replied, "I am brutal to show you this, my love, but you are wrong to say you are the fool in this case. The honest idiot is me. Mainly, because like you and everyone else, I thought to be the Lord and Master of the Haus was the place of luxury and power. As you now can clearly see, it is anything but that. The Founders were indeed the clever lot. They understood that the man that can be the heart of this foul place should possess a Palace the reflects the evil souls of those he commands. However, that said. Noah, I'm surprised at you. You of all people surely can appreciate the truthful treasures that surround you. Don't you see these bars? They are made of pure silver. Each inch of them created by years of sacrifice and hard labors. Both from the Dungeon Master that molded the metal to the child and the innocent submissive that lost it." I reached out and gently caressed the glimmering cage.

Noah gasped then bellowed out, "Are you saying these are the melted collars of the, oh my God. So, that's why there is the law that all collars be returned to the Throne of the Fur when the owner falls. They use them to decorate this fucking tomb they call the Mortar Palace. For Christ's sake Mad Maxx, this is abomination."

A plumped, overly healthy rat ran past my boots as I replied, "That it is, Noah. Now, get off your knees and recompose yourself. Use that key to undo these locks. I need to attend my Court and visit with my jester. Hurry up, dammit. We have better things to do then peer at my royal subjects like the common voyeurs."

Noah sucked in his breath, sniffed loudly then took to his boots as he said, "I will obey your will, Mad Maxx. Before I follow you inside though, can I beg your mercy. If you intend to add my head to the moldering skulls that inhabit this cell, would you do it quickly please."

I laughed out loud then replied, "In a hurry to get to the place where you are free of this horrible reality are you, Noah?"

He shook his head while placing the key into the lock and said, "Ja, you are correct that I want to escape Mad Maxx but not from knowing the truth about the Mortar Palace. I'm merely want to be released from the rancid smell of it. It stinks." He swung the gate wide as he finished his statement.

Florian called out from his place on the Mortar Thone, "Ah, if it isn't my old buddy Mad Maxx. Who is that fellow with you? Is this one of your latest interests? I thought you were supposed to be bringing home the wife, not the swinging dick. I suppose you are too stupid to know the difference, ja?"

I growled in reply, "Shut the fuck up Florian. That's no way to welcome the honored guest into our home, is it? Where the hell are your manners?"

Florian laughed wildly and said, "I think I left them in my pants, Mad Maxx. Tell you what. You go find them and then I will stop acting the unruly brute. Otherwise I must demand you get him out of here. Well, unless you intend to give me that beautiful noggin of his to me to play with."

I threw my crutch across the cell. It collided with Florian perfectly, knocking him from his place onto the floor. He rolled without hindrance until he came to the stop at Noah's boots. I watched the Head Master shaking appearing too frightened to move while he stared into the court jester's empty eye sockets.

With a snort I began to snicker as I said, "I think Florian likes you, Noah. Don't worry my beloved. He is aware you belong to me. Stop fawning over that bone head and come over here. I need your help to move something."

Noah responded in the trembling voice, "Mad Maxx, who is, I mean was Florian? Does he haunt you? Is that why you speaking to him just now?" I noticed his pallor had gone white as the sheet.

I halted my trip to the furthest corner of the Palace and said in the irritated tone, "Are you blind, Noah? That is

11

Florian right there that you're looking at. I don't know what the hell you talking about. Ghosts, God, Santa Claus, those are all things found only in children's imaginations. I cannot be haunted by imaginary things, fool. Now are you going to yap with Florian all day or are you willing to get over here and do the task I brought you along to do for me."

Florian gurgled then yelled out, "Don't you dare, Mad Maxx. I know what you are up to. You've brought this man here to distract me but I tell you it isn't going to work. That is mine and you know it. If you take it from me, then you and I are going to fight. I promise you cannot win this battle, little King of nothing." That pissed me off.

I hissed back, "You better remember that I can crush you anytime I wish, Florian. Maybe this time I don't ask Birgit to glue you back together, ja? This ting I come to take has always been my and never yours. I only let you borrow it for the moment. I must take it to hide elsewhere because your big mouth told the secret. I wasn't gonna punish you for that insult, but if you insist in making this harder than it must be. Well, then I happily can rethink my decision. I mean it."

Noah interrupted the argument with the hushed whisper, "Mad Maxx, uhm, this thing you need to retrieve. Is it, uhm, that body bag you standing over? If so, then may I ask the identity of the one that occupies it? Is it, uhm, the rest of Florian?" He was trembling so badly by this point I thought he was about to collapse there onto the stoney floor.

With the evil chuckle I replied, "You're correct about the thing I want to throw out. As for that other question, nein. Florian's flesh was long ago food for the rats. Don't let him get to you, Noah. He's nothing but hot air without any bite. Hahaha." I kicked the body bag and the end where the head once was leaked out the river of green and yellow liquids.

Noah covered his mouth, made the sound of retching then rasped out, "Goddamn that's ripe. Where do you desire I take this, uhm, item, Mad Maxx?" I saw him look about the cell while being barely able to hold back his stomach contents.

I sighed loudly and then replied, "We must take this one to the silver well. There cannot be any evidence of her left anywhere within the Haus walls. There isn't much more time we can wait to do it either. If I've timed this correctly, we can smuggle her out of the Palace through the back Dungeon door without being spotted. I think the Guard will be too busy doing the daily shift change to notice us slipping past them. We must travel quickly to the playground. Behind it is the cover of the woods. However, if we make a single misstep before we can reach that place, well brother. It's been a pleasure to know you."

Noah's face melted from serious fear to that of absolute terror as he said, "So, you are saying to be caught with this, uhm, thing carries the death sentence, ja? Since you are the Master of the Haus, and above most rules regarding ending the life, it must have been one of those that are of the highest levels. I'm guessing this was either the Voter or Elder. You refer to it as 'she.' You know there is only one female leader

13

that's been unaccounted for within the last year. I dare say that smell indicates this person died not too long ago. So, I think that's must be your, uhm, I mean to ask you. Is that the missing Voter Agnette in the bag?"

I limped over to the wooden privy all the while snickering as I replied, "If you are wondering that. Then perhaps any Fur Kings that come by to visit for the tour of the Palace may assume this to be this thing's identity also, ja? Good thing that you understand. So, now that you realize the seriousness of this task. You can appreciate that we better get the lead out or the Guard will sure be damned happy to put some into us." I reached into the hole of the crude toilet and removed the skull that had her boney jaws propped open by wadded up hundred-dollar bills.

Noah rushed over to the spot behind me and picked up the decaying bag. He gagged loudly but managed to heave the weight over his shoulder like the rotten sack of grain. I turned around and displayed my trophy to him. He stared at me wide eyed and appearing too frightened to speak.

I opened its mouth, removed the valuable packing and in the most feminine voice tone spoke for her, "Ah, nein, my little lamb. Why are you taking away all the things I ever loved? How could my son treat his loving mother so badly? Shame on you, Christian Axel."

With a snort I turned Agnette's skull to gaze upon my face as I replied angrily, in my regular voice tone this time, "Now, now mother, what have I told you about complaining so much? You wanted to be adored completely, and I have seen to that desire thus far. I tell you we were betrayed by Florian. I must apologize, but like it or not you must blend in with the others for a little while. Fear not though, mother dear, I'll soon return you to your personal throne. Then you can resume your feeding off the foul things the come from the hard labors of your loving son."

I knelt then rolled her head like the bowling ball across the cell. She came to rest next to another that I thought Noah would recall knowing in the recent past.

I chuckled as I said, "Ah, look there, Noah. Agnette is the woman of uncompromising tastes. She chooses to visit with your brother Olaf and mother Evelyn. I bet they are going to spend hours bitching behind our backs of the poor treatment their sons and brother give them. Ah, that's not right. As you can see, they have been granted the special place in my Palace and are among the most important in the court of their Mortar King. Well, don't look surprised. None of them appreciated their places of luck in life either. Why should they have gained any wisdom in death? Well, never mind them. Use that key to lock up behind us. Then once we are safely out of the Haus, I will need you to return it to me. Come on, let's get the fuck out of here. Florian, I will be seeing you soon."

I heard Florian yell after us while Noah and I practically flew back the way we'd come, "You sure will, Mad Maxx. The clock is ticking. Tick, Tock, Tick Tock."

Obviously, since I sit here with you today, Meine Liebe, Noah and I managed to make it to the back door and across the yard without anyone witnessing our frantic run. I managed to maintain the appearance of bravery though it was one of the scariest trips I'd made toward the playground since that day Julius found me there years before.

You see, when Claus told me that he'd heard I'd stashed my mother's head in the Palace privy. I denied it because being found guilty of killing any leader carried the sentence of burning at the stake. Not even me, the powerful Mortar King, was immune to this punishment. That is if any evidence were discovered that I had indeed ended her life.

While I wanted to believe Claus was the one man that wouldn't wish to see me dead, I couldn't be sure of it. I didn't trust anyone by this time in my short life. Nor should I have. Even my beloved Cary had let a tiny little bit of power go to his head. I'd given Claus the one thing he desired above all else. I was left to worry that if he didn't intend to use that information he'd gotten from Birgit, who no doubt she was told by Florian, that rat bastard, then why did he ask me about it in the first place?

Plus, he had told me he wished he was strong enough to go down to my Palace and see the truth of it personally. The second Mad Lucus told me Claus had recovered enough to return to walking around unaided, that made me the nervous man. I knew what had to be done, the moment I was able, no matter the real reason behind his interests in my mother's whereabouts, he'd find me innocent of the claim I'd killed her. Yikes.

Sadly, in my stressful attempts to see this crime covered up. I'd unintentionally pulled Noah into the scheme. I honestly wanted to believe he was truthful in his claims that he loved me and was the loyal man until death. But as you know already, I'd heard those bullshit lines before.

Eventually, everyone that ever said that to me ended up hurting me far more than skin deep. I honestly believed that Noah was going to be the newest in the long line of those that had broken my heart.

I painfully understood that his knowing this dangerous business about my mother had given him the perfect blackmail betrayal device. Though it was not expected to be that day. I knew that sooner or later he'd end up getting involved in some plot with me. Only then could I find out if he really was the man of his word. More likely than not, he'd only pretended to care for me in his effort to use me to reach whatever lofty thing he'd been trying to obtain in the first place.

These were the dark thoughts that consumed my thinking as the two of us rushed across the yard heading for the wooded area behind the playground. The trees swallowed his huge frame many moments before I caught up with his rapid stride. Despite his carrying all that added dead weight, the cumbersome crutch and pronounced limp left me the straggler between the two of us.

When I finally made it to the safety of the thickets, I was immediately struck with fresh terror. Noah was nowhere to be seen. It didn't seem possible that he could outrun me to the extent of becoming invisible.

With the trembling in my knees I halted my wild dashing and craned my neck in every direction. I didn't dare to call out for him for fear that some passerby or even the Guard would hear my cries.

Then I heard him faintly giggling. His sound was coming from behind the grouping of hearty brush to the left of me. I quickly headed for that area full of dread. I thought I was about to step into the center of Russian rifles all pointed at my head. Surely, Noah was laughing over his success of leading me right into my doom, ja?

Yet, as carefully squeezed through the thicket, the firing squad isn't the situation that greeted my eyes. There in the center of the small clearing was the burley Head Master. He'd carefully placed his forbidden cargo on the ground while he joyfully examined his natural surroundings. The very ones all his life he'd been cruelly denied.

I watched him in awed silence. He put out his arms and twirled with his eyes turned toward the blue winter sky. His smile of innocence and thrill was breathtaking to behold. It was then I saw that his face was moist. This was from the slow river of happy tears that caressed his cheeks.

In that moment, I imagined, the near middle-aged man magically became the delighted little boy once again. Noah was drinking in the sights with the eagerness, and hope that had almost been beaten out of his soul by my grandmother's sentence.

I would've been satisfied to view this wonderful vision for the rest of my shitty life. That wasn't possible of course. So with the pang of guilt in my heart I approached the celebrating man. We had to deliver our stash to the silver well before even considering taking the nature break, ja?

After catching his attention by clearing my throat I said in the slightly whispered voice, "Noah, we must get moving before we are spotted. You know what will happen to us if they do."

He stopped his spinning and replied in the excited tone, "Ah I know this, Mad Maxx, but it's all just so beautiful. I never imagined being free in the outside world would be like this. I never want this feeling to end." His eyes blazed with awe and blissful stun as they darted about taking in the scenes around him.

With a nod I responded, "I promise to do everything in my power to see that it doesn't. Now, grab that bag and follow me. Stay close this time. You get lost out here and you'll freeze to death before I find you. I should've recalled that the temperature can be brutal on the flesh when covered by nothing but the leather harness. My apologies for that oversight, lover."

His smile didn't fade while he stood dare shivering in the frigid air and said, "To become the icicle that has all this to keep him company for eternity wouldn't be the bad way to go, Mad Maxx."

I chuckled then replied, "I cannot argue with you about that. However, let's try to live a little bit longer before we go seeking the void, ja? Come on with me before I forget myself and attack you like the hungry bear."

Noah suddenly frowned but picked up the bag as he said, "Then you still are thinking of killing me, Mad Maxx? Like you did my brother, mother, your own mother, and Florian. Do you plan to add my head to all the others that I saw in that horrific cage they call the Mortar Palace?" He groaned while he adjusted the weight on his broad shoulder.

I didn't reply to his question but instead took off hobbling toward our ultimate destination. The truth is, I really hadn't quite made up my mind regarding what to do with him. He'd learned my most devastating secret. Leaving him alive and hoping he was something I'd never encountered before, the man of true loyalty, was simply too dangerous to do.

Yet, ending his life over the crime he'd thus far never committed. That wasn't fair either. In all my days I'd never had such conflicting emotions over doing the things that I had to do to survive.

With Noah, however, I just couldn't find the strength to admit I'd let this loose end remain so for far too long already. While we slowly traveled the foot path through the woods I braced my resolve to finish Noah and be done with this entire shit show.

Thanks to my low spirits over this necessary task, I barely glanced back at the Head Master tailing me. Each time something new appeared within our surroundings I could hear tiny sounds of thrill escape his throat. The bird that flew past us, the early spring flower, the trickling stream flowing through the melting snow, all caused him great delight. The more he demonstrated childlike wonder, the harder it was for me to harden my heart against him.

Then the light breeze began to blow. The familiar scent of his aftershave wafted across my nose. I breathed deeply of that smell that seemed to bring me into a calming peace within. I wanted to run away from him or throw things at him to make him leave. I knew one of us had to become scarce before I would be forced to do something I honestly didn't wish to do. I knew neither of those actions could solve this problem between us, but I did wish it in the repeat while we continued the journey.

Then suddenly the remnants of the silver well came into my view. It was too late to demand Noah drop that mess that used to be my mother and leave me be. Now that he'd been given the location that would bring about my doom if he were to tell anyone, his fate was sealed. Just as was my own if I didn't do what was necessary to assure he would never speak a word of my crime.

Noah saw the ancient watering hole and let out the ecstatic squeal and said, "Look there, Mad Maxx, what is it? There are so many stones laying all around. It is made of mortar, ja? Is this the secret way to get under the Haus maybe?" He rushed past me and halted at the edge peering down into it with the curious expression on his face.

I limped up next to him and said in the somber tone, "Maybe. Do you desire to go down there to find out?"

His face became even brighter with thrill as he nodded and replied, "Sure I would, Mad Maxx. If this is the secret way in and out of the Dungeon we could use it to escape into this beautiful place anytime we wanted. Just think, all this would belong to us, and no one could tell us nein. Freedom Mad Maxx, Freedom. Did you bring a rope or is there one around here I could use?" He started glancing around the base with hope in his expression.

I felt my chest start aching as I replied, "There isn't any way to the bottom other than to drop, Noah. I command you to lay that trash you carry there on the ground. Then you will go to the edge and jump in. Do this now, before I lose my nerve to demand that you obey me." The first tear erupted from my left eye, followed by several more the moment I saw the look on his face that indicated he fully comprehended my intentions.

His beautiful face held its cheerful smile as he said with voice tone tinged with sorry, "Ah, okay. I think I understand now what this was really all about, Mad Maxx. Please, I beg of you. Don't weep for me. I die today the happy man that I thought I never could be. I've seen the sky and felt the grass. I've known the touch of the most wonderful lover anyone could desire. I've even lived long enough to see that distressed little boy I trained become the strongest man and King that ever lived. I swear to God above, that I've done the best I could do given the hard path chosen for me. I am grateful to you for giving to me everything that was wonderful in this brutal life of mine. Can I be so bold as to ask that you kiss me one more time. I know I haven't earned it but I wish to meet my end with the taste of you on my lips.

I thank you for the mercy of it, even if you say nein to this final request."

With a tremble in my voice tone I replied, "If I kiss you, Noah, I fear I won't be able to do what must be done. I love you so much to remain that strong. Though I'm sure you don't believe that given that I've ordered you be executed."

Noah chuckled and maintained his peaceful grin as he responded, "But I do believe you, when you say you love me, Mad Maxx. The tears you shed for me, they started from your left eye. When someone is crying in happiness the first drop flows from the right. When in grief or terrible pain, always the reverse is the truth. Do you see my tears flowing opposite to your own, my love. I am feeling joy not anguish, ja? I want you to let go of this guilt you feel over this. It isn't the truth that I end my life because you command me to do it. I do this because I love you and that means I trust you. Obviously you must believe it will bring you comfort to demand I do this or you wouldn't send me away, ja? That is all I want for you. To be as happy as you have made me. So, again, I say thank you for the mercy you've graced me with, my Lord. I hope you come to visit with me on the other side. May you live the long and happy life." He began to climb over the edge of the silver well as he finished his tender words to me.

He took the seat on the crumbling lip and swung his legs into its deep mouth. Then he closed his eyes tightly and mumbled the prayer. I watched him making his peace with his maker stunned into the trance of disbelief.

The hundreds of brutal memories flowing across the wheelroom screen told me this was the correct thing to do. Getting rid of the man sure to cause me further pain without having to expend any energy was the gift I'd rarely encountered.

However, the heart of my flesh couldn't bear to lose this possible treasure. I kept thinking if Noah was willing to obey me to the point of taking his own life only because he thought it would make me happy. Then surely he was the one I'd been looking for all along.

Only mere moments before he let his body slip off into oblivion I yelled out full of desperation, "Halt, Noah. Don't move. I'm coming to help you."

He nodded and turned to glance at me appearing relieved as he replied, "Oh thank you for this mercy, Mad Maxx. I'm afraid to die. I admit it. Your push will grant me the peace of mind that I don't have your last memory of me being that of the coward."

I limped to him and put my arms around his waist then whispered into his ear, "You misunderstand, my love. I've not come to murder you with my own hands. I'm here to take you within them and this time I swear on my honor, I'll never let you go." With that I engaged him in the most passionate kiss I'd ever given in my life.

With great caution I guided him from the ledge never breaking from our fevered cuddling. I was determined that if that edge failed before I got him to safety, I'd gladly go with him. With the squishy thud, he slipped off the well wall into the thick mud from the freshly melted snowpack.

A gasp of shock escaping him when his flesh was met by that freezing muck. He stared into my eyes for the moment, appearing enamored and full of ardor. Before he could speak to me, I attacked his lips with heightened exhilaration. The gloriousness of our mouthy embrace was sweetened by the taste of our salty tears of gratitude.

Noah had proven that even the threat of death couldn't persuade him to break his words of loyalty to my commands. More than that, when faced with the fact that the man he loved would order him to die, his final words were those meant to comfort his would be killer.

I had decided his love for me was pure, honest and above all complete. There was no way in hell I was going to part with something this wonderful. Not on your life. In those moments on that fridged morning, with the remains of my uncaring mother there to witness, Noah became my confidant, my best friend, my truest lover, and my world.

I allowed myself to forget that Noah was the male. I used my weight to force him to remain under me with his back on the wet earth. Our heated caresses kept the cold winds at bay while we fully explored each other's flesh with firm groping and heavy petting.

Noah was moaning full of ecstasy while I plied his washboard stomach with nips and kisses. His hands gently encouraged me to continue my trip toward his groin. No doubt, he thought I was willing to grant him another oral service encounter. His eagerness was heightened upon my sudden attempts to undo his heavy belt buckle.

The Head Master reached down and happily completed this difficult task for me as my hands were still in bandages. The moment his leather breeches were unhindered by both his belt and the buttons of his fly I slipped off his lap.

His confusion was evident after I rolled him to his face. He tried to get up, but I moved to quickly pinned him by taking the straddle across his upper thighs. I then dropped and draped my frame over his own. His anxiety calmed the second I returned to my enthusiastic adoration of his neck and upper shoulders.

Noah let out the sounds of thrill then mumbled, "Please, Mad Maxx. You are torturing me here. I cannot return your kissing from this angle. I thank you for offering the back rub, but I've got something more sensitive that I'd rather you fondle." He chuckled sounding dreamy.

I moved to his left ear and after giving the light lick into it whispered, "And I will indeed see that your pleasure is attended to, but first I'm going to seal our deal by claiming your virginity. I command you to remain still but I demand that you relax. There will be pain. That's regretfully unavoidable. However, I'm going to grant you the mercy that I wasn't the day I was broken in by Peter. I never go anywhere without the best lube available to anyone in this accursed land. You'll also be grateful to know that I'll use it liberally."

Noah whimpered sounding honestly frightened as he cried out, "Wait, Mad Maxx. Are you saying you are going to fuck me here? Right now. Oh, my God, I'm not ready for this." He began to wriggle under me.

I laughed softly, swatted his backside, and whispered to him, "Easy dare, sweety. This will be over before you know it. I suppose you thought I'd always give you the perfected Priceless blow job without ever demanding a return for that coveted service? I think your anal virginity is the fair trade for the amazing sexual thills I'm willing to grant you, don't you, lover?"

The Head Master stopped his thrashing immediately, and then he replied in the strained voice, "If you say it is, then it is, Mad Maxx. I thank you for the mercy of it. Though before you do this, I must beg you grant me the mercy of covering your ears. I'm afraid you'll be ashamed of me when I cry out like the little bitch you about to make me into."

That made me near fall off his back in howling laughter. While my mirth was the appreciated break from my sinking feelings of being the monster that rapes the unwilling, it did nothing to calm my would be victim. He flinched and gasped upon feeling me reaching into my jacket pocket to retrieve my expensive lubrication bottle.

I held the item where he could view it with ease and said, "See this, Noah? I hold your salvation in my hands, but unfortunately, I cannot give it to you."

He groaned like the wounded bull as he replied, "Why do you deny me this comfort after telling me you possess it? Unless you are the sadist that enjoys watching my torment."

With a chuckle I responded, "And if I am, what of it?"

Noah shook his head then said, "Nothing at all, Mad Maxx. You are the man with the experience and power in this situation. If watching me suffer is your pleasure then I give it to you without complaint and thank you for the mercy of your brutal touching." Another groan escaped his throat when I withdrew the bottle from his eyes.

Then I leaned in close to his ear and whispered, "That was the correct response, my little plaything. Now, you are far too hasty to bleed and cry out in pain I think. Be patient. We will get to that part of this game soon enough. However, it isn't sadism that prevents me from offering you my comfort. My hands are nearly useless with injury. If you desire to endure this harsh initiation into sex with the help of the magical slippery liquid. You will need to prep me, and then yourself, lover boy." I kissed and nipped on his earlobe.

Noah lifted his face from the ground slightly and glanced at me as best he could due to his position as he replied, "I'm most grateful to do anything that will make this less horrible than I expect it to be. Does this lubrication cause the penetration to become painless? Does it numb the flesh, maybe?"

He flinched when I let out a loud guffaw then responded, "Nein, don't I wish it did. A million times I have thought such a wonderful invention as the numbing lube should exist. That said, without it, you will discover that anal sex is the closest that the male can come to appreciating the agony of childbirth the female is cursed to suffer. So, stop fooling around playing in the mud, Noah. Roll over and help me get ready to take you for the ride. Giddy up, my pretty pony. Hahaha."

The Head Master sucked in his breath and I slipped off his back. He rotated to his side facing me. I handed him the bottle of lube and he held it up close to his face, examining it in the light. I chuckled over the expression of curiosity in his gaze. I was thinking once, long ago, my stance of confusion and fear must have been similar. If you recall, Ryker wasn't real clear about the meaning of that stuff to me as I had been with Noah.

His gawking of wonder was interrupted when I cleared my throat and said, "You are stalling. This cock isn't going to prep itself and if you don't get on with it, then I'm gonna fuck you without the luxury it can offer."

Noah nodded and with the sour expression on his face hurriedly began to undo my breeches. I watched him with unveiled humor in my gaze, while he pulled me free of encumberment. He didn't take his eyes off my exposed manhood for several minutes.

Then his brow raised as if curious and he glanced up at me and said, "Either I've nothing to fear or you aren't honestly interested in penetrating me, Mad Maxx. I say this with respect. Have I done something to turn you off?"

I rolled my eyes and replied, "Oh, I apologize that sitting in the frozen mud, next to the rotting corpse, with you staring at my dick, trembling like I'm the rapist, isn't what I would call the sexy fantasy, Noah. If you wish to turn me back on, you need to do a lot more than breath on it, you know. I mean I realize you are the virgin. But hell man, you own a cock yourself. Tell me, does it get hard randomly or do you have to encourage it to behave like the oak tree?"

Noah shot me the weak smile, then opened the bottle of lube as he responded, "Okay, I had that coming. It was stupid of me to expect the man with your vast experience in this kind of sexual tryst could gain erection just by willing it. I don't know what I was thinking." He poured the slick stuff into the palm of his hand and without hesitation reached out and started stroking me.

His fridge flesh caused me to yelp and then I replied nearly coming unglued over this most disturbing situation, "What do you mean by that? Do you think I fucked everyone in the Haus? Nein, they fuck me. Noah, there is a difference, you know. In fact, you're about to find that out very shortly."

Without breaking off his attempt to incite lust in me he furrowed his brow and said, "Uhm, I apologize for not thinking before I spoke, Mad Maxx. I didn't mean to insinuate that you are the whore or anything, I swear it. I only meant that I've heard for years the rumors of your excellent special service skills and that you never leave any of your lovers unsatisfied or sometimes even, uhm, breathing. I merely assumed with such amazing powers, you'd need no assistance to play the stud."

I rolled my eyes and blew out my breath full of frustration, both over these stupid rumors that follow me everywhere and the fact that Noah wasn't getting me to the place I needed to be, as I yelled out, "Goddammit, Noah. You are terrible at the hand job. How the fuck can this be when I know you only been permitted release into your palm before today? As for that other bullshit you've heard about me. Well, I cannot lie to you. When I do this with you today, you will be only my third penetration experience and my first like this. The other two I wasn't the aggressor, nor did I even realize what was going on till it was over. I cannot even recall the details, just that I think I enjoyed it." I pushed his worthless hand off my cock and sat forward grabbing both sides of my head to stave off the growing irritation within me.

Noah sat there staring at me in disbelief for several minutes before he said in the near whisper, "You mean you never done this, I mean anal sex, before? But I thought, I mean I saw Elder Jonas kissing you those two times, and you said to him you gave the Fur King Claus the blow job. You are skilled beyond imagination with the oral service, that I know personally. Your kissing, in all the right places, with all the finesse of the sublime artist of the flesh. I don't understand. I know Peter must have trained you to do everything expected of the catamite or else Xavier would have ended you before you got the chance to kill him."

I sighed loudly but didn't even glance at him as I replied, "If I were the one about to be penetrated, then you damned right I'm the overused bastard, Noah. However, this place at the top during intercourse, in that I'm regretfully the novice.

Almost the virgin for the vagina and pure as you are in regard to penetration of the male. I suppose it is for the best that I cannot get it up to do as I said I would and take your maidenhead. I know you are straight. I've never enjoyed being forced to submit to their lusts. I really don't believe I can live with the idea that I'd be no better than these fiends that raped me if I do the same thing to you. You don't want me to find my pleasure at your expense, and I don't desire to play stud to someone that doesn't truly want me to do it either." I felt like I was going to start weeping like the lost soul as I listened to the factual statement I was confessing to him.

Noah's face took on the expression of adoration as he said, "Oh, Mad Maxx, I cannot express the sorrow that comes over me to hear this terrible truth. I suppose I'd realized it would be the case, no matter how much I wanted to believe the fevered gossiping of the Haus. I think it was easier to imagine you the powerful stud that topped those arrogant bastards that claim leadership than to consider they misused you more foully than I ever did. You say to me that you don't want to find your climax inside of the lover that doesn't wish to receive it. Well, then you are in luck because I swear to you this honor of becoming your first true lover, I not only accept but I honestly yearn for it. I beg of you, Mad Maxx. Make me your sexual plaything, and don't stop until you are satisfied completely." He leaned in and kissed my lips while taking hold of my manhood firmly.

His most skilled actions were still not causing the stir of interest in the right area for this thing to happen after many minutes. Noah was becoming visibly upset that the "bird was dead in his nest." I had to grab him by the shoulders and stop the man from dropping to my lap to attempt the unseasoned blow job.

The Head Master halted his misguided behaviors and said in the frustrated tone, "Didn't you hear me, Mad Maxx? I told you I consent to this. I don't do this because you command me. I love you, dammit. I honestly do. I long to be with you in every way possible."

With a bitter chuckle I replied, "I'll remember you said that, Noah. Hopefully you will too. The last thing I need at this moment is for you to end my chances of mount by biting my dick in the attempt to perform skills you haven't been trained to do yet. This problem we are having isn't the new one and has nothing to do with you. Here, apply this lube heavily to the point of my entry. Then you get like the dog, over there. Wait for me to take the spot of the stud and whatever you do, don't look back. I think it best you don't see what's coming. Sometimes pain is partly psychological."

Noah's face fell into the expression of anxious caution as he said, "Am I to understand you're trying to say that not all the rumors I've heard about your sexual prowess are incorrect?"

I shrugged then replied, "Depends on which ones you are referring to."

He shuttered and snuck another glance at my flaccid penis and said, "Whatever you about to do to see that your tool for this project is of the sturdy construction, I would beg of you to keep it to the barely acceptable levels."

That made me laugh wildly as I responded, "Ah, you have heard that I'm the grower of giant wood, ja? If I confess this tall tale may be the truth of it, do you still grant me permission to plow your field, Noah?" His eyes reflected a bit of fear while he nodded and removed his breeches.

Then while prepping as I told him to do, he called out to me, "I know you are the novice to this type of intercourse, but if you know of any, I beg of you to give me advice that can be useful to prevent me from behaving the coward while playing your mare?"

I looked up into the clear blue sky and pulled up the image of beautiful Annette as I replied, "Other than using the entire tub of lube, you mean? Oh well, you can grit your teeth, count, grip the ground, and keep telling yourself it's almost over. Oh, and I won't judge you if you cry, Noah. I do every time, but don't tell anyone, dammit."

The Head Master hid his head in his burly arms the moment he saw the flash of my movement coming toward him. I sighed and glanced down at my semi-erect cock. This was proving to be the harder task than I ever imagined it would be. Okay, I never thought in a million years I'd be fucking the male of our species. Yikes!

Nothing was working to gain my lustful interest in penetrating Noah. The truth was that I felt I had to do this. Though I did believe he loved me for real, I wasn't sure that I could totally trust him yet. I needed something to hold over him, in return for the thing he could now use against me if he wished to. I knew he could deny that he'd breeched the rules of no contact if push came to shove. The blow job I gave to him left no evidence of it.

However, if I could perform this act and take his anal virginity. That could be proven. Then I could rest easy knowing if he dared to share our secret of the silver well. I'd see him sold off to play mare to the Russians before I was sent to face the fiery death, ja?

I realize this wasn't the romantic reason to lose my penetration virginity, you know what I mean, nor to take his. That was just too bad for your stupid Master, Meine Liebe. This foul deed was the sure way to keep down my fears and keep Noah out of my often overly paranoid radar.

So, there I was, on my knees behind the trembling brute, unsure what to do next. In the past experiences playing the top, I'd simply stood there. Both females had taken care of the work to get my part where it needed to be. I knew where I was supposed to put it (duh), but to be honest, I didn't want to hurt the man. It seemed to me the place I needed to enter was far too narrow to fit inside. Even if I wasn't even close to full potency.

Noah shivered while he yelled out, "Is it over yet?"

I sighed loudly, then replied, "I haven't even started, Noah. Dammit, be quiet. If you make too much noise we will never get this done."

He nodded into his arms and said, "I understand, Mad Maxx. Remember, I do this because I want to. I love you. I honestly do. Please be gentle."

His words caressed my ears and I felt them flow through my veins. I gazed upon the flawless flesh of his well-toned buttocks. They appeared not so different in beauty to that of Annette's. Though I had to admit, she'd left me so long before I could hardly remember her gorgeous bottom perched on that bathroom countertop.

I reached out and groped his backside. He flinched but held his place and his tongue. The smooth skin sent shivers of thrill through me. I increased my rubbing on him, and to my relief I got the notice that my cock was getting the message at last that I wished to mate.

This alleviation of my fear that I'd remain impotent was quickly replaced with apprehension. That unruly dick of my always been the overachiever. If I didn't do something to offer some mercy to my virginal partner, he wasn't going to be my buddy for too much longer, hahaha.

Without notifying Noah of my intentions I used the only thing available to mildly stretch him for ease of entry. The Head Master's head come up with suddenness and he let out the loud bellow as if in great pain.

I swatted him in the back of his head lightly and growled out, "Shut up, dammit. Why are you acting the fool over only the thumb? Do you want me to lose my erection before I even get started? Keep screaming like I'm killing you and that's gonna happen."

Noah quivered and returned his face to his arms before mumbling out, "Oh, my God. That's the digit you using and not your dick? I'm not gonna make it without screaming I just know it."

I winced upon hearing him say that as I replied, "If you scream, I fear I will lose it too. Look, no matter what happens keep your mouth covered, okay? I've done all I can to make this as easy as possible, but there isn't any way around the pain. Are you ready and are you absolutely sure you want to do this? I won't think you the coward if you say nein. This isn't going to be fun for you. I understand that more than I am happy to admit."

He nodded wildly and though muffled I heard him saying, "Hurry up and do this before I lose my nerve. I am sure, I swear it to God and to you, my Lover and King."

I took the deep breath, placed my part over the target and with all the strength I could muster thrust forward. Noah seized up immediately. He made choking and gagging noises while I held my position with force, refusing to be ejected by his objecting sphincter muscles.

The both of us trembled in our spots. Him from pain, and me from the unexpected strength required to gain entry into Noah. What was worse is only the tip of my penis had managed to penetrate at that point. Yikes!

After what seemed like hours, the initial tightness began to loosen slightly. I didn't hesitate to thrust further. Noah yelped, groaned, clawed at the mud, and shook like the newborn calf under me. I felt terrible to be causing him such great trauma but there was also the sense of victory that I'd managed to penetrate to the halfway point.

Then without any warning, I was pulled from within him. This strange experience caused me to gasp and spasm almost as bad as Noah was. Though my behavior was from the sudden ecstasy that was filling me to the point of sheer lustful madness. I wanted this man, more than I had ever wanted anything, even chocolate, in my life.

The drumbeats of the inner beast thumped in my ears. I began to match their rhythm thrusting with eagerness into Noah. He wailed several times and cried out that I was killing him. I heard his pleas for respite but I simply was too overheated to entertain calming my onslaught.

That interesting thing about this first time with penetrating something other than the mouth or vagina was I didn't reach my climax with my usual unnatural speed. In the situation with Annette, and Gretta if you believe that lying bitch, I came so damned fast I barely had sex at all. Too bad for old Noah. This wasn't the case for his initiation into sex.

I must have humped on him like the horny rabbit for five to six minutes solid before I felt the signs of coming release. My spine tingled with exhilarating delight just second before my groin exploded in the earth-shattering, toe-curling orgasm. I moaned out in thrill louder than Noah was screaming for mercy.

With the shout of joy I fell forward and held Noah in the cuddle from above without uncoupling. He was still groaning, and trembling in my grip. I felt satisfied, and sleepy as I plied his sweat drenched neck with gentle kisses.

His shivering halted and then he mumbled out, "That was it? Is it over?"

I chuckled then yawned as I replied, "Ja, you belong to me now, Noah. I took from you something you can never have back. I thank you for the mercy of it. You know, I never loved anyone as much as I love you right this minute."

Noah lifted his head from his fleshy gag and responded, "I hope you mean that, Mad Maxx. Ever since you come to me and asked me to be yours, you are all I can think about. I want you so badly, it's driving me insane, I swear it." I uncoupled and withdrew from my mount.

With the glazed over vision I watched him spin around till he faced me, then I said, "It isn't fair to leave you unsated after you've kindly attended my own urges. I'd let you lose your own penetration virginity if I were in the condition to see to it. However, the doctor says it will be another two to three weeks before I can repay you in equal service."

He smiled at me and quivered sporadically for the moment then replied, "You're worth the wait, Mad Maxx. It'll give me something to look forward to, ja?" I crawled over to him and dropped my head into his lap.

Noah heaved in sheer thrill the second my mouth assaulted his manhood. I pushed him to his back with firmness and employed every skill I possessed in the oral services. He offered no quarrel but this time his yells were from pleasure not pain. He climaxed as heartily as I had done, only mere moments before.

Once he was spent, he reached down and pulled me up to his level. He wrapped his arms around me in the cuddle. We both lay there on the frozen ground in silence, enjoying the warmth of our loving embrace under that beautiful winter sky. I didn't want to move from that spot for the rest of my life. I believe Noah felt the same way. Had it not been for the threat of freezing to death, and other pressing matters, I think we might have remained there for hours more.

However, when at last I noticed his shivering was getting heavy I spoke up and said, "Noah, we must finish the task we started. Before I leave your arms, can I ask you something?"

He nodded and then with a chuckle replied, "I think I've proven there isn't anything I will deny you, Mad Maxx, ja?"

I joined him in the mirth for the moment then said, "I need to leave somethings with someone that I can trust. Things that I will need desperately but will be denied me after I'm forced to name the regent and become the prisoner within the Mortar Palace. I wonder, if you would be capable of storing them for me, and brave enough to continue our love affair till I either escape or I am killed?"

Noah sat up with suddenness and fearful concern in his expression as he replied, "I had forgotten about that law, Mad Maxx. Oh, my God. They will lock you away in that horrible place you showed me, won't they? Of course, I will do anything you ask to make sure you are as comfortable as possible. As for remaining at your side as your lover, I already swore that. Happily, willingly, and honestly, I would like to add." He reached out and caressed my cheek softly.

I nodded then said, "But do you possess a place to hide the things I give to you to hold till I need them?"

He nodded, "Ja, I do, but, my love, they will lock you away where I cannot reach you to give them back when you ask."

I chuckled then pointed at his discarded leather pants, "They will, but you already hold the key that promises they can never part us. As long as you are truthful about having the secure place to store it."

Noah's face broke into the huge grin as he responded, "Thanks to your labors, I believe I'm now capable of smuggling you anything you need. The key, the lantern, blankets, the turkey dinner, my sister if I had one." I interrupted his silly joke by swatting him on the shoulder.

I laughed out loud, "Stop playing, Noah. I'm not so big as all that. Tell me though, did I hurt you? I worried that I was being too rough. I didn't see much blood but some is to be expected. That should end in about three days. If it gets heavy enough to require stanching the flow, go see the doctor, ja? He is the trustworthy soul. If you tell him I said so, he'll stay quiet about the reason for the visit."

He had to work hard to end his giggling as he replied, "There won't be any reason to be making the doctor calls, Mad Maxx. I admit in the beginning it was painful as hell. I thought you were trying to cram the tree up my ass. But truthfully, after a bit, the pain subsided to the dull roar of mere discomfort. I think if that is the worst that I can expect, I'd happily let you find release this way anytime you wish. Oh, as long as you bring lots of lube that is." He smiled then leaned forward and kissed me lightly on the lips.

I furrowed my brow in confusion as I said, "Wait. You mean the pain calmed the longer the sex went on? That's doesn't seem right. It never gets better when I endure it. Aren't you cramping and burning like hell this minute?"

Noah shook his head and shrugged his shoulders as he replied, "Nein. I mean I can tell you have been there, don't get me wrong. However, there isn't any sensations of irritation nor stomach pains. Do you think something is broken?" His expression became that of worry.

With a groan I took to my feet and said, "I don't think so, Noah. Maybe the problem is mine. I've been told by others that this agony I suffer from penetration isn't supposed to be the case after so long being misused as I have been. Unless you notice the things I warned you to watch for, you will be no worse for the wear. Uhm, but I do think I should tell you something important. If you do intend to service me in this manner in the future, you'll need to get the enema kit. Also, for the next few days, if you need to pass gas, uhm, be near the bathroom. Or at least, have the clean pair of shorts to change into quickly."

His eyebrows went up in shock as he said, "Thank God you told me that just now. I was just about to let one rip to make sure everything was still working correctly."

I groaned and replied, "What is with all the farting today? Did the Haus cooks fuck up the breakfast eggs that badly? Christ sakes, Noah, I cannot believe you'd think to befoul our beautiful memory with the grossness of rude smells."

Noah walked over and stood by the body bag as he chucked and replied, "Well to be honest. I didn't think you'd even notice since the stench with this one laying around. I thought surely it would overpower even the worst I could produce."

My eyes ran across the decaying plastic as I said, "Speaking of that garbage. Untie the ropes. There is something inside I wish to keep before we make her disappear forever."

Without hesitation he did as I asked. The closer he got to freeing the corpse, the more the rancid scent of rot filled the air. Noah covered his nose fighting the waves of nausea that overtook him but refused to quite attending his task.

When the last knot was undone, he pulled open the false winding sheet. His sounds of pure shock filled the air, as the stacks of cash tumbled out onto the slushy snow. He cast the bewildered glance at me. I stood up and walked over to pick up a few of the gore covered bundles.

Noah shook his head and said in the whisper, "Where did all this money come from, Mad Maxx? Did you rob the Elders or the Haus bank? Is that why you really needed to get this hidden away? What is left of this thing you say is your mother isn't identifiable. So, this money was the real evidence all along wasn't it."

I nodded and then with the chuckle threw one of the wads in his direction, "Here you go, lover. You can now claim to be the rich, sex toy you always dreamed of being, ja? Nein. I didn't steal this money, Noah. This that you see is what this bitch charged the Vampire to buy her son like he was nothing more than her used furniture. Well, too bad for her that she couldn't handle the torture that her actions has condemned me to. She gladly gave to me everything she had, in the vane effort to keep me from killing her. Too bad for her that what I thought was the fair price wasn't nearly as expensive as she'd sold me away for. Equal for equal, Noah, remember? She gave me life, then she took it away. So, I returned the favor. Gather up the cash and then toss that useless bag of crap into the well. Get dressed before you freeze to death. I suppose we'd better get to sneaking back into the Haus before someone notices we are missing."

He nodded and then held up the stack as he replied, "Sure thing, Mad Maxx, but what am I supposed to do with all this money? Hide it in the bushes maybe?" He glanced around seeking a good spot for stashing.

I laughed with much humor and responded, "I thought you said you had the place big enough to smuggle your sister, if you had one, into the Haus?"

Noah stopped his wandering eyes and his face took on the serious expression as he replied, "I tell you I could comfortably play the wife of the bull elephant thanks to your harsh lesson this morning. All kidding aside, I could break down these bricks and stuff them into my pants. Once I get into my room I'll hide all of it in the chest of the Golden Buckles. As for the key to the Palace. That will remain on the only thing of worth I ever had before today. I'll place it on the silver chain I took from the corpse of my neglectful mother and keep it next to my heart. It should be kept close to the place I store its rightful owner, ja?" He shot me the glance of adoration as he said that.

I clutched my chest and said, "Awe you keep speaking romantically like that, lover, I'll get lustful to have you again While it sounds like fun to help you poke all the paper in the place no one ever thinks to look for it, we simply don't have the time for it right now."

Noah broke out into wild laughter for the moment. Then with the mischievous grin he picked up my mother's corpse bag. Without so much as the groan of stress, he tossed her over the lip of the well. I listened in eager anticipation until at last I heard the faint sound of splashing. That concluded my important meeting with Agnette. Ha!

Though I had been kidding, I did end up having to aid Noah into getting some of the last of the hundred dollar bills into the back of his pants. Inside the clothing not inside him. He does have the pretty bubble shaped bottom, but I couldn't stop the giggling over the sight of his stuffed derrière.

After a bit of teasing and rough horseplaying, the two of us took off down the path leading back to the Haus. For fun, we pretended to be engaged in the friendly game of kiss chasing. I confess, I was the loser on purpose.

Luckily we were able to get inside the back door of the Dungeon without anyone spotting us. The second we were safely within her dark hallways once more, we broke off from our traveling as the team. I did glance back several times, while I headed for the stone staircase. Noah was made of stronger stuff. He kept his eyes forward and rushed for the sanctuary of his barrack's room without stopping.

I felt the warm fuzzy feelings that I'd long forgotten upon imagining the things that money I gave him could buy for us. These childlike thoughts distracted me from noticing the figure that had been spat out of the shadows. I barely hobbled up the first step when I heard:

"Ah, your Majesty. I've been looking everywhere for you. Would you be kind enough to grant me audience for a few moments. There is something of importance I'd love to discuss with you."

My air left my lungs and I trembled full of near maddening anger as I turned to face the one I recalled owned that voice.

Sigrid stood there doing her best to offer me the kindly smile. With the groan I glanced up the stairs, realizing that I wasn't capable of outrunning this "pegging rapist" from my past with any speed.

Like it or not, I was going to be obligated to grant her request that I listen to her offer.

Chapter 19: The Collar King

I stood there staring at Sigrid more than a little pissed off that she'd dared to bother with me after all this time of smartly keeping her distance. She batted her eyes, appearing to do all she could to seem the adoring fan of the Mortar King.

This silly behavior was useless to gaining her the affection I'd stupidly granted her years before. I was no longer the naïve little boy that was easily misled by women. She'd given me the painful lesson that one should never judge the book by the beauty of its cover and I'd learned it to perfection.

With the angry snort I responded, "Since I am at the disadvantage of being able to either remove myself from your presence nor to make you disappear easily, then I suppose I will be forced to listen to your request, Mistress. Before you speak another word though, you better beware, my honey. Seeking me out and reminding me that I dislike you, isn't good for your continued good health."

Sigrid grabbed at her ample bosom while sucking in her air attempting to appear shocked as she replied, "Why, your Majesty. I am surprised that you would still be upset over that minor misunderstanding between us. It is the truth that me and Gisla were the bullies to you in the closet. However, not only was I rightfully punished for that dishonorable behavior, but I have matured. I can honestly say that I regret many things I did in my misguided youth. This situation that causes you alarm upon seeing me is among the top of things I wish I could take back. In fact, once not long ago, I attempted to approach you to offer my personal apology. You ran away before I could provide that service. You remember, the one that I and Gisla grievously denied you as the little boy. Well now you are the handsome man and I am the single lady. If you could find it in your heart to forgive me, my Lord, I swear to you I can be the most grateful of your loving subjects." She took a few steps toward me while dropping her smiling face coyly.

I backed away and used the crutch as the barrier as I said in barely restrained fury, "Halt, you stay the hell away from me, Mistress. If you dare to touch a single hair on my head, then I will not be as merciful as Rolf was to your mane. He merely shaved it off. I will remove it for good along with the source."

She immediately stopped coming toward me and replied with a pouting expression on her face, "Your Majesty. I must beg your mercy. Tell me what it is that I can do to end this discord between us. I swear to God I am happy to do anything you ask of me to demonstrate I'm your humble, loyal and above all, remorseful servant." She then fell to the graceful kneel on the floor in front of the first step just inches from me.

I glared at her then said in the spiteful rage filled tone, "I see you're still as deaf as you always have been. Perhaps not hard of hearing but maybe mentally deficient, ja? I told you already, Sigrid. The only thing I demand of you is that you remove yourself from my presence for good. Go away, damn you. Leave me alone and I will be satisfied to forget you ever existed at all." I attempted to go up the step but nearly tripped when my bum leg failed to follow smoothly.

Sigrid rose with speed and blocked me from falling with her forearms. The unexpected sensation of her touching me sent me right into the absolute terror. I spasmed and jerked wildly which further threw off my balance. In the misunderstanding that she was my savior from the unintentional misstep, rather than the complete freak out reaction, she grabbed me around my waist.

No doubt this innocent action of the Mistress was viewed as yet another traumatic event because it was just too soon after that harsh situation with the Stasi. The flashback of epic strength had blinded me to reason. Without restraint I burst into tears and began to wail loudly. This unmanly display of distress didn't phase the Mistress in her attempts to pull me off the dungeon staircase.

The second she had me to the safety of level ground, Sigrid withdrew her hold. I dropped to the floor and rolled up into the fetal ball. All the while my heavy sobbing with the screams for help continued to echo off the rocky walls.

Somehow Noah heard my anguished shrieking. He came running from out of seemingly nowhere. The Head Master took no time to evaluate the situation. The only thing he could determine is that his lover was upset, and that this female standing over him was the cause of it.

I heard the sound of flesh colliding with bone. It was followed by the faint thud of heavy weight taking up the spot next to me. This noise caused me to glance with frightened curiosity as to the proximity of Sigrid.

My tear drenched eyes took in the sight of the haughty Mistress laying in the unconscious heap not more than inches away. I was too panicked to realize this wasn't some sneaky ploy to continue what I'd wrongly perceived as her attempting to assault me. With a gasp I scooted away from her, frantic to escaping the helpless woman.

Noah raced my direction and quickly scooped me into his arms. This alarmed me even worse than before. My hero was immediately pelted with the series of bites, swats, and cursing so bad I'm ashamed to repeat the things I called him. Ever the calm personality, Noah took my unfair blows without complaint nor attempt to prevent me from them.

Instead of begging me to end my cruelty, he hauled me away from the scene. He cuddled me gently close to his chest that was covered in the sweat of his anxiety. It would occur to me later, he'd been at least as terrified as I had been upon arriving to find me in such a state.

As Noah traveled down the hallway, Dungeon Masters and Mistresses hurried toward their leader full of wonder over the racket. He saw the small group of them approaching and halted.

He ignored my blows and said in the hushed tone, "Your Majesty, please get ahold of yourself. There are about to be witnesses to your behaviors. Remember you are the Lord and Master of us all. I swear to you, I will not allow anyone to harm you. I love you more than my own life. I will lay it down for you without question nor quarrel, ja?"

His true words of affection reached my overwrought mind. They wrapped around me like the blanket of invincibility. A sudden surge of strength came over me and this quelled my dramatic display instantly.

I looked into his eyes and replied, "Oh, my God. Noah, put me down your fucking idiot brute. What the hell is wrong with you? I could see you whipped for daring to lay your nasty hands on the Master of this Haus."

Noah dropped his head and returned me to my own boots without delay. I stood over the hulking man glaring at him appearing more than a little perturbed. This was the picture every Mistress and Master found upon their arrival to the scene.

Dungeon Mistress Edelle gasped and dropped to the kneel while hand motioning the others around her to follow as she cried out, "Your Majesty, our apologies for daring to interrupt your correction of your unworthy subject. We heard the clamor and were unaware of the source. With your permission we beg you the mercy to allow our release. We shall remove ourselves, so that you can continue your discipline without the insult of our useless presence."

With a snort of disgust I eyed the elderly woman trying to seem irritated as I replied, "You and your dungeon kin are indeed the useless bitches. There doesn't seem to be one among you that can boast the decent sense of hearing. How long must your Master yell for help before his commands are heeded?" I nonchalantly wiped my face dry with the back of my bandaged hand.

The Dungeon Master Johannes glanced up at me and said in the frightened tone, "We beg your mercy, your Majesty. We shall remain more vigilant in the future. We accept your judgement against us for the oversight. In the meantime, do you desire we arrest our Head Master and take him to the pit to await punishment at your pleasure?"

I blew out my breath and pretended to be perturbed beyond comfort as I shouted out angrily, "Shut up, Johannes. This crew of so-called Dungeon Masters and Mistresses are among the shoddiest bunch of useless heaps of flesh I've ever seen. There is no wonder with this idiot hailed as your leader, one cannot expect better, ja? I'm your Dungeon Master Supreme and your Lord and Master. So, that means when you fuck up this reflects badly upon me. That dishonor isn't something I'm eager to endure. Well, no problem, which can be easily remedied. Noah, you have one hour to pack up your things. I will return to collect your worthless carcass shortly. Beware you motherfuckers. I won't tolerate any more excuses nor mistakes in the fulfillment of your duties to me. You can all be assured I intend to give the harshest five-month lesson in manners to this improperly trained bastard you call your leader. When he is returned to you, he will be humbled, sublimely experienced, and finally capable of running the proper dungeon in my name. Master Johannes, since you seem to think yourself the spokesman for your brothers. I temporarily turn over to you the place of power this beast currently holds. You shall be henceforth called the Head Master and the welfare of *Das Haus*

Miststück (*The Haus Bitch*) is in your hands. Do the job with honor and dignity without failure or Noah's punishment will seem the mercy compared to the terrible things I will do to you. Now, everyone get back to work, dammit."

The Dungeon Masters and Mistresses took to their feet and practically ran in the opposite direction. Except for Noah and Head Mistress Birgit that is. I stood there appearing furious over the kneeling Noah. During this role of playing the disappointed Supreme Dungeon Master, I pretended to ignore the elderly woman for many minutes. If I was to pull this rouse off, fooling the clever Birgit was of paramount importance, ja?

I finally cleared my throat and said in the hateful tone, "You wish maybe to say something worm?"

Noah kept his eyes to the floor as he replied in the shaky voice, "Nein, your Majesty. It isn't my place to question the commands of my Lord and Master."

I nodded and the most brutal expression I could muster broke across my face as I mockingly responded, "Then I must wonder why you are still groveling like the little bitch your truly are at my boots instead of getting your lazy ass up to do as you were told."

Head Mistress Birgit interrupted me before I could further berate Noah, "Your Majesty, at the risk of inciting your anger I must report to you something you may not be aware of already with regard to former Head Master Noah."

Birgit's odd statement caused me to snap my attention at the elderly lady as I barked back, "Oh? well my dear Mistress, please by all means, tell your Lord and Master his business. Afterall, you surely are more fit to know my own subjects than I am, ja?"

She grimaced but replied in the calm tone, "You are correct to remind me of my place, your Majesty. That said, I still desire to say that if you intend to remove this man from the security of the Dungeon, you risk his life. If your intended punishment was to see him executed, than I must beg your mercy for this dishonorable attempt to interfere with your best judgement, my Lord."

I howled in laughter over her statement, then after getting my mirth under control I inquired, "And you speak up for this idiot's life, why, Mistress?"

Birgit dropped her head lower and replied, "Noah is the Haus submissive half-breed, your Majesty. The honorable Queen Ingrid decreed he was to remain the resident of the Dungeon and to remain untouched for the length of his natural life. I don't wish to insult you by reminding you that once his kind is above ground level, he is immediately stripped of his Dominance. If you desire to see him collared black, then please forgive my interference. However, the black collar must choose the mate, which as you are most likely already aware, Noah is forbidden. He cannot fulfill his duty to the Haus, and likely without constant supervision would attempt to anyway. Such abomination carries the sentence of burning at the stake for the one that touches him.

and for this man, he will be sent to auction to be used in the most foul of ways."

I approached Birgit slowly with the expression of pure fury on my face as I growled in response, "To be used in the foulest of ways you say. Ah, you mean like you witnessed your king mistreated during his incarceration in the Mortar Palace, my Lady, ja? So, are you saying you believe this nothing half-breed's dignity or life is of more worth to protect than your Lord and Master?"

The Head Mistress audibly gulped as she replied in the frightened whisper, "Please, your Majesty, I didn't mean it the way you are hearing it."

I dropped to my knees before the kneeling woman and cooed back in the dangerous sounding tone, "Oh? Then what did you mean by it Birgit? Maybe if you choose your words more carefully I will more fully understand your intentions. Then again, hearing any requests coming out of the mouth of one that has enjoyed far more blessings then she earned from her Master is disruptive to me. But don't let me stop you my dear. Go ahead. Speak up for this bitch, and I promise to listen."

Birgit trembled slightly and drew in her breath before she whispered, "I've known this man since he was the little boy, my Lord. He is the Head Master that is well loved and kind to all the children cursed to wear the silver. If you wish to see him sent away to suffer as I know you already do, it is your right. I gladly give up my own life if only to see you obtain the smallest of comfort in the hellish fate you suffering. This you must know, your Majesty. However, I admit to you I swear this affection I feel for you is almost equal in my regard to this Head Master. If it is blood you desire in compensation for any insult he has done to you. I beg of you to take it from me in his place."

Her confession caused me great shock. I stared into her eyes fatigued by the years of hard living for several minutes unsure how to respond to her. I had intended to visit with Claus to verify the things Noah told me of his situation. Birgit's unsolicited information solved that issue for me. There was no longer any question that my new lover was the honest man in every way.

The elderly lady groaned softly and shifted. Her sounds of discomfort tore me from my deep thinking. I broke my gaze from her own and took back to my boots, hand gesturing her to do the same.

The grateful woman smiled nervously and made noises of struggle as she slowly stood up. I watched her do this apparently painful action with some pity. It wasn't the good thing to be young in the Haus, but being the elderly that was still expected to follow protocol had to be hell too.

With the sigh of frustration I glanced at the kneeling Noah and said, "If you weren't listening Noah, than I wish to inform you that Head Mistress Birgit has admitted she is in love with you. She even goes as far as to say her affections for you are similar to that she has for her King. What do you have to say to that?"

Noah didn't look up from the floor as he replied, "I am grateful to the Head Mistress for her kind words regarding this worthless worm. I thank her for the mercy of it."

I chuckled and said, "That is the proper protocol you spew. Interestingly, you can show manners when you need to. If you had remembered them in the first place, you'd not be in this dangerous situation. Ah, well, no matter now, because you are in big trouble, Noah. You have no choice but to obey the orders of your Lord and Master, but he commands you break the Haus law that you never leave the dungeon. Seems to me, you might go ahead and complete your rude tempting the fates. Tell Birgit you love her back. Then, when no one is looking, take her for your lover."

Noah's head popped up with the expression of pure shock on his face as he breathed out, "Wh…Wh..at? Your Majesty, I, uhm, did I hear you correctly? I apologize but I thought you just told me to sleep with the Head Mistress? Does this mean you do intend to see me sent to auction?" His eyes began to fill with water upon believing I was betraying my promise that I'd never let him go.

With humor in my tone I replied, "You hear my words correctly, but don't listen to them, Noah. I said to do this with Birgit when no one is looking. I know my beloved Head Mistress well. She is the honest soul with a heart bigger than the moon and sun combined. More importantly, she is the perfect keeper of the secrets that can end the lives of those she cares for. The lovely lady says she loves you enough to suffer in your place. She speaks up for your best welfare at the risk of my brutal punishment. She also admits you have honorably lived the life of hard labor without the mercy of the lovers touching. Ah, so here is the solution to that most unfair sentence that curses you."

Mistress Birgit gasped and said in the hushed tone from behind me, "Your Majesty, please, you are embarrassing me and this poor boy. If this is your intention than you can consider it done to perfection. I beg of you to end this cruelty. I'd rather be whipped than become the subject of such foul discussions."

I turned around abruptly, frightening the poor old woman to nearly dropping back to her knees as I replied in the slight fury, "Are you telling me that taking this beautiful man to your bed to adore your flesh with his loving touch is more horrible than the punishment of tasting the kiss of my cane, Mistress?"

Birgit whimpered and kept her worried sight glued to my left hand as she responded, "Nein, I don't mean to insinuate that I prefer to be beaten, your Majesty. I merely say to you that Noah is young enough to be my son. You are wise beyond my understanding, but I think you see me through rose colored glasses if you missed that I'm no longer the beautiful girl in full flower. I'm the wrinkled prune without anything left of value to offer the lover."

I saw a tear escaping her left eye and roll down her heavily creased cheek. I reached out to catching her water and she flinched.

With the expression of adoration I caught her gaze and softly caressed her face as I replied softly, "Father time has not erased the vision of perfection you truly are, my dearest Mistress. You are old enough to possess experience that this poor fool cannot imagine in his most fevered dreams. The smoothness of the flesh matures into the folds capable of hiding sexual mysteries that books of unmatched heat could be written of it, ja? I wonder when was the last time you were adored in the way a woman should be? Do you even recall? I lament such a waste of the treasure if you cannot. I do love you, Birgit. Because of this, I refuse to force you to obey any command that causes you the discomfort you have voiced to me. I ask only that you consider taking this boy and make him into the man he has long since earned the right to call himself. I swear on my honor I never demand that you tell me you've done this or not for Noah. I grant you the mercy of your dignity and your choice. The two things neither of these brutes before you have the pleasure to know, ja? I also take away the suffering you doing over this unjustified fear that I intend to injure your Head Master. I am the Lord and Master of this Haus and I am the Dungeon Master Supreme. I can and will remove Noah from this hell hole. He will safely receive the lessons I require him to learn. Rest assured, I'll make sure he is completely protected from the retaliations of the Fur Throne. Trust in your King, Birgit. Now, go in peace, my love." I rapidly took up her left hand and lightly kissed her knuckles.

The elderly Mistress blushed while she responded, "Forgive me for forgetting that you are far more than the foundation of this Haus, your Majesty. You are the Priceless of prophesy. I humbly ask that you ignore the silly things I said to you today. I suppose I should chalk up my weakness to the residual mother inside of me that demands to be kindled. Noah, dearest Head Master, mind your Master well. If you serve him without restraint, I can attest that he can be as generous as he can be brutal."

Noah nodded slightly and replied in the most reverent sounding voice, "I thank you for the mercy of your wisdom, Mistress. I owe you great favor in return for the one you intended to grant to me this day. Anything you desire that is within my power you need only ask and see that I will make it so."

Birgit smiled affectionately at Noah and responded, "Return to the little silvers as wonderful as you are is the only thing I want, Head Master. Be safe in the world up above and remember yourself and the terrors that will come for you if you don't." He nodded while the sweet old woman hurried back the way she'd come, satisfied there was nothing more she could do or say.

Once the Head Mistress was beyond the place of hearing us speaking, Noah said, "Mad Maxx, are you okay? Did that woman I hit harm you?"

I chuckled and tore my eyes off the retreating Birgit as I replied, "I've told everyone in this dungeon I intend to take you upstairs and this is all you think to ask me? Noah, beloved, I must wonder what goes on inside that pretty head of yours. As you can clearly see, I'm fine. It was the overreaction to an old nemesis you happened upon is all."

He frowned deeply and said, "If it is permitted, I do wish to know why you told the Masters and Mistresses that you're removing me from my post. The Mistress Birgit speaks the truth of it. I'm forbidden to leave. I go if you say I must, but Mad Maxx, I must be collared if I do. Is this your pleasure? Have I offended you that badly to deserve enforced submission that I cannot fully comply with? I am far too old to be trained to do proper black collar duties."

That caused my giggling to grow heavier as I replied, "Noah, you silly thing. There is no collar black nor silver that ever walked the hallways nearly as trained to provide beautiful service as you already are. However, that is irrelevant because you have proven you are quite able to perform the task I'm going to assign to you, lover. You will be leaving this dungeon for the remaining amount of time that I have above ground. and you won't be wearing the collar made of either color. I'm going to make sure you maintain your status as the respectable Dominant."

The Head Master narrowed his eyes and took on the expression of confusion as he responded, "How can that be possible? You words are the law, but only if your regent can speak them for you. Has Lucus agreed to inform the Fur King that the law forbidding the half breeds to wander about uncollared is to be abolished? I ask that with respect, Mad Maxx."

I shrugged and motioned him to rise as I said, "I have no idea if that pervert would or not. That's why I don't intend to bother asking him about it. I have a safer idea to make this happen for us without risking your place of honor. The Mortar King is granted two Dungeon Masters. I've named the Voter Byron and his burly brother Voter Friedrick to these positions. But I've decided to recant the name of one of them and claim you in his place. That way you will have permission to visit with me in the Palace without having to sneak in to see me. Next, once I have formally announced your appointment, you will immediately offer your submission to Matz in the sacred rite of the Golden collaring ceremony. You will temporarily grant him the responsibility of protecting your status as the Dominant. He will be your champion and since you cannot officially speaking for yourself the Elders cannot bitch that the half-breed is breaking the Foundation laws by appearing in the Haus population uncollared because you will be kind of."

Noah gasped and his eyes went wide in terror as he replied, "Wait. If you make me the Mortar Dungeon Master, I cannot ever return to my place as the Head Master, Mad Maxx. Not that I'm complaining but you cannot allow that idiot Johannes to be in command of training the little ones. He isn't as careful with the children as I am."

With the heavy humored tone I responded, "It is far easier for me to get the sitting Fur King to change the rules and grant you both positions than it ever would be to get that monster Lucus to voice the overturning of the half-breed foundation law, Noah. Don't stress over this. You'll be returning to that shitty hovel you call your home sooner than you want, I promise you that. With sadness, may I add. Have a little faith in me, will you?"

His beautiful face lit up with joy as he replied, "No one knows King Claus better than you do, Mad Maxx. If you say he will make this happen, than I've no fear it won't. I'll happily go with you above and do whatever job you assign me without quarrel, and with joy in my heart. I thank you for this wonderful gift you give to me." He almost forgot himself and approached ready to adore me with his lips.

I pushed him back gently then said, "Easy there, Noah. The walls have eyes, ja? You must always be vigilant and give no reason for untrue rumors to spread about you. If gossiping starts that claims you've been unfaithful to your sentence as the untouched, I cannot be sure I could save you. Not yet anyway. So, promise me on your honor that for the next five months, you'll be extra careful. You are to speak to no one without my approval and do nothing without my command."

The Head Master nodded and replied, "Of course I swear this to you, Mad Maxx. There won't be any trouble. Everyone knows that to be caught fooling with me carries the death sentence for them too. You've nothing to be worried about."

With the hushed tone I said, "You are the respected Master down here, but up there is a different world. There are plenty that gladly would risk their lives if only to see you suffer while hurting me in the process of it. Come to think on it, Birgit is right about one thing. Keeping you under trusted and constant surveillance isn't the bad idea. You go back to your room and pack up your things. I said I'd return for you in an hour, but I'm going to need until five o'clock to get the things in order for your safe retrieval. Take some of that money I gave you to hide and go to the Dungeon commissary. Buy plenty of that wonderful aftershave I love and get several outfits that are worthy of the personal servant of the Mortar King. Get the suitcase to carry the fortune I gave to you and fix the compartment within to tuck it out of sight."

He nodded and leaned in to whisper, "And do you want me to buy the enema kit too?"

That made me chuckle as I replied quietly, "Nein. There will be questions about your asking to get that item, Mister Untouchable. Leave the procurement of those things of pleasure to me. No one even bats the eye when the Priceless catamite go seeking such foul devices for my use, ja?" Noah grimaced but nodded that he understood.

He then shot the nervous glance back toward the staircase and said, "What of that Mistress I knocked out? Surely, when she wakes, she will wish to see me punished for hitting her."

I groaned but replied, "Ah, shit. I almost forgot about that idiot. Let me handle Sigrid. Hopefully she was being honest in her offer to do anything to gain my forgiveness. Or at least the illusion that I'm willing to let old hurts slide. Okay, lover, go do everything I said."

Noah hesitated then with the sheepish glance said, "That woman that upset you is very beautiful, Mad Maxx. I know she has done something to cause you to dislike her, but I doubt there is anything in this world she could do to me that would make me wish her to disappear. I could look at her all day."

I reached out and swatted him harshly as I growled in reply, "You forget yourself, lover. You are my plaything exclusively. Keep those lovely eyes to yourself or I'll remove them and keep them in the place I am sure they never stray again. Besides, you know nothing about women. That one you dare to fawn over is the monster in a female's clothing. She'd fuck you over with brutal violence. It'd make that business I give to you earlier seem the gentle cuddle in comparison. Trust me, I found that out the hard way."

His eyes flew open wide in surprise and he glanced back her direction again as he said, "Really? He certainly did fool me. Thank you for correcting my error. Damn, how does he appear so feminine and how the hell does he camouflage his cock I wonder? Tape maybe?"

I rolled my eyes and nearly yelled out in irritated frustration, "Oh, my God. You are beautiful, Noah, but dumb as the post. Stop fooling around with stupid questions about crossdresser secrets and get your ass in gear will you? I'll see you at five. Go." I pointed in the direction of the Masters barracks hall.

Noah flinched then mumbled, "Okay, Mad Maxx. I'm going but please don't be angry with me about looking at that man. He makes for a lovely lady and I'm not the man with much experience to tell the difference. Besides, you did try to trade me off to that old lady Birgit. You say you don't share your things but what if she'd taken you up on the awful things you suggested? Would you expect me to go with her? How is that any different?" He started to leave to attend his duties.

With rapidness I blocked his retreat and replied, "Noah, Birgit is the only woman in the world I'd trust with my life. If you'd been so lucky as to have her choose to be with you, no one, not even God, would ever hear of it. That you can be sure of. Listen, you left me innocent as the little boy when you could have denied me such mercy. Even though I've suffered countless times being used as the sex toy to satisfy the lusts of perverted males my first taste as the penetrator was with the female, not the male. I will heal soon. Then you will be granted access to do to me the thing I did with you this morning. It was my desire to give you the gift of losing your penetration virginity to the gender you claim to prefer, as I did. What that wonderful lady lacks in youth, she makes up for in gentleness and patience. You could do far worse. In fact, you think to want to fuck that nasty thing that hates men but show distaste upon the thought of sharing the bed with the woman that could take you to paradise without breaking the sweat. Ah, Noah. You truly are untouched not to realize this is the truth of it."

He shrugged then leaned into my ear and whispered, "If she is such the Goddess, Mad Maxx, why don't you taken her to be your lover, ja? Perhaps, like me, you don't desire to wake up in the morning laying in the bed next to your mother either. All though, to be fair, unlike in your case, my mother was ugly on the outside too." He snuck a quick pecking kiss on my ear and rushed off before I could threaten to punish him for saying that and doing that.

There I stood fretting for far longer than I should have, unsure how to handle Sigrid. Though I didn't want her to demand Noah be punished for protecting me, however misguided that may have been, he did mean well. I also wasn't willing to allow her to go pegging me again to prevent that from happening.

The sounds of her faintly moaning alerted me to her returning from her unconsciousness. Like it or not, I was going to have to do my best to talk her into forgiving and forgetting this incident. Yikes.

Quickly I hobbled back toward the steps. I arrived just in time to see the groggy Mistress attempting to rise from the floor. With urgency I hurried to aid the woman to accomplish this without further injuring herself.

She glance up the moment she felt me take hold of her by the upper arm and said softly, "Oh, thank you, your Majesty. I guess I must have slipped or something. Tell me, how do I look? I'm worried that I'm the ghastly sight. Apparently, I caught the edge of the stone step with the bridge of my nose, ja?"

I winced upon noticing the gash in the center of her beak as I replied, "Don't stress over the tiny cut, Mistress. A little soap and water will clean it right up. It doesn't seem deep enough to require stitches. I doubt you'll end up with the scar over it. Seems to me your beauty remains flawless even if you did get a nasty bruise." Sigrid wobbled for the moment but indicated she was stable enough to stand on her own.

With slow caution I let go of her arm then inquired, "How you feeling now? Should I see if I can get one of my Dungeon Mistresses to escort you to visit with Doctor Attila?"

Sigrid smiled slightly and shook her head while she said, "Nein, but thank you for being the gentleman to make such an offer, your Majesty. I beg you to ignore my clumsiness. I'm completely embarrassed that you've witnessed my less than graceful moves. Despite all that, I wonder if I could be so bold as ask if you'd grant me a few moments of your time. I wish to give you the offer I think you'll find worthy of entertaining."

A small chuckle of relief that she didn't appear to recall Noah punching her escaped me as I replied, "Well, Mistress. I dare not leave you here until I am sure you won't pass out again. Why don't you take these moments to say what you've chased me down to say. However, I must tell you, Sigrid, you surely missed your calling as the saleswoman extraordinaire. Very few that have that job title could claim such dedication as to throw themselves at their customer's feet as roughly as you have done, ja?"

Sigrid's eyes twinkled as she broke out into uneasy sounding laughter then responded, "True, true, your Majesty. Well, I would consider that career but I had another more prestigious one in mind. Perhaps, you will believe I'm far better suited to do it than becoming the common barker for cheap material objects."

My intrigue over her words was obvious in my expression as I replied, "You don't say. What position in the Haus is it that you were thinking I'd be capable of appointing you to fill? The thrones of both floors are filled to capacity. Are you seeking placement here in the dungeon?"

She shook her head and smiled even more brightly as she said, "I suppose my duties, if you were to generously appoint me, would often include trips down here. However, it isn't the Dungeon Mistress that I want to lobby you for. I was thinking to offer my services to your Majesty, as your trusted tongue. If not as the one that gives voice to the Haus Law, then perhaps you may consider making me your Queen?"

My face fell into complete disbelief and I took a few steps back before I replied in the near whisper, "You are offering to become my regent or even my Mortar Queen? Why the hell would you want to be such a thing in the first place, Sigrid? You are the desired beauty with a wonderful future ahead of you. If I were to grant you either request you'd be condemned to the short life full of nightmares with the most violent end no doubt."

Sigrid frowned and fixated her pretty eyes into my shocked gaze as she growled out, "Before you quickly dismiss my honest offers, your Majesty, I think you should be made aware of something. I happen to know that bitch Gretta and that cunt Cora are looking to see you neutered, shamed and then buried under miles of mortar. I refuse to voice the many reasons I desire to see both these Queens fail but be assured I hate them bad enough I'd gladly suffer being the imprisoned Mortar Queen. If only to gain the place close enough to cut there fucking throats. However, you give me the honor of becoming your voice. Well then I can swear on my soul I not only will get you the best deal possible given the restraint of Haus laws, but I also will stop at nothing to use my place as Mortar Regent to send the two Queens right to hell where they both belong."

I allowed my famished eyes to wander down her gorgeous frame for the moment, then I returned my attention to her gaze and replied flatly, "You really expect me to believe anything you say to me, Sigrid? You screwed me over once, and no doubt will happily do it twice if I let you. I'm not stupid enough to believe your hatred for Gretta and Cora is the truth of your change in attitude when it comes to me."

The Mistress snorted then in the flash unzipped her oversized jacket. I stood there stunned to stupid when she threw it open to reveal she wore nothing under it. Her perky, well-formed breasts of the most impeccable shape held me in the trance of lust for several moments of awe-struck silence.

Sigrid permitted me to examine her assets unhindered as she finally said, "Before you say nein too hastily, your Majesty, I wish for you to remember there is far more difference between me and that arrogant cousin of the Queen Lucus than merely our agendas. Everyone in this Haus thinks you are the homosexual that loves being drilled, but not me. I know the truth of your nature. That little boy I played the nasty prank on was willing to marry me if only I'd say, ja. Well, your Majesty, today you get your darkest wish. I tell you, ja. Make me your Queen if you wish or take me as your equal partner in the way only the Mortar King can. Don't try to lie to yourself or me. I know you'd love to be enforced to

71

grant your special services privilege to the Regent of your preferred gender."

My throat had gone dry from ragged breathing, but I managed to squeak out, "Can you give me a little time to consider your most generous offer, my Lady?"

She giggled then closed her coat abruptly before she replied, "You have five months, and not one day more, your Majesty. However, if you wish to come by and grant me a private audience, I will give you my complete resume. I think you'll agree, I'm the best suited for either position I'm interested in filling. Oh, I meant to say, every position that you could have interest in filling." She covered her mouth with her palm and shot me the coy glances as she said that.

I felt my head nodding while I barely said in a raspy tone, "Uhm, ja. I think I may have to fit you into my busy schedule. I suppose it couldn't hurt to take a look at what you have to offer. I mean to say, investigate fully the benefits of choosing the Mistress instead of the Master for the job as Regent."

Sigrid lowered her hand and grinned widely as she exclaimed, "Ah, you are the wise King indeed, your Majesty. I am certain after careful consideration you will come to the conclusion that I am the right pick to defend you as your regent. I am grateful that you granted me the mercy of an audience with you. Please, allow me to extend an open invitation to you. I'll wait patiently for your attendance to this matter. Now, I've taken up too much of your time already. I will withdraw from your royal presence with your permission, my Lord." She curtsied gracefully and I waved her off in the gesture of release.

The Mistress ran her eyes over me appearing wanton for a second. Then without another word she took off up the steps leaving me behind to contemplate this most unexpected offer. I might have held that spot dumbstruck with the looping vision of her naked flesh caressing my memory had it not been for the slight tap on my shoulder.

I turned around and found myself face to face with Mistress Birgit. The elderly woman wore the peaceful smile and the expression of humor on her wizened face.

With the growl of irritation in my voice I said, "And? Can I help you, Mistress?"

Birgit chuckled low then replied, "Lovely frau, that Sigrid. Too bad she isn't Mortar Queen material. I hope your Majesty isn't foolish enough to be seriously thinking of sleeping with her. I believe you'd find yourself wondering who is fucking who."

My breath rushed out and I groaned in response, "You are maybe the smartest person I've ever met, Mistress. Now we both have found agreement in something. I repeat, what can I do for you? Surely, you aren't sneaking around in the halls looking for chances to point out the obvious to your Lord and Master."

The Head Mistress shook her head and quelled her mirth as she replied, "Of course not, your Majesty. I was trying to catch you before you left to ask you if you'd spoken to King

Claus lately. Also, I thought if it was alright with you, I think the Palace could use the cleansing done by the experienced professional. Me and Vivianna would be most happy to see that it's tidied up. You know in case the honorable Claus wanted to take a tour of your court."

With the knowing nod I kept my gaze on her own and said, "Ah, okay I understand, Mistress. Uhm, I thank you for your most loyal service offer but there will be no need for you or your sister to expend so much energy. I, uhm, happen to know Florian hired the worthy maid earlier today. The palace is spick and span. The honorable Claus is more than welcome to come see that all is in order himself."

Birgit smiled then replied, "That certainly explains why our beloved Monarch bothers to pay us his unworthy servants the unannounced visit. I thank you for the mercy of your kindness, your Majesty. I beg of you to grant me release. I believe you have better things to do than stand around yapping with old ladies, ja?"

My own face lit up brightly as I said, "Not quite yet, my Lady. Before you go I wish for you to get me a few items that are not easily acquired without many questions asked. Can I trust you to do this for me with both haste and stealth, my dear?" Birgit nodded and I leaned into her ear to whisper the list.

When I had completed this request I pulled away and Birgit's smile returned as she replied, "You know I meant what I said to you earlier, your Majesty. Noah is the loveliest of young men I've ever been blessed to know. I beg of you to treat him well. He's more than earned generosity and kindness."

That caused me to chuckle as I said, "I think I shall be the judge of that, Mistress."

Mistress Birgit smirked and then winked as she replied, "I think you already have and I say that with both respect and the promise of silence, your Majesty. Don't look so surprised that I know what you're up to, Sire. You forget this old bird has been around for centuries. I can see the way his eyes follow you and the return adoration showing in your own for him. I worry that if I figured out this game, if maybe others not so understanding will do it also. Where the hell do you intend to store that innocent boy while you're held hostage to Lucus's will, darling? Perhaps you hoped to hide him in your closet, right next to that enema kit you want me to acquire for him?"

I nearly choked on my spit as I said in the hushed whisper, "Mistress, you go too far with your accusations. I have no interest in the Head Master other than to have the burly bodyguard. You must be aware being the Mortar King carries great risks. Besides, you already know my nature. I do not find the attention of males sexy."

The elderly lady snort laughed then replied, "Ah, your Majesty. You must forgive this old woman her silly thoughts. My brain is getting soft, ja? Of course, you don't intend to find comfort in the arms of that sweet man that's almost more love starved than you are. He is just so easy to adore, I already confessed to you he's slain my dusty old heart. I will say nothing more of it. However, I do insist, even at the risk of punishment, you give me the answer to where you plan to store him above? Those rats that live on every floor will gnaw the flesh right off his bones if you don't put him into the impenetrable vault."

I rolled my eyes and with the childlike stomp I whined, "Dammit Birgit, why do I always feel like I'm being scolded by a mother whenever you speak with me? You got to stop that. If others were to see me bending to your advice, they won't respect my authority."

She shook her head then pointed the boney digit into my face as she replied angrily, "Stop behaving like the little boy and I will end my preaching to you, Maxximillian. Listen to me, honey. I think you are doing a wonderful thing for Noah. I'm not trying to talk you out of it. I merely am asking you to be sure you aren't doing more harm than good for him. I know damned well you're in love with him, and him with you. I'm truly happy for you both, and I wish to see the relationship safely continue. There is only one sure way to protect him from vicious attacks of the physical nature or rumors that will get him hurt. Order him to be confined to the apartment with me and Viviana when not in attendance to his King. We are the most elderly ladies in the Haus. No one will think any hanky-panky is going on with him sharing the rooms with his grandmothers, ja? We are on the fifth floor. You know getting up there without high status nor permission is nearly impossible."

My shoulders slumped and I dropped my gaze to the floor as I nodded and then responded, "You would make the far better King than me, Birgit. I never would have thought of such a clever cover. I apologize to have acted the ass to you earlier by shamefully asking you to take Noah's virginity. I take you up on your generous offer to command he be housed with you and your sister Vivianna. I also beg your forgiveness for insulting you as I have done." I fell to the kneel before her.

Birgit gasped then reached out and backhanded the hell out of my head as she croaked out, "What the fuck are you doing, Maxximillian? Get the hell off your knees, fool. The King never apologizes, not ever. Damn boy, perhaps you need to visit with the Fur King for lessons in the proper way to rule more than that old bitch needs to go snooping around in your kingdom."

I nearly went face first into the floor in my haste to return to my boots as I quickly said, "Uhm, okay, so you are released Birgit. Go on, go dammit. Before I forget that I love you like I do and send you to the pit for striking your King."

She slapped at the air and snorted but turned to leave while mumbling, "He threatens to send me to the pit? Well, don't I feel neglected that my beloved King wouldn't treat me with the same affection he has his natural mother. I was hoping to get told soon I'd be entertaining guest on the throne next to Florian." Birgit continued to mutter to herself long after she was too far for me to hear her lamenting my lack of violence toward her.

I glanced at Maxximillian and said, "That woman is crazy. How could we not love her?"

Maxximillian snorted then said with the huge grin on his pretty face, "She might be full of dementia but that dame has got spunk, I'll give her that. Had you whining like the little bitch you truly are. You know I think you aren't cut out for this gig as the King, motherfucker. You didn't jump on Sigrids's offer. Why? That babe is built like the brickhouse and hot to trot. Yet, you do all you can to obtain the favors of that jive turkey, Noah. I think you confused as to where you are supposed to put our cock, daddy O. Maybe it's time you move over and let this cat run the show, you dig?"

His insane speech made me cringe as I replied, "Seems to me, if we were to leave it up to you there would never be any relief for the *fleischpuppe (translation: meat puppet)*. You aren't old enough to recall the dirty trick that bitch played on us. Eventually you will learn that wisdom comes from making mistakes, son. In these dangerous situations to come, there is no longer any room for that. So, experience must rule out your youthful impulsivity every time. Don't fret over it. I'll always share the wheel with you whenever there is the need for speed. Otherwise it is for the best that you let me handle the more complex problems."

He put his hands up into the air and blew out his breath in frustration while saying, "Fine. We'll do this your way, pops. Just don't come crying to me when this loser winds up on the wrong side of the grass. We better stop this useless gum flapping though. You have plenty of dicks to suck before you're forced to return to crash at our pad and lick the nastiest of them all."

I turned around and flashed the expression of confusion at Die Brutal and said, "Can one of you get the translation book so I can understand this unruly bitch's language? Do you think he's autistic or something? Nothing that comes out of his mouth makes a bit of sense."

Die brutal shook his three heads and then Mad Max replied, "Nothing that goes into yours makes sense to us Mad Maxx. I'd like to ask about this crazy shit you are pulling with the Head Master myself. However, I'll never get that chance to because you'll never remember to turn off the speakers, you fucking idiot." I gasped and swung my head in every direction full of fear that someone had been eavesdropping.

Upon finding no other soul hanging around taking notes on my inner dialogue, I sighed the breath of relief. Then with great care, and slow progress I made my way back up the steps. The moment I put the boot upon the lushly carpeted first floor, I heard yet another voice I recognized hailing me from somewhere in the fast moving foot traffic.

I decided whatever this fellow wanted to speak with me about, I wasn't interested to hear it. Rudely I pretended to not notice Eric's frantic waves and begging me to wait till he could get near enough to visit.

The big clock on the wall indicated it was nearly three. With a groan of disgust, I hurriedly headed for Matz's old apartment. It was time for the Haus whore to get to work, and I couldn't afford to be late. There was no way I could easily explain coming into a sudden fortune to my pimp without being forced to share the unfair cut with him and the other Wolves.

The way I saw it, that was my blood money. I would be damned if any of those useless pricks were taking more of the bite out of me than they already had. Besides, I had far bigger plans on the best use for that cash. Matz wouldn't approve of my designs and I didn't wish to end up having to kill him over his bitching over it either.

The residents of the Haus managed to block my route of escape from the determined fourth floor Dominant. Eric practically ran hurtles in his wild attempts to catching up with my rapid pace. Before I could protest the man had managed to place himself between me and the destination I preferred he didn't know existed.

I halted and glared at the top man from the team leaders of the FBL while he smiled then said, "Oh, thank God I've gotten your attention before I lost you among this mess of flesh. I swear you can move like the wind even with the impediment of that oversized crutch, your Majesty."

With the frustrated eye roll I replied, "So, you've decided to interrupt my important schedule to give me underhanded insults, have you Eric? Well, go on. Tell me that my clothes, though out of date by hundreds of years look impressive on my svelte frame. Or maybe you desire to say that my bandages are sure to be all the rage in the Haus culture this year because I make them appear fabulous."

Eric chuckled nervously but obviously didn't take the hint because he said, "Your sense of humor is one of the things I've always appreciated fully, your Majesty. That said, I don't want to waste your time with small talk and gossiping."

The sounds of indignation escaped my throat as I responded, "Ha, you claim that, but yet here we are, Eric, aren't we? There must be too much lead in the Haus water pipes because I do believe everyone is going deaf. But regrettably not dumb. Get out of my way and leave me be. I'm all favored out today. Try again tomorrow or if you think this simply cannot wait. You can take up your cause with Florian, ja?"

This pushy Dominant replied in the fussy voice, "Ah, that name isn't familiar to me, your Majesty. So, since you are already perturbed, it seems to me I've nothing to lose by just stating my case. Do with it as you please."

My eyes vent wide in pure disbelief of Eric's lack of notice that he was flirting with death as I responded, "Oh, why thank you for the mercy of permitting me the right to behave as the King that I am."

He backed up one step and put up his hands in the signal of surrender as he replied rapidly, "Hold on, your Majesty. I didn't, I mean I. Oh fuck it. Look, I wanted to offer you my services as your potential regent is all. I told Kay this was idea was stupid. Why the hell would the Master of this Haus consider naming me his trusted tongue, anyway. That is what I said to him. Kay made it sound like the perfect match that you'd surely be thrilled to accept though."

The fury rising within me suddenly turned off as I said with rising curiosity in my tone, "Am I to understand you're willing to backstab your most coveted FBL member the mighty Mad Lucus? Eric, have you lost your mind? Do you realize what that vicious motherfucker will do to your gay men's group the minute he hears of this attempt to betray him? Isn't that the life work and love of you and your husband Kay?"

Eric frowned but nodded his head slowly as he said with venom literally dripping from every word, "I dare that snotty bitch to try it. He's will find out real quick Kay and me are the unbeatable team with the connections that run far deeper than that thin blue blood in his veins. He doesn't scare me, Sire. Now, are you willing to entertain my proposal or should I go see this fellow you called Florian and speak to him first. I confess I'm unsure of the protocol required to see my honest offer is taken in with serious consideration."

I put up my hand and signaled him to be silent as I replied, "Nein, I think it best I manage this one personally. Florian isn't in charge of matters above ground anyway. Tell me, Eric. What makes Kay think you'd be the better choice as regent than the powerful cousin of the Queen of England? Hurry up and state your case, dammit. I don't have all fucking day."

Eric smiled with sudden glee as he responded in the rapid fire speech, "First. I thank you for the mercy of hearing me out, your Majesty. Second, simply put, you share the same vision for this Haus as we do. Abolish slavery, end torture, stop the murdering of the helpless, and cessation of purchasing children from human trafficking sources. You name me your regent and I will use your power and voice to see all this is accomplished. Furthermore, Kay and I are in the honorable monogamous marriage. You will be free of enduring unwanted attention from me or anyone else. I will protect you with my own life if necessary. Come what may, I remain loyal to my Lord and Master." He dropped into the semi-graceful kneel at my feet as he finished his attempt to gain the title as Mortar Regent.

I stood there staring at him for the second then motioned him to rise as I replied, "All good arguments, Eric. Can I have a little time to think on your offer or do you expect the answer today?"

The pudgy middle-aged man grunted as he stood up and said in a friendly tone, "Oh, my goodness, your Majesty. I wouldn't believe you were being honest with me if you said ja without considering this important decision for many weeks or even months."

With another frustrated eye roll I said, "Again, you attempt to offer veiled insults, Eric. Tell you what, while I mull over your most interesting offer maybe you should brush up on your manners, ja? You better. Because the next time I see you and you dare to insinuate that I'm the liar, you will get that meeting with Florian. Good day to you. Tell Kay I said hello." I took off without waiting for the man to respond to my dressing him down.

I barely arrived at the apartment door before the clock chimed on the hour. Without hesitation I knocked on the wood softly. It swung open immediately. Roland's dower face was there to greet me. The smile of thrill quickly replaced his expression of discord the moment he recognized it was the talent that had arrived at last.

He backed away and waved me inside while saying, "See Matz, I told you he'd make it on time. Maxx isn't ever late for work. You worry too much and bitch to the extreme."

Before I made it past the Violinist I placed the stiff elbow into his gut. His air expelled with force and he went to his knees. Matz, Valitin, Magnas, and Cary stood there staring in shock at their flailing Wolf buddy unsure what the hell to do over that sucker punch I'd thrown.

I reached out and slammed the door shut then turned toward the pack as I yelled out, "Where the fuck have you motherfuckers been? Well, while you useless bitches have been sitting around here stroking each other's limp dicks, I've been approached by two Dominants that should've never gotten the chance to know me by my first name much less force me to grant them audience. Why do I pay for protection I'm clearly not getting?"

Roland gasped and rasped out, "Mad Maxx, you got to cut us some slack brother. None of us knew where to find you. Matz said you took off out of here like the rocket to the moon. What were we supposed to do? We assumed you didn't want us around or else you'd waited around till one of us arrived. Or at the very least, tell Matz where you were headed."

My eyes tore away from the stressed appearing pack members and took focus on the struggling Wolf. Without the word I reared back my good leg and kicked Roland in the face with strength. He sputtered, flopped and cursed while blood flowed in rivers from his mouth and nose.

Matz wailed out, "Mad Maxx, please stop this violence. It's not Roland's fault. If you must take out your aggression on anyone then it should be me. He speaks the truth. I didn't give them orders to seek you out because I thought you desired to be left alone."

I turned and shot him the glare of caution as I exclaimed, "Shut up, Matz. You are far too eager to receive the punishment for shit that you're not fully responsible for causing. Roland here has no issue with beating up the little fellow that cannot defend himself. Seems that chronic bad behavior has resulted in his wrongly thinking I too will tolerate his bullying. Well no more. This shit of failing me and assaulting your own will stop today. Roland, get your stupid ass up and go clean yourself up in the bathroom. Hurry up, dog. The customers will be arriving shortly. I doubt they paid to watch the boxing match loser lick his wounds, ja?" I kept the furious eye on Matz as he rushed by me hell bent to help his lover to obey my command with quickness.

The second the two of them were clear of the room I returned my attention to the remaining three and said angrily, "Any of you want to add to this one way conversation? If not, then I think you should be getting your asses out into the hallway to do your jobs of greeting rather than guarding."

Valitin and Magnas hoofed it past me without argument. Cary, however, just couldn't hold his tongue. I drew in my breath near ready to breath fire as he took the spot in front of me.

He shook his head, crossed his arms and with the sound of disbelief in his tone said, "I get that you must convince the Haus that you are the man to be respected. But Christian, baby, you need not lord your power over your friends."

With the loud sigh I shook off my fury then replied calmly, "Ah, you are so right, lover. It's unforgivable for me to demand that the men that I pay do the job they were hired to do. What was I thinking?"

Cary sucked in his air and said, "Uhm, I'm not sure that's the response I was seeking but, okay. I'm just saying that you need to stop losing your temper with us all the time, baby. This isn't the time to make enemies of your only honest allies, ja?"

I nodded then motioned him to approach as I breathed out sounding defeated, "Again, you speak the truth. I suppose I'm so grouchy because I'm sexually pent up. You know what? You could fix that problem for me, and then I would be better able to manage my temper, ja? What do you say, lover? Are you up for the quicky?"

The Shadow King grinned but seemed apprehensive over my suggestion as he replied, "You know damned well I'm eager to be with you, baby. However, that bitch Friz is due here any minute. It'd have to be so damned quick it could win the Olympic medal for speed."

I approached him and ran my bandaged hands down his flesh as I responded, "When Roland and Matz free up the room, I'll make you the first customer of the day. We'll make Friz wait his turn. There are perks to being not only the Master of the Haus but her only working hustler, ja?"

Cary quivered with thrill and nodded then said, "You have no idea how bad I want you right now, Christian. If you are being serious, than count me in."

With a sudden move I wrapped my arms around his waist and pulled him into the deep kissing. Matz came out of the bedroom to find the two of us engaged in heavy petting on his fancy new couch.

He gasped then called out in the loud whisper, "What the fuck are you doing Cary? Not only does Mad Maxx have clients, but if that bitch Friz saw you necking with your dark bonded, you know what could happen. This action is forbidden between the Dominant and black collar submissive."

I broke from my mouthing Cary and replied in the breathless tone, "Matz, you are getting forgetful brother. This lovely man is the mercenary. He isn't collared nor Dominant. Therefore he cannot be off limits to anyone in this Haus. Be the dear and tell the boys at the door to hold off Friz for about seven minutes more. Oh, and then you can make yourself scarce as well. Maybe use this extra time to remind Roland his abuse of my pimp is the insult to me. He ever hits you again and I find out about it, I will give him twice the beating." I returned to my action already in progress without interest in hearing the response.

The moment the overtly confused Matz had completed the orders I gave him. I ripped Cary's shirt open and plied his skin with heated kisses. The Shadow King moaned and writhed under me, very clearly appreciative of my efforts to seduce him.

Then I found my way back toward his sensitive ears and whispered to him, "You must have been told that I'm incapable of providing you penetration service, Cary."

A loud disapproving groan escaped him as he replied, "Ja, that damned doctor read me the riot act when he thought it was me that caused your injury to re-open. I swear to you, baby, I want to kill that bastard Jonas more than anything. He's the callused brute to misuse you the way he does."

I nodded then responded, "Ah, so you don't believe me either when I say the DJ raped me, not the vampire? That's regrettable to know."

Cary grabbed me by the upper arms with suddenness and forced my eyes to gaze into his own as he said, "Christian, honey. Everyone is aware you killed those two collars in the psychotic fit because Jonas forced himself on you while they watched without offering to pull him off you. This memory you have of invisible DJ is merely the stress driven delusion. I wish you'd stop claiming such a thing exists."

My expression remained lustful as I replied, "Whatever you say, lover boy. Now, as to that minor issue that you admit you're aware of. How can we get around that? I've got the itch I need to scratch and you certainly are the man with the tool to see me released from the torture of it, ja?"

The Shadow King's look of concern softened to that of mischievous humor as he responded, "If I give you the skilled remedy then what shall you give me in the return service, baby? Hmmm?" His eyes ran down my chest until they sat upon the evidence of my interest in seeing that this trade happened between us.

I leaned down into his face and said, "I go first. Then I will see to your urges after I finish the last customer of the day. Deal, ja or nein?"

Cary's face fell and he whimpered in response, "You want me to wait in line? Come on, Christian. That's unfair and to be honest not very sexy to think about."

With the evil chuckle I replied, "What's the matter, lover? You don't enjoy the sloppy seconds?"

He glared at me angrily and said flatly, "You mean the foul fifths? If we're being honest with each other here, than ja. I am not eager to be nothing more than another man on your long list of conquests, Christian."

His response caused me to take on the expression of pity as I nodded then replied, "Ah, ja, I can understand your misgivings, lover. So, tell you what. How about we do something that no other man coming here today can lay claim to paying to enjoy from me."

Cary's eyes narrowed as if he'd become suspicious as he said quietly, "What the hell could that be? I've seen the skilled services they are buying, baby. everything but fucking you proper has been purchased in one form or another."

With the demonic cackle I replied, "The thing I desire from you isn't for sale on the menu. I cannot be penetrated but you certainly are healthy enough to be yourself, lover. I want to fuck you instead of being fucked. What do you say? Are you ready to serve your King to his complete satisfaction?"

The Shadow King shook his head wildly, "Nein. You ask for anything else from me, Christian and I happily will do it for you. But being your mare, forget that shit. Never gonna happen."

My mirth ended abruptly while I glared at him barely able to contain the anger in my voice, "Why not? You may like it. You won't know until you try it. Besides, you don't bother to listen when I tell you being the bottom isn't pleasant to me. I think it only fair you allow me to explore this new avenue with you before making the rash decision about it."

He dropped his gaze appearing suddenly shameful as he whispered, "I can assure you that being the one penetrated isn't sexually thrilling to me."

Through gritted dentures I hissed out, "Oh? And how is it that you can be so damned against something unless you've already tried it. Which couldn't be true. Since I seem to recall you were the complete virgin to homosexual sex when we bonded not more than six months ago. I've not been guilty of taking the mount, so, again I demand you to take the position of submission. We will discover if you are right about disinterest in stepping into my role right now." I attempted to roll him to his face with force.

Cary struggled with all his might against my actions. His refusal to obey my command further excited my urge to use him for my base urges. The two of us battled as roughly as we had in the beginning of our troubled relationship for several minutes. Until at last, the Shadow King believed he was about to lose his bid to remain the top man between us.

He called out in the desperate sounding tone, "Christian, enough. Okay, I confess it. I know I don't enjoy anal sex because I've already tried it a few times with someone else. It was awful, and I don't want to ever do it again. There, are you finally satisfied that I'm telling you the truth when I say I'm not interested in quelling your lust that way?"

I halted my actions with promptness and bellowed out full of fury, "You went behind my back and let someone else take your penetration virginity? You are nothing but the fucking dog. Get away from me, Cary." I punched him in the side barely able to control my rage over this insult.

The Shadow King wailed from the blow then replied, "Stop acting the jealous lover you certainly aren't, Christian.

From what I recall you never seemed interested in doing that with me before today. Plus, you have a lot of gall calling me the dog when I do believe you have several cocks waiting for your attention right outside the door. How do you think that makes me feel being forced to watch my lover ridden hard every day in the Haus by those with the money or the power to pay for it."

I glared at him while chuckling without the sound of real humor behind it as I responded, "I suppose you didn't consider the cost when you thought to ride the Collar King pony express to the third floor, ja? You say that you love me but then refuse to return the service I ask of you because you didn't enjoy it. However, I find it incredibly painful, humiliating and unnatural to endure it but give it to you because when I say those words I fucking mean them. Get out of my sight, Cary. I'll deal with you once I'm finished with my tasks of making sure you and these other ingrates are not thrown into the streets to starve."

Cary dropped his shoulders into the slump and said, "Christian, I am. Well, an apology at this point sounds empty. I suppose there is nothing I can say or do to take it back. Oh, shit, I have no idea what you want from me. I never have. I do love you. I really do. I wish that you could believe that without constantly questioning it."

I pointed at the door and roared, "Get out, dammit. I said I will deal with you later. So go, wait in line like the good customer that understands he must pay to play, Cary."

His head snapped up and he glared at me with the barely restrained tempest in his gaze, "I'll go with pleasure, your Majesty While you entertaining the swine, I'll be turning over the seat cushions in the effort to scrape together enough change to cover the amount you're charging to be blown by the Master of the Haus." He stood up with speed and rushed for the door, slamming it behind him with such force it nearly broke the framing.

Matz stuck his head out of the bedroom door and very quietly said, "Damn that was brutal, Mad Maxx. Will you and Cary be okay? I mean I don't mean to pry or anything, but you boys were loud enough I think the fourth floor may have heard some of that argument."

I laid my head back on the couch and blew out my breath into the air then replied, "Can I not do anything without being questioned endlessly about it? Matz, leave Roland to recover on the bed. I need you to go down to the Dungeon to retrieve some things the Head Mistress has collected for me. Go get them then hurry back."

The pimp walked into the room slowly while saying, "Sure thing, Maxx. However, how you intend to service the clients? It may be a bit uncomfortable performing with Roland hogging the bed, ja?"

A chuckle erupted from my mouth as I replied, "You couldn't sell the penetration services. There is no need for the comfort of the mattress. The couch will provide adequate staging I think. Now, go do as I asked without giving me grief, please. Oh, and send in that asshole Friz before you go. Damn I think I have the migraine coming on."

Matz raised his eyebrows and said, "That excuse only works for the females, Maxx. I'll be back soon. Make sure to send them away smiling. It was the serious chore to get the customers to believe you would be here given the rumors they've heard about that Stasi mess, you know." I nodded that I understood his anxieties, and the pimp took off to seek out Birgit without further quarrel.

I heard Friz enter the room before I could see his unsightly frame approaching. With the deep breath I left my place sitting on the couch and took to my boots. There was no secret that I hated this client slightly more than almost any of the others. He was notoriously rough with me, and deeply into thudding with an extra interest in humiliation. Yuck!

The cruel Dominant stopped in the entry and smiled at me then with the wink said, "Ah, there you are, pretty Mad Maxx. Aren't you the sight for sore eyes. I wonder before we begin this pleasure service might I bend your ear for a moment?"

"I've rolled my eyes so many times this afternoon Friz, I swear I can tell you what color my brains are. So, go ahead. Tell me what foul sexual thing you want to add extra to this service call. Just be aware, talking dirty to you costs extra and I charge by the number of words." I motioned him to take the seat I'd just abandoned.

Friz chuckled then walked toward me without any sign of fear while saying, "You always been the crazy bastard, haven't you? I think that may be one of the few things of quality you possess with honesty." I started to rear back to strike him but the man was expecting my fury.

He blocked my blow and quickly retaliated by grabbing me by the balls. Then he covered my mouth with his free hand to muffle my cries of pain. He squeezed till I was robbed of breath from the torture of it and leaned into my ear.

Friz whispered in the humored tone, "Now that I have your complete attention, you schizophrenic freak, you should listen closely to every word I say. Only I'm not the one who will pay for each one. You are. There is the rumor going around that the place as your regent may not be fully committed to the snotty bitch Lucus. Well, I must say that makes you far more interesting to my dark interests than you ever have been before. Now, I realize you'll be getting tons of offers. Choices for the weak minded can be difficult, I know. Hey, are you paying attention to me, idiot?" He began to twist my parts until I nodded unable to do anything else for fear that he'd damage me permanently if I tried.

The bastard chuckled, then resumed his demands only loud enough for me to hear, "Anyway, as I was saying, I'm gonna make this real easy for you. You are going to stand before the Fur and Silk during the internment ritual in five months and call out my name just like you've done many time right here in this shitty little apartment. If for any reason your simple brain let's this important information slip away, than I suppose that creepy husband of yours may have to be told of your dishonorable career choices, ja? I wonder, are you capable of understanding what it is that I'm telling you, boy?" I quickly nodded and did all I could not to faint away from lack of air. That shit really hurt you know.

Friz nodded back than said, "Good boy. Now, I'm gonna release you. If you thinking to call in your brutes or retaliate in any way it might be best for you to re-consider it. I wrote the note with all the things necessary to see you all punished without mercy. I left it behind and instructed my wife Audrey to turn it over to Jonas if anything bad were to happen to me. This entire situation will be our little secret. I bet you know all about those, don't you? You've been sucking the cocks of your uncles and cousins since you could barely walk, but I doubt you've the intelligence to understand how fucked up you truly are. All you Schmidt motherfuckers are the inbred morons. That's fine though. Finally we've found one with some use. Oh and I do intend to enjoy you to the hilt." He let go of me and pushed me away from him with speed.

I fell to the floor gasping and cradling my aching parts. Friz walked over and stood above me glaring down with the nastiest smile tugging at his lips. I quickly rolled to my side, both to protect myself from further assault and to prevent him from seeing into my eyes.

He knelt down behind me and said, "Aw, don't pout. You are so ugly when you do that. I do believe I've paid for the oral services. I think it in your best interest to make sure

I don't feel ripped off or as I just proved to you I can and will return the favor."

Fritz roughly snatched me by the shoulders and turned me to face him. I glared at him full of quiet rage. He smiled and began undoing his breeches buttons, while chuckling under his breath.

I sucked in enough air to speaking and rasped out, "You put that in my mouth and I'll end your quest for power immediately."

The brutal brute reached out and took up my head by the hair on the back of my head as he replied, "You almost as hard headed as I am right this moment, boy. I think you'd better put your tongue to better use than issuing useless threats. I've got you backed into the corner and you know it. Go ahead, say another Goddamn thing to me other than thank you for the mercy of allowing me to service you, Master, and watch to see if I'm the one suffering emasculation, boy." With that he forced himself into my mouth.

Obviously, I was not in the position to refuse him his demands. Not at that moment, anyway. Though while I endured another of his usual scenes of humiliation, I was making plans to gain the return of head service. As far as I was concerned, Friz's days on earth were numbered, whether he believed me capable of doing it or not.

Once he believed he had completely dominated me, he reached his climax. I refused to leave my place on the floor while he said several more disgusting things. He was attempting to use demeaning language in his effort to break my self-esteem into tiny bits. I pretended to be upset by his silly games.

Yet, if he really wanted to destroy my confidence, he'd have to get up far earlier in the morning to do it. Peter was my original trainer. No one was as good at finding weakness and exploiting it as that man is. Fritz was the novice in comparison. Ha!

The moment he was out the door, I sat up and shook off the foulness of his memory. Matz quietly slipped into the apartment and took the seat across from me with the expression of worry on his face.

I popped my neck, groaned over the mild discomfort still clinging to my man parts, then glanced at him and said, "What is it now, Matz. You look like someone ate your grandmother. Out with it."

He shook his head then replied in the near whisper, "All your customers have cancelled, Mad Maxx."

That caused me to take notice as I yelled out in surprise, "Huh? Did they say why?"

Matz nodded then dropped his gaze to his lap as he replied, "Uhm, ja. It seems that Cary was so pissed he told all them you weren't available. I haven't had time to call them all back, but before I go groveling with false excuses, Maxx, you must put the leash on the Shadow King. He's forgotten his place both in service to his King and in the partnership with his Wolf brothers."

I snorted then took to my boots with speed as I responded, "You seem to have read my mind, Matz. Where is that ungrateful bitch at this moment?"

Cary's angry voice called out from the doorway, "He is within hearing distance, Mad Maxx. If you got something you wish to say to me. Here I am." The Shadow King was flanked by the stressed out looking Valitin and Magnas.

With a snort I replied, "Ah, you wanted to continue our discussion but didn't agree that I had the right to demand you wait your turn, ja?"

The Shadow King approached me and bellowed back, "What's the matter, Maxx? Wasn't Fritz's interests enough to scratch that itch for you? I'm tired of playing second fiddle to your whims. We are going to settle this discord while you are still fresh enough to give me your full attention."

I motioned for Matz to throw me the paper bag he'd retrieved from Birgit. He quickly tossed it and I caught it midair. Cary became enraged to the point of stupidity over my seemingly ignoring his attempts to start the fight with me. He came charging my direction, practically blowing smoke out of his nostrils like the mad bull.

Rapidly I stepped aside. Then I placed my boot in the direct path of the furious Wolf. He didn't have time to react with effectiveness. His frenzied stride was terminally interrupted. Cary let out the wail of indignation as he spilled to the floor face first.

Without a single sound I calmly threw myself upon his writhing frame. He cursed me, but he'd not regained balance enough to end my retaliation assault. Then to every Wolfs' surprise, I jerked the chain leash attached to the silver collar from that bag. Cary was stunned to silence and stillness when he felt me slip that manacle around his throat then lock it closed.

No one in the room moved nor spoke while they watched me roll off their subdued brother. I took up the slack in the leash and glared at the still bewildered appearing Shadow King angrily.

"There are many foul things I must suffer thanks to my fate as the wretch that was leveled Priceless. However, I refuse to continue down this treacherous path without the mercy of proper protection. Cary you swore your undying allegiance to me and were condemned by the actions of our Dark Bond. If you now regret the hast of your choice of lovers than welcome to the hell that is my world, sweetheart. I'm going to make Goddamn sure you keep your promises of loyalty to me and only me. Get up. You've decided to behave as the poorly trained canine and therefore you'll be treated like one. What is the matter Wolves? Didn't you realize that your King could turn the wild beast into the coddled pet using only the sound of his voice? Well if you find that fascinating, wait till you see the magic trick up my other sleeve. Matz, you will follow behind the Shadow King and your Lord and Master. There are two collars with the leashes in this bag. It is time to go collect its owner. Since apparently, one guard simply isn't enough to do this job correctly. We about to capture the rare grizzly bear and tame that bitch too."

Chapter 20: A Pack of Wolves

Cary laid there on the floor appearing too stunned to say or do anything. Matz also seemed too surprised to find the will to obey my command. This unexpected disruption in my attempts to make the living for myself and the numerous little ones wearing black collars in my name, certainly was not appreciated.

I had told Birgit to purchase the Gold collar and the chain leash for Noah. He was already aware that to bring him to ground level, certain rules in the Haus laws would need to be artfully bent. Though I hadn't spoken with Matz about his important role in my plan, I hadn't been worried too much about the possibility he would refuse my wishes. We had the long history of troubles between us, but no matter what the situation, I had come to trust that the Wolf pimp was the man of his word.

Sure, he had raped me back in the early days of my place as Dominant. Yet he was only the human. He was capable of terrible mistakes, which was the truth of it. I'd had a few far worse ones under my own belt. Yikes! In the end, Matz had always managed to pay me back for any pain he'd ever caused me. Often in ways he wasn't even aware of if he'd be willing to do the Gold collar ritual and give Noah the opportunity the taste of life above the dust of the dungeon stoney hell. Well, I had decided that would clear the slate between us for goo. That's how I planned to lay out my request to him anyway.

Now, that would solve this issue with my lover Noah, but it wouldn't correct the errors of the Wolf pack. They all had continually let me and the black collar children down. Sometimes to near deadly and very deadly results. This had to stop immediately. These assholes were burning the hole in my pocketbook and I was getting nothing for it.

Therefore I had Birgit get me that second collar that Cary was currently sporting. Truth is, I really had expected to be locking that band of silver around Roland's throat. He was going to halt his abuse of my buddy/pimp Matz whether he wanted to or not. I assumed the brutal Wolf wasn't going to be that easy to persuade that I meant business. Hence, I was going to put a fucking leash on that stupid prick. I knew the rest of the Wolves would fall into line upon the sight of the biggest of them being humiliated.

Then Cary insisted on being the volunteer for my dramatic display of showing that I was fed up with them all. I won't lie. I was doubly pissed at my Shadow King by this point. Not only did he continue to demonstrate the lack of respect for my authority over him. He had even gone as far as to behave the publicly jealous lover. He'd always been aware that I was the unwilling catamite to many of the men in power. I'd never hidden my shameful career path from him either.

All that aside, dough, this bullshit of dismissing my paying customers over the insult of calling him out for willingly whoring around. Ah, well, that motherfucker was really lucky I love him like I do. Otherwise, instead of collaring that shithead, I would have removed his head. and then I would have decapitated him too. Hahaha.

After the very few moments of silent freaking out from the Wolves present, finally Valitin spoke up in the breathless tone, "I told you the Mortar King would kick your ass, Cary. Dammit. Why did you go and ruin the day as you have? Don't we treat you as our equal brother? I don't know about you other fellows but I'm with Mad Maxx. This gang has got to stop cock blocking each other. If wearing the collar and leash will retrain each of us to watch each other's backs like we used to. So be it."

I turned around and glared at the skinny Voter in training and growled out, "I agree with you in every way, Valitin. So, you willing to put your neck where your mouth is? I can call down to the Head Mistress and order another collar with ease."

Valitin dropped to the kneel immediately and then replied calmly, "If it would please you, your Majesty, I'm your subject to do with as you desire. I thank you for the mercy of it."

The eyes of Magnas went wide as he quickly fell to his knees next to his brother and mumbled out, "This is also my answer, your Majesty. I am grateful for your attention to this unworthy servant of yours."

Matz sucked in his breath the second I spun my head to turn my hateful expression upon him. He snuck a quick glance at the freaked out Cary on the floor and then refocused on his reverent brothers.

He cleared his throat, turned his sight upon me and said flatly, "If you waiting for me to fall to the floor and beg you to collar me, your Majesty, forget it. I realize whatever you got up your sleeve has already been decided, likely long ago. Your anger with us is more than justified. That I cannot nor will I ever argue. However, before you do your worst, just know it won't change my mind about how I feel about you. I've always loved you from the day you come visit me looking to save Karsten from debt. Tomorrow, the day after, and the eons can pass and that emotion will grow stronger. However, I refuse to act the horse's ass as if suddenly kissing yours will save me from the inevitable. Do your worst. I've earned it and I accept it on my feet not on my knees." I broke out into maniacal sounding laughter for several seconds over his words.

Cary and the other Wolves shot each other frightened glances. Matz just stood there staring at me without any sign of discomfort in his expression. For the little man, who was capable of enduring Roland's mean right hook, he was a tough bastard, I'll give him dat.

Once I got my mirth under control I snorted then said to Matz, "You know me far too well, brother. Okay, you say you are ready for my judgement? We shall see very shortly. Come with me as I already commanded. Don't make me repeat the order the third time or you will regret everything you just claimed. Cary, get your lazy ass off the floor and take your place three paces behind me. Ja, like the good little Haus sexual plaything you are so hell bent to become. Magnas and Valitin, you boys get into the bedroom and attend your injured brother Wolf. It would seem that you're

105

getting off work early. Matz can reschedule the clients for tomorrow after I'm done re-adjusting this so-called Wolf pack. I assure all you sons of bitches when I'm finish, there will be no more slacking around here. Now let's go, dammit." I jerked on the chain leash with brutality.

Cary whimpered but took to his feet with speed. I raced for the door, ignoring the remaining pack members still crouched on the floor. I didn't even bother to check to see if Matz was minding my orders. I knew he wasn't stupid. There was no doubt in my mind that the slightly built redhead was holding up the rear of our strange parade.

Though I had no idea what the Shadow King was thinking, I had to assume forcing him to behave in this shameful way was infuriating him to no end. His place as the second most important man in the Haus had cultivated the dangerously inflated ego. It was not fun to have to be forced to deflate it so cruelly. That was just too bad for me and certainly for him.

I watched in feigned interest as every collar and Dominant fell to the kneel around us while we traveled to the Dungeons. The initial fright in their expressions quickly turned to humor the moment each saw the identity of the one following on my leash. Soft giggles, and hands covering smiles of evil delight, broke out in our wake. Even if I had ended that march of shame before reaching our destination, then released Cary from my punishment, his reputation was in tatters. There had been enough witnesses to spark the gossiping that before dinnertime would be the raging inferno of exaggerated facts.

For that moment I wondered if I had perhaps gone too far. I was more than aware by this time that Cary's rise in the Haus wasn't the plan of his engineering. His power mad wife, Roselina was the brains between the two of them. With her husband the official Shadow King, and her Dark Bond with the likely future Silk King Rolf, she'd climbed the ladder from total obscurity to first lady of that rat hole in less than one year. The birth of the undisputed biological Prince of the Mortar Shadow King assured that Roselina had successfully put herself in line to inherit either or both thrones.

Her lust for control and quiet push for gaining that power had been so skillfully employed. Even me with the most paranoid of minds, hadn't realized it. It was too late to block her rise, and I do love Cary. Parting with him was out of the question and impossible thanks to that rule about dark bonding. Roselina was just one more evil heart I was about to be forced to do my best to dodge.

However, doing that without making Cary's life more hell than it was about to be already would be difficult. Cary hadn't learned yet that being Shadow King had serious drawbacks. Yikes! This humiliation of being collared by his Mortar King wasn't something that I thought Roselina was going to take laying down. An addition to the plan already in progress rapidly formed within my mind. Like it or not, everything he'd ever known was about to become alien to him.

The moment we reached the stone entry of the Dungeon staircase, I stopped our journey. I turned around to find Cary had dropped to the kneel. His demeanor indicated he was completely mortified and more than a little despondent. Matz on the other hand had stood his ground, refusing to take to his knees yet again.

Matz glared at me and said, "You sure it's safe for you to attempt going down though steps, your Majesty? That leg of yours appears less than sturdy. Perhaps, we come back to hunt for bears to slay when you've had a few more days to re-gain your strength, ja?" He crossed his arms seemingly honestly more interested in my good health than wishing to appear insulant.

With the diabolical chuckle I replied, "Ah, I need not stress myself with the trivialities of this expedition. Not when I have the perfect retriever hound on my leash that is. Cary, you go down below and find the Head Master. Tell that idiot his King demands he follow you and grant me audience. Do not dare come back saying you couldn't find that brute. If he is not located in his shitty little barracks nor among his moron brother Masters, then try the Dungeon commissary. Whatever he is doing you tell him he is to drop it immediately and mind my orders. Go." I dropped the leash and the Shadow King took off quickly seeming unwilling to anger me further. About damned time.

Once Cary's figure had been swallowed up by the darkness of the stone steps, Matz began sighing loudly. I unconsciously winced. I'd known this man long enough to know that was his typical response anytime he was about to light into the list of complaints he had over some behavior he disapproved of.

I glared at Matz as I said with barely restrained irritation in my voice, "Ja? You got the frog in your throat? Stop with that noise. It's giving me the headache."

The Pimp returned my gaze of displeasure as he replied, "Drop the acting job, Maxx. There isn't anyone around for you to try and impress with it. You're not fooling me in the least. What the hell is really going on? I mean I do agree, it is time to call the boys to account, but collaring Cary? Was that really necessary? You do realize he will have to fight for his life thanks to you making him look weak among these assholes. I thought you honestly cared for him. This isn't like you at all. You've become so different. Sometimes I wonder if you haven't been replaced by a double. Same face, but without the heart."

I rolled my eyes then said curtly, "Matz, when will you ever learn to trust my best judgement? Have I ever let you down?"

He snorted then responded in that whiney tone of his that I hate, "Uhm, ja. You give great honor to Magnas and Valitin but treat me like I'm nothing more than your slave. That funeral party business was just as humiliating for me as this leash you put on your Shadow King. I mean I get it. You needed to replace Freidrick and Byron, and I'm not even gonna ask why you name those two brutes your champions. That blows my mind so bad, I've tried to forget you did it. However, you could've named me and Roland instead of them. What have they ever done for you? Nothing is what. They don't care about the collars the way me and Roland do.

We could've done so much for them, but you acted as if we were almost your enemies. Why?"

His wrong assumptions made my temper heat up as I spat out, "You couldn't even protect yourself from your own lover, Matz. How do you expect me to believe the second that bitch Gretta were to threaten you, that you wouldn't fold up and maybe even join her team? I am not willing to start with my issues with giving Roland any power. You wear the evidence that he's not good leadership material on your face."

Matz dropped his folded arms and he took the step toward me appearing aggressive as he bellowed back, "You don't know about the personal troubles between Roland and I though, do you? That isn't even relevant because you dare to insult me by claiming you think I would be such the pussy to fear Gretta? Seriously, Maxx? I think you forgotten it was me that hounded Lucus day and night to see you freed from the Palace. Do you think that bitch didn't already say she's see me burned at the stake if I didn't relent my bid to help you? I told her to fuck off, and I see you standing in front of me. So, am I such the blow over? I think not."

My eyes never strayed from our stare down as I took the step toward him and growled in response, "Why did you never tell me there was such a thing as the annual Stasi Party, Matz? You also neglected to inform me I was in danger of becoming the Mortar King. For that matter, you never told me that Peter was once the Fur King. How dare you keep such important information from me? I thought we were friends."

His face fell into the expression of confusion and he stopped his slow approach as he stammered in reply, "What is this you say? Who says that Peter was such a thing? That's the first I ever heard of this. Holy shit, if that is true, that's not good news. As for the Mortar King and Stasi Party, shit I didn't know such horrors existed until you taught me about them. I think you forget I have only been the Haus resident for the last four years, Maxx. I'm still learning all the bullshit rules, laws and unfortunately pit falls, myself. I dare say being your damned friend has put me on the fast track to becoming wiser than I ever hoped to be, far sooner too."

I halted my stance of aggression the moment he said that and after a moment of consideration I said in the cautious tone, "I thought you said you spent hours in the Haus library reading."

He nodded then snottily replied, "Ja, I do. However, you forget I study the books trying to learn about the career of dentistry. You know, the thing I can never be. Okay, to be fair. Sometimes I also read the steamy romance novels, but you better never tell anyone about that, dammit."

With the snort I shook my head and said, "Fuck, Matz. You really should've cracked at least one manual on the Haus politics."

The Pimp rolled his eyes, "You too, fool. Guess we are both the idiots, ja? So, where does realizing that put us now? No where. That's where. It's past the point of being helpful to go running to fix the unfixable, isn't it. Thanks to our oversights, and our hurry to save everyone else, we're going to end up the losers. You will be locked away to rot in that hell hole Cary told me about. Old Matz here, well I'll have to eat Roland's shit or find myself the homeless corpse. Wishing I could go back and undo all the stupid crap I've done or not done won't prevent what is coming. I kind of wanted to spend our last few months together making fun memories, not ending our relationship on the sour note, you know." His voice had softened several octaves as he finished his words to me.

With the shoulder shrug I dropped my gaze to the floor and said almost in the whisper, "You always been the most honest criminal I've ever known, Matz. No matter what punishment is coming, you never shy from it, nor attempt to lie you way out. I wonder, if that gift of your strong heart couldn't be harness to use for something other than getting dark deeds accomplished."

Matz glared at me angrily then replied, "I'm the man that breaks the rules because I have no choice, Maxx. I've told you it's not the life I wanted, but it is the one I'm stuck with. There is no secret crown, nor a pot of gold waiting for me at the end of any rainbow. Mother nature was unkind. Nothing about me is special. So, accuse me of foul behavior all you want. I won't argue that you say the truth of it. I also refuse to apologize for doing what I must to survive. However, you remember, it is only by luck you are not me and I am not you."

I nodded then returned my focus to his defiant face and said calmly, "You always sell yourself short. That is maybe your other most enduring quality, Herr Egg Farts. Well, we will see if over the years to come you are correct in your assumptions that you lack anything of coveted worth, ja?"

Matz's eyes vent wide as he breathed out sounding incredulous, "What the holy fuck are you talking about, Maxx? Have you gone psychotic again? I already told you there isn't a future for either of us. In fact, neither of us will know the ultimate fate of the other. I doubt you will be getting much gossip while holding down the Mortar throne. Unless one of the monsters that come to visit and use you for their pleasures decides to yap while they rape you that is. Even then, why they would bother to report the death of a no account street rat that once was blessed to call you friend is beyond me."

I began to respond to his misguided statement but was interrupted by the sudden appearance of the Shadow King. He stepped out of the staircase with Noah following closely on his heels. I snatched up Cary's leash before he could say anything. He dropped his face to hide the redness in his cheeks. I couldn't tell if that flushing was due to extreme embarrassment or from rising fury over my actions against him.

Honestly, at that moment, I didn't care which emotion was causing him pain. What was done was done. To withdraw from my mistaken choice of punishment at this point would have made this bad situation even worse.

Instead of giving him the time to do anything impulsive and stupid, I motioned Noah to approach. The big man obeyed quickly, dropping to the reverent kneel at my boots as was proper protocol to do.

I glared at him then said in the booming voice, "Rise, Head Master. You do me no service of worth on the ground. I wish to visit the Voter's floor. There is business I must attend to there. You shall carry me and my Shadow King will follow three paces behind. Matz, you are going to join us but remain behind Cary one pace. Anyone gets out of step then they will find themselves supping with the Guard. Now, let's go, you are all wasting my time." Noah didn't hesitate to take to his feet and scoop me up like the bride.

Cary smartly held his tongue, and for maybe the first time in his life, Matz didn't argue. The four of us were on our way to accomplish the next thing I had on my agenda.

As we traveled up the main staircase to the fifth floor. I snuck a quick glance at the clock on the wall. It was already four thirty. It took all I had to hold back the groan of dismay caught in my throat. The possibility that I was about to run out of time to see my latest plan to completion was nagging at me.

For whatever reason, that entire day had been full of unexpected complications. I was starting to think that my stint in the Palace would begin before all the loose ends could be tied off securely. I simply couldn't have anything else go wrong. It was worrisome to realize I was fast running out of ways to repair weak points in my plots.

Noah as always was graceful and quick in his gait. We were on the Voter's platform before I had too much time to stress over my latest problems. The moment we arrived I motioned him to take the left turn and head for the end of the hallway. He nodded then rushed toward the destination of my choosing.

Just as we reached the dead end of that floor of swank, oversized apartments I put up my hand to gesture the halt. Noah responded immediately. Cary and Matz were so busy gawking at their surroundings both ran into the hulking Head Master. He was pushed slightly forward by the force of that two man collision from behind.

Cary let out the quiet gasp and backed off but Matz let out the loud curse word. Noah held his ground, and tongue appearing unwilling to do anything unless I told him he could. With the eye roll over the poor manners of my travel companions I notified the Head Master he could return me to my feet.

Once I was back under my own power I craned my neck around. My eyes came across the thing I was seeking without much effort. Without explaining to any of them I hailed the middle aged black collar attendant I recalled was named Nele.

She hurriedly came to my command and dropped to the kneel as she squeaked out, "Your Majesty, how may your unworthy servant be of use to you?"

I chuckled and eyed the heavy wooden door next to me as I replied, "Do you still serve the throne of the fifth prince of the Fur, dear lady?"

Nele nodded but kept her eyes to the floor as she said, "Ja, I do, Sire. It is my pleasure to serve for all my life the throne I was assigned to in my youth."

That response made me laugh loudly as I replied, "Ah, the joy it must be indeed. Since that prince is not much trouble these days to be looking after, ja? Tell me something, dear lady, have you had any news of the Honorable Kilian's condition? Is he expected to return to his duties as the Voter, soon?"

The black collar attendant shook her head and whispered, "Nein, your Majesty. I've been informed it is likely he will remain in the care of the medical facilities for another year or more."

The tisking noise escaped me as I shot a glance at his empty apartment door and said, "Well, that's unfortunate news to hear, dear lady. The Voters are surely suffering deeply from the loss of their brother's voice in the Council, ja? If these important leaders are unbalanced the Haus residents lose out too. That cannot be permitted to continue. Dear lady, I command you to go above and seek out the Honorable Elder Jonas, please. Tell him that his husband, the Mortar King, requires an immediate audience with him. Go ahead, my love. I'll be waiting for your return. I thank you for the service." She glanced up and offered the nervous smile but then took off in near flight in her attempt to obey my order.

After her departure, Matz whispered out, "What the fuck are you doing calling that monster down here? If you want to see us murdered at least show a little mercy and toss us over the banister with your own hands, Maxx." I shot him the humored glance and noticed he, Noah and Cary were observably trembling.

I snorted then angrily replied, "Look at you chicken shits. All about to piss your pants over my inviting that blow hard down for a meeting with me. Jonas hasn't any power compared to that I hold in the single palm of my hand. Yet none of you act like frightened children in my presence, do you? In fact, two of you think nothing of fucking me over in the repeat. I'll have you know there are plenty of incidences I could've seen you burned alive for daring to impart upon me. Stop this fear reaction I witness this minute. Or I'll give you each something to be afraid of. I mean it."

Matz started to reply but his anxious expression fell to full on terror. I watched in fury as all three of them dropped to their knees. Each had been keeping his eyes out for the arrival of the Vampire. They saw him coming before I did because I had been facing them in the dressing down. With a groan of visceral disgust I turned around just in time to see the fast approaching Elder.

The Vampire yelled out, "Maxximillian, what is the meaning of this shit? You know damned well I hate coming down here. Then to further insult me you think to force me into the company of these two criminals and Noah. Why the fuck is he up here? Wait, and that one is wearing the silver collar on your leash? Okay, that's it. I'm calling Doctor Attila. You've lost your Goddamned mind, yet again." He then turned around to head off to make that call to my physician. (Yikes.)

In the frantic sounding cry I called out, "Jonas, wait a minute. I'm not having a fit. I've got a good cause to seek the visit with you, but you've got the better one to entertain my request. If you leave, you will never find out what it is that I've come to bargain for and with what I'm willing to pay."

That stopped the Vampire dead in his tracks. He quickly returned to traveling my direction, the sly smile breaking out across his pointed face. I refused to demonstrate any expression that could further demonstrate the weakness in my position of making the deal with this devil.

He ended his journey several paces away and motioned me to join him. I was grateful to heed his command in this case. I was in no hurry to have my crew hear me attempting to persuade Jonas to give me the thing I wanted. Nor did I want them to know the details of the payment he surely was going to extract if he agreed to give it to me.

The moment we were far enough to speak somewhat privately, he shot a menacing glare at the three as he growled out, "So? I'm listening Maxximillian. This must be a pretty big deal if you think to offer me a bargain. Out with it. I'm listening."

I sucked in my breath then leaned in close as I whispered, "I wish to place the temporary Voter in Kilian's spot. It isn't likely he is going to ever return given the severity of his injuries. Though it is within my power as the

Mortar King to do this, it would require I get Lucus to voice it."

Jonas's eyes lit with sparks of fury as he replied flatly, "Ja, what the fuck does that have to do with me? You expect me to endure that pervert's lust in your place to gain his approval? If that is what you about to asking me, be warned, I'll kick your ass for even suggesting it, much less interrupting my nap to come down here in the first place."

That nearly made me choke as I replied quickly, "Oh, my God, Jonas. Nein. I'm not stupid. Give me a little more credit than that dammit."

The Vampire nodded then leaned toward my ear and said in the soft voice, "I never said you were that. Crazy as a bed bug is what you are. The insane are unpredictable, aren't they? Ja. So, if you want to raise some fool to play the temporary Voter, again I ask you, what the hell do you bother me for and what the hell do I care who sits on this empty throne? Now, you look to replace the crown of the Fur, I'm happy to murder Lucus and fucking Claus to see you name me the King." He pulled back and grinned at me evilly.

With the snort of frustration I shook my head and replied quietly, "I won't say that you already owe me this favor I'm about to ask, but you do. That bitch Kilian and his late brother misused me in the foulest of ways. That was your fault, as much as the fact that the Voter floor is lacking one prince. However, I am willing to forget all that or at least try to. There is no reason to kill Claus. He is already the dead man. You show patience, I imagine Cora will slip down the steps soon enough. you've no need to tempt the Haus punishment to end the life of that pervert Lucus either. Besides, if anyone gets that pleasure, it'll be me. What I need from you over this naming of the new Voter is your backing. If you say you heard Lucus voice approval, Claus and Gretta will believe you even when that royal idiot denies he did this. All he needs is one Elder to witness."

Jonas glared at me for the moment then whispered in response, "I'm not going to respond to the bullshit you say about Kilian and Reece. Not that I'm against doing this for you. If nothing more than to piss Lucus off, but I got to ask. Why didn't you ask Leo? I know him and so do you. He'd not charge you nearly the hefty fee that I will. You are losing your mind, ja?"

I groaned then whispered back, "Stop torturing me dammit. Of course, I'd rather ask anyone but you, dad. But Claus and Gretta wouldn't believe the word of Leo or Malfred. Justus has reason to seek revenge on me. You on the other hand, they will think the way you have. Neither will believe I'd dare to bargain with the man that will make me suffer for it."

His smile went wider as he leaned into my ear and said, "Oh, you can be assured I'll enjoy torturing you for this, little Maxximillian. Okay, here is the opening bid. You will come home in one hour. Then we will discuss, in detail, what you will owe for this favor."

I shook my head and whined out, "Nein. You tell me this minute what it will take. I refuse to accept the open-ended deal with the likes of you."

He ran his tongue into my ear, causing me to shutter, and cooed out, "Take it or leave it, Christian Axel. You need me, not the other way around this time."

With another quiver of disgust I spat out, "Fine, just so you know Jonas. I'm not medically capable of giving you the full special services yet. If you thinking of raping me, I'll see you staked in the heart for it."

He chuckled low and replied, "Hahaha. If I want to fuck you, I will do it and I dare you to stop me. But you need not worry. I'm not in the hurry to break my toy. Not yet anyway. I merely want you to come with me to dinner, not to my bed. Now, if we are done with these early negotiations. I will leave you to the task of notifying the fool that will think himself or herself lucky. Oh, wait. I nearly forgot. I will need that idiots name, won't I? Otherwise I cannot claim to be the witness to their rise, ja?"

I cleared my throat nervously then said in almost the mumble, "I will need the fifth-floor apartment keys before you go. Oh, and the man I am naming fifth prince of the Silk is Matz."

The Vampire's eyes nearly bugged out of his head as he exclaimed loudly, "I knew it. You are in the active psychotic cycle. What the fuck are you thinking giving that Wobben's scum the voice in Council, Christian Axel? You know what?

Forget it. No deal." He started to leave but I grabbed his arm with quickness and spun him to face me once more.

I took the deep breath, batted my eyes sweetly then said in the soothing tone, "Awe, come on, baby. Don't tell me you are jealous. You are though, aren't you? It does make me feel special to know you still care enough about me to allow such a tiny thing cause you to behave the angry lover. However, I can promise you, I don't desire to place that Wolf on the throne to cause you emotional injury, lover. This personal insult is aimed at that arrogant prick Lucus. He hates that man almost as much as he does you. I thought you of all people would enjoy this cruel game I'm playing with that pervert. Admit it. It is the clever plan. Placing yet another Wolf in his way will help block his attempt to grasp at things that are not his, ja?" I leaned in and kissed him softly on the lips while never breaking contact from his infuriated eyes.

Jonas moaned out as if in pain then grabbed me by the back of the head. He held me hostage before him, staring at me hard for the moment. Then his expression of anger softened to that of barely vailed lust.

He sighed loudly and licked his lips before he replied, "So, if you confess that you don't belong to Lucus. Who owns the Mortar King? I want to hear you say it, Christian Axel. Loud enough that I can hear it."

I reached out and grabbed him by the crotch, rubbing his growing interest with lustful vigor as I gasped out, "I am the property of my blood bonded, husband. These other men will fall but in the end there is only you that can claim me body and soul."

Jonas let go of my hair and snatched me roughly by the chin then growled in response, "You are the terrible actor. You really think you can seduce me so easily? I do believe that famously silver tongue of yours has become tarnished and rusty from lack of use. Repeating the truth of our relationship to me isn't going to work. The one thing I desire from you, you've never granted me access to. It is also the fucking thing I cannot forcefully take. You give me that willingly, then I can make your life less the burden than it need be. How many times must I tell you this before you listen?"

I forced my eyes to begin to water as I whimpered out, "Please, Jonas. I don't understand what you are asking of me. You demand that I turn over my special service rights to you and become your donor. I did these things, but still you were unsatisfied with me. You bring in other lovers to mistreat me in our wedding bed. Still, I forgive you for this, but that's not enough. You ravage my flesh, drink my blood and stomp on my ego. I stand here saying despite all the horrible things you've done to me, I still think first to call you, my honorable husband, whenever I need the trusted partner. If this leaves you empty and feeling slighted. I beg of you to tell me the thing that will prove to you that I'm your honest lover."

The Vampire smiled and pulled my face closer to his as he said in the low throaty growl, "Better, but yet I hear the fakery in your voice tone, boy. Try again to make me believe you are finally falling in love with me the way I have always loved you. Maybe you can fool this old bat, but I doubt it. I simply know you far, far too well. You cannot give me something that you don't really have." He reached out and placed his clawed hand over my chest.

I gasped and let the false tear run down my cheek as I replied softly, "It beats for you, Jonas. Surely you realized at last that I have a heart. Remember you were there when they laid Heidi and Henry to their eternal rest. Was that only the clever acting job too, do you think?"

His expression turned into one of interest as he leaned into my ear and whispered, "I want to believe you have matured enough to find honest adoration for me, but I cannot. There is nothing left of you. Just the empty void that is encased by the pretty flesh camouflage. I will confess to you this disaster that I hold in my hands is partly of my own making. I was far too violent in my haste to create the perfect lover to feed all my darkest desires. In my misguided efforts I've destroyed the very thing I loved the most. I thank you for the offer, but I must woefully decline it. I'm getting too old and tired to chase after dreams that never will come true. Come see me when Doctor Attila gives you the medical release. I may not be capable of capturing the heart of the ghost, but I do intend to live long enough to enjoy the meager pleasure I can still suck from him. Goodbye for now, Christian Axel." He released me and strode off at full speed in the attempt to thwart my response.

I let out the loud wail and rushed for the banister. Jonas heard this unearthly cry even from his place many paces away. He turned to see what had caused me to shout like that. Upon noticing I'd gotten his attention once more, I rapidly took the straddle over the railing.

The Vampire's face fell into complete terror and he roared out sounding desperate, "Nein, stop the Mortar King. Don't let him jump, dammit."

Noah, Cary, and Matz broke from their startle over the events happening they were witness to. Each man come flying in my direction. I let out another ear shattering scream and leaned closer to the edge. All three brutes stopped abruptly. They were fearful that any sudden movement may result in my taking that leap that I was threatening.

I glared at them briefly then turned my attention back toward the frantic Vampire as I yelled out, "If you don't believe that I love you with all my heart, Jonas, then I see no reason to keep fighting for my life. Without you, I may as well be dead. Stay back you assholes. This isn't any of your business. My husband doesn't want me anymore and I can have no other until one of us is dead. I swear to all of you, his happiness is my only my purpose. Since he is in misery over his choice in partner then it is my gift to him to grant him the only relief possible. Jonas, I pray you enjoy the peaceful, and long existence, full of happiness. I regret that I could give you none of those things." I glanced down and closed my eyes pretending to say the silent prayer. Ja, thank you Noah for teaching me this most useful trick. Hahaha!

The Vampire saw this and despite his earlier remarks that I was the poor actor. He fell for my unrehearsed attempt to appear suicidal over his saying I was the lost cause to him. Jonas came running faster than I thought him capable of doing. He halted his wild race only inches from my dangerous perch there on the fifth-floor banister.

His expression was that of both fear and desperation as he calmly and slowly said, "Christian Axel, honey. Listen to me. Please get off that barrier and return to this side where you are safe. If you fall I cannot bear it."

I kept my eyes closed tightly and forced more tears to fall as I wailed out, "Nein, you don't love me and you say I am the liar when I say it to you. There is nothing left for me. Turn away if you don't wish to watch."

Jonas gasped softly then with unusual gentleness in his voice tone replied, "I apologize for doubting your words of affection for me, Christian Axel. It was wrong of me to do it. I believe you. Now, please, baby, come off the ledge."

I shook my head violently allowing it to shift me into the slight rocking movement. Everyone present sucked in their wind. They all assumed I was going to fall on accident before I got the chance to jump on my own power, ja?

Before that could happen I whimpered out, "But do you love me, Jonas? Really? If you did, you'd find it no hardship to go to dinner with me tonight as you said you wished to. You'd also not question the wisdom of my desire to make Matz the fifth prince of the Silk. A real partner that cares for his husband would have already given him the keys and be off to put on his best dancing outfit for the celebration with his lover over this wonderful news. Instead, you laugh in my face and question my motives. Go away. Let me die without the insult of hearing you pretending to care about me, because you don't."

Matz let out the gasp of sheer surprise, only slightly louder than Cary and Noah. I couldn't see the looks on their faces upon hearing of my intentions, but I bet it was worth seeing. Hahaha.

The Vampire stood silent for the tiniest moment then he said in the defeated sounding tone, "Okay, baby. You are right. This idea of yours to make the Wobben's boy the temporary fifth prince is wise. Here, open your eyes and watch me. I'm giving him the keys to his new apartment as we speak. I'll notify King Claus and Queen Gretta of the Mortar Regent's approval, and every man present shall keep his fucking mouth shut about the details of that, ja?" I wasn't looking but I think he likely threw the threatening glances at the Wolves and Noah when he said that.

I waited a few more seconds before I opened my eyes. They focused just in time to witness Jonas digging into his pockets to retrieve Kilian's apartment key. The First Fur Prince holds all the extra apartment entry sets for the fifth and sixth floor you know.

Matz stood there wide eyed appearing in complete disbelief, while the Vampire handed him the item that marked his ascension. He shot the stunned glance at me, and a small but anxious grin come over his face.

The Vampire than dropped to the kneel before him and mumbled out, "Welcome to the Voter's floor Honorable

Prince Matz Wobben. May your reign be long and peaceful. Nele shall be your personal assistant. Anything you require to make your stay here more comfortable, she will fetch it for you. The Hall of Records contains the section marked 'for Voters only.' You should go there and study the books on Haus law immediately after you have settled in. Council meetings are every Monday at five pm sharp. Do not be late. Refusal to attend your duties are punished severely upon the third unexcused absence from leadership conferences. Any other questions you may have, your brother Voters can answer. I suggest seeking out Rolf due to the shaky nature of Friedrick and Byron at this moment. Gretta is the busy wife and soon to be mother. As for Peter, do I really need to voice the reason you should avoid him at all costs?" He returned to his boots upon finishing his generalized induction ritual for all princes of the Silk.

Matz's mouth dropped and his face turned pale, but he managed to reply in the slight stammering tone, "Uhm, I thank you for the mercy Honorable Elder Jonas. I give my full affection, thanks and loyalty to the man that grants me this unbelievable gift, his Majesty Mad Maxximillian. Though I am aware I'm unworthy of this raise to leadership, I wish to ask am I to understand I'm to assume the full powers of the fifth throne, unlike the Voters in training Magnas and Valitin?"

Jonas chuckled bitterly as he responded, "If that crazy husband of mine will get his ass off the railing, than the answer is ja, Matz. You will be filling in for the ailing Honorable Kilian until and if he returns. When that day comes, you must relinquish his throne back to him, along with all the trappings of it, without quarrel. Do you understand and agree to this minor stipulation?"

Matz nodded rapidly and replied, "Ja, ja. I do. I thank you for the, uhm, vow and mercy of this, Honorable Elder."

Jonas turned his attention back to me, still sitting on the ledge as he said calmly, "There, see, it is done just as you asked. Now, there is no illusion that I don't love you with honesty. Apparently, you feel the same way. I desire nothing more than to take you out for dinner to show off that our marriage is stronger than it's ever been. What do you say, Christian Axel? Won't you agree to forget this silly bid for the dangerous divorce and return to the safety of my grateful arms?"

I nodded and carefully swung my leg back to the solid floor as I grunted the reply, "I agree to your return service for this favor, you've done. Ah, and these men have witnessed our contract so there will be no wriggling out of the details of it. I give my promise to go to dinner with you tonight only. That's more than the fair price for making this official claim that Matz is risen to fifth prince. May it be known that all negotiations are closed with regard to this situation. I thank you for the mercy of your more than fair price. I'll see you in one hour, lover." I winked at him while doing all I could to keep the expression of slyness off my face.

The Vampire appeared stunned for the moment then he angrily yelled out, "Why you dirty little bastard. You tricked me into getting almost nothing in return for this expensive favor. Do you realize what I'm going to do to you the second I get you alone?"

With the shrug I responded nonchalantly, "Everything short of killing me, just as you always have done, Jonas. Now, if you don't mind. I have a few things to clean up before I meet with you for dinner. Oh, you are buying, ja? I'm broke at the moment. However, if you are also tight in the pocketbook I'd happily accept the rain check."

Jonas's veins were popping out on his forehead as he shouted, "Nein, I'll be waiting for you at the apartment, boy. Don't be late or so help me. Shit!" He pounded the air with his fists then stormed off down the hallway in the direction of the staircase appearing furious beyond reasoning.

Me and the other fellows stood there sneaking each other glances of humor in the wake of the Vampire's departure. It was the truth I was playing with fire pissing Jonas off as I had done, I knew he'd calm soon enough. That's because I was aware I was not quite through with my need for his valuable claims as a witness. He didn't know it, but he was still the man with all the best cards in his hand.

The second thing I desired him to lend his name to wouldn't be as easy to get him to agree to. I had to assume he'd rather see me fly off the top of the Haus, than to come to officially stand as witness to Matz protecting Noah's Dominance with the Golden collaring ceremony.

To be assured this part of my plot went off without the hitch I was pretty sure I'd end up having to break that medical promise to Doctor Attila. There was almost no chance that Jonas would do as I asked him for anything less than a fuckfest with me playing the main attraction. Yikes.

Anyway, I had decided before I threw in the towel and gave into his risky demands I would pull out all the stops to try and avoid it. That kind of seduction requires far more time, work, and possibly threats than I was willing to participate in with the audience. This dinner with him was my best opportunity to either take him my hostage or him to take me as his.

As usual Matz was the first to break the silence between all us when he said in the shocked sounding tone, "Maxx, uhm, I don't know what to say. You have made me the Voter a full fifteen years before I could even think to qualify even if I ever did. It is a historical moment, and I'm now the legend just like you are. Such an honor, for me? Why? I mean, I don't wish to sound ungrateful because I certainly am not. It just so unexpected and frankly unearned, I think." He fell to his knees clutching his new apartment key close to his chest tightly.

I glared down at him and with the snort replied, "Matz stop the groveling, you fool. I merely gave the job to the right man for it. About time this floor was filled with a heart seeking to improve the lots of the Haus peoples, all of them, not just those with big wallets, ja? Who better to understand the plight of the poor and helpless than one that until a moment ago was one of them? Never forget where you came from brother. Today I gave you back the fortune stolen from your family, and restored honor to your name. You are no longer beholden to Roland's whims because you are Master

131

of this glorious palace here in the sky. He cannot hold his money nor place in his home over your head any longer. Sadly though, in my haste to grant you the power and cash lacking in your life, I've likely screwed over my own future earnings, ja?"

Matz startled and looked up at me full of confusion in his expression as he responded, "Huh? Seriously, Maxx? You think me so shallow I'd quickly forget the man that raised me to Heaven? Nein. nothing shall ever change between us. This I swear before you and these good men here. Anything you ask of me, consider it already done for as long as fate allows me to walk the earth."

I nodded then replied in the cautious tone, "Ah, that's good news to hear, Honorable Voter Wobben. Because it seems that I have two favors already to ask of you. They are above the big one you already grant me daily." I winked at him over that veiled reference to his role as my pimp.

He smiled with joy and said, "I always keep my oaths, your Majesty. I live to serve. State your orders and watch me obey them to the letter."

I pointed at Cary as I replied, "The first order of business I need you to attend deals with this brother Wolf of ours. He is in immediate need of constant supervision and re-training. He's allowed many in this Haus to cloud his understanding of his role as the Shadow King. Plus, I think there are some close to him that are not interested in seeing he manages his powerful position successfully. It's come to my attention, his life and therefore my own are in peril if he is permitted to continue to live as he has been. You have this fortress, on a floor that is hard to reach for assassination attempts. I beg that you take him in as the constant lodger until I'm safely incarcerated below. After I am where those seeking to knock me off the stone throne cannot reach me, he can be returned to his family. I insist he repay this kindness you show him by continuing in his job as security for the Wolf pack dealings."

Matz shot the quick glance at Cary and nodded as he said, "Ja, this is something I too have been concerned with Maxx. It's the wise decision to provide him the sanctuary in the coming storm. Consider it done. I'll send Magnus and Valitin to collect his tings. Best the break from Roselina and his children be done without notice."

Cary let out the whimper and whispered, "You are separating me from my wife and kids? Why Christian? In what way have I offended you so badly you think to punish me this severely?"

I glared at the Shadow King as I growled in reply, "You hold your tongue, Cary. I didn't grant you permission to speak. One day you will come to appreciate the favor I've just granted you. But for today you will do as you are told without complaint. Matz will answer your questions as soon as you are settled in. Though I doubt you'll bother to understand this is for your own good. I know you far too well. The only thing that makes me feel better about that, is thanks to the ones that honestly love you, you'll live long enough to realize this is a mercy not punishment. Now, Matz, that second item I require?" He nodded as he returned

133

to his feet and took up Cary's chain leash upon seeing my hand gestures to do it.

I cleared my throat, shot the nervous glance towards Noah and then said, "I expect you will allow Roland to move in with you. I strongly caution you to tell him to get bent, but you won't. So, that means all my Wolf brothers will be up here on the Voter's floor attending important Haus business daily. This will leave me vulnerable to attack while I am busy with my own duties as the Mortar King. I'm going to require protection, and that doesn't come cheap. Rather than spending your new fortune hiring thugs that will be loyal only to the money. I wish to assign the man of impressive reputation, massive size, and undying loyalty to his Monarch. Noah is the man that meets this criteria to perfection. However, there is the problem of his loss of status as Dominant once above the Dungeon level."

Matz's eyes went wide and he turned his attention to the Head Master as he whispered, "Do not speaking another word, Maxx. I already know where you going with this conversation. I saw the collar of Gold in Birgit's bag. I wondered the meaning of it, but now it makes more sense than I ever could have contrived on my own. I say to you, ja. It's my honor to assume responsibility for this worthy Dominant. Though, without the Elder witness, the status transfer isn't legal."

I nodded and replied flatly, "You already heard the answer to that loose end if you were paying attention to my drama queen moment, ja?"

He chuckled then said, "Ah, the dinner with Jonas. Okay. So, if you are successful in getting that fiend to agree to this. Where is Noah to live when not acting as your bodyguard? I suppose you want me to give him the bunk beds with Cary?"

With a grimace I shook my head and replied, "Nein. You already have enough roommates I think. Noah is to return to the dank hell from where I've stolen him after I no longer require his services. It is best that he remain in the company of his own kind while doing this tour of duty, ja? Birgit and Viviana were granted the use of the Silk Queen's old apartment on this floor. These lovely ladies have agreed to give him his own space within their own. After you collar him, his welfare will no longer be your burden. At least not until you relinquish responsibility for him in five months, which I demand you give me your oath you'll do without argument."

Matz spat into his hand then held it out toward me as he said with the smile, "We have the deal, partner. Now, that's all done. Let's open this door and see what wonders I've come to own, before I wake up from this wonderful dream, you know." I shook his paw as he chuckled over his statement of disbelief.

I groaned and then replied in the mildly sad tone, "This excitement is all yours and Cary's to enjoy, Matz. I regret that I do not have a second to spare you. I must see that Noah is safely deposited in his temporary new home, then rush upstairs to cement the deal. You heard from Jonas you have access to the Voters' files down in the Hall of Records. The moment you boys are settled in, get your ass down there and look up the ritual for the Gold collaring Dominance transfer. Be ready to do it to perfection at nine thirty tomorrow morning. Please promise me you will do this. Oh, and hand that bag of Birgit's to Noah. He will need to be the one to provide the collar, and the other stuff in there is mine." He nodded as he handed his bundle to the Head Master but the expression on his face was one of disappointment.

This was the greatest day of his life. I understood and felt terrible that I wasn't in the position to be there for the glorious moment he took his first steps into making his dream come true. That was just too damned bad for him and for me. I was going to have to settle for hearing the story of it later.

As I motioned Noah to take up his place behind me to follow in silence. I realized there would be plenty of time for such wonderful listening material. It offered me some peace, terrible as it was, to know Matz telling me his stories of untold future glory would be of comfort in filling the years of nothing coming for me.

You may recall, the Voters and Elders are the only Haus residents with permission to visit the Mortar Palace. Ah, I see that look of sudden understanding in your eyes, Meine Liebe. Hahaha. Indeed, I'd made Matz the Voter for more reasons than you'd assumed, ja?

Besides the few I'd mentioned to him. I'd thought of the way to continue working as the Hustler if Gretta tried to break that contract I'd made with her. With my pimp granted undisputed right to continue our association. I also could continue my work to cleaning up the misuses allowed by laws. Plus, he'd be capable of smuggling in the clients in the event I was prevented from leaving to attend to them on the first floor after dark as agreed when the residents slept.

With Matz put far beyond the reach of Mad Lucus being capable of putting an end to our association. Yet another good reason to make him Voter, ja? I was quickly approaching the door of the next leg of this long journey to fix the mess I'd created by demanding the Mortar King coronation. Yikes!

Noah had trailed behind me, in complete silence. He'd not spoken a single word since being called to attend me earlier than expected. I motioned him to knocking on the Head Mistresses door and stood away slightly as we waited for her to answer. The elderly woman didn't delay in her greeting her unexpected visitors.

Her smile was beautiful as she laid her tired gaze upon the handsome Noah and said, "Ah, there you are my dearest brother Master. Me and my sister have been nearly ready to faint in pure excitement over this most wonderful gift of enjoying the company of one we truly adore. Vivianna is still busy preparing the spare room but I want you to know it's decoration is all up to you. Change it to your liking. Our home is now yours." She took to her toes and kissed him lightly on his cheek, which is the proper way to greet a dear friend in the Haus culture.

137

Noah blushed and then said in the soft tone, "I thank you for your warm welcome and the mercy of your kindness, Mistress. I'm sure whatever you fine ladies have done to prepare for this worthless man, is better than I've ever dared to hope for."

Birgit stepped aside and motioned him to enter as she replied, "Your Majesty, would you honor your grateful subjects with the pleasure of your company?"

I chuckled then nodded while I followed Noah inside the apartment saying, "Well, how could I deny such a lovely invitation? I must caution you though dear Mistress that I cannot stay for long. There is pressing business I must attend very shortly. However, I'd love for Noah to offer me the short tour of the arrangements you've generously made for him. If it'd not be too much of an imposition to ask him for it."

Birgit stifled the chuckle and shot me the glance of mischievous humor as she said, "I'm sure this young man would never tell his Majesty nein. Come with me, and I'll direct your both to the Head Master's room. Vivianna should be finished by now, and we'll give you a moment of privacy for the inspection. After that, perhaps you'd meet us in the kitchenette if you wish to enjoy a cup of hot tea before departing, ja?" She led us down the opulently decorated hallway to the dark wooden door at the end.

Vivianna came out of the entry and nearly fainted upon seeing the three of us there as she squealed out, "Oh my God.

I didn't hear you coming. I think I may be having the heart attack."

Birgit chuckled and yelled loudly, "Oh stop the dramatics, sister. You wouldn't have heard the elephant stomping through this apartment you so stone deaf."

Vivianna continued to grip her heaving bosom as she replied, "Huh? What did you say? Speak up sister. You know I cannot hear you when you whisper like that. Stop playing. You're embarrassing me in front of our guests."

Birgit rolled her eyes and glance at Noah as she said, "I think you are already aware, but there is the evidence of it. If you in need of anything from Vivianna, you'll be using your lungs to full capacity to get it. I'll take my sister and go make that tea. You boys play nice, ja?" She shot me the smile and blushed while snatching up her sister's hand.

I watched in some mild humor while the two elderly ladies beat the hasty retreat. Noah stood there silent as usual without any expression that could be read on his face.

The moment I was sure even Birgit couldn't hear me, I said to him, "Well? You want to carry me across the threshold, lover? I'd be the one to show such the romantic gesture, but I fear I'd bust out my stitches hauling your brute frame, ja?" I chuckled over such the funny idea of my skinny teenage ass managing this huge man's weight.

Instead of answering me with the wicked retort. Noah scooped me into his arms, and I'll be damned if he didn't do exactly as I kidded. Once through the door, he kicked it closed in reverse as if the angry donkey. He smiled at me sweetly, then leaned down while lifting my head to meet his. Noah assaulted my mouth with vigorous kissing. I eagerly returned his lippy embrace. The passion between us was quickly building into the unquenchable fire. He took off carrying me across the oversized room heading for the luxurious bed. When he reached it, he threw me onto the comfortable mattress and leapt like the hungry leopard. I was held to the spot by his heavy weight while he continued his ravenous smouching.

We hadn't even taken the second to examine the beauty of our surroundings before the two of us were ripping at each other's clothing. No doubt this impulsive sexual attack would have progressed to full on intercourse of some sort had the small alarm clock on the fancy night stand not gone off. That annoying and sudden sound startled the both of us out of our momentary loss of discretion.

Noah rose from his place as aggressor and hit the button to shut up that time piece as he exclaimed, "Goddamn it, that scared the shit out of me."

I chuckled and said, "I hope it didn't. these sheets are far too nice to soil, lover." He returned his attention to me, grinning in the most beautiful way.

His calming laugh chimed out as he replied, "The angels in Heaven are jealous of Noah this day, Christian. The gorgeous trappings of this bedroom are trimmed with the treasure of the rarest splendor. When you leave me here alone soon, I fear you'll cause this vision to become dimmed to commonness."

I swatted his huge arm playfully as I said, "You use that tongue of yours with perfection to stroke this man's heart and ears. I wonder how skillful you'll be with it in places far more discerning."

He leaned down and nipped my bared chest gently as he replied, "Stay with me a bit longer and we can find out, ja? Perhaps you'd find it useful to grant me further favor this day by granting me the first lessons in the art of the oral services?" He glanced down at the buttons on my trousers that were straining to hold back my lustful interest in him.

With a groan of truthful irritation at having to turn down his most wonderful offer I responded, "Don't I wish. That training will have to wait though, lover. Tell me when I sent Cary to retrieve you had you acquired the things I told you to get? Is the money safe?" I ran my bandaged hand down his well-muscled chest and watched him quiver with delight.

Noah sucked in his air as he forced out the words, "I did get the things. I was packing up when the Shadow King sent for me. I never leave my barracks without locking up tight. Should I go back tonight to bring everything back here?"

I continued to pet his flesh softly as I replied, "Nein. My love, you must never leave this apartment without being on my leash. There are many in this Haus that would happily see you put to the grave. I fear I've removed you from one prison only to place you into the gilded cage. If you say the stash is secure for now, then so be it. Tomorrow after your collaring, we will go get it together."

He moaned out in pent up lust as he said, "You've given me the memories that will sustain me for several lifetimes. You never need to think I'm ungrateful for the providence you given me, Christian. If you say to remain in this magnificent home waiting for the chance to attend the one I love with all that I am, so it shall be done without complaint nor quarrel. I thank you for the mercy and the affection a million times." He leaned down and brushed his lips over my own then nuzzled my neck gently while taking deep breaths.

I ran the bandaged hands through his hair and said in the giggle, "What are you doing, Noah?"

The Head Master mumbled into ear, "Taking in your scent, Christian. Your smell drives me wild. I swear I could die the happy man if there was some way to bottle it to thrill over whenever you are away." The tremble of surprise overcame me as I pulled him from his place to stare into his eyes.

His adoration was evident as I whispered out, "I think the same of your own odor. It is the thing that brought me to the knowledge that I must have you for my own."

Noah's face fell into the expression of peace as he smiled and replied, "I think it must be because of the cuddling we did when you were the child. Nothing ever brought me such joy as those moments after our wrestling. Do you remember? I'd hold you in my lap…" I let out the loud gasp.

Suddenly, the rich tapestries that lined the walls of the Silk Monarch's room faded into the stone walls of the dank Dungeon cell. I felt Noah's strong arms around my tiny body. There in the damp straw in the center of that horrible prison, I sat on the Head Masters lap. His pleasant voice softly sang a song in a language I couldn't understand. He was petting my ravaged flesh and rocking me like the little baby in his gentle hold.

To my absolute surprise there was a piece of delicious chocolate in my little hand. I snuck the glance up at my huge jailer. He looked back at me with the affectionate smile on his face. The smell of his cheap cologne was mixing with the wonderful scent of that candy. It was confusing to be finding this loving comfort granted by the one that often was brutal in his lessons. Yet, in my short life of extreme violence and despairing isolation, his adoring embrace was the only kindness I'd known since my brother had died…

Noah shook me hard and glared into my refocusing eyes appearing terrified as he said, "Christian? Can you hear me? What happened? You went unresponsive. Do I need to call the doctor?"

I waved him off and whispered in reply, "Nein, Noah, I'm alright. I think that this was the trance, but I've recovered. Uhm, tell me something, love. When you say you enjoy smelling of my flesh can you describe what it is? I mean is there anything similar to it in comparison?"

He let out his wind as if relieved then with the small smile chuckled and said, "Ja. I swear to the Gods, you smell just like the finest, uhm, chocolate."

Chapter 21: Unholy Union

I stared at Noah with my eyes narrowed in suspiciousness as I said, "I smell like chocolate to you, do I? How interesting is that? It seems like lately a lot of people been mentioning that delicious treat when speaking with me. Mostly the ones seeking to taking advantage in some way or another. I wonder something, did you perhaps pick up some sweets and this is your way of trying to entice me into promising you the favor for it?"

The Head Master appeared startled over my words as he said in the stammer, "Huh? Why would I do such a thing, Mad Maxx? I thought we are the honest lovers. If this is the truth of it, then I'd have no reason to use trickery for any reason. Especially not for such dishonor as you suggesting to me. You asked me the question and I answered it. Your scent is reminiscent of that desert, period. I meant nothing more than what I said."

I glared at him angrily feeling the fury starting to rise within my chest as I growled out, "Don't attempt to lie by saying you weren't aware of my fondness for chocolate. How dare you act offended that I call you out on the foul deeds you are indeed guilty of doing. I've just recalled you giving me the sweets after you'd pulled that sexual wrestling game on me. That's why I didn't remember you until recently, isn't it? You drugged that stuff to assure I couldn't remember and tell on you for it." I pushed him hard and he backed away from me appearing suddenly quite frightened.

He didn't break his terror filled eyes from my own as he replied, "Nein. Please, Mad Maxx, you must believe me. Despite that horrible misuse of you for masturbation I did no other crime against you. Not ever. In fact, I was only made aware of your interest in the chocolate sweets after I found you munching on some of it not long after you arrived in the dungeon. I had no idea where you got that candy bar, but you had one. I took it from you and you attacked me, but I returned it to you after our training session. It calmed your crying and I cuddled you in my arms while you held it. I sang you the song my mother once sung to me when I was young. You liked it so much you offered me the bite of your candy. I realized this was the bonding moment for us, and every day from then on I brought chocolate to treat you for doing well. You were always the loving soul that was willing to share your prize with me."

I gasped then interrupted him before he could finish his tale, "Wait. Did you eat any of that chocolate I offered you? I mean the first time I offered it?"

He nodded and said in the anxious sounding whisper, "Uhm, ja. Of course I did, Mad Maxx. It would have been rude to refuse your sweet offer. I apologize if you think that was wrong to do. I mean, whatever you'd done to earn it, I suppose I had no right to share in the spoils of it."

With a groan I replied, "Did you notice anything odd happening after you swallowed that chocolate?"

Noah gulped and cast his eyes downward as he nodded then said, "You don't remember, do you? If I say what happened after that, I fear you might not love me anymore."

I closed my eyes and braced as I responded, "I was the virgin when Peter locked his collar around my neck. My innocence was proven, so no matter how bad you may think your behavior towards me after eating that drugged candy may have been, it wasn't the worst you could've done, ja?"

He nodded as he took the deep breath then replied, "Drugged you say? Well, that does little to relieve my conscious over that horrible day in the cell. You see I took the nibble of your chocolate to keep you calmed. Within only a few moments, I noticed you looking at me with those big beautiful blue eyes of yours. I swore I could see into the heavens through them. Before I could stop myself I, uhm, I pulled you to my lips and started kissing you. You struggled and whimpered. No doubt you were frightened by my doing that to you but you didn't attempt to attack me as you usually did back then. The more I tasted your lips, the more desire I felt to possess you. The demon of lust overtook my good senses, and the rest you say you recall. The wrestling happened. I wanted you so badly. I'm truly surprised I managed to keep it to rubbing on you superficially. Your obvious terror over the mock intercourse business, and my deep interest in doing far more caused intense guilt within me. I swore I'd never do it again. Yet every day for several after that, you offered me some of the candy bar you always seemed to have stashed in the straw. Each time, I took the bite. Each time, I couldn't stop my overwhelming need to stroke you. Then one day, you didn't produce the chocolate.

147

You seemed despondent over the lack of having it. So, I started to bring some each visit. The smell of it on you as you ate it drove me mad with desire. I brought the candy and gave it to you for the job well done, and when you smelled of it, the beast in me took over. And so the ritual repeated itself for all those years. I don't know why you think to call me your lover and be this good to me after all the evil I've done to you, Mad Maxx. For what it is worth, I'd do anything to take it back, but I cannot."

I opened my eyes and set them upon Noah as I said in the gentle tone, "It's okay Noah. It wasn't you fault, not completely anyway. Claus and Ingrid were giving me the drugged candy bars so they could hypnotize me more easily. I'd been hoarding some of the tainted treats, and you my love were the accidental victim of it." I reached out and stroked his arm lovingly.

He flinched at my touch but looked up while shaking his head and replied, "Nein. I refuse to blame chemical reasons for my behaving the brute toward the helpless, and innocent child, Mad Maxx. There has to be something foul within my soul to begin width. Otherwise I'd kept my hands and other parts off your little body. It's unforgivable and I am damned well aware of it." He started to tear up and his cheeks turned bright red in humiliation.

The chuckle of humor broke from my throat as I said, "You are too much, Noah. No wonder I love you like I do. Any other man would happily accept any excuse provided him to escape the victim's righteous anger. However, this time, the reality is you were conditioned to adore the joy that drugged chocolate provides just as I have been."

He stared at me appearing flabbergasted as he breathed out, "Are you really hell bent to insist that my affection and longing for you are nothing but the trick of the trainers tainted sweets? If this is what you believe, then I beg of you to release me of your command. I don't desire to live with the idea that you don't really love me, nor do I love you back. Our adoration for each other is not the feeling driven by drug addiction." I noticed his tears were falling fiercely and his breathing labored from obvious inner turmoil.

I sat up and wrapped my bandaged hands around his waist then leaned into his ear to whisper, "I already told you I will never release you, Noah. Stop this lamenting. I command it. No matter what brought us together, we are one now, ja? I see no chemically altered chocolate laying around in this room, and yet, I want you more than I wanted anything else in my life. I wish that you could see the truth. You are not the willing child molester you thought you were. I offered you this explanation only to provide you some comfort, but not to make you doubt that our love for each other isn't real. Oh, never mind. It doesn't matter, does it? Kiss me, you fool. We will forget the past just as we always have, ja?" He nodded then met my lips in the passionate mouth groping.

For several minutes we grew ever more heated in our heavy petting. It was as if we were two men that been adrift upon the ocean surrounded by water, but without any suitable to quench our terrible thirst. We had avoided the madness caused by partaking of that forbidden salty fluid while lost upon the sea of life. But at long last, we thought we found the savior oasis in each other's arms. We sucked and licked at our lover's flesh, drinking deeply of our lustful sweat sweetened by cupid's arrow. As expected when engaging in things that are taboo for good reason, insane wantonness was the reward we reaped in abundance.

Noah ripped off my shirt, then my breeches. I offered no struggle while he forced himself between my legs. He paused his wild necking long enough to release his engorged member but pulled his leather pants only as far as necessary to relieve the pressure off his erection.

Once unencumbered he moved forward, causing my ankles to find the perch on his broach shoulders. I gasped and shuddered full of interest in his offer of taking the position of Dominance over me. For that moment I nearly lost my good judgement. Doctor Attila's warnings were burned away by the fires of my raw lust. Yikes.

Thankfully Noah was the man in control in more ways than one. He let out the groan of pent-up desire as he grabbed his manhood. Then he took up my own within his strong grip. I joined him in his sounds of ecstasy, while he vigorously stroked both our parts in unison. It wasn't any surprise that his skillful action didn't take long to produce glorious results. All I can say is that between the two of us, my stomach got bathed in the copious amount of the finest skin moisturized that afternoon (gross and hahaha).

When he found his apex, not long after I reached mine, he withdrew from his place of straddle. I lay there panting and moaning still enjoying the lingering sensations of pleasure while he took the spot next to me on the bed.

He put his big arm around my chest and nuzzled my over sensitized ear, then whispered, "I apologize for the mess, Mad Maxx. Give me the second to rest, and I'll go to the bathroom to find the rag to clean you up. I thank you for the mercy you've just given me."

I chuckled as I replied, "You thank me? For what? I was happy to play this game of target practice with you, lover. All I had to do is lay there. If only all my trysts were this wonderful, I'd never have need to complain again."

Noah frowned then kissed my cheek as he said, "I assume you referring to the terrible things Jonas will do to you shortly, ja? Or perhaps Lucus later? Oh, Mad Maxx. Tell me how can I help? What will stop these brutes from causing you trips to the infirmary on a regular basis? You need only to say the word, and I'll pitch them both over the banister without feeling the least bit of remorse for it." That caused me to startle.

I set my eyes on him as I said with great authority in my tone, "Noah, this isn't the time to attempt playing the part of the jealous lover. You already saw what happened to Cary for engaging in such deviltry, ja? The dark business I endure at the hands of those perverts is the burden I must carry alone. Swear this minute to never ask me about anything that goes on between me and others behind closed doors unless I direct you to do otherwise. My life, and special services rights are not always min to control. I shouldn't need to tell you any of that. after all, you were the one that dropped me onto the floor of the one that began it all."

He winced but nodded as he replied, "You say the truth of it. I give you my word to never seek information nor to judge anything you must do to survive. I realize this affair between us isn't the natural one. I dare say if given the opportunity neither of us would have even considered such actions as we've taken with the other. That said, I'll not apologize ever again for wanting your affection as I clearly do. I agree with these things you say of our sad situation. We are not freemen. We are the prisoners of this accursed Haus. I think God will forgive us for loving the one we are width, since we cannot have the one want."

With the mild giggle I said, "I believe that is the saying I've heard on one of Leo's records. However, I must tell you. There is no God, Noah. There certainly is the Devil though. I'd love to chat and cuddle with you all day. Yet I'm not only married to that demon but I've got a date with that bat bastard very shortly. You must have read in your bible that Satan doesn't forgive lateness in the damned souls he claims, like your benevolent deity does, ja?"

Noah sucked in his breath as if punched as he replied, "Ah, tell me, Mad Maxx. When did the doctor say you'll be ready to, uhm, you know, again?"

I glared at him as I responded in the surprised tone, "He said at the earliest not for another two to three weeks. Why?

You worried I won't be honest in my return for your services to me the moment I am able? Come on, Noah. Give me some credit. I may not enjoy playing the pin cushion, but I'm the fair lover. You'll be the first on my list for the payback, I swear it."

He shook his head and winced again as he replied in the near whisper, "That's not why I asked. I, uhm, wondered about that request you made of me earlier today is all. The one about me seeking the frau to give my penetration virginity to. You know, before I come to know you that way. If I only have the two to three weeks, well I have been told that wooing the female is the tricky thing. Plus, finding one that'd be willing to keep the secret and accept the risk associated with it will make it far more difficult. Oh, my God. I think I do need to be seeking that unlucky girl quickly, ja?"

I rolled my eyes then snorted out, "You damned fool. You already cum twice today and already your mind wanders to conquering the silken fields of forbidden flesh. What a horny beast you are and I thought I was the sex fiend extraordinaire. Ha. Well, for your information, lover. Your only good option I've already pointed out to you. Birgit is a fine woman of still handsome features. Coaxing her into this beautiful room to couple with you shouldn't be either the hardship nor result in the dangerous outcome. Besides, I see no way for you to do as I wanted you to do otherwise. You cannot leave this apartment without me or the Wolves at your side. It will be really hard to find any woman much less one that meets such high standards as have unfortunately been set for you, ja?"

He shook his head vigorously then said, "Stop that, Mad Maxx. Birgit is too old. That suggestion is just wrong and gross too. I mean she is sweet, kind and no doubt the gentle soul. But I find no desire for her. My cock would go limp the minute she took off her dress. I squirm just thinking of the terrible wreak of withered skin that surely her clothing hides from my sight." He shuddered slightly as he said that.

I shrugged, then replied, "Ah, you are too picky, Noah. I've had to tolerate the touching of some far older than Birgit. They were men to boot. Trust me, had any of them possessed even the fraction of the assets she does, I'd gotten over the disgust of it. I already told you. I won't command you to do this. However, you're time is running out to explore the pleasure the mysterious female can gift to the male. If I were you, I'd fuck that woman, eyes wide open, with every light on in the Goddamned apartment. In fact, I'd likely not stop sexing her until the poor gal escaped my lust through death from natural causes. Hahaha." He swatted my arm playfully then rose from the bed, headed off to seek out the items to clean up our indiscretion.

Once Noah had aided me into making myself presentable, I gave him the quick kiss goodbye. I gave him strict instructions to remain behind the locked doors of the apartment until I came to retrieve him for the collaring ceremony in the morning. It was regrettable that I couldn't stick around for that cup of tea Birgit offered me to enjoy. Jonas, however, wouldn't tolerate me being tardy. So, I took off for the Dungeon Mistresses front door from Noah's room like the back of my jacket was on fire.

154

I rushed down the Voter's hallway headed for the private staircase of the Elders, when I heard Matz's cries for mercy ringing out. His new apartment was located near to my destination, so there was no need for me to break off the journey to investigate his fearful sounds. The closer I got to his residence, the more clearly I could make out the outline of two large brutes. They appeared to be using tag teaming tactics to prevent the slightly built Voter from escaping their bullying him. My speed increased to the limping run the moment I recognized one of Matz's assailants was the sadistic Byron.

Before any of the three saw me coming I yelled out angrily, "Halt that bullshit this minute. Byron, you mind your Master. Let the Honorable Matz alone or so help me I'll see you sent to the pit for daring to harass that Voter."

Byron turned his attentions away from the irritated Matz and set his beady eyes upon me as he growled in response, "You call this nothing the Voter? By who's authority has he been given the right to befoul the fifth floor with his unworthy presence?"

I arrived upon the scene just as he bellowed that. Two things were immediately brought to my attention. The first was the identity of the second thug bothering Matz. Fritz stood there staring at me with a shit eating grin on his face while I approached. He appeared calm and full of humor despite my obvious fury over this situation.

The other thing I noticed was that Roland was also present among this throng of thugs. I hadn't seen him at first because he was lurking in the shadows, just behind the haughty Fritz. I didn't need to hear anything he wished to say because his expression was doing plenty of hateful talking, trust me.

Without warning I reared back and backhanded Byron so forcefully he nearly fell to his knees. The sound of my injured hands colliding with his burly jaw echoed off the hallway walls. Every man present, including the usually unflappable Fritz, ducked and cowered upon witnessing my overt sign of displeasure toward my Dungeon Master.

The roar of intense rage erupted from my throat as I shouted out, "There is your answer, you insolent dog. Fritz, Roland, what the fuck are you boys doing this far above your status? Hmmm? I think you both better crawl back into the hole you came from before your Lord and Master of this Haus decides to see if you worms can fly, ja?" They nodded their heads but cast infuriated glances as me while rushing off toward the exit back down to their levels.

Neither was dumb enough to challenge my authority with so many powerful allies within shouting distance.

The second those two idiots had left the area, I returned my attention to the sulking Byron and said, "I believe you have forgotten your place Dungeon Master. Matz has indeed been risen to the lofty place of fifth prince. The Elder Jonas has witnessed his ascension by orders of your Master. Not that any of that is any of your business. It would seem that you and I are in great need of the unfriendly visit, servant. tomorrow at eleven o'clock you will meet me in the Hall of

Records. Do not be late. If I must come seek your audience you will not enjoy the results of it. Do you understand?"

He nodded while dropping his gaze to his boots as he replied, "Ja, I do, your Majesty. I thank you for the mercy of it."

I glared at him hard then responded in the harsh tone, "I know nothing of mercy, Dungeon Master. If you don't move your big ass out of my sight this instant perhaps you'll forget the meaning of that word also, ja? Leave and do not return. I mean it." I pointed in the direction of his own apartment several paces away.

Byron shot the menacing glance toward the new Voter but wisely decided to obey my command. He stormed off, clearly annoyed that he was being corrected in front of one he viewed as less than himself. It wasn't lost on me, that he likely was further pissed that our renegotiations had been put off yet another several hours. I was more than aware that motherfucker been seeking my whereabouts ever since the rumors of my release from the clinic had made the Haus rounds.

It had been my intention to give him the attention he was looking to have. That entire day, as I have said, hadn't gone as smoothly as I'd planned. Like it or not, Byron would have to wait his turn to do his best to kick my overused ass.

Matz broke me from my deep thoughts while I was watching the brute retreat, "Maxx, uhm, thank you for, uhm, always being there. Those guys were surely about to end my wonderful day before I had even an hour to celebrate it."

157

I snorted as I replied, "What I wish to know is how any of them knew of your good fortune before it's been formally announced in the Great Hall at dinnertime as is the custom."

He looked at the floor appearing shamed as he mumbled in response, "Oh, it was my fault, Maxx. Cary got pretty upset when I forbid him to leave to go pack his things. Rather than fight him over it, I, uhm. Well, I locked his leash around the bathroom towel rack. Then I hurried to his apartment and demanded that Rosalina gather up his personal effects. She was like the viper when informed her husband wasn't coming home for the next five months. Anyway, I suppose it goes without saying Cary's stuff and me were tossed out of her home like yesterday's garbage, but with more force, ja. Roland heard the clamor and came running thinking some of the black collars were in trouble. I told him the good news and he didn't receive it any better than Cary's wife did. The fight broke out. He was throwing me and my own things around the third floor hallway when Fritz come upon us. He'd been coming to see if you had any available slots for tomorrow afternoon for, you know, entertaining. So, he attempted to end the brawling, but then suddenly that bastard Dungeon Master of yours came out of nowhere. Roland shouted out that I'd stolen the fifth throne by misleading the, uhm, insane Mortar King. Maybe you need to be getting to that appointment you have with Jonas?" He shifted anxiously and started chewing on his lower lip, the way he always does when stressed.

I rolled my eyes then with the sigh replied, "I swear you boys fight worse than children. Okay, so you have your hands full, but as I expected. You also appear to have this mess under control."

He nodded swiftly then said in the sure sounding tone, "Ja, Maxx. This drama is nothing. Though it could have gotten bad had you not come by when you did. I cannot beat three of them and I stupidly penned up the one man that can provide proper protection if necessary."

I shrugged then replied, "You better remember that brother. You're the honorable Voter now. There are plenty in this hell hole that would enjoy hearing your eulogy, ja? I know that Cary is upset at you and me this minute, but he is good Haus stock. He always obeys his betters, when threatened with severe punishment. Don't forget that it's far easier to gain forgiveness from the slighted friend on this side of the grass."

He chuckled then said, "You, as usual, are right, Maxx. I'll go have the heart to heart with our distressed brother. Then he and I will head down to the Hall of Records to do some studying. See you in the morning, I hope." He shot me the worried glance.

With the groan I responded, "Jonas doesn't scare me and he shouldn't frighten you either. The only thing powerful about him is his body odor."

Matz gasped then said in the near whisper, "It isn't the Elder that concerns me. I'm aware he wouldn't dare risk losing you with so much at, pardon the pun, stake for him. Lucus, on the other hand, I wonder what the fuck he may do to you the second he finds out you've gone behind his back.

That fucker is shadier than Jonas ever hoped to be in his best nightmares."

I grimaced than just before I took off to return on the journey to my original destination responded, "You worry about the wrong man, Matz. The one that is the bogey man of the moment is that bastard Fritz. Oh, and that sneaky DJ needs to be dealt with soon too. I'll be there in the morning. Don't embarrass me by fucking up your lines, ja?" With that I left Matz to clean up the mess I'd made by collaring Cary during my hissy fit earlier.

At last I made it to Jonas's apartment door. I stood dare for the few minutes attempting to brace my nerves. It was the truth I told Matz. I wasn't frightened of the Vampire like I had been as the little priceless boy. That didn't make dealing with his notoriously grouchy old ass any easier though. There were still plenty of yellowing bruises and tender healing cuts all over my flesh from that nasty business that left Heidi the corpse. I was in no hurry to add further injury and any situation with Jonas often resulted in unnecessary violence.

Finally, I dared not wait any longer to get this foul meeting over with. I knocked gently, doing as I always do whenever I'm forced to visit with him. I silently hoped he'd slipped in the shower, banged his head and was already playing poker with the other fiends in Hades. That day my secret wish hadn't come to pass. I barely began the wrapping on his door before hearing his obnoxiously loud footsteps approaching to answer.

He wrenched the wooden slab open with undue rapidness. To my complete surprise I saw him standing in the entry with the sheepish grin on his hairy face and the handful of blood red roses in his claws. No words passed between us as he pushed the bundle of fancy flowers at me. All I could do was stare at his offered gift sure that any perceived move on my part would be viewed by him as the act of aggression. As I said, I was in no mood for enduring his wicked backhand.

When I refused to relent from stoic stillness for several moments, his smile melted while he rolled his eyes and thrust the roses at me appearing irritated, "Christian Axel, what the fuck is wrong with you? You behave as if you never received the token of affection from me before. Here, take them. I bought them just for you." He pushed the roses at me again.

I refused to take them and backed away as I growled in response, "I've been told that the spouse gives this gift because he has committed some kind of grievous act that breeches his wedding vows. If it is alright with you, I prefer to keep that tradition intact. Go ahead and confess your indiscretion. I will become righteously incensed by it and you'll become angry that I don't just accept you are the insensitive cad. You'll start the fight that will end in blows. Then when you've calmed your temper, I'm crying in the pool of blood from your beating, I'll make the usual excuses for your bad manners, while I accept your meaningless trinket in lieu of the proper apology."

Jonas's expression became incredulous as he said in the exasperated tone, "You cannot be serious. I've gone through a lot of trouble to get these in the gesture of my truest affection. Yet, instead of gratitude I get sarcasm and disrespect that has become far too common the response from you."

With the loud snort I replied, "Ah, I see. Now, what exactly did you hope I would say, dad? Perhaps something like 'Oh, thank you for the mercy of giving me the dying weeds. It's the perfect service return for all the trauma, terror, and damage you and your friends have done to my flesh and soul all these years. No matter the painful assaults, nor brutal attentions you so callously call love.' Well, heck pops, all is forgiven and forgotten because you read my mind. these stinking flowers are way better than having a mouthful of healthy teeth."

The Vampire dropped the roses on the hallway floor and glared at me full of fury as he said through gritted fangs, "You are pushing your luck with me, boy. You don't want to be treated like the treasure, than I happily behave as if you are nothing of worth."

The chuckling began low in my throat as I replied, "But that wouldn't be the truth of it, now would it, my dearest. I'm worth my weight in mortar, but since your rightful husband took to wearing the foundation crown, you are completely encased in the burden of stone. Best you remember our marital roles have changed most drastically since I wore your bat collar, sweet wife, because I sure do."

He let out the loud gasp and hurriedly grabbed me by the upper arm as he whispered out in the frightened tone, "Be still, Christian Axel. Don't you ever say that shit out loud again. What if someone were to hear you?" The Vampire nervously craned his head all around seeking out anyone that may been within listening distance.

I could barely hold back my wild cackling as I said, "What is this? Is the mighty Jonas the fraidy cat that everyone will figure out the thing he's been frantically trying to hide? Guess you should've thought twice before you tricked the desperate little Priceless into your bondage bed, ja? You raped me into the blood bond thinking I'd be married to the female before I officially began my reign, didn't you? Well, my time is almost up and I am still without the ring on the hand of the mythical beauty. Thankfully, when the Elders come for me in five months, I'm not the bachelor though. I do have the husband that the Haus will gladly fill their Mortar Queen's throne with. Do you think they will expect us to have many children, love? Oh, we will have to change that masculine name of yours. I'm kind of partial to Johanna, but I'm not the brute husband that doesn't take into consideration the happiness of his dutiful wife."

Jonas let out the terrified sounding wail and dragged me into his apartment with force. He slammed his door while tossing me away from him wildly. I fell to the floor, laughing so hard I couldn't catch my breath. once he was certain we were fully alone, and not likely to be overheard, he turned his panicked attention back to me.

Without moving from his place of blocking his entrance he said, "How did you find out? Ah, wait, Claus told you, didn't he? That bastard."

I continued to giggle as I nodded then replied, "Ja, he did. Though to be fair, I would have figured it out on my own, had I not been, uhm, distracted over far more pressing matters during the last many months." Slowly I began to return to my feet as I said that.

He sighed loudly then turned his eyes toward his ceiling as he responded, "I suppose it isn't relevant the way you discovered this disastrous situation. Only that it is quickly becoming unfixable."

With the humor filled tone I replied, "Why Jonas, my dear wife. Didn't you say earlier you wanted me to love you the way you always have loved me. Well, guess what. Since I am the King, you will soon become the Queen. With you in the spot of submission to your husband, I do intend to return all that wonderful adoration towards your body in the equal service. If the idea of submitting to my unholy lust isn't something that incites sexual eagerness in you. No worries, sweetheart. You do remember they have heavy chains, and chemical solutions to assure you fulfill your role as my mate, ja? In fact, in this light, I suddenly noticed you are very attractive. I think I'm getting hard just imagining you trembling under my mount. Ah, the sounds of your screams for me to be merciful with my excited thrusts will drive me mad with passion for you. If that isn't the correct expression of true love for the helpless spouse, than perhaps you shouldn't have been my trainer in the proper return for that emotion. Hahaha."

The Vampire's eyes gleamed with deep rage as he spat back, "There are five months left before I'm to become such the creature as your Mortar Queen, Christian Axel. I suggest you wipe that smug look off your face and remember who it is that you poke fun at. I am still the Fur Prince of the first throne. Claus could die and then I will become the Fur King. If that happens, I can prevent being sent below as your bitch. Or better jet, maybe I'll decide remaining youthful isn't as important as becoming the widower. The Haus doesn't need the Mortar Throne, nor the Collar King."

I stopped my mirth and locked my eyes onto his gaze as I replied flatly, "It does not, I agree. So, get to doing your worst, Jonas. I've grown tired of playing these boring bat and mouse games with you. Kill Claus, kill me, kill yourself, or bend over and suffer my vengeance for a change. It matters not as far as I am concerned. No matter which outcome, I'm the loser."

Jonas's expression soften slightly as he took the deep breath then responded, "I wouldn't be so sure about that, Christian Axel. There is more than one way to skin the cat, you know. Anyway, you know the laws as well as any Elder. You've always been the clever boy. I have faith you'll figure this out before it's too late. However, where does that leave us in the interim while we await your final judgement in June when you turn eighteen? Are you certain you wish to name that pervert Lucus your regent? Can you trust him? I think not."

I shook my head while refusing to break from our stare down as I replied, "Could you trust Kilian to be your own, my dearest Queen? Don't act as if you are shocked I figured out what that snake was doing slinking around your door. That is also the reason you were desperately trying to get me to marry Mott before I killed that silver and placed the Torture Mistress Amanda in her spot. Too bad I didn't save you by condemning her, ja? This embarrassing matter can be solved easily. Give me Anna, and a few other mild concessions. you'll be free of your burden as the honorary Mortar Queen, and I'll just have to be satisfied with the bride of Dracula baring my demonic babies."

Jonas shook his head and bellowed out angrily, "Nein, I will never agree to let you blood bond with that diseased bitch. Besides, she doesn't meet the criteria of the foundation laws to be crowned the queen. I command that you choose the female that does on the eve of your incarceration."

I sneered at him as I replied, "You mean that Kraus baby, ja? Fuck you, Jonas. I mean that literally too. You better start investing in the fancy lube, lover boy. I'm will misuse you in every way and often. I am the lusty beast you know."

His gaze lit up with the fires of fury as he shouted, "You might find me more of a challenge than you assume, boy. Threaten me again, and perhaps I remind you why you wear those dentures."

With the evil chuckle I responded, "I'm the young stud, who grows in strength. You, pops, are the old nag that soon will crumble beneath my hooves. Are we done measuring our cocks yet? I'm famished and you promised me dinner."

Jonas broke from his barely restrained anger and chuckled as he replied, "Damn. You are the most beautiful creature that ever walked the earth. No wonder I want you like I do. If you were not under doctor supervision I would attack you right here in the living room floor. I suppose I will have to be satisfied with the pleasure of showing off my good fortune to the no accounts of this Haus in the Great Hall. Before we go, tell me something. Besides that stupid request to name Anna your queen. What other favors were you going to ask me to grant you?"

I shrugged then I said with the yawn, "Depends on the price you intend to charge to get them."

He groaned loudly then with the click of his tongue replied, "Power suits you, Christian Axel. Sexy, mysterious, and strong as you may have become, I don't care for this gap between us that grows ever larger. Speak your demands and I will consider them carefully. Be reasonable. I cannot offer the fair charge for things that I'm unsure I'm able to provide you in the first place."

That made me snort as I grumbled, "Why not? You certainly have done exactly that to me numerous times in our history together. No one else can give me the things I want, or I wouldn't bother to haggle with you over them in the first place. Tell me the terrible toll you'll extract to see my interests quelled and I will readily agree to it, as I always have."

He narrowed his eyes suspiciously then with the slow nod replied, "Once you are healed I want you to come to me every late afternoon. You will attend to me in any way I desire, without argument or hesitation until you are rendered incapable by Haus law. I will accept nothing less than total submission to my will during our hours together. Do you agree to this?"

I shrugged then said, "I must return to Lucus each night by nine. His contract supersedes any arrangement we make here today. So, I will need two things before I commit to this agreement with you. First, I need to know the scheduled hours I am to attend you and when you expect me to start. Second, I want it in writing this time. I never make any fucking deals with you or anyone ever again without the paper trail to protect my interests."

The Vampire chuckled with great humor as he replied, "You have learned that lesson the hard way, ja? Okay, If you must be back with that fiend by nine, I want the hours of six until eight forty five. That will give you fifteen minutes to clean up the messes I intend to make of you. Hahaha. I want this pleasure to begin tonight. As for the contract, I'll happily sign in blood for it. Your turn. I know what I am buying, but what am I paying for it?"

I put up one of my bandaged hands and shook my head wildly as I responded, "Wait the damn minute you fucking monster. This deal cannot begin tonight as you state it. Do you believe me too daft to realize if I say ja, you can technically breech Doctor Attila's medical commands? I will concede to your terms with the stipulation, you cannot force me into your nasty mount until I'm released medically. Otherwise I'm willing to enter into this contract with you, with no further provisions made."

Jonas's eyes vent wide as he breathed out, "Holy hell. What exactly are you about to demand of me? This lack of interest to balance our arrangement more in your favor makes me nervous. Hmmm, alright. You make the fair case. I'll keep my hands and other parts out of the place forbidden by your doctor. However, I demand that you grant me permission to be notified by him personally the moment you are deemed fit for your duty as my plaything."

I rolled my eyes and with the irritated sigh replied, "Sicko. Fine, you have the deal. Now, about dinner. I'm ready if you are, pops."

It was his turn to halt the conversation as he put up his clawed hand and growled, "Oh no you don't, boy. We will go fill that greedy stomach of yours the second you answer my question. What is it that I've just agreed to do?"

I dropped my eyes to my boots and mumbled out, "Uhm, witness the Gold collaring ceremony between Matz and Noah in the morning. Oh, and force Gretta to sign the law King Claus will put forth that allows the Dungeon Headmaster to serve the dual duties as the Dungeon Master attendant for the Mortar throne."

Jonas went pale as the ghost appearing faint as he whispered out sounding flabbergasted, "You've got to be kidding me. Why the fuck would you sell yourself to me to torture at my will only to get favors for that useless bag of

169

nothing? What has Noah promised you? Surely, you realize anything he swears to isn't even as valuable as the air he wastes to say it. Wait, did he trick you into promising him these things in order to gain the worthless honor of wearing the Golden Buckles?"

I lifted my head and glared at him angrily as I replied, "Whatever you need to believe so be it, Jonas. Makes no difference to this arrangement between us, does it? I'll hold up my end as long as you do the same. I warn you though. If you dare to breech this contract. I will make damned sure you are punished to the full extent of the Haus law. Plus, once you are held prisoner with me down below. I vow I'll make your putrid existence far worse than you ever have my own."

The Vampire appeared to recompose himself as he said, "There is no need for you to threaten me, boy. I'm the man of his word. When do you expect this collaring ceremony to happen? Ah, quickly I must assume or you wouldn't be here without the fight tonight, ja?"

I nodded, "Tomorrow at nine thirty in the honorable Voter's apartment. I'll attend this farce dinner with you as the payback for backing my raise of Matz, but when you arrive in the morning have all that we've agreed in writing with you. We'll ratify it den. As for that law I wish to see passed. Claus will pen it and have it ready for Gretta's signature by the weekend. You have plenty of time to bully that bitch into doing her fucking job."

Jonas smiled then held out his claw towards me as he said, "Fair, and done. Now, my beautiful boy. This foul business is settled. Come take my hand. You are famished and I'm eager to fill you to bursting. Let's go." I groaned with dismay but limped forward to accept his offer to aid me down the steps.

He quickly wrapped his arm around my waist and forced my own around his. With the evil grin he pulled me along next to him headed for the Elder's staircase. I didn't bother to protest his overly friendly embrace. The truth was, without the proper cane, I was at risk for becoming the memory if I dared to go down the steps alone.

I was grateful that he decided to take this particular route. I'd grown weary of the sight of every resident falling to their knees as I traveled through the overcrowded Haus hallways. These steps were forbidden use by anyone except the leaders. For at least the first leg of our journey, I could be sure, no other soul would either block our path nor witness this unsavory display of the Vampire's affection.

At first silence was between us, but by the time we'd reached the fifth floor platform, Jonas insisted in assaulting my ears.

He cleared his throat then leaned in close to me and said, "Admit it, Christian Axel. This is nice, you and I cuddled together, leaning on each other for support. Don't you desire peace and adoration over the threats and brutality that cause us constant strain? Why must there always be discord in our marriage?"

Without taking my eyes off the next step at my feet I replied in the irritated tone, "Because you constantly trying to suck then fuck me, Jonas. I'd happily stop fighting with you if you'd let me alone. But that's never gonna happen, is it? It is natural for any creature to do its best to escape from something unpleasant."

The Vampire drew in his breath as if offended then responded, "Aw, you hurt my feelings saying that our lovemaking isn't fun for you. You don't appear that upset to spread your legs for every other dick on the thrones."

I shook my head then growled out, "Call me the whore all you like, pops. It's your fault that I wear that hat in the first place. Before you forced me into your wedding bed, I was known only to Peter and Xavier. This disgusting life I lead began after you locked your bat collar around my neck, remember?"

The Vampire halted with suddenness and looked at me appearing shocked as he replied, "I do indeed recall the details of our first meeting, boy. It is you that forget how eagerly you sucked my cock in the garden bushes while still claiming loyalty to Peter."

With a shrug I said, "I didn't hear you complaining at the time. What the hell is this really about? I know you, Jonas. Something is bothering you, so say it and relent your attempts to tease out information you are really seeking through insulting me over things I cannot change. Nor be wholly held accountable for engaging in."

Jonas briefly looked over the side of the narrow staircase then with the bit of anxiety in his tone replied, "Are you really, honestly gay, Christian? Please, if you ever felt anything for me, you'll answer this question without attempting to mislead me. I must know the truth."

I felt the jolt of surprise as I stared at him nearly stunned to stupid stammering out, "Do you, uhm, think that I, uhm, am?"

He turned to gaze into my eyes as he nodded then responded, "Not at first. I mean you still cry like the baby every time I take you. But you seem to be sharing the bed with almost as many men since you broke your metal as you did when submissive. You turned down the chance to make Mott your wife and then claim to have blood bonded that dead girl despite the intact cock cage. During that funeral business, you had complete power to do as you wish but take no female for your own lust. Instead, you pair up every available bride with unworthy Russian grooms. You didn't even blink upon receiving the most tempting offer from that lovely Mistress Karsten. I don't know what to think anymore. It is almost like you intend to refuse all possible mates including the one you already are unofficially spoken for. Then the way you look at Cary, and now Noah. Well, to be painful truthful, I'm concerned."

Another round of cackles broke from me as I replied, "Ah, okay I understand. You aren't really that worried that I'm the schwuler. This fear you voicing is related to that rule that if I don't choose the worthy female, they will make you play the role. Or perhaps, you are jealous that I might be interested in any man but you. Well, don't you get your pretty little panties in the bunch, sweetheart. Once you're down in the Palace with me, I'll only have eyes for you." I made the kissy face at him.

I pretended to not be the least bit rattled by what he'd said. Though in reality, his words bothered me the great deal. It had been anxiety causing to discover my lustful interest in both Cary and Noah's touching. That alone was good reason to be frightened, but hearing that Jonas was perceptive enough to notice it was scaring me.

I'd been capable of ignoring the evidence that my sexual preference had been changing rapidly. Since I was forbidden the company of the females, I'd convinced myself that any port would have to do in the storm.

However, with my ability to penetrate the male proven by that tryst with the Headmaster. I was beginning to wonder if I'd turned the corner I couldn't easily return from. Jonas did have a point while it seemed I could find desire for the woman's build, I'd turned down plenty of opportunities that likely would have remained private information.

What I couldn't understand is if this sudden giving in to the pitiful existence as the catamite was the real deal or merely conceding in to things I felt I couldn't change. Then again, maybe, he had a point. Had I unconsciously decided to punish him for everything he'd done to me by drinking the poison myself?

All that aside, the Vampire suspecting I had affection for the untouchable Noah. That was more than alarming.

174

Admitting to such the crime as being the Headmaster's lover was the outcome I was not in the hurry to face. This was the moment I had to swallow my pride and say whatever necessary to save my flesh from becoming the fuel for the Russian's winter stove. Yikes.

Jonas's expression turned serious as he glared at me and said, "Just this once can you answer me without tempting my fury, Christian Axel? Are you gay, ja or nein?"

I sucked in my breath and cast my eyes to his chest as I replied in the lamenting tone, "That's a complicated question, and the truth of it really doesn't matter anyway. As you said, there isn't a single girl in the Haus capable of meeting the legal requirements to become the wife of this idiot Mortar King. You already stolen everything else from me. If you don't mind, I'd prefer to keep my personal preferences to myself. You do with me as you will, and I will play that I enjoy it as always and just as I do for all the rest of these nasty bastards that have me in the compromised position."

He nodded appearing cautious as he responded, "Believe it or not, you have managed to calm my anxiety despite doing all you could to evade my question. I'm grateful to know there is still hope that one day the Haus shall have her Priceless line. Okay, I'll not ask you about this again. Just promise me that you'll use more discretion when engaging Noah as your protection while traveling the Haus. If I thought there was more between the two of you than merely the bodyguard partnership, others may think the same, ja?"

I feigned the expression of insult as I replied angrily, "Noah? You think I'm interested in that surly brute? Come on Jonas. He looks like the shaved down grizzly bear. I prefer my lovers to be slender and fuzzy."

Jonas chuckled then leaned in and kissed my lips lightly as he breathed out, "Ah, well you are in luck. I meet all those requirements to keep your attention. Unfortunately for you, I like my boy to be slender and smooth, ja?"

I growled out, "And toothless apparently." He swatted my cheek lightly then dragged me down the steps while laughing in the most evil sounding tones.

We arrived at the Great Hall with plenty of time left on my clock for him to make the most public spectacle of our time there. The new head black collar waiter Nicholas gracefully seated us at the Elder's table. To my dismay, none of the other fur princes were present to alleviate some of the pressure put upon me to keep Jonas company.

He calmly took the menu from my bandaged hands, then disrespectfully placed my order for me. I sat there fuming over his lack of proper manners for one that was above him in status. There wasn't shit I could do about it and he knew it. Both agreements I'd made with him prevented me from voicing any discontent in his treatment of my royal person. Like it or not, I was his plaything until I found release to return for more of the same in Lucus's hold. Ugh.

Once he'd secured our dinner selection, he stood up while clicking his crystal glass to demand silence. All eyes in the Hall turned to him, and the silent hush fell over the crowd.

Jonas cleared his throat then said with the huge grin and loud booming voice said, "Good evening my dearest brothers and sisters. I thank you all for granting me your undivided attention. I have the most wonderful news to share. The young Master Matz Wobbens has been blessed by our reigning Mortar Monarch this very day. By order of his Voice, Mad Lucus, the Honorable Wobbens is assigned to the role as fifth prince of the Silk Thrones. I've witnessed this legal rise with my own eyes. Let's all rejoice in this most wise appointment of this worthy Dominant." The crowd broke out into scattered applause.

Jonas returned to his seat and winked at me with the wickedest of smiles on his face. I rolled my eyes over his silly thrill at shoving the stick right up Lucus's ass. Though it is the custom to formally announce the filling of leadership thrones over dinner in the Great Hall. He was aware that my regent, Matz and that shady bitch Gretta were supposed to be present when he did it. It was bad manners but not illegal to do it as he'd done.

However, I knew he was doing far more than merely ignoring the proper protocol. I saw him eyeing the mass of diners before he'd decided to take this action. He was making sure none of the above were present to dispute his claims before it became the latest hot gossip. The Vampire was behaving shady in the barely veiled effort to avoid open conflict with Lucus who swore to the Gods he'd never would have done such the thing as raise Matz. I'd never tell Jonas this to his face, but I secretly thought it the clever move.

Jonas leaned into my ear then whispered, "There is your payment in full for this night of pleasure I gain at your expense. I wonder, will you still believe Matz was worth it when I send you home later?"

I glared at him and replied flatly, "Keep talking sexy like that and I'll be incapable of keeping my hands off you, lover. Whatever deviltry you've got planned I beg of you to get on with it. I've had a long difficult day. I am not in the mood for your bullshit games."

The Vampire grabbed me by the back of the head and forced my lips to his own. He engaged me in the open mouthed kissing with far too much of his nasty tongue. I endured it with stoic calmness, returning his sloppy adoration as best as I could without vomiting.

When he decided to break off the disgusting display of a public display of affection he whispered breathlessly, "Get under the table and give to me what you once gave to Lucus. Nein, do better than you did for that asshole. Do not tell me this isn't possible. Doctor Attila only blocked me from taking out my lust on you further south than I've requested." He pulled away then hand gestured the kneeling command.

I glanced around at our fellow diners nervously then whispered back, "Jonas, please don't make me do this here. I'll happily attend to your urges back at your apartment, as many times as you wish. It's rude to perform oral services in this hallowed place. You know that. Plus it erodes my authority as their reigning king to behave the bottom man in public."

He chuckled and nodded as he replied, "Oh, I am aware of that, boy. However, that doesn't change the fact that you've agreed to do all I ask without quarrel nor qualm. So? Perhaps you desire to breech our agreement? I'm certain the punishment I could see done to you, would be far nastier than sucking my cock in front of an eager audience."

With the groan of irritation erupting from my throat I responded, "I fucking hate you, Jonas."

The Vampire laughed while pointing at his lap as he said, "Not yet you don't, but the night is still young, ja? I did promise to fill you up. Best get to dining while it's still warm."

I let out the sigh of surrender, then slid out of the chair to the kneel at his boots. I attempted to crawl under the table but he grabbed me by the hair on the back of my head before I could. I was held hostage in his grip, unable to refuse his wishes without getting into the violent fight. To my absolute horror he turned in his seat, unbuttoned his breeches, then pulled me toward his unsheathed manhood.

Jonas purred out, "Stop stalling, your Majesty. If you don't hurry up, you'll have to stir up my lust again." He grabbed his erection then with his hand full of my mane forced me forward while pushing himself into my mouth.

The Dominants sitting in the tables around us noticed the pornographic show almost the second Jonas began his

179

sex on me. The room broke out into loud gasps, followed by waves of titillated giggling. Despite the gross sounds made by this raping of my head ringing in my ears, I could hear wooden chair legs scratching across the floor. I couldn't see them but I realized many in the room had quickly left their seats. It was pretty expected given the novelty of this display, most were in the hurry to gather around to watch the free show. Ugh.

I closed my eyes and attempted to go away to the place deep within. There was no reason for me to suffer this shameful act fully conscious. By now I was the expert at performing oral services on automatic pilot in front of others thanks to many, many terrible experiences with it. Jonas, however, didn't think it fair to allow me this tiny bit of mercy.

He let go of his member and used my hair to pull me off him then said in the pant, "Look at me, boy. I want to see your pretty blue eyes adoring their husband while you blowing me dammit." my glare of pure hatred met his own upon hearing his command.

He smiled at me then pointed at his engorged cock, "That's more like it. Now, don't forget to adore my hodensack with that talented tongue of yours. Show your subjects, just how much you love me, and enjoy sucking me off every chance you can get." With that he jerked my head back towards his interested parts.

Well, Meine Liebe. There was nothing I could do but obey him. He had me dead to rights, and I knew it. As usual,

I dealt with the humiliation like the expert sexual artist I'd become. Though I could feel my flesh heated up with the signs of embarrassment, I refused to allow the Vampire's latest indignity reach further than skin deep.

After all I'd been through from the first incident in Peter's ropes to the Palace, hustling for the collars, and the dreaded Stasi, I think I handled this minor incident pretty professionally. I engaged him in the blow job telling myself this shit wasn't even close to as bad as I'd already survived. Who in that Haus didn't already have either firsthand knowledge or at least some truthful ideas of the foul things I did on the daily basis with far too many male partners?

The life of isolation and chronic rape in that horrible palace was looming before me. There was nothing worse that anyone could do, not even Jonas, than to put me in the desolate cell. As I felt Jonas's thigh muscles twitching to indicate he was reaching his apex, I decided to give him the taste of the life he was soon going to be condemned to suffer next to me.

The Vampire let out the loud moan of intense pleasure. As predicted, he held me captive to his groin as he unloaded his lust into my mouth. I held still and waited patiently for his claw to release me from his grip. All around us the crowd broke out into excited whispers, and scattered clapping echoed through the Hall. Jonas's rigidness from his orgasm slowly relaxed while he panted and chuckled under his breath.

Then I felt him let me go. I rapidly rose from his lap and glared angrily until he noticed me staring at him like that. His eyes were glassy with the expression of relief written on his face. He wiped his brow of the light layer of sweat that had settled there and shot humored glances at the many people standing around us.

Jonas then returned his attention to me and said, "That was lovely, boy. You are truly the benevolent Monarch to share this loving act before so many of your adoring subjects, ja?"

With the loud hiss I spat at him in the fierce stream. My aim was true and before he could respond, the Vampire's eyes were pelted with the mix of his spent seed and my copious saliva. He let out the cry that sounded both surprised and agonized. That shit will blind you, ja? Hahaha.

I than yelled out in fury, "Oh, I agree completely, lover. But what kind of King would I be if I didn't share my deep affections with the man that is the most deserving of it?" With that I stood up and returned to my chair while casting the dangerous glances at all the loitering watchers.

Within mere moments of my defiant action, our table was cleared of unwanted company. Everyone rushed back to their tables and the usually boisterous talk was tuned down to the subdued levels. I sat there staring at the sputtering Vampire. I chuckled quietly while watching him grabbed everything, including the silken tablecloth, in the effort to clear his vision of that nasty mess.

He growled and fumed under his breath for several moments, then said in the furious tone, "That was uncalled for, boy. I could see you whipped for daring to assault an Elder."

I snickered then replied, "Go ahead and do your worst, dad. You really should have seen that cuming."

Jonas halted his attempts to wash out his eyes then to my surprise laughed heartily as he said, "You are the most insolent little bastard I have ever known, but Goddamn you are funny as hell. You missed your calling as the comedian."

The shock of hearing him humored despite my public show of aggression caused me to pause. I'd assumed he would backhand me for that at the very least. I sat there with my mouth hanging open unsure if he expected me to retort cleverly or if it was wiser to stay silent without tempting him to beat me any further. I determined it best to keep my smartassed responses to myself, for the moment anyway.

Once he managed to regain his sight, he leaned in close then said calmly, "Don't ever pull that shit again or I'll forget how much I love you."

I nodded then replied in the barely restrained tone, "Exactly."

Jonas leaned back into his chair, stared at me strangely for the moment then sighed as he said, "I want to eat our meal in peace, then dance with you for a bit. after that, I'll walk you up the stairs and return you to the care of the idiot Lucus. There is no reason to ruin this beautiful night with verbal arguments, you can never win, ja? Here, give me your hand and we'll shake in agreement that your disgraceful behavior is forgiven and forgotten." He put out his claw in offer of the truce.

I snorted then replied in the irritated tone while reaching out towards him, "Sure thing, pops. However, I don't do either of those for your bad manners…" my sentence was interrupted by Jonas in the most heinous of ways.

Before I could react, he'd snatched me by the wrist. In the most rapid move I'd seen him make in many years he opened his mouth and latched onto my lower arm with his pointy teeth. I let out the wail of terror as the pain of his bite rushed up through my nerve endings. The Vampire sucked enough blood to fill his cavernous maw to capacity.

Just as abruptly as it began he ended his toothy attack and let me free of his hold. I pulled away and cradled my aching arm to my chest stunned to stupid. Jonas's crimson stained lips bent into the sadistic grin. Then he returned that favor I'd granted him moments earlier by spitting his sanguine load into my eyes.

I yelped and as he had done, grabbed wildly for something to free me of that sticky liquid. Jonas slapped the table and howled in laughter over my disgusting predicament.

While I used the sleeves of my jacket to wipe my face he said in the tone of intense humor, "Didn't I promise you'd have the bloody good time tonight, Christian Axel? Now stop acting the fool and eat your dinner. I feel like dancing."

I glared at him in silent fury while Nicholas carefully placed our plates of food in front of us.

The rest of that first date with Jonas was relatively uneventful. I was full of the gloomy feelings over being forced into agreeing to the contract that was unfair in that he got five months for almost no real work on his end. He chattered on endlessly about everything from the weather to his plans to redecorate his bondage room in the apartment. I sat there pretending to listen with interest, but honestly if it had not been for the delicious food – I was not lying about being hungry as hell – I likely would have fallen asleep from boredom.

Luckily for everyone there in the Hall that night, no one was stupid enough to approach either of us after that gross blow job business that is. By the time, Jonas had stuffed himself with rich food and drank down two glasses of fine vine, he was ready to hold me his captive on the dance floor.

Dutifully, and without complaint, I accompanied him to the center of the Great Hall. I shot the anxious glance at the stage. It's large red curtain was drawn leaving me to wonder if that hideous lion cage was hidden behind it. It took all I had not to think about the horrors I'd endured only the fortnight before in most spots of that accursed room.

Several times, while forced to follow Jonas's lead, I felt that I may explode in the screams of terror that lurked just below my surface. Try as I might, even the smooth rhythms playing over the Hall speakers couldn't drown out the sounds of Heidi's dying gasps, nor the grunts of those Stasi men taking their turns raping me into unconsciousness.

Suddenly in mid twirl, Jonas halted his fancy footwork and pulled me close to him. He stared into my eyes appearing to be concerned. I trembled in his arms, unsure if he intended to kiss me or bite me again.

Then he sighed and said, "Not a single snotty retort nor any fight out of you for the last hour. You are a million miles away, Christian Axel. Tell me where is the boy I love this minute?"

My voice broke slightly as I rasped out, "I'm just tired, Jonas. I told you this already."

He nodded then cast the glance at the stage and replied, "Oh, my God. Forgive me, my darling. I wasn't thinking. This isn't the happy place for you to be is it? Here, come with me. I am the idiot for not realizing, never mind. We'll call this visit off early. Until our contract is satisfied, we'll either dine in our home or have the picnic outside, ja?"

I teared up and nodded as I barely mumbled, "I thank you for the mercy of it, Jonas."

The Vampire pulled me into an unusually gentle hug then whispered, "I know you think I'm the brute and I most definitely have earned that belief from you. Yet believe it or not, I do honestly love you with all my black heart. You should've said something about this calloused oversight of mine. Ah, but then again, I should've been more empathetic to your trauma, ja? This terrible pain your demonstrating isn't my pleasure. If only you could find true affection for me, I could be the light that leads you out of this darkness you suffering needlessly."

I shook harder from the effort it was taking me not to break down into the blubber mess as I panted out into his chest, "Please, Jonas, get me out of here. I'll do whatever you want but I must leave before I fall apart in front of everyone."

He nodded then rapidly whisked me from the Great Hall, not slowing his pace until we'd arrived at the main staircase. Nothing was said while he clung to me tightly leading me up the steps. All around us, the residents melted to their knees. All the while I fought hard to maintain my demeanor of fierceness.

But I was quickly losing the battle. Bitter tears rolled down my cheeks and unsung sobs of despair caused my breathing to appear labored. Each time my flesh quivered from that rising tide of psychological torment, Jonas would clutch me more tightly. He seemed to be reading my body language better than I thought him capable. The strangeness of this unexpected appearance of sympathy from the usually cruel Vampire was unsettling.

When we reached the door of the apartment Lucus had stolen from me he maintained his stance of comfort. I shuddered and pitched slightly while he knocked. My regent opened it and stood there staring no doubt full of confusion at the sight that greeting him.

He stole the anxious glance at me then looked to Jonas as he said, "What's wrong? Has something happened to Christan Victor?" He started to come at me with speed.

Jonas blocked his approach and held on tight as he replied calmly, "Christian Axel, is fine, Lucus. He needs quiet and the good night's sleep is all. He also requires the sturdy cane to travel those treacherous steps. Since you are apparently too cheap to provide his majesty with that important medical device, I insist you allow me to get one for him."

Mad Lucus's initial expression of concern melted into that of irritation as he growled, "As you wish, honorable Elder. Now, unless you desire to insult me further. May I humbly request you return my ward to me please."

Jonas looked at me briefly then with the slow nod replied, "Of course. However, I must warn you. The boy should not be trifled width. He's agitated enough thanks to my stupidity. For that, I must apologize, but not to you. Christian Axel, I'll make this error up to you in the way that demonstrates I'm truly sorry. Hopefully, you'll accept my offer and forgive me." He let me go and I wiped my eyes with the clot covered sleeve of my jacket unsure if I was hallucinating this scene.

Mad Lucus motioned me to enter the apartment, but I stopped before going inside then mumbled back, "I think you should know I hate roses, Jonas. Chocolate is the proper gift if you really wish to win my favor. After all these years you should've known that." I retreated swiftly through the entry without waiting to hear his response.

My wild pace didn't slow until I was safely behind the closed door of the Master bedroom. I set my grieving eyes upon that horrific cock bed of Lucus's and fell to my knees before it. The unwilling sex partner of the two brutal men that thought this abomination was the work of art couldn't be my fate. I wouldn't accept that. The heart wrenching sorrow of the lost soul I'd become gained the upper hand at last. I rolled into the fetal position and wept until I could find no more fluid to make the tears.

While I violently lamented the probable outcomes of the future too horrific to believe. I lost control of rationality and my thoughts became those of pure desperation. Many times I considered the hefty price I was prepared to pay my brother Byron if he could manage to get me out of the Haus.

Insanely, I also wondered if I should offer to forgive the DJ for raping me to near disability if he'd showed me the exit he used to come and go as he pleased.

Then I imagined the comfort I could gain by accepting Sigrid's bid to be named my regent if she could assure me that she'd give me regular access to her special services rights.

Guilt overtook me while I realized that if such a dishonorable agreement could be reached with that sneaky Mistress. Noah might find me less interested in granting him relief of his own lack of affection.

189

After all, I'd sold myself into the foulest type of sexual slavery to the Vampire to make sure Noah wouldn't go without my honest affection. I had already decided Jonas's alleged ties to the Russians and Stasi would ultimate protect him from being forced to play my queen. Even if it turned out I was errored in this belief I knew I'd kill that bat the second they locked us behind those silver lined bars.

Just before sleep overtook my fatigued flesh, Cary came into my focus. His love for me and my own for him was not the trick of chemically altered chocolate. Nor was that scene with him in Roland's apartment bathroom the act of last resort. I knew he would be devastated if he were to discover the secret affair I was carrying on with Noah behind his back.

Both of the men I cared for were risking their lives to help me achieve the best outcome given the limits of my deplorable situation. I eventually concluded I needed to slow down, gain command of my unruly emotions, and use the utmost caution before taking any further actions from that point forward.

Worst of all, I knew that I wasn't the only one who would pay the ultimate price for my epic failure by claiming the Mortar throne. To my deepest anguish I understood if I wanted to survive long enough to locate the escape from this trap I'd stepped into that Florian's court was about to become crowded beyond his wildest dreams.

Chapter 22: Brutal Flames

I never made it to bed that night I'd made the deal with Jonas that saw Matz rise to voter and assured Noah could be by my side until I was forced into the Palace. Nein, I ended up crying myself to sleep right there on the floor next to Mad Lucus's hideous cock bed. It felt like the weight of the world was crushing me into the fancy velvet carpet as the captive cockroach, ja?

When the soft sounds of rapping at the door alerted me to consciousness the next day. I found I'd gained no true comfort by that unmanly display of severe mourning. I laid there for several moments hoping against hope that Mad Lucus would decide to grant me the mercy of the peaceful morning. Well, you should know that bastard by now and I certainly did. Such a luxury as leaving me alone wasn't something he'd ever entertained in our sorted history together.

I couldn't prevent the audible groan from escaping me when I heard him call out in the calm tone, "Christian Victor, honey. It's six thirty. You need to take your medication and eat the breakfast your lamb Geraldine has sent up. Plus, I desire to visit with my beloved King for the little while before he goes running off to do what the hell is anyone's guess, ja?"

It took all my strength to hide my deep irritation as I replied, "I need to shower and change clothes, Lucus. I'll

191

come visit with you after I've completed my grooming rituals."

The door opened a crack and his voice boomed out, "You know better Christian Victor. Those hands of yours are still wrapped in the bandages. Until the Doctor releases you from them, you're incapable of taking the piss without some aid. I'm asking with politeness to enter, but I think we both know I'm not obligated to. Like it or not, I'm the only one qualified to see to your basic care. Do recall we have the formal agreement as well. It's not even close to nine o'clock yet."

He didn't wait for my response but instead entered the room. I rolled over to face the intruder with the unmistakable glare of fury in my expression. Mad Lucus crossed his arms haughtily while engaging me in the silent stare down.

I allowed this bullshit attempt at intimidation to continue far longer than I should have before I finally cleared my throat and growled, "You are the deluded bitch if you honestly think I've no better candidates to speak my desires Lucus."

Mad Lucus's eyes went wide as he stammered in response, "What is this? You think to hurl empty threats at me in the rudest tone? Ah, that's understandable that you've become the unruly brat that believes himself free to do as he pleases, ja? This is why I must not give in to any of your misguided desires. Just look at you. I've permitted only the few hours without any supervision and you've not enough sense to do even perform the simplest of tasks. Christian

Victor, everyone knows that the floor is for stepping on and the bed for sleeping."

A snort escaped me as I replied, "I threaten nothing, you idiot. You can choose to ignore me all you wish, my lord. There are others around this hell hole that are just as worthy and I dare say more than a little willing to help me wipe my ass. No doubt they'd understand that such gross functions aren't supposed to incite thoughts of the special services, you fucking pervert."

Mad Lucus screw up his face as if he'd eaten something that tasted bad then said in the whiny tone, "Not this again. I thought we'd come to the agreement that there would be no more arguing between us. I'm weary of it and surely it's not the joy for you either. Look here boy, the sooner you end this insane belief you have any chance at the quality of life worth living without my help, the sooner we both will be as happy as possible given the limitation of our situation. What more must I do to demonstrate no one can love you as much as I do?"

I began to laugh wildly as I exclaimed in disbelief, "My Gott. If this treatment I've endured since you came into my life is your attempt to show deep affection then shit, I need to seek no further enemies Lucus. Even the bat's violent embrace is softer than yours has been. You fool yourself if you think I'm going to quickly dismiss the recent offers to name the regent that has the shorter list of offences against me. Given the three that have thrown their names into my top hat, it's impressive that you're still at the top of the most evil of them all."

Mad Lucus gasped loudly then yelled, "Huh? Did you say there are three that think to claim what is mine? I demand you give me there names immediately Christian Victor. That's the directive."

With the mild groan I took to my boots while I spat back at him, "Go fuck yourself. You forget that I'm Dominant and the triple crowned, but I didn't forget. Not this time, fool. If you desire to know the identities of those more qualified than you are to play my tongue, then you can use the clever skills you've so loudly bragged to possess to do it. I think you'd better hurry and get to using that huge nose of ours to sniff them out though because soon I'm obligated to give the Haus my decision. As it turns out, your well thought out manipulation of the idiot Priceless wasn't as perfect as you'd assumed, ja? Now, I'm feeling grimy and I'm starving. If you insist on getting your thrills at my expense during my baser functions then let's get on with it. I'm a man of my word. I will give you no further fuss until the clock strikes nine. However, it'd be wise to recall that contract between us ends on June 27th. The next day you no longer have any say in what comes out of or goes into my mouth unless I say so. Ha!" I took off toward the bathroom without looking back to see if Mad Lucus was following.

Of course he did trail me, thankfully in sullen silence. I knew it was dangerous to alert that pervert of his sudden competitors. That was the calculated risk I was willing to taken with the hope it would result in the less harsh treatment while in the hours of his control. I only had the five months left to discover the man or woman that could give me the better deal. Until that terrible day I found myself forced to name the life-long abuser I needed to find comfort in any way possible.

At that time, I blamed Mad Lucus's unyielding bid for absolute power as the cause of all my pain. In truth, he is more guilty than anyone else, save one man. That idiot would be me. Not even that royal bitch had done as much to destroy any hope of a future of worth for me than I had. Though without his help I doubt either of us would be sitting here tonight, my Liebe. Take that as you like. Good or bad, that day I did not killed Mad Lucus in the hallway after discovering he'd been tailing me for years was perhaps the bigger mistake than visiting Jonas to ask his help to escape Peter's clutches.

Anyway, the morning I confessed to him I had other offers for regent was the quietest one I'd encountered while in his possession. He sulked the entire time he assisted me in my grooming services. His irritation was my celebration. I'd never grown accustomed to having to endure his nasty interest in being involved in the private matters. Just knowing that I'd gotten a little revenge for all the humiliation he'd heaped on me daily was the invigorating tonic I needed to regain some of the strength I'd lost since that Stasi business.

By the time I'd finished the tasty pancakes Geraldine had sent to me for breakfast, my broken spirits had found some mild healing. The sound of his chime clock announcing my hour of freedom had arrived sent me limping with fresh speed for the apartment door. I was bracing my pounding heart for the coming battles of the day when Mad Lucus's high pitched yell stopped me in my tracks.

"Wait the damned minute Christian Victor. You cannot leave without this or you'll find your death trying to travel, dammit." I turned to see him holding up another copy of that flimsy cane he seemed to favor.

I rolled my eyes and replied angrily, "Keep it Lucus. At least this way I will expect to fall down the steps instead of being shocked when I'm taking the boat ride across the river Styx later tonight."

Mad Lucus tossed it across the room and it rolled until it stopped at my boots. I stood there glaring at him defiantly for the few moments, then left without picking it up, slamming the door behind me.

I didn't get two paces down the hallway before I heard Mad Lucus's muffled bellow of fury calling out from within the apartment. That caused me to chuckle with great humor that I'd managed to frustrate that fucker into losing his so-called unflappable cool. Hahaha.

That said, I didn't get six paces further before I realized my victory was the hollow one. It was the truth that my leg had become the disabled mess. Rushing around in the uneven limp was causing my hips to send angry complaints about their unfair burden. I didn't return for that cane though. I was too proud and stupid to admit I'd made the mistake refusing Mad Lucus's offer of that useful tool. The realization of the severity of my error didn't completely sink in until I reached the fourth-floor platform. I stood there looking at the many steps leading up to the Voters level damning myself for being the pig headed fool I truly am. There wasn't any possibility that I could safely climb towards Matz's place. Unless I did it on my knees like the uncoordinated baby.

"Looks like you could use a little help there Mad Maxx."

I nearly jumped out of my skin as the voice of Fritz called out from behind me. With the startle I turned around and found him standing there. He held out a cane that appeared to be of the sturdy sort fashioned from the finest dark oak and topped with the carved image of the bird of prey.

Fritz's face broke into the evil appearing smile and said, "I beg of your Majesty to accept this humble token of my honest affection." He then dropped to the kneel at my boots while holding that beautiful cane above his bowed head.

I blinked a couple of times to see if I could clear my vision of this likely hallucination before I stammered out, "Do you have nothing better to do other than following me around like the sneaky snake you are?"

He chuckled low but didn't raise either his head nor from his knees as he replied, "There isn't anything more important than being available to offer service to my Lord and Master."

That response wasn't the one I'd expected, at least not from this creature. However, I was careful not to allow Fritz to know he'd surprised me with his generous offer. I had to assume this gift was anything but free. I quickly decided that as long as his price was fair, I'd be willing to bargain for this necessary item. Allowing him to know I wanted the cane would surely put me at the disadvantage in our haggling, ja?

With a steady hand and the feigning of indignation I snatched that fine object from his outstretched paw and growled back, "Ah, well that's good that you've finally learned to demonstrate proper manners, worm. I'll honor you by accepting this useless trinket you're offering. I'd never wish it to be said I'm the monarch that doesn't appreciate the unworthy attempts of his subjects to show respect that I'm owed."

Fritz nodded then said in the humored tone, "I'm thrilled you've granted me your mercy of acceptance of my gift to you, Sire. However, I would respectfully ask that you grant me the minor return service for this, uhm, useless offering."

I glared at him as I replied, "You call it the gift but then ask for recompence? So, you are not only rude but you are also stupid, ja?"

He snapped his head up from the bow and his irritated glare met my own as he responded in the barely veiled tone of anger, "As you say, your Majesty. It's not for this unworthy subject to argue with his Lord and Master's opinions of this useless man. I said this is the gift and I don't relent that claim. Please keep it with my blessing without fear that I seek payment. It's my desire that it serves you as well as it has me."

I snuck the surprised glance at the cane then returned my attention to Fritz as I asked, "I wasn't aware that you have difficulty walking. Have you managed to recover enough to part with it?" My eyes vent about examining his kneeling frame for weakness with the dubious expression on my face.

Fritz shook his head nein as he responded, "Nein, I've never had need for the cane, Sire. I meant being in possession of it meant I was able to find cause to speak with you without going through the usual protocol expected to gain an audience. Listen, your Majesty. I swear that I'm only interested in getting the moment of your time. I want to discuss the matter I believe could be of great interest to us both."

I sucked in my breath and broke from his gaze to examine the pretty cane while I replied in the bored sounding tone, "Fritz, cut the crap. You could've paid Matz far less than this gift must have cost you to visit with me privately. What is this all about? I must warn you that giving me the sturdy crutch isn't nearly enough to sway me into turning my back on Lucus in your favor."

He shook his head nein, then took on the serious expression as he said, "I wouldn't dare to expect such the honor could be purchased so cheaply as that, Sire."

With the nod I replied, "Good that we agree. So? You're wasting my time. Say whatever it is that you paid the pretty penny to tell me. Otherwise go see Matz and set up the meeting with me the proper way. I've got important things to attend to, you know."

Fritz turned his head in every direction as if to assure himself we weren't in danger of being overheard then he leaned in closer to me and whispered, "Tell me something Sire. Do you like my wife Audry?"

My eyes went wide as I barely was able to breath out, "Fritz, if you are about to offer up that ugly bitch that calls you husband than I suggest you rethink it before you say something you cannot taken back. My right to name the regent isn't for sale for that nasty proposition any more than it is for this fancy wooden babble."

He gasped loudly then took to his boots with such suddenness it nearly sent me scrambling for cover.

"Nein. You misunderstand my meaning for asking that question, Mad Maxx. I'd never be so daft as to believe you'd find desire for that harpy much less be willing to name me your regent for granting rights you technically already have as the Mortar King." He said rapidly in the loud whisper.

I didn't bother to conceal my shock as I responded softly, "If not, then what the fuck do you care if I like her? It's not my bed she shares and thankfully not the space I usually occupy either. That's your burden."

Fritz nodded with vigor as he replied quickly, "Unfortunately you hit the nail on the head, your Majesty. I assume based upon your reaction to the thought of her presence that you aren't a fan of hers, ja?"

I shrugged as I cautiously said, "I confess she's not someone I wish to know better than I already do. That's not such a revelation though. I think it's not the secret there are few in this Haus I think of with fondness. To be brutally honest, Fritz. You are among the many I detest enough to consider sending to hell almost on a daily basis. Now that you know that, are you still interested in taking up time I don't have to bitch to me about your regrets over marrying the unattractive, vicious Audry Baus?"

Fritz winced then dropped his gaze to his boots as he mumbled in response, "I suppose that's fair. I've not been the gentle benefactor while taking my sport with you, ja?"

I leaned in close to him and replied flatly, "Woof, woof."

He stifled the chuckle then glance at me appearing embarrassed as he said, "I refuse to apologize for enjoying the services I purchased with honesty. Sadism and humiliation are my pleasures. Last time I spoke with Matz, he didn't indicate you're opposed to playing the part as my slutty dog as long as I paid the fee. If my continued place as your occasional client in your hustle is the threat to see us become the trusting partners than I happily withdraw from that pursuit."

The sigh of resignation escaped me as I softly replied, "Nein. I don't desire you stop paying for services that I offer and you desire. If I erased the names of every man that I dislike from my client list I'd be the pauper in mere hours, ja? Okay, that's settled. I'll politely ask you to explain your reason for asking me about how I feel about Audry once more. Answer quickly or I'm leaving. I already told you I'm the busy king, dammit."

Fritz nodded then he leaned into my ear and whispered, "I wish to become the widower without anyone suspecting that I'm not the grieving husband. It's my belief you are the only man that can make this dream come true."

I pulled away from him with the surprised gasp, "Are you asking me to kill your wife? What the fuck? Is she that bad in bed?"

He chuckled nervously then replied, "You know better, Sire. My reasons are so obvious that without your help I'm sure to be implicated if anything were to happen to the future Silk Queen. Now that you've put that death sentence on Gretta, the Baus are the next in line to taken the throne. Audry's rise is sure to happen the second they pull Justus's baby from that idiot bitch's loins. Tell me something Mad Maxx. Do you really think that Audry will be merciful to you after witnessing the terror you inflicted on her predecessor?"

I trembled slightly at the thought of that most likely scenario then responded, "I see your point Fritz. However, I still don't understand why you'd even desire to stop this from happening since ending Audry's rise will also stunt your own. Your family line, the Fincks, aren't even close to next to take the voters floor. The Haus will raise Karsten as the only viable Baus candidate for the Silk and I dare say your chances to woo that angel are non-existent. Claiming to be the legal consort to the Silk Queen isn't as bad as being

202

the life-long first floor nothing you'll remain if Audry were to, uhm, go missing. I suggest you stop drinking so early in the morning Fritz. You're obviously getting the wet brain from it."

The shady Dominant chuckled bitterly than shook his head and said, "Your little trick of forcing that blood bonding with that no account silver collar ended Karsten's chance of taking the Silk throne and you fucking know it. That's why you ruined her like that, ja? Come on, Mad Maxx. Give me some credit. I'm not the total idiot you seem to take me for. It's occurred to me that you've been expecting this request from me since the funeral of the late queen and prince of the mortar throne. Well, here I am with the answer you wanted to hear. Just name the time and place. Fritz is your willing accomplice to see that the Baus's are passed over in favor of the Finks."

I furrowed my brow then leaned in close to him as I whispered, "I think Audry has gained a few too many pounds. Perhaps you should encourage her to take walks in the garden, ja? If you are too worried that informing your wife of her extra baggage than I'll do you the favor of breaking it to her politely. I'll be hanging out at the yard playground tomorrow around sunset. I'm interested in giving my new bodyguard the tour of the swing set, you know. He's the novice to such luxury. Oh I know I spoil my subjects but that's a weakness of mine. No doubt your lovely wife will soon come to appreciate my experienced ability at giving people everything they have earned and so much more." I pulled away and winked at him.

Fritz nodded while the wicked smile spread across his face and replied, "Enjoy the cane, your Majesty. I dare say its elegance is matched only by the man that it graces." He bowed low for the moment then without further comment took off down the steps headed back to his place on the first floor.

I watched him retreat for the few seconds then practiced with the aid of my new sturdy tool for the moment. It was the pleasure to feel secure in my ability to navigate independently. The huge clock on the Haus wall indicated I'd tarried far too long. With the rapid steps of sureness I hurried up the staircase ready to engage in the first of many meetings on my agenda that day.

My arrival at Matz's apartment was uneventful thanks to the early hour. The Haus Dominants tend to be the lazy bunch with so many servants living among them. The halls and staircase were already teeming with hundreds of black and silver collared unfortunates but there wasn't the single unhampered neck among them.

The fifth floor apartment of Birgit was likely abuzz that morning fueled by the anxiety of Noah's upcoming collaring. However, before I went to retrieve my new lover I needed to visit with the disgruntled Shadow King. I had no fear that Noah would mind my command to remain in his room until I arrived to escort him. Jonas wasn't due until eleven and my meeting with Byron at eleven thirty. Both of these difficult situations were far enough in the future that surely I could calm the anger that Cary's notoriously pissy behavior would incite in me, ja? Or so I hoped anyway.

I lightly knocked on the door and to my relief Matz answered almost immediately. He said nothing as he moved aside to allow me entry into the apartment. The newly minted voter didn't need to say anything. His hallow eyed expression told me that he'd been praying I'd realize his plight. I could only imagine the nervous sleeplessness the frail, skinny Matz had suffered being forced to share the enclosed space with the angry, well-muscled ex-door guard.

Before I could ask, Matz pointed at the door that I assumed was the entry for the loo. With the nod of understanding I hurried to that room. The weary Wolf rushed off in the opposite direction to barricade himself behind his sturdy bedroom door, no doubt. He'd been around me and Cary long enough to know that this was likely to get ugly very shortly.

I halted my journey long enough to take the deep breath before entering to engage with the Shadow King.

He must have heard me arrive because he'd been crouched in the blind spot just behind the door. The moment I came inside with him he pounced on my back. I hadn't expected this assault and therefore hadn't braced for the added weight to my own. We both went to the tiled floor with the loud crash.

"Goddamn you surly bastard. I think you broke my leg. Get the fuck off me this minute or I'll kill you." I wailed out partly in pain and partly from anger.

Cary wrapped his arms around my neck then started squeezing with strength as he growled in reply, "You first, motherfucker. How dare you collar me into the silver, forbid me from visiting with my children, and give me to that ugly Dominant to use for his pleasures like I'm nothing more than the common whore. I cannot believe you did this to me simply because I gave my virginity to the more eager and fairer lover. I don't recall you ever asking for it, nor did you ever demonstrate interest in obtaining the promise of monogamy from me in the first place. You expect me to remain the chased underused boyfriend while you grant access to your body to everyone under the roof. Well, I guess my sexual services became the important thing to you only because you knew another found me desirable. Ah, and you call me the jealous bitch? Ha. Well I'm gonna make you choke on those false words of love you've given to me, you duplicitous asshole. We'll see which of us is the more humiliated as you die at the hands of the collared nothing and I find the honorable death at the stake. See you in hell sweetheart."

I flailed helplessly in his tight grip as I gargled out, "Cary, stop this. Let me explain. Ugh, I cannot breathe. Let me go dammit."

He responded by putting more determination in his blocking my airway as he growled into my deafening ear, "Now you know how it feels to be me. Loving you is like smothering painfully slow while your boots stomp on my heart. The only way to be free of this burden is to find the peace of our graves. Die already will you."

With the fight rapidly leaving my air starved muscles I rasped in reply, "I'm trying. Thank you for the mercy of it."

I barely finished that sentence before the darkness of unconsciousness overtook me.

My eyes fluttered open after a brief dance with the void. The sight of Matz hoovering above me was there to greet them. His worried expression told me that Cary's assassination attempt had been nearly successful.

"Tell me Mad Maxx, are you in any pain? Speak to me brother. Shit, blue just isn't your color." The Wolf exclaimed nervously.

I nodded then replied in the strained tone, "I've never heard you say that when you were fucking me. I thought you loved looking into my pretty blue eyes, Matz."

Matz's face relaxed from that of fear to one of anxious relief as he responded, "Ja, that's true but I prefer that hue remain above your nose Maxx. Can you move? Do you think anything is broken?"

I glanced to the left and discovered my attacker laying there appearing to be taking a nap. There was the growing spot of purple across his ear with blood oozing from a wound that indicated the skinny Wolf had decided to break up our little misunderstanding.

I groaned then sat up slowly while I replied, "Only my pride, Matz. Shit, how hard did you smack him? I warn you. If you've killed him, I will be pissed off. His anger outburst was a bit over the top but not totally without validity."

The Voter Wolf gasped as he said, "You cannot be serious, Maxx. Cary is lucky it was me that caught him

207

assaulting the Mortar King and not anyone else. What he just did carries the penalty of death. He knows that and so do you. It's not only legal to end him for this crime against you, but I could be in trouble for not finishing him off."

Cary's voice weakly called out, "Then you better get to it Matz before someone finds out you are breaking the law."

I rolled my eyes as I responded, "Always eager to play the drama queen aren't you, Cary? Matz, be the dear and make yourself scarce. I think the Shadow King has gotten his complaints out of his system for the moment. If I need further assistance from you, I'll hail you with the blood curdling scream of terror, okay?"

Matz shot me the glare that indicated he wasn't impressed with my attempt at humor as he took to his feet, "As you wish, Maxx but just so you know if he kills you. I'm will kick both your asses the minute I get to hell after I expire on that stake right next to that idiot Shadow King of yours." He stormed from the bathroom grumbling under his breath that everyone but himself were 'completely nuts.'

I cleared my sore throat then said, "If I speak are you going to listen or are you insisting on taking the impromptu road trip to hell with me and Matz in tow?"

Cary didn't open his eyes as he replied, "You can say whatever you want, Christian. I need the second to rest before I return to murdering you."

With the mild chuckle and the double take of the bent towel rack discarded on the floor next to Cary, apparently the weapon Matz used to change my Shadow King's mind about hearing me out, I responded, "Guess I'd better talk fast then. Please believe me when I tell you that I didn't collar you and give your care over to Matz merely to see you humiliated in retaliation for seeking attention in another's bed, beloved. It's the truth I was angry that you continue to question my authority and I confess that collar was meant for someone else not you. But that doesn't change the fact that I'd already intended to assign you to Matz. Not for his sexual abuse, but for your protection."

The Shadow King's eyes flew open and he turned his head to set them upon me as he said in the infuriated tone, "Ah, well I'm glad that Matz interrupted me before I got the chance to listen to your pathetic attempts to lie your way out of this. Go ahead Christian. I'm eager to know the person this collar was intended for. Oh no, wait a minute. Don't bother with that worthless detail of this fanatical tale. I'm more interested to hear you try to explain why if you didn't mean to collar me, you fucking did." He sat up and lunged at me with speed.

I managed to back away from his grasp as I yelled out, "Because you wouldn't stop acting like the dumbass, that's why. Goddammit Cary, be still and hear me out just this once will you? If only you were as patient as you are handsome wouldn't I be the luckiest bitch in this Haus when I call you my true lover?"

Cary's attempt to regroup and make another grab at me was immediately halted. He blinked hard and then rubbed his angry bruised ear gently appearing to be in the brief shock.

He then snuck the quick glance at me before mumbling, "You really mean that, Christian?"

"Mean what? That you're the impulsive asshole? Ja, I do," I replied.

Cary shot me the snide glance as he said, "Nein. You think me handsome and you called yourself my true lover."

I rubbed my reddening neck and replied, "Well your affection has gotten a bit rougher than I enjoy as of late, but ja, I meant what I said. Too bad my feelings for you are misplaced. I must tell you it sucks to discover I suffer from the silly crush rather than be able to boast I'm the trusted partner of the man that loves me back. To think everyone in this Haus believes me the seducer of unparallelled prowess. That's utter bullshit since I cannot manage to win the heart of the only person I really want to call my own." I threw up my hands as if giving up my bid to win him over.

Cary's face took on the expression of anxiety as he quickly responded, "Nein, Christian, please don't say that. I do love you. So much that it hurts."

I nodded pointing at his wound as I said, "I can clearly see that. So, if you admit it, then why do you continue to battle with me instead of being next to me, Cary? Do you honestly think I'm so cold that I'd do all you've accused me of over such the petty thing as playing bottom to another lover? You're right. I never asked you for the promise of monogamy. I didn't request you give me your penetration virginity. I certainly promised neither of those things to you in return."

He nodded and cast his attention to the floor as he responded, "That's the truth of it, but if not over jealousy then why have you condemned me to the silver? I would think after you knew of the terrible price I paid to escaping it once, you'd never stoop to returning me to it."

With the long sigh I replied softly, "Soon the Haus will come for me, and they will carry me below. They will lock me into the Palace and throw away that key. There isn't any reasonable escape for me my love, I've come to accept that truth. One of the only comforts I've managed to bargain for is regular visits from my gorgeous Shadow King. The problem is that if anyone were to be seeking to gain the upper hand into what name comes from my mouth during the regent naming day they would need the strong bargaining chip. I've stupidly announced to the entire Haus of my deep affection for you. That made you the perfect target for such deviltry, along with the biggest threat to Mad Lucus's attempts to gain my attention exclusively. Then there is the danger that wife of yours is interested in replacing her roving husband as first Prince of the Mortar Throne."

Cary looked up into my eyes with suddenness appearing startled as he asked, "What? Are you suggesting that Roselina intends to assassinate me? Why the hell would she do that? If she did, than you'd have no further reason to see our family treated as Haus royalty. You choose me as your Prince of the Mortar Throne not her as the Princess."

211

I shook my head and stared at him with unwavering harshness in my expression, "Stop lying to yourself brother. Roselina set you on this path of destruction at the side of your Mortar King. Don't you recall it was her suggestion that you offer to Dark Bond with me? Though you didn't believe I'd choose you, she suspected I would do so. Then after she reaped the benefits that you will pay for the rest of your life, long or short as it may be. She quickly blood bonded with Rolf, the second prince of the Silk Thrones. That son of ours, I hear the rumor that he thrives, ja? I suppose your lovely lady neglected to inform you that all males that claim blood lines to the Mortar King, and his princes are also royalty of the stone throne. That boy of yours is the current second prince, right after his father the Shadow King. If you were to expire, or let me say when you do, he will be rise to take your place. If you find the grave before he reaches the age of minority, and if this unlucky king of yours also has an unfortunate mortal accident, his mother will automatically become the regent to the infant Mortar Monarch."

Cary began to visibly tremble as my words sunk into his conscious.

"You realize you are suggesting that Roselina intends to see me murdered, ja? That's the intense accusation that has no proof behind it Christian. Roselina loves me, even if she isn't in love with me. Come on, think my love. Even if she's faking her feelings for me, no mother with any heart would desire to condemn her helpless baby boy to that horrific fate this Haus calls the Mortar Palace." He shook his head with vigor doing all he could to deny the dark truth he wasn't able to ignore any longer.

I very slowly began to approach the Shadow King that was heading for the melt down as I said softly, "Cary, if you cannot care for your own fate or for my own, I beg of you to relent your refusal to see that I tell no lies for the sake of your little boy. He's the innocent among this pack of vicious predators. You and I must survive until I'm safely buried far beyond any plots Roselina and her allies may have to see your son condemned in our place. Please help me, help yourself and him, I forgot. Forgive me that I never asked. What did you name that precious child of yours?"

Cary lifted his tear strewn face to greet my own approaching one and said through trembling lips, "I named him Christian Axel after the only man before him that ever brought me as much joy to hold in my arms." I rushed forward and caught him in my embrace before he could collapse onto the floor overcome by the weight of grief.

I held him tightly while he wept loudly. It was hard to listen to the sounds of his anguish. *Though I never told him to this day, Meine Liebe. This pain he suffered at realizing that the one he thought he could trust never loved him I could empathize with fully. Poor Cary was the victim that I once had been with my misled belief that Agnette would come to my rescue.*

Once the worst of his weeping had calmed down I leaned into his ear and whispered, "Thank you for honoring me as you have done. Though I think that your son deserved to carry on the name of the man of a more dignified reputation. What do you think he will say to you when he's old enough to discover the story of the whore that came before him?"

Cary sputtered through his tears in the failed attempt at the bitter chuckled then replied, "I said I named him Christian Axel, not Mad Maxximillian, my love."

I swatted his shoulder playfully then nodded as I responded, "Ah, you choose he follow in the footsteps of the killer rather than the seducer, ja?"

The Shadow King pulled out of my embrace and stared into my eyes, "There is not a hell of a lot of difference between them is there? I've heard it said that a rose by any other name smells as sweet. Perhaps in your case too many are hasty to call you by anything other than your truthful moniker."

That caused me to raise the eyebrow as I replied, "And what would that be?"

Cary frowned then growled out, "Survivor. Christian if my son is capable of enduring a fraction of the horrible things you have, then you can be damned sure I'd be the proudest papa that ever walked this unholy Earth."

"Who is the seducer now, ja?" I moaned out just before I pulled his lips to my own.

My lustful kissing quickly turned into the heavy petting session between us. Cary offered up no quarrel, appearing to enjoy the deep attention my eager lips were paying to his exposed fleshy spots. His breathing had become labored and his breeches zipper strained to contain his interest in going further than necking.

I ended my soft assault to whisper out, "This action cannot be completed as it has in the past. I'm still too injured to service you the way you prefer, lover."

Cary groaned in frustration over my resistance in his attempt to gently push me to my knees as he replied, "The Stasi didn't break that beautiful mouth of yours. I'd be content with finding my release inside you that way, ja?"

My head shook nein as I said, "I'll grant you such pleasure after I get mine." I pushed him away from me with force.

He stood there appearing confused as he stammered, "Uhm, okay. I suppose that's fair."

Cary fell to the kneel and reached for the buttons of my breeches. I slapped his hands away. The expression of irritation came over his face immediately. For several moments he sat there on his knees staring at me in silence.

I refused to break from his gaze as I finally said, "Are you pissed off because I denied you the easy route to see me satisfied? If I wanted the blow job, then I'd have asked for it specifically."

The Shadow King's glare became even more hateful as he growled back, "Am I supposed to read your fucking mind, Christian? So, the hand job then, ja?" He again reached out to undo my pants.

I repeated my quick swatting of his hands. He rose to his boots with swiftness. His face turned red from the underlying anger he felt over my continued denials. I watched him ball up his fists that hung limply at his flanks. I was pretty sure he wanted to punch me out but thankfully for him he held his temper in check.

"You sure are sexy when your pissed, lover. However, we don't have time for this arguing. As you can clearly observe, I'm aroused already. There isn't need for more foreplay. You know I keep the lube bottle in my jacket's right pocket. Hurry up dammit. If you don't get me prepped quickly you will end up with blue balls. Jonas isn't late for appointments, even the ones he doesn't wish to attend." I crunched up my shoulders to allow my vampire jacket to slip off easily.

Cary rushed forward and took me roughly by the upper arms. He slammed me into the wall harshly sending all the air from my lungs in the single loud rush. I stared into his infuriated eyes baffled as to his reason for his appearing offended.

"What the hell is your problem? Let me go this minute. That hurt dammit. I'm gonna lose my hard on, you know." I gasped out.

His mouth drew up into the sarcastic appearing smile, "I already told you, Christian. I don't enjoy anal sex and I'm not going to submit for it. Not for you and not for anyone else. I see where this is going. You bend me over the sink and fuck me to bloody. Then later, after you return to the

216

beds of one of your many other lovers, Matz forces me to endure more of the same. Well, if that is the plan, you can forget it. I'm not the compliant silver whore just because you put this piece of metal around my neck. Kill me if you must, but I am never going to play mare to any man."

Maxximillian pushed me off the wheel and my expression turned dark as he replied in the angry tone, "You know, man, you're nothing but the hypocrite. All these many months you never listened when I told you hell no. I think to call in the return favor one time and you're tripping out. I'm the Master of this Haus, you dig? So, that means you will take it anyway I demand, jive turkey. Now, get your greasy fucking hands off the threads before I lose my cool." The perfect shard then headbutted Cary with all the strength he could muster.

The skull collision caused the Shadow King to release his grip on me. He staggered away the few paces, groaning and rubbing his newest injury. Maxximillian recomposed himself and let the jacket finish dropping from his arms to the floor.

"Lucky for you, motherfucker that I've lost my wood. This time, I give you the pass but next time I say bend over. You better fall to those hands and knees like the little bitch, or I'm gonna feed you to one, you dig?" Maxximillian glared at Cary with the fires of hell raging in his tone.

The Shadow King backed up until the wall on the other side of the room ended his attempt to retreat.

With the expression of terror overcoming his face he breathed out, "Christian? What is happening to you? Sometimes I think I don't know you anymore. Last time we spoke, you believed yourself neutered. Then you return and not only won't submit to my interest but you want to play the top man. Now you're talking weird. Are you taking your medication? What good is that idiot Lucus if he neglects your medical needs."

Maxximillian spit onto the floor, then with the evil sounding chuckle replied, "There isn't anything good about that freaky deaky turkey. As for what is happening, ah, well listen up Daddy O. You need to take the chill pill and stop this jive talking. Ain't no one buying it, fool. Tell you what. Maxximillian will break it down for you. I'm the Casanova with the groovy moves every stone fox and closet queen wants to boogie with, you dig? If you ain't willing to do me the solid by creating motion in my ocean, that's a bummer. I hate to be accused of being the flat leaver, but man, you're out to lunch if you think I'm will become the priest. I'm totally wally wally blood and dolly for you. But I've got to get my groove on before the old man comes to take back the car keys, you dig? I'm going to get my kicks wherever there's action to be had. So, don't be the bunny and stop dripping in my Kool aid, catch my drift? You better close the shades about that medication bullshit too. I ain't bananas so mind your potatoes."

Cary stood there wide eyes with his mouth open. I confess, even I had no idea what the hell Maxximillian had just said to our Shadow King. For several troubling moments, we just stared at each other. Neither of us spoke

218

nor dared to move from our spots while he was distracted watching for quick moves by the Shadow King, I made my move. With the loud grunt I pushed Maxximillian away from the wheel and took possession of it.

I glared at Cary then said full of fury, "I wanted this last few moments we had together for Gott knows how long to be pleasant. However, as usual you managed to thwart my good intentions. It's maybe the surprise for you to learn of the truth of our precarious positions of weakness. I realize you are upset as anyone would be given these circumstances. Yet, I don't have the time to do any more stupid dances for dominance with you. Perhaps it's for the best that we start this separation without the sweet moments of holding each other in the cuddles of intimacy. Hopefully, during the long five months to come you'll finally stop taking my honest love for you for granted, ja? Matz is the top man, and since you deny me the coveted place as your stallion. You better not dare to give in to playing his mare or I swear I'll murder you for it."

Cary's eyes went wide as he rapidly replied, "Wait what is this you saying about separation? I'm only here on the floor above the one you sharing with that devil Lucus. Am I to understand you aren't going to visit with me? And how the hell do you expecting me to deny any special service requests that Matz may make of me? You collared me in fucking silver, then hand me to him like I'm the piece of property to trade. That makes him my Master, ja? To refuse his desires means swift and painful punishment. If you don't want him fucking your lover than you shouldn't have done this to me."

219

I chuckled evilly then I said, "That's the strange reason to claim you're helpless to stop unwanted advances made by your Master, Cary. I've noticed you've demonstrated no problems telling me nein in the repeat. I dare say my swing with the whip is far worse than any man in this Haus. So, am I to believe you fear Matz's fury more than you do your true King? Ah, if that's the case then you are not only the fool, but you are also the moron. I happen to know you'll never be asked to service your Master Wobben in that capacity. What the conceited bitch you've become. You know, not everyone thinks you're sexy. Especially, those of us that know you best. That nasty attitude you've cultivated as of late is the real turn off, lover."

Cary's face fell into the expression of deep hurt. Then he dropped to his knees and covered his face with both his hands. I watched him without any indication of stress as his body began to tremble and quite sounds of sobbing filled the air.

With the slight trembling in his voice Cary whispered, "If it will prevent you from abandoning me. I'll submit to your desires, my Lord."

I shook my head and made the tisking sounds as I approached the weeping Shadow King.

"Wrong answer. Terrible reason. Worst timing, lover. You wanted to play the top between us. and still you think only to bully me into feeling pity for you when I've called you out on your bullshit. The advanced lover understands in any relationship there must be equality. Sacrificing one's own comfort in the effort to see your partner gain some is the truest sign of full maturity. Apparently you're still only the impulsive little child. That's okay. Don't worry my pretty little baby. I still love you. Luckily or unluckily, I've not been permitted the luxury of maintaining my innocence. I've proven hundreds, perhaps thousands of times, that I comprehend the complexity of the romantic bond. Therefore, I mercifully grant you the next five months to catch up with me in my wisdom. You'd better grow the fuck up. Because the next time we meet, I will expect you to be the man you've thus far failed to become. Now, get off the floor and follow behind me like the good little bitch you honestly are. Come on Peter Pan, you're wasting time I no longer have to spare with your childish tantrums." I patted him on the head in the gentle but condescending fashion.

Cary stood up and did as I told him while weeping quietly the whole time. We exited the washroom to find Matz sitting on the fancy sofa of the Voter's apartment. He shot the look that appeared sad at the Shadow King and sighed loudly.

I snorted then said loudly, "And? Go ahead Matz. Say whatever you're dying to say but do it fast. I've got to head down to the Dungeon Mistresses place to collect that dog Noah before that creepy Vampire gets here. That is unless you desire to spend a bit of alone time with him."

Matz grimaced then replied, "You know damned well I don't. I just wanted you to know that the walls of this haus are not so thick as you'd think. Not that men on the moon couldn't have caught at least the gist of that shouting match you boys had a moment ago. It's not my business, but when the fuck did you take up the habit of desiring to play stud to the studs? I thought you're the straight man."

With the loud guffaw I said, "Why you concerning yourself with my personal carnal interests, Matz? Oh wait, I know. You're offering to give me what this motherfucker won't, ja?"

"Hell nein. I'm certainly not. However, should I put that on your list of services you'll offer to the clients?" He narrowed his eyes while waiting for my response.

I shook my head and allowed the chuckling of bitter humor to fill the room as I replied, "You think yourself clever don't you? Questioning me about my sexual orientation isn't the smart thing to do, Matz. All you should've taken from that discussion between me and Cary is that you are to do nothing more with him than watch his back. He is commanded to do the same for you. But if I find out either of you did more than lay eyes on the other's backsides, I'll remove them from their sockets. That's a promise. Beware, Cary belongs to me exclusive. He will learn that lesson or I will end his studies for good." I jerked on his leash harshly and the Shadow King let out the soft yelping noise.

Matz nodded slowly then said, "I swear on my honor that Cary won't be molested while in my care, by me or anyone else. I wouldn't have done such evil even if you hadn't demanded such the thing. He's the free Wolf even if for the moment it's wise to let the Haus believe him the collared submissive."

I growled deep in my throat while I walked briskly toward Matz, with Cary in tow. I handed his leash to the newly minted Voter. Matz's eyes darted nervously from me to the Shadow King as he took firm hold of the chain.

Once that transfer was completed I leaned down into Matz's fear filled face and gruffly said, "If only you'd been so inclined to such integrity towards your friends when living under my roof, I'd not have as many nightmares with your name on them, ja? I suggest you avoid alcohol, brother. You know that stuff will kill you. Fuck up this time, and you'll find out why they call me Die Brutal and not Die Merciful. I hope you learned your lines for the gold ceremony. If not, you've got ten minutes to. I'm going to retrieve Noah. If Jonas arrives before I return, tell him to keep his fangs on. I won't be late."

Chapter 23: Monstrous Monarch

I took off down the fifth floor hallway headed with eagerness to retrieve my new lover Noah. Despite my recent disagreement, and vicious head aching with my ungrateful Shadow King, my interest in getting my baser urges sated was undeterred.

Of course, it was pure silliness to think that I had any time for the romancing. Jonas was never late to his appointments, even if he didn't wish to meet them. The clock was ticking and my burly babe's neck needed to be decorated with my brutal wedding ring of gold, ja?

I approached the doorway of the apartment that housed my elderly dungeon mistresses Birgit and Vivianna. Before I could wrap on the wood it flew open. There stood the deaf Vivianna staring at me as if I'd been beamed down by aliens.

"Oh my Gott. Your majesty." she bowed low then continued her comments sounding panicked, "I must apologize for taking so long to answer your calling. These old bones aren't what they used to be, you know. My sister Birgit is with the head dungeon master this moment preparing him for his sacred ceremony. She begs that you allow her a few more moments to see that he's ready."

I furrowed my brow and replied, "What the fuck are you yammering about woman? I only just arrived and knocked once without much vigor I might add. You couldn't have heard the stomping of the elephant much less that mild rapping I did. Your mind must be playing tricks on you."

Vivianna startled then said, "I suppose it could be. They say the elderly's brains grow soft over the years. I also admit this you saying about my audio ability is the truth of it. However, I must beg your forgiveness because if this is the case, then my delusions are of the shared kind. It was my sister Birgit and Noah that sent me with haste to answer your hailing. They insisted you'd been pounding on this door for many minutes before this useless old lady could arrive to let you in."

That was a bit of strange news, but to be honest at that moment the serious implications of her report didn't sink into my hormone riddled mind. I carefully pushed Vivianna aside and entered the apartment without addressing her statement.

"Tell your sister and that idiot Noah they've had plenty of time to prepare already. If they don't get their lazy asses out here this minute, I'll thank them both with my cane for wasting my time, dammit." I growled as I briskly rushed toward their overstuffed loveseat.

"Ah, you've become the impatient monarch, ja?" I heard the voice of Birgit calling out from down the hallway.

"I'm the busy man, woman. Tell that bitch that's already received far too many blessing from his king to move his ass before I'm pissed enough to give him a fresh lesson in how to do that," I bellowed out in the thwarted lust driven tone.

With suddenness Birgit stepped out of the shadows and into my full view. My breath froze within their lung prison. I blinked several times unsure if I was hallucinating but no matter how many times I tried to clear my sight, what I was seeing remained.

The elderly lady was clad in a beautiful and sheer nightgown that I'd only ever imagined in my most fevered adolescent dreams. It was of the expensive fine silk and covered with hundreds of intricately embroidered pink roses. My fervent gaze traveled over each inch of Birgit. Without an ounce of shame nor attempt to hide my interest I drank in the delight of the way it clung with perfection to the mysteries that makes the woman the most sublime of creatures on this Earth.

Birgit stood there allowing me to enjoy the scene with the sly smile pulling at that corners of her well-worn mouth.

I sucked in my air and whispered out, "You are the Goddess fallen from the Heavens, my lady. Your beauty is matched only by your cruelty. Why do you torture this worthless man by demonstrating such treasures he can never possess?" I felt my knees go weak as I said that.

Birgit chuckled low, "Forgive me, your majesty, but it's you that are the master of cruelty. I'm not the foolish maiden that's so easily flattered by the pretty words. There was a time that I could perhaps slay the man without trying, but that time is long passed away. This dusty rag of flesh is far too ravaged by water over time to be of value to heat the blood of anyone other than the buzzards seeking their dinner."

Well she did say that, Meine Liebe, but while she did I saw her milky eyes fill with water. Deep in my heart I knew, Birgit understood I truly meant everything I'd said.

Before I could argue that her attempts at appearing meek were unwarranted, Noah stepped out of the hallway from behind her. If the unexpected sight of gorgeously mature Birgit sent me into lust driven madness, seeing him and even more what he did next nearly caused me to orgasm without further prompts.

The stud of masculine perfection was wearing nothing more than the tightest leather britches. His muscle clad chest heaved and glistened in the light, appearing to emit a glowing aura.

Noah approached the angelic Birgit and without a moment of hesitation took her by the upper arm. He swung that silk clad woman in the move so graceful it appeared he was attempting to begin to tango with her. She swooned in his embrace. Noah caught her melt so perfectly it was as if the two of them were the same person. Birgit allowed her head to fall back just as Noah's lips swooped down and took possession of hers.

My feet felt as if they'd been taken hostage by the floor. The two of them frantically caressed each other. The pounding of my heart was the only sound louder in the room than the that of Birgit cooing out in the wanton tone while Noah's tongue examined her mouth and neck.

It took an extra second or two before I realized Vivianna had placed one of her wizened claws upon my shoulder. I let out a shocked cry the moment I understood she was reaching toward my, uhm, overly interested manhood.

With much force I jumped away from her encroaching touch as I yelled out, "What the holy fuck do you think you're doing woman? Unhand me this minute, Gott dammit." I swatted her liver spotted fingers with my bandaged wrapped ones.

Noah lifted from his task of seducing Birgit and called out in the breathy tone, "Vivianna, my beauty, I've only a few more moments left before I must leave you lovely ladies. Come to receive my appreciation for your fine hospitality and leave the king unmolested."

Vivianna shot me the look of distain as she replied, "It's too bad, my lord, you aren't as brave as your cock nor your willing servants either. The taste of the forbidden could be yours, but the frightened little boy that owns the most magnificent of weapons doesn't have a clue as to how to use it properly." She glanced at the straining crotch of my breeches then, far faster than I knew she could move, rushed over to join in with the pawing pair.

Noah pulled Vivianna close and pelted her copious folds of flesh with lippy kisses. He did this without a single pause from his groping of the willing Birgit. It felt as if the air in the room had been sucked out. I couldn't draw the breath. That water that been filling my knees was threatening to send me sprawling to the floor, along with the feeling of smothering, you know.

It took every bit of strength I could muster to tear my eyes away from the heavy petting of that oddest of threesomes. Clumsily, I turned and fled out the way I'd come in, slamming the door to close off the sights I was certain I didn't have the courage to witness.

You'd think after so many years of being forced to see, and be involved with, the sexual scenes of the wrong gender of my preference. I'd been more than thrilled to watch my sexy Noah taking on two of the most wonderful females that ever lived. Well, believe it or not, my flesh was willing but my spirit was just as Vivianna said, weak.

I won't try to lie and claim that jealousy sent me running away that morning. Nein. The truth that I'd been trying to hide from myself all those years had caused my flight. If you haven't figured out the secret that I wasn't ready to admit to that day, then you're not the smart woman I believe you to be Meine Liebe.

Master Max turned me around in his lap and stared into my eyes as if seeking the answer. I bowed my chin into my chest as I whispered, "You can't have sex with anyone unless they are paying you to do it, forcing you to do it, or..." my voice trailed off.

Master Max shook me gently as he replied in a soft tone, "Finish that sentence, Meine Liebe. Prove to me you understand the thing not even Noah understands."

I glanced up into his steel blue eyes that were filling with tears as I said flatly, "You are doing to them what has been done to you. You say you don't want to force the unwilling but that is a lie. Rape is your fetish, but you need to believe it's not what it really is. You need to be in complete control from start to finish. The only way you can truly feel satisfied is when the victim can't deny, judge nor escape your every desire while swearing to you that they are a willing partner. That's why you ran away from Birgit, Vivianna, and Noah. They truly wanted to be with you, but they were the ones controlling the situation, not you. Had they been afraid of you, you'd have happily fucked all three of them."

Master Max sniffed loudly then dropped his gaze to his lap as he nodded and said, "Very good, Meine Liebe. I'm happy that you've realized this without my needing to insist upon it during our love making. I refuse to apologize for the things that cannot be changed, but I wish to thank you for the many years of sacrifice you'll be forced to endure to feed my limitless urges."

I shook my head as I replied glumly, "But what happens if I do enjoy having sex with you for real? Then what? Will you divorce me and leave me here to rot in this hell?"

Master Max snorted loudly then so smoothly I almost missed it, popped my bare thigh with his cane, "If I ever believe you are truly loving my brutal touching I will make it hurt till you fear seeing my face much less my cock. Now are you done bothering my ears with the worthless sound of your voice? Or perhaps you may wish to take the moment to sate my disgusting urges, hmmm?"

I wailed out in both shock and pain, "Nein. I thank you for the mercy, Master."

He spun me around in his lap until my back was against his chest as he chuckled and replied, "That's exactly what I thought. You never forget that lesson and we shall get along just fine, ja? Hahaha."

So, there I was standing in the hall outside of that apartment of forbidden delights trying to catch my breath when suddenly I found myself flung face first into the rich carpeting of the floor. The force of the blow to my back knocked the senses out of me for several moments.

Through my confusion I registered the sounds of baritone chuckling hovering just above me. That mocking noise caused my blood to boil with the most intense of fury.

Though muffled by the maw full of the synthetic floor covering I yelled out, "I'm going to kill whomever the shady bastard is that thinks he can dare to use violence against the master of this house."

To my surprise the culprit reached out and pulled me back to my feet. I reeled in the near faint but quickly regained full consciousness. As my view returned to me, I slowly began to recognize the face of the man that both laid me low and then returned me to standing.

"Byron, you dirty motherfucker. What the hell? Are you feeling suicidal?" I growled out while pushing him away with strength.

He stood there grinning with the evil twinkling in his eyes saying nothing as I recomposed my royal self.

"I'm not going to repeat the question. You better start explaining, not that there is any excuse you can offer. I mean it bitch."

With the mild snickering he said in the calm tone, "Shut up brother. You had that coming and you fucking know it. As far as I see it, you're lucky I still desire to use you for my pleasures or you'd already be supping with the devil after I threw you from that banister." He pointed at the flimsy iron bars only the few feet away.

I aimed my eyes on him then responded angrily, "I'm going to pretend that I didn't just hear you attempt to threaten me, brother. As it is you are the one that should be thanking the Gotts not this idiot man. With only the whisper I could see you flayed and fed to the yard dogs. Now, if you are quite through playing the fool, get on with voicing your reasons to insist in risking your good health by bothering me. But hurry this up, Byron. You have my attention. I'm quite eager to hear what the fuck is so important you couldn't wait to discuss it later today during our prearranged appointment."

The burly Voter's cruel smile melted into the frown as he replied, "I've heard the rumor you intend to see the Council grant that bitch Noah the position of mortar palace guardian. This is only gossiping, ja? If not, then I think waiting until you decide to breaking yet another appointment with me, I've every right to force you to reconsider this stupidity at any time I can corner your sneaky ass."

With the air of arrogance about me I responded, "You dare to question the decisions of your lord and Master, brother? Buzz off irritating little fly, before I swat you into oblivion." I waved the bandaged hand at him.

This sent Byron into the spasm of fury. He growled low in his throat and ran at me with speed. However, I expected this move. By this time, I'd come to know my half-brother's behaviors far better than one should ever know another's. Without much effort I stepped out of the way of his charge in just enough time to prevent him from recalibrating his own movements. This led to him missing his target with completeness. His huge frame collided with the wall.

The sound of his crash must have alerted the occupants within Birgits apartment. Because almost immediately Noah flew out the door with the expression of worry written across his face. His focus moved from his king onto the cursing Byron with the speed of the apex predator. Noah didn't hesitate nor waste time asking questions. The misguided Voter was taken hostage in his vice-like grip before he even realized the headmaster had come to my rescue.

Byron thrashed and pitched with all his might. That did him no good. The headmaster's hold on him wasn't broken. To be honest, I think Noah was most probably the strongest man in all the house back then. Despite his constant working out, and liberal use of the muscle building steroids, none of it was any match for the perfect genetics and hard lifestyle of that sexy lover of mine. Hahaha.

This went on far longer than it should have, before I finally lost my temper and yelled, "Enough of this cock measuring, both of you. I'm the busy man. This shit is wasting time I don't have. Noah let that bitch alone and follow me. Jonas will be arriving at Matz's place any fucking minute. Byron, if you must play games, perhaps you'd be more successful at winning them if you played with yourself."

Noah released his hold on Byron the moment he heard my orders. Byron turned around and sucker punched the headmaster in his washboard gut. To his shock his blow didn't appear to phase Noah in the least. Instead of falling to his knees fighting for breath, the huge man offered him the most insulting smile I'd ever seen on anyone's lips.

"Are you satisfied? Or perhaps you wish to hit me again?" Noah said in the mocking tone.

"Turn your back on me half breed and we will see if you tough enough to withstand the fall from the top of this house," Byron threatened back.

I stepped between the feuding pair and growled, "Are you two as deaf as the honorable Vivianna? I said stop your foolishness, ladies. Come on Noah. Byron, I will see you after I've witnessed this useless motherfucker's collaring." I took off in the direction of Matz's apartment without looking back to see if Noah was following me.

I knew he and my bitter brother were tailing. Noah because he knows his place, and Byron because he's the dumbass that never has figured that out.

The three of us arrived at Matz's door at the same time the Vampire did. Jonas's face wore the expression of mild humor as he took in the sights of me and my entourage. He politely backed away and used the hand signal that he was permitting me to do the honors of knocking.

I shot the glance of caution at Byron as I reached out and banged on the wood with the head of the cane Fritz had gifted to me. Jonas's ever vigilant beady eyes were drawn toward that magnificent walking tool.

"Ah, it would seem that miser Lucus has decided to invest a tiny bit of his immense fortune on our beloved King, ja? That is a fine piece of art you're holding, your Majesty. Perhaps after this foolishness is done, you'd grant me the honor of examining it closer?" The Vampire cooed out.

Matz opened the door and bid us to enter as I replied, "Fuck you, Jonas. I know damned well you are thinking to confiscate my property. Well, forget it bat. The only way you getting the look at this cane is when I shove it up so far up your ass it comes out your eye sockets."

Jonas laughed hardily while I pushed passed him with speed, "My Gott, what a nasty mouth you've grown Christian, ah, Victor, is it? I certainly hope later tonight you're gifted tongue isn't too worn out to bathe my eager ears and other parts with that promised perversion. You know I love it when you speaking dirty to me, boy." He reached out and swatted my hindside before I could get clear of his aim.

Matz, Noah, Bryon, and even the brooding Cary shot me the glance of worry upon their witnessing the Vampire's attempts to anger me. I decided to ignore Jonas's bad manners. I knew he was hoping to cause me to lash out at him, like I tend to. This was no doubt his pathetic last ditch effort to gain the legal excuse to refuse to witness this most important collaring of Noah. I was well aware that no one in that room wanted to see Noah raised to his rightful status. The man's potential power was dangerous to each of them, though for different reasons.

I suspected that Jonas was more than a little aware that if there developed an alliance with the headmaster I could see him placed on the Fur Throne as king one day. That was the one thing the Vampire desired as much, if not more, than the elixir of eternal life.

Matz worried about my sudden interest in Noah because he couldn't be sure the man would keep the secret of our shady hustling business. Plus, I assumed that like every motherfucker in the house, Matz hoped to warm his skinny ass with the fur padding too in time.

I think it's unnecessary to explain why my Shadow King viewed Noah's appearance in my life as the threat. He's always been the jealous bitch.

As for Byron, though I often didn't give him the credit he deserved as the clever bastard, he was no doubt well aware that something serious was going on between Noah and me. I'd not gotten around to informing him of the change of heart I'd had about my appointment of him and Freidrick as my palace masters. Yet somehow he'd found out about it. This was causing me anxiety. It's not that I'd already figured out that Byron's spies around the house, as well as his constant stalking, was going to making it hard for me to keeping any secrets from him.

However, since I'd only discussed this information with Jonas and through him the Fur King Claus, I now had to be concerned that one or both of them were working with my evil brother. That means the promise Byron was making to see me freed from the Haus to the outside as his willing bitch could be not only the false promise I feared it to be, but it could also mean that this was another trap set for me by those clever perverts. Though I couldn't for the life of me understand what the fuck would either Claus or Jonas gain by allowing my half-brother to use me as his tortured fuck toy.

Anyway, these worrisome thoughts kept me occupied while Noah took to his knees at Matz's feet. The fear that the newly minted Voter would fail to perform the sacred collaring properly was for nothing. Matz kept his word to me. I was proud of the Wolf when not even once he faltered in his promises before his high ranking witnesses to answer for his ward Noah.

My pretty lover's answers to his new guardian questions were voiced with perfection too. The entire collaring went quickly, smoothly and without any hesitation from either man. In fact, the gold ring was around Noah's thick neck and locked closed before anyone of us realized the ceremony had come to the end.

I tore my wanton gaze away from their exploration of Noah's beautiful flesh and shot the quick glance in Cary's direction. My heart flip-flopped for a second when I discovered him standing there behind Matz silently staring back at me. It may have been in my guilty imagination, but it seemed Cary's expression was of the accusatory type.

I wasn't granted the time to worry that Cary had noticed my attention to Noah's collaring proceedings weren't of the innocent kind. Jonas had taken advantage of the awkward moments just after this holiest of ceremonies to slip up close to me.

He leaned in and whispered into my ear, "When you come home later tonight, I've got the surprise for you."

Without moving any muscles but the ones that rolled my eyes upward I sighed and replied, "You always seem to think that, but you are mistaken Jonas. I've seen it and believe me it's not shocking nor is it worthy of bragging about."

Jonas smiled then said with the soft chortling, "You are so sexy when you try to insult me. I want you to know, I appreciate the effort, but it's unnecessary to attempt to stroking my hodensack this way. I confess your mouth is seductive in the extreme, however even your supernatural gifts fall short unless you're on your knees begging through your tears for mercy. That I will never grant you."

Without a word I turned around and punched the Vampire in his face. Jonas let out the cry of surprise then fell backward onto his ass. Every man in the room sucked in their wind while I calmly limped over to taken a place above the scrambling Elder.

I tisked, then leaned down toward Jonas and said dryly, "You may find my mouth of interest honorable Elder, but I care nothing for your own. Next time you think to behave the brute during the hallowed rituals of this house, best you reconsider it. Bad manners equal swift and painful lessons to remind you of them. Get your disgusting flesh off the Honorable Matz's floor and recompose yourself in the dignified way expected of one of your level. Noah, you have ten minutes to go to your room and dress in something appropriate for the rats that live above ground in this hell hole. If you're one second longer, I'll see your flesh beaten to bloody. Matz, I thank you for your perfect service. I believe the payment of my Shadow King for your pleasures as agreed has also been fulfilled. Therefore unless you wish to renegotiate, which I suggest you reconsider if you do. Our business is done here, ja?" I didn't breaking my deadpan gaze from Jonas as I finished my comment.

Matz replied to me with the slightest stutter, "Uhm, ja, ja. I'm satisfied that you're the man of your word. I'm grateful for your mercy, your majesty."

Jonas shot Matz the hateful glance then turned his furious eyes at me as he growled out, "I must beg your forgiveness honorable Voter for my most rude behavior."

Matz bowed his head low and responded, "Forgiveness granted honorable Elder. Think nothing of it. You're always the friend of this worthless man, ja?

I lifted my brow and with the mocking tone said, "You hear that Jonas? Matz is your ally and grants you something I never will. No matter how much you beg."

Jonas snatched the end of my cane with suddenness as he yelled out, "That's because I never would beg you for a fucking thing you ungrateful bastard. Make damned sure you bring this with you later. I believe your suggestion earlier is a valid one. If you're lucky I might even lube it up first." He jerked the end harshly.

I managed to remain on my feet despite the Vampire's attempt to knock me down. After regaining full balance I sneered at Jonas and replied, "Well now you saying something that perks my interest at last. Instead of empty brags, I'll finally will get the piece of wood capable of seeing me sated in your bed." I kicked the Vampire in his upper thigh with my good leg then took off at full speed for Matz's door.

Noah rushed ahead of me to offer to hold it open as I exited. The moment it closed behind us his expression filled with fear as he said, "Mad Maxx, do you think it wise to anger Jonas? I mean, I don't question your will, but I worry he may be serious in his threating to injure you further by torturing you with your cane." He pointed at the walking stick.

I clicked my tongue then glared at him coldly as I replied, "The clock is ticking bitch. Up to you if you wish to waste your precious time waiting to hear of business that's none of your own. What happens between me and my husband remains to be seen. However, I do know what I'm going to do to your tight little ass if you fail to return in another eight minutes. and believe me you won't enjoy it."

Noah barely waited for me to finish that sentence before he tore off toward his apartment. I chuckled for the moment, but my moment of mirth was interrupted by the Vampire and Byron exiting Matz's apartment together.

Jonas's usually condescending gaze softened upon seeing me still lingering in the hall. He slowly approached with the shady Byron trailing behind him.

I pretended to look past both of them as I said, "Ah, it would seem that the fifth floor is the busy highway today. I wonder if perhaps the Council should consider widening the lanes up here before someone has the fatal accident, ja?"

The Vampire nodded then replied, "Maybe. Perhaps you should ask Lucus to bring that up to the queen next time she dares to show her face around either of you vicious cunts."

I snorted then said, "Speaking of the devil, have you seen that bitch Gretta lately? Do you really think she's avoiding me? Nah, she's never been the smart one. I suspect I'll be running into her soon enough."

Jonas smiled widely showing off all his pointy teeth, including the two fake ones he'd gotten to replace the ones

I'd knocked out, "I suppose it'd do me no good to remind you that playing nice with her is expected. Now that she's expecting. After that, well no one denies she's earned her punishment from our Mortar King."

I glanced over Jonas's shoulder to look upon Byron as I responded, "If every piece of shit in this Haus gets the death penalty they have coming from their Lord and Master, I'm going to be the busy man while this problem with traffic will be the thing of the past."

Jonas shrugged then turned to stare at the Voter before returning his attention to me as he said, "Byron, listen to me carefully. This youngster you see before us isn't the same one that disappeared behind the hallowed doors of the Great Hall a few weeks ago. I've no idea who he is, but I suspect he's not one to be trifled with. I suggest you don't attempt to push him too much or you'll be the fellow pushed too far. I'll be waiting eagerly for your return to our bed later tonight my dangerous beauty."

I stood there refusing to budge as the Vampire leaned in and put his lips onto mine. He halfheartedly pawed at my chest but there wasn't any real urgency to his touching. His kissing though was full of vigor. Though it angered me that he was insisting on forcing this indignity in front of my bastard brother, I eventually returned his lippy affection if only to end this silly scene.

After he was certain he'd embarrassed me fully he released my mouth from his exploration of it. Then without another word, he hurried toward the staircase headed back to his lair on the floor above us.

Byron stood there in sullen silence while the two of us watched the Vampire retreating. Then before he had the chance to offer complaints, Noah's voice rang out down the hallway. He was shouting in the horrified sounding tone. Every hair on my body raised to attention as I practically flew in the direction of my lover's distressed cries.

Byron to his credit, didn't require any orders from his king to take up the position of guarding my back as we hurried to aid the obviously freaked out headmaster.

The scene that greeted us upon arrival at Birgit and Vivianna's apartment was surreal. The huge Noah was cuddling the limp body of the lady of his house to his chest as the mother does her sleeping baby. His eyes were wild with fear and behind him Vivianna ran from the apartment emitting the loud wails of grieving.

I yelled out before reaching the three of dem, "What the fuck have you done fool. Put her down before the Guard get here. Killing the honorable dungeon mistress carries the death penalty. Why Noah? Oh shit, why?"

Vivianna's shrill voice called back, "Nein, leave this man alone, your majesty. He's done nothing to my sister. I found her collapsed on the floor when she didn't arrive to share breakfast and tea as we always do. I think her heart has failed her. I couldn't revive her nor could Noah. Oh my Gott. Don't leave me dear sister. I cannot go on without you," she fell to her knees while gnashing her teeth and pulling at her hair.

Noah stopped his flight and with great gentleness laid the deceased Birgit on the floor at his feet as he said, "May the angels come to guide you home honorable lady. Rest in peace, our father who art in Heaven knows you have more than earned this glorious reward. Amen." I arrived at his side just as the tears began to roll down his cheeks.

Birgit had managed to dress in her usual dungeon mistress uniform before the reaper had come to claim her for his own. I stood there staring down at the fallen lady feeling the tug of grief pulling lightly at my heartstrings. Though her age was advanced enough to expect her demise could happen any time, the suddenness of it still was the surprise, ja? I shamefully wondered very briefly if the strain of her apparent dalliance with my lover had hastened her trip over the river. I quickly forced that idea from my consciousness as I took to the kneel next to her corpse.

"Is what the honorable Vivianna saying the truth of it Noah? Was Birgit already dead when you come to change your clothing?" I whispered to the headmaster, even if I realized the answer to my question without his saying so.

He was still wearing the leather dungeon master breeches and harness he'd left Matz's apartment in.

Noah nodded then said solemnly, "Ja, your Majesty. There has been no foul play here. Birgit has complained many times in the last few weeks that the teeth in her jaw were going bad. This was because it'd been aching. Then one of the silvers below told me last Tuesday she nearly fainted during seduction classes after gripping her chest saying that she couldn't breathe. The Haus doctor will most likely diagnose her death has been by heart failure."

With the long sigh I shot a glance at Byron that had just arrived to the scene as I replied, "Fair enough Noah. Well, as you said, the lady has more than earned her escape from this hellish population she served with honor all her life. Byron, go fetch Doctor Atilla and do this quietly. No reason to alert the nosy that will surely come flocking to try to get their sick desires fulfilled by seeing the corpse of the head mistress, ja'?"

Byron nodded and unusually without any argument hauled ass to see my orders minded.

I watched the saddened Noah softly caress the cooling flesh of his lost lover for the moment. It's likely I'd happily stayed there at their side in the trance of disbelief until Doctor Atilla arrived. However, the loud weeping of Vivianna pulled me out of that place of numbness.

Slowly I took back to my feet and approached Birgit's grieving sister. She had fallen to her bottom with her back firmly pushed into the wall next to the still open door of their apartment.

I held out my hand toward her and said softly, "Come beloved mistress. Birgit has gone to the Green Fields. She'd never forgive you if she knew you dishonored her memory by behaving as the ill-mannered baby over her finding peace before you have."

Vivianna turned her wet, swollen eyes toward my own as she wailed out, "Nein your majesty. I cannot go on without her. I heard you tell Byron to send for the doctor. Stop him. I tell you, I won't let him take her away from me."

A long sad sigh escaped me as I leaned down and looked into her face then said, "Dear lady, you must end this insanity immediately. Birgit cannot remain here in the hallway. The flies will seek her out for their dinner and I dare say the black collar maids won't appreciate trying to keep the smell of rot down. Get off your ass and calm yourself this minute. I've found myself in need of the new dungeon mistress. The silvers will never mind your authority if you show them this display of weakness."

Vivianna's eyes went wide as she breathed out sounding incredulous over my words, "You cannot be serious, my lord. I'm not capable of taking the place of my sister below. Did you not hear anything I've said? I cannot go on without my sister. We've never been parted, and I refuse to leave her side now. Leave me be, damn you. I'll kill you before I let you take her away from me."

A sudden numbness overcame me. I stared into her face wizened by the years of hard labors, pain, sorrow and could see the unbreakable strength of defiance glaring back at me. After checking to make sure that Noah was still distracted by his own flood of emotion, I returned my attention to the newly minted head mistress.

In the most authoritarian tone I could muster I pushed the bandaged hand back at her and roared, "Get up dear lady.

Mind your master or face the severest of consequences for denying me what is mine."

Vivianna startled for the second but then as she'd been trained to do through more pain than most can imagine, she took my offered paw. I pulled her to standing, then motioned her to follow at my side. The mistress minded like the loyal dog as I briskly traveled beyond the sights of the headmaster and her fallen sister.

Once I was sure we were beyond any chance that Noah could hear or see us I halted and turned to Vivianna.

"Dear lady, you and your sister demonstrated kindness to me in my darkest hours. I want you to know, I never forget the debt I owe you both. Tell me, did you enjoy living above the heads of those that once crushed you beneath their boots?"

Vivianna nodded then sniffed loudly as she replied, "There are no words strong enough to explain the gratitude Birgit and I had for the favor you delivered to your unworthy servants, my Lord."

I reached out and softly caressed her wrinkled cheek as I said, "And what of the beautiful young man I sent to warm your bed? Did his efforts to make you feel desired bring you to ecstasy?"

Her sallow skin took on the pink hue of the blush as she whispered, "It's bad manners to discuss such things your majesty. However, I say to you, Noah reminded my sister and I of the things that we'd long forgotten. What he lacked in experience he made up for in eagerness to please. I cannot speaking for Birgit but I must thank you for the mercy of it."

I nodded and caught one of her tears with a minor portion of my fingers not wrapped in linen as I replied, "Ah well, I say to you that the gratitude is well received by your monarch. So, tell me fair lady, with all the favor I've bless you with, and could bless you with, do you still desire to defy my orders to taken up your sister's mantel as the head dungeon mistress?"

Vivianna dropped her gaze appearing ashamed as she said softly, "I cannot live without her, Maxximillian. You maybe could understand better if you'd ever known the pain of losing the only person that truly loved you."

The low growl began deep within my throat as I leaned in close to Vivianna and said in the furious tone, "How dare you insult me by addressing me in common. Furthermore you compound that error by assuming I know nothing about loss. You neither deserve my favor nor my mercy."

Vivianna lifted her gaze and stared into my eyes that blazed with fury and said, "Nein, I don't but I thank you for granting it to me anyway. Good luck, your majesty. If there is the Gott in Heaven, I will beg him to show you favor. Goodbye."

With the howling of the demons from hell I swung my cane with all my strength aiming it for the elderly woman's head. The sturdy bird of prey at the heavy end met it's mark with outrageous effect. Vivianna let out the loud grunt just as the splatter of blood and brain matter exploded from her left temple.

Quick as the wind I spun in a full circle with my leg outstretched. The toe of my boot aided by the power of my motion sent the collapsing and blissfully unconscious elderly dungeon mistress right over the edge of the Voters' banister. Her dying flesh fell in silence until it was halted with suddenness by the floor five stories down.

The sounds of screams of terror rose through the air from those far below. I stood far enough away from the scene of Vivianna's swan dive to not be visible to anyone looking up. This was one crime I was careful not to have blamed on me. I was aware that the murder of the dungeon mistress, especially my own, carried the automatic death sentence.

I did my best to feign the expression of pure shock before Noah came running. I was certain by now he'd heard the commotion from the first floor. After all the collective yelling that the mortar dungeon mistress had jumped to her death from the banister was so loud by then, I thought even Vivianna would have heard it. Well I mean if I hadn't killed her that is.

Noah rushed to me, his face contorted with terror as he yelled out, "What happened? Are you injured Mad Maxx?"

I shook my head then glanced at the banister doing my best acting job as I replied, "I tried to stop her, but damned these bandages. I couldn't keep the grip on her. Oh my Gott, Noah. I've lost both of them. What am I going to do? The silvers are doomed without a trustworthy mistress to look after them." I fell to my knees in the, not completely false, expression of frustration.

Noah stood there unsure if he should weep harder or maintain the stoic posturing in the effort to offer me strong comfort. I sat there quietly listening to the chaos spreading all around us. This was the mess I'd not expected. Losing these two important allies at the eleventh hour of my own plight toward permanent incarceration was most unfortunate. Though I admit to you that I loved both those ladies more than I should have, I was at that moment beyond pissed at them for leaving me like they had. Had such the tragedy happened to the boy I once had been there would be no consoling me in my grief.

However, that little crybaby had died right next to that poor virginal girl that had agreed to marry me before being raped to death by the Stasi. The day that Xavier's dungeon mistresses died, I felt nothing but irritation that their freedom from pain meant extra heaped upon me.

Well, there was one other emotion that I felt that morning. You may have forgotten but Birgit was Byron's mother, ja? Ah, well I'd sent him to fetch that nice Doctor Atilla without any care that his rightful place of weeping over her was granted to another man. But not just any man. The one fellow the Byron had begun to realize was his truest rival for my attentions. Not even my desire for his pain killing drugs, calming nicotine nor promises for freedom were strong enough to pull me away from the allure of pleasures I was discovering in Noah's powerful embrace.

Noah helped me back to my feet, and together we returned to guard the helpless remains of the amazing Birgit. Even in death, that lady managed to appear as the sleeping Goddess. To this day I cannot tell you where the woman nor her sister came from, nor who they had been in their life before the house. Even Claus claimed he didn't know the answer to that, though I asked him many times. All I can say is I understand like few others can why my brutal father Xavier loved Birgit so much he spared her and her sister Vivianna from the curse of the silver by painting them black. He must have adored her more than even my own mother because when push came to shove, he exiled them to the dungeon instead of sending them to the circuit when Ingrid pulled rank on him. Or perhaps, it was his affection for that bastard son Birgit bore him. No matter the reasons, not a day goes by that I don't thank Birgit for being the angel she honestly was to me. Even if her boy has done all possible to make me sorry Xavier ever set his sights on her.

So, in the last act of generosity to me, Birgit's sudden exit bought me the extra week of freedom from having to renegotiate with Byron. He may be one of the biggest monsters in the house, but even the worst criminal can love his mother. That bitch may not have appreciated her while she lived, but to his credit he did take her parting with the proper emotions. After, Doctor Atilla wrapped her in the death shroud and had the Guard haul her to his office for examination, Byron withdrew to his apartment to grieve. No one saw or heard from him for the next seven days.

That was more than a bit of good fortune for yours truly. At that moment, there was a great deal on my plate. With the

Vampire starting to hoover far too close, that murderous agreement I'd made with Fritz, and Ruslan demanding audience with me over some other serious matter, I really needed the break from whiny over demanding brothers, ja?

Oh, and then there was that unfinished business I had with superman. I hadn't forgotten I owed that motherfucker the ass kicking for daring to taking more than he deserved without asking politely. That said, since he wasn't the fellow that was easily found, I'd decided to deal with the more pressing problems first. I assumed I'd have time to seek him out before the end of the week. I certainly hoped he was enjoying the last few moments of his life. Cause I was going to make damned sure he wasn't going to thrill at the end of it. Hahaha.

Once I'd given Doctor Atilla my statements about the things I'd witnessed both with Birgit and the suicide of Vivianna, Noah, and I hightailed it down the stairs headed for the Hall of Records. I'd managed to send word through the late Birgit's fifth floor black collar maid to have Ruslan meet me there. I was in the hurry to find out what the fuck was so complicated that the Captain of the Guard required my assistance to deal with it.

While Noah and I stood around loitering in the Great Hall till Ruslan arrived, I hazarded questioning my lover about the sight that greeting me earlier that morning.

Noah frowned when I asked him about his tryst with Birgit and Vivianna but with some prompts finally told me the story, "I swear to you Mad Maxx, I didn't make any

252

advances toward the ladies, after you left, I returned to my room to study my lines for the collaring ceremony as you had commanded me to do. Several hours had passed and I was pretty sure I'd be capable of doing the ritual with honor."

So, I decided it would be best to take the shower before trying to get a few hours of rest before sunrise. I'd gathered my bathing tools and headed down the hallway toward the bathroom. Birgit called to me from behind the closed door of her room. She was reminding me that she was in possession of that enema kit you'd wanted me to become familiar with. I thanked her but she refused to bring it out to me. She demanded I come into her room to retrieve it.

I argued through her door that going into the lady's bedroom that late at night was undignified, but Birgit continued to say if I wanted that kit I had no choice. Eventually, my desire to please my king led me to do as she insisted.

Ah, Mad Maxx, the sight that greeted me once I entered was, well there are no words."

I snorted loudly then bellowed, "There better be. If not then make some up you bastard. How dare you leave me hanging like this. I want to know what the hell happened next." I swatted his shoulder hard enough to cause me to wince.

Noah grinned sheepishly then replied, "Uhm, well, you saw that gorgeous housecoat, ja? She was wearing only that while posed on her bed in the most suggestive manner. I quickly averted my gaze before she could see my terror. It wasn't that I was afraid of that her nakedness would revolt me, but that the second I saw her like that she'd realize I liked what I was looking at."

I nodded then snickered as I said, "And did you enjoy the view truly? Or was it merely the lighting? I mean Birgit was, what, seventy-three or so?"

Noah blushed and replied, "She said she was seventy-nine until next month."

I nearly choked on my spit as I gasped out, "Birgit was eighty? Nein. I saw her nearly naked too, Noah. She must have been funning you. There is no way her body could be that fine when she was nearly the ancient mummy."

He shrugged then with the grin replied, "Why would she tell a lie? Especially since she shared that bit of information with me before we, uhm, you know, made love."

I slapped him on the back and chirped out happily, "You serious? What a lucky dog you are. Tell me, was it wonderful? Did you fear breaking her? Ah, stop fooling around. I want details, dammit."

Noah's smile melted to the serious frown as he responded, "Mad Maxx, I love you more than I can say, but I really think it's wrong to discuss the details of the gift that great lady gave to me. It's something very special and now

254

that she's gone, it feels like I betray her for saying as much as I have already."

I shook my head vigorously as I replied, "Come off the high horse, Noah. Vivianna told me, uhm before she jumped. That she gave you this so called gift also. You know come to think on it, if you did the deed correctly, it was you that was doing all the giving and those ladies all the taking. Spill it or I swear I'll beat you black and blue for denying your king his desires."

Noah sighed then with suddenness his eyes seemed to turn glassy as he said, "Though I tried hard to avoid looking upon her flesh, she insisted I stop behaving the coward. I stood there staring at her in the awkward silence wondering what the hell she thought she was doing. Then to my surprise she said, 'do you focus on the cruelty done to me by age or does this man before me ignore his eyes and see with his heart?'"

I gasped then whispered, "Birgit had such the way with words, ja? And? What did you say to that?"

Noah's sweet smile returned as he replied, "I didn't say anything. At least not with my voice. Before I could think better of it, I rushed to her. I tell you Mad Maxx, for all my life I've imagined what it'd be like to hold the soft flesh of the female in my calloused rough hands. In those wonderful moments, I forgot that Birgit was old enough to my grandmother. I didn't care if doing this could send me to the circuit. Nothing mattered but embracing that angel and making her my own forever. I had no difficulty worshiping her with my lips or caressing her softly with my hands. I thank you for the mercy of giving me the useful lessons in those skills. However, when it came time to consummate my physical affections for her, I was left confused. Honestly, I only had some idea where to seeking the proper place to enter her. I suppose I thought my cock would just automatically know where it was supposed to go."

I began to laugh wildly, which immediately caused Noah to both blush and to clam up. This was cruel of me to find humor in his virginal innocence but damn me I couldn't help it. After all I was far beyond the overused whore of the worst kind despite being more than twenty years his junior. Hearing this forty plus year old man tell me he thought his cock would seek out the hole to complete intercourse without any input from him was fucking hilarious, ja?"

I admit I laughed too, far too loud and far too long given that not long before that moment I'd been ignorant of the terrors of intercourse myself.

Once I'd managed to get my inappropriate mirth under control I demanded he continue his story. There was no doubt I'd hurt his feelings but because Noah is the loyal man to his bones, he let go his bruised ego and followed my command.

"Birgit realized that I was the novice. She leaned into my ear and begged me to go slow because she was the advanced age of seventy nine. The idea she was too fragile to tolerate my advances frightened me to near uselessness. This did nothing to detour her from taking me to the place of pleasure with her. She directed me to roll to my back. I did as she requested, sure that the best I was about to get was the consolation blow job, you know. Which I was happy to accept, since I knew that such a thing wouldn't injure the generous lady. However, to my pleasant surprise, the moment I was positioned Birgit took to the straddle over my groin. She politely took the second to re-man me with her skilled and generously lubed hand. Once I was ready for the mount, Birgit slipped me inside her palace of fur. I didn't have to do anything but lay there and enjoy the sensation of engaging with another that had always been denied me. I am embarrassed to admit, it didn't take but moments to lose control. I fear that first time wasn't much fun for Birgit, I came so fast."

I stared at Noah feeling struck to dumb as I blurted, "That first time? Wait the minute. How many times did you and Birgit fuck?"

Noah chuckled softly then replied, "You mean how many times did we make love? Ah, well I think I can say at least four times, but that last one was only for her benefit because after being with you a couple times yesterday, my engine was running but the tank was empty."

That caused me to nearly faint as I said in the near whisper, "Four times with Birgit? But if you couldn't come anymore, what the hell was Vivianna doing claiming you took her for your lust too?"

Noah sucked in his breath then replied, "Ah, well you see after Birgit wore me down, she began to feel guilty to be

257

enjoying my favors without sharing with her sister. I suppose you realize too late these woman didn't do anything without considering the other. I assured Birgit I was too worn out to sleep with Vivianna though I was willing. So, she called in her sister, and I brought her to orgasm with my mouth and digits. I wasn't as skilled at this but Vivianna swore it is something I'd learn to perfection with time and their patient instruction. But I suppose now that they are gone, I'll be left incomplete." He dropped his head and covered his eyes as the tears of grief overtook him with suddenness.

I rolled my eyes and then slapped his fingers away from his face as I growled out, "Stop being the idiot, Noah. That permission I gave you to lose your penetration virginity to the female was the one-time thing anyway. I dare say you've taken that mercy I granted you farther than I believe I said you could. I'm happy that you've become the man with the gender of your obvious preference. However, now that you have it's time to wake up from that velvety dream to face the hairy reality baby. Even if Birgit and Vivianna still could view the grass from this vantage, I'd demand you never have sex with them again. You belong to me, remember? I don't share my things. So, dry your eyes and be grateful that I'm going to let your greediness with those gorgeous females slide. Do that again and you'll not find me so eager to forget or forgive."

Noah winced but nodded while saying, "As you say Mad Maxx. I thank you for your mercy though I don't deserve it."

I snorted hatefully and replied, "Damned right you don't, fool. I suppose you can thank me for my mercy later when I bend you over and fuck the brains you don't have out of that pretty head of yours, ja?"

"My goodness, your majesty. No wonder all of your allies fear the sound of your name. Don't let him get to you Noah. His majesty surely doesn't intend to see you sent to the circuit nor does he enjoy the idea of becoming winter fuel for the Russian Guard," Ruslan's voice called out from the entry of the Hall of Records.

I rolled my eyes then bellowed back angrily, "I'll thank you to mind your fucking business while I correct my subjects Ruslan. I believe you've forgotten your place as badly as this dog has. Perhaps I should send both of you for the remedial courses down in the pit."

The huge Russian came forward into our sightline with speed and dropped into the graceful bow before me as he replied, "Forgive my momentary loss of sanity, your majesty. There is no excuse for my bad manners. I throw myself at your feet begging for your mercy."

I waved him off as I responded trying to sound bored, "If I weren't already far too busy to see your flesh ripped off your backsides, you'd find no mercy from me. That said, for the moment, I'll consider holding off on making you squeal like the pig. Now, stop pissing me off and tell me what the hell are you bothering me for in the first fucking place." I slammed my cane into the floor to make sure he understood I was beyond irritated over the weirdness of this meeting.

Ruslan's usual humored expression suddenly turned dark as he replied in the hushed tone, "Your majesty, I've come to you in good faith that what I've discovered is something you'd punish me for not telling you before acting upon it."

That got my attention as I approached him quickly and said, "Ah, so? Are you waiting for me to read your fucking tiny mind? What's the problem, dammit."

The Russian groaned then replied, "I stumbled upon a plot to murder you and your Shadow King."

With a snort I laughed as I responded, "Oh is that all? Tell the bitches to take a number. I cannot believe you broke me from my important tasks to telling me something you could easily handle yourself. Or better yet, take it before the Fur King. Isn't punishing the criminals his fucking job anyway. Let me guess. He's too frail to sign the death warrant you hand to him, ja?"

Ruslan shook his head slowly as he stared at me appearing anxious, "You don't understand, your majesty. The culprits are not within his domain to punish without going through you first."

I stood dare feeling quite confused as I replied, "Huh? Wait, are you saying that you're thinking that Ivan or other Guardsmen are thinking to destroy me and Cary? If so, then I believe that falls under your authority, and not the responsibility of the Mortar King."

He nodded as he said, "It's not Ivan, my Lord. However, you are correct that some of the would be criminals are guardsmen. If they were the only players in this plot, I'd of course handle the situation with vigor and violence. Yet there are several of your subjects involved in this particular plan."

With the anger rising within me rapidly I rushed the brute and yelled into his face, "Are you trying to claim the collars are daring to speak deviltry against the sovereign who suffered unimaginable torture so that they may know better treatment?"

Ruslan dropped his gaze to the floor and nodded slowly as he replied, "Unfortunately that's exactly what I'm claiming. Some of my best men have sworn that these criminals have been holding secret meetings designed to construct the fool proof plan to end the reign of their Mortar King. My sources report there are at least ten Russin guardsmen and their recent silver brides involved in this plotting."

I shook my head violently, "No way Ruslan. I don't believe this. How can you be sure your sources aren't trying to mislead you? This makes no sense. I can believe the Dominant families or any of the sitting leaders seeking to re-seal the Mortar throne, but the collared people? If they kill their king they lose their voice and protection from the Silk Queen's wrath."

Ruslan's brow furrowed and his frown deepened as he replied, "Your majesty, I must confess to you that I believe the real mastermind behind this plot is jet to be named. My men tell me there brothers and the silvers involved seem to believe their lots will be improved if they remove you and Cary in favor of Cary's newborn son." I interrupted the Captain by yelling out,

"Fucking Roselina is behind this. Gott damn that bitch. She's gone too far with her desire for power this time. Well, alright so be it. You know what they say Ruslan, if the child isn't satisfied with what is in their hand and they insist on reaching out to take from his brother, then you smack his hand so hard he never dares to steal what doesn't belong to him ever again. Come on Noah. Oh and you shall call all the Guardsmen together including that useless prick Ivan. Meet me at the edge of the property where the Mortar King has so generously provided the newlyweds with plots to build their new cottages. Be there in thirty minutes. I'll accept no excuses for being late."

I started to haul ass toward the door of the Hall when Ruslan yelled out, "Wait, your majesty. Should I notify the thrones of your intention to interrogate the accused?"

Without turning around I growled in reply, "If you thought that was the proper protocol you should have done that before calling out the thunder of the foundation. Get your lazy ass in gear or I'll retire you by dusk, you dig? Nein, you won't because your replacement will be tasked to do that for your grave motherfucker."

The moment my boots entered the main hall of the first floor I let out the roar of intense fury. Every collar dropped to the prostrate immediately, and every traveling Dominant to his knees. I glared at the bodies strewn about before me feeling my blood coursing coldly through my veins.

I yelled at the top of my lungs, "Worms. Buzzard food. Useless pieces of shit, all of you. How dare you consider to rise up against you king? Ah, well that's to be expected since you think me nothing but the toothless baby that sucks the bottle and dick while pissing his pants, ja? That's the unfortunate vision of your all powerful monarch to have. I've tired of the false stories, and lack of respect I'm receiving from my worthless servants. Noah, you go to the dungeon and pull every single one of those monsters from their tasks. Tell them there supreme master orders them to gather every single fucking collar in this hell hole together in the place I've demanded the Guardsmen are to report to. You have twenty-five minutes to have this completed. I warn you, do not permit even the youngest brat in this house to slip through your fingers or so help me you'll suffer in that bitch's place. Go now, you stupid pig." Noah took off like the bullet from the gun.

I turned my attention back to the now trembling audience at my feet, "Did you bitches go deaf? If you wear no metal I suggest you remove yourself from my sight while I'm still feeling generous enough to set you free. However if you are collared, get off the floor and line up at the front door. Your glorious and merciful King is taking his loving subjects outside for the outing of a lifetime. You may thank me later but for this minute, mind me motherfuckers!"

The entire first floor took to their feet and ran, not walked, in mass headed for the most unprepared front door guards. Ivan and Jonas must have been alerted by one of the retreating Dominants of my sudden aggression toward the collars. They came running down the main staircase heading my way with looks of terror in their expressions.

Jonas called out loud as he could hoping that I'd hear him over the chaos of the many bodies rushing like mad people for the house exit.

"What the fuck are you doing Christian? Did you forget to respect the dead? End this nonsense immediately. There isn't supposed to be any noise for the next seven days. I thought you adored the dearly departed dungeon mistresses."

I laughed maniacally then shouted back, "I don't give two fucks for those fucks, Jonas. The dead enjoy the silence no matter how loud the living care to be. Now be the good little bat and bugger off while the men attend to the unruly children that disgrace this house."

I took off in pursuit of my fleeing subjects refusing to further entertain questions from men that I outranked by miles.

Though I did my best to ignore them, Jonas and Ivan insisted in following behind the frightened mass being driven like cattle by their king. I noticed they kept a safe distance and also had definite expressions of total confusion over my behaviors.

This would have brought me some humor had the situation not been of the grave sort. It's the truth that I'd grown weary of the chronic disrespect and constant plots to see me murdered, or worse. Even if I knew deep inside that this time the trouble had been contrived by the most unexpected of foes. I knew Roselina had managed to spread her poison further than I'd anticipated she could. All this in her attempt to seize control of the throne that was not ever intended to be hers or anyone related to her in the first place.

I may hate wearing the metal crown of the Mortar Palace, but dammit, I've suffered enough to have earned the right to it, ja? And I was going to be damned before I would let that no account black collared tramp interfere with my designs to continue to grace it.

Noah ever the loyal man, and Ruslan the most dedicated of Captains, followed my orders to the letter. Both arrived with the entire population of collars, dungeon masters and mistresses and all Russian Guardsmen in tow. If you'd been the plane flying over the Haus that day, I'm sure the view would have been one to boast to your grandkids about. At least a couple thousand people stood there at the edge of the grass covered lot, staring into the freshly cleared barren earth of the half built new cottages.

With the single step onto the bare dirt, I took the deep breath then turned to face my subjects.

I stood tall then bellowed out, "Noah. Bring me the youngest yard dog you can find. Do not return here without one or suffer for it." I watched with the humored expression as the huge man took off in the sprint to obey my orders.

Ivan came barreling out of the crowd and without any attempt to adhere to proper protocol he screamed at me, "What right do you have to confiscate my property, Mad Maxx?"

I looked down my nose at the haughty Russian as I said without acknowledging his presence, "Ruslan, take two men and retrieve three barrels of petrol. Bring them back and saturate those two completed cottages with their contents. Go now, you worthless idiots." Ruslan, Bora, and Shasha tore off in the direction of the Russian guard shack with speed.

This latest order caused Jonas to step forward from his place of hiding among the crowd.

He joined his butt buddy Ivan in protest as he yelled out, "Are you off your medication, boy? What are you thinking trying to burn down the houses you gifted the Russians? I'm warning you to end this madness before you anger these gentlemen after all that trouble you went through to gain their favor."

My evil laugher echoed across the silent land as I replied, "You believe my actions mad do you? Ah, well shows what you know, batman. Shut the fuck up before I'm forced to remind you of your place, petty prince of nothing." I glared at Jonas defiantly keeping the wary eye on Ivan while Noah quickly returned with the pup I'd requested wriggling in his burly grip.

Jonas was obviously confused by my refusal to submit to his or Ivan's authority. He knew that since I'd become the King and demoted Ivan, technically neither of them could stop me from wielding my power.

The moment Noah reached the spot next to me I shot the look of fury at the trembling crowd and shouted, "Noah, let this puppy go. He will rush toward the humans that he sees. You and your men will bring every silver collared female the dog chooses from this mass of useless worm shit until I tell you the number I have in mind has been reached. If you catching any girl attempting to flee from his affections, bring her to me immediately. Let this game of dog and seek begin."

Noah gently released the eager German Shepard pup. The hush fell over the crowd as ever eye of the females wearing the ring of silver fearfully watched the fuzzy ball of fur rush in their direction While every other set of peepers were glued to the terrifying sight of three huge Russians adding the coat of deadly accelerant to the newly minted cottages only a few feet away.

With a wide grin I pointed in the direction of Roselina and said, "I'm feeling a bit lonely up here without the single kinsmen to guard my back. I believe I see my most honorable sister over there Noah. Be the dear and fetch her for me. Oh and while you're at it, I'd appreciate it if all of the collars with the ties to their king were gathered up to stand with me during this most auspicious display of just how powerful their monarch can be anytime he wishes to flex his muscles, ja."

Chapter 24: Choice Cuts

My goodness. The Mortar King is certainly a bit crabby these days, isn't he? Well, that's to be expected given that he has got too much to do, and not enough time left to get it all done. He thought he'd managed to gain enough loyal followers to help him accomplish the impossible. Guess, he thought wrong. Or maybe, the false allies are wrong.

Mad Maxximillian has always found himself being forced to endure horrors in the dark. Those who never see the light often become blind. The tortured boy that is now a brutal man has been consumed by the darkness and learned to use senses other than his eyes to see through it. Numbness comforts his twisted soul, while brutality and hatred feed it. The Haus's ancient prophecy has finally come true. The population of perverts had created a demon, but that is exactly what the founders realized it would take to rule over this hell they call their home.

The only thing left for the Priceless Mortar King to do is to rise from the inky blackness that has borne him. He knows he must prove he's the one they've all been waiting for, and he will. By illuminating the unbelievers when he sets their world on fire.

I watched in silent humor as Noah and his dungeon masters sliced through the crowd. They wasted no time seeking out the ever increasing number of collars that hoped to share in my fortune of the false power of the Mortar Throne. All the while, that eager puppy rushed about the masses wagging his tail and jumping at the frightened people. Each time he started to approach someone they trembled, fearful that he'd chosen them to attend their lord and master.

Noah arrived first, with Roselina. She was holding the new born son of my Shadow King tightly to her bosom. Her tiny toddler daughter followed them keeping her pretty little eyes on the antics of the wandering puppy. I returned the glare of defiance of her shiftless mother while motioning her to taken the spot behind me. Next, Ruslan delivered his beloved wife, Matilda. Both she and her anxious husband quietly went to stand with Roselina without being instructed to do so.

A no account dungeon master herded the bonded pair of Rudolf and Samual my way. I motioned these fellows to join their kin. Neither man offered argument nor hesitated to obey. I gave the bunch of nothings that call themselves dungeons masters a few more moments to fetch my Shadow King. When after at least five minutes, I didn't lay eyes upon Cary. I bellowed out angrily, "Noah, there is one missing among my kin. Are you as useless as you are stupid? Where the fuck is he?" I set my fiery gaze upon the headmaster.

Jonas called out to me, "Oh. shit, I must apologize to your majesty. Hold on, I'm on my way."

I sucked in my breath and rolled my eyes as I replied, "I wasn't referring to you, pops. Obviously, I'm standing here in the sunlight, but yet cannot see my shadow. I meant where the fuck is the Prince of the Mortar Throne?"

Noah took to the bow before me and said in the soft tone, "Sire, his majesty wasn't gathered up with everyone else. I wasn't aware you required his presence."

I quickly backhanded him with enough force to nearly rebreaking my healing bones as I yelled in fury, "I ordered you to round up every fucking collar in the Haus. I suppose if you're insisting upon it, I'll happily show you I am the man of my word. Ruslan, take this bag of useless flesh to the Pit and give him five lashes. Next time, his aching back will remind him to mind my words blindly instead of thinking for himself."

Ruslan shot the glance of worry at Matilda but wisely decided not to further test my patience by hesitating. He motioned Noah to follow him, which the headmaster did with haste. I kept an eye on the two as they traveled to the back entrance of the dungeon for a few moments. Then returned my attention to the punishment already in action.

Sasha stepped in closer to me and whispered, "Do you wish for me to go find Cary and bring him to you, your majesty?"

I growled back, "Nah Shasha. I just sent my headmaster to be correct as the reward for obeying my orders to the letter. Of course I want you to go get that idiot. You'll find him on the fifth floor in the Voter Wobben's care. Do not return here without him or you'll be joining Noah."

Jonas arrived and tried to take up the spot right next to me. I spun around to face him with the expression of extreme irritation on my face. He shot me the arrogant smile immediately. Without saying the single word I lifted my cane and used the end of it to push him backward. The Vampire's grin faded as I forced him to join the group of captured kinsmen and kinswomen.

However, he didn't dare to deny my physical command. At last, and maybe only for that moment, he realized his power was insignificant in comparison to my own. The Elder knew if he tried to fuck with me during this justified exercise of my rights as both the Collar King and Dungeon Master Supreme I could legally see him to the Pit for it.

Ah, but Meine Liebe what I wouldn't have given to have him give me his usual lip that day. I was itching to see scars on his backside after all the ones he's gifted me with. Too bad for your useless Master that the bat isn't as stupid as he looks. He managed to curb that overinflated ego just enough that I couldn't find just cause to making my darkest dreams come true.

I startled then asked, "But couldn't you have made up some reason? He wasn't even supposed to be there, right?"

Master Maxx chuckled bitterly then replied, "You are right. He had no business to be there, but as the Elder he had the authority to go anywhere he pleased in the Haus or on her grounds, ja? So, his presence there wasn't good enough to see him whipped to bloody. Understand Meine Liebe if ever any of the kings or queens of the thrones demands punishment for Dominants, at the level of prince or princess they must prove some serious rule or law been broken. If I sent Jonas for nothing more than being the rude and being a nosy bastard, I'd receive far worse than anything I'd seen done to him."

I responded by nodding only. I'd managed to ask a question without being given permission to speak and not been punished for it. I assumed, rightly, it best not to push my luck by repeating that mistake.

By the time Sasha had rushed off to get Cary, the German Shepard puppy had selected his first silver female to play with. The tears immediately erupted from the teenage girl's pretty eyes when I motioned for her to come kneel before my feet. She didn't offer to further displease her king by hesitating to obey my command. Though I was unsure how she managed to do this without falling down she was weeping so hard. Hahaha!

That playful puppy managed to pick at least three more to serve their king's pleasure by the time Sasha finally returned. Cary was moving with speed behind the burly Russian appearing awed and confused by the strange sight that greeted him.

I expected my disgruntled Shadow King to cause the scene and earn himself some punishment for it. You can imagine how surprised, pleasantly so by the way, I was when he took the spot next to Roselina and his children without any attempt to speak with me. I nodded the silent approval at him. He returned my thanks by dropping his eyes to the ground. I thought it figured that he was still behaving like the sullen bitch over my well-meaning attempt to protect him from, well that she-wolf in the lamb's fleece he called his wife and best friend.

The puppy continued to wander about the collars, stopping ever so often to offer snuggles to the female wearing the silver manacle. His final pick wasn't as easily selected as the other nine had been. He ran in every direction putting his nose high in the air as he rushed to the very back of the huddled mass. I sent Bora to follow him to his final choice. No doubt the girl I was interested in meeting had taken advantage of her position further from her sisters by slowly retreating to the back of the crowd. Too bad for her, I was in no hurry. I'd have waited all day if necessary for my loyal subject's nose to sniff her out. There was nowhere left to run and no place to hide either.

Once ten beautiful silver collared females were in the position of prostrated kneeling before me I motioned Bora to collect their tattle tale. That pup had done his job to perfection and deserved to be rewarded properly.

Bora captured the joyful ball of fur and approached me until I pointed at the Haus and said, "Take this young fellow to the apartment of the Elder Leo. Tell him that his nephew wishes to gift him with the most loyal subject the Mortar King has ever known. He'll make the wonderful companion for the King's hound Der Makellos."

Ivan shouted, "Nein. Bora you will do no such thing. Take that mutt back to the pup shack where he fucking belongs. You may have the right to tell these nothings what to do, Mad Maxx, but you do not have the authority to confiscate things that belong to the Guard."

With the sneer and sound of thrill in my tone I replied, "Bora, you best obey me or you'll be keeping the head master company for the rest of the day. Sasha, you will deliver Ivan to Ruslan. Tell him to give this brute twice what he's given Noah. You may use as much force as you like to make sure this rude motherfucker keeps his date with the Captain of the Guard. Maksim, Isoff and Grisla, come forward. It's time to repay the debt you owe me for the glorious favors I've lavished on your unworthy and overly furry faces."

Sasha walked over to Ivan prepared for the fight. The ex-Captain glared at his onetime subordinate appearing ready to resist this arrest. His uncanny sixth sense saved his sorry hide because instead of refusing to follow his fellow Russian, he stormed off in the direction of the dungeon entrance. Sasha was forced to run to keep up with him.

As I watched Ivan doing his best to remain the tough bastard in front of the captured audience I chuckled and said aloud, "Damn, the swing and the miss. No worries Florian. I'll get you the Captain to guard your palace forever soon enough I think."

Isoff frowned then cleared his throat before he said, "What do you desire we do with these?" He pointed at the shivering silver girls face first on the ground.

I turned and faced him with such suddenness he instinctually flinched as I bellowed out, "Did I grant you permission to speak, worm? I think not. Be still, damn you."

Isoff dropped to the kneel with speed and muttered the apology followed with the heart-felt plea for mercy over his bad manners.

I ignored the mistaken Russan and instead turned my attention to Roselina.

"Ah, dearest sister. Be the angel and come forward please. I'm in need of your most advanced wisdom in these most important of matters." My tone had abruptly changed to the of the cooing sound from the initial harshness toward Isoff.

Roseline glanced at Cary with the expression of confusion and attempted to hand him his son. I put up my bandaged hand in the signal that she halt her behavior.

"Bring my adopted son with you dear lady. I've woefully neglected to formally recognize the first prince of my Mortar throne. There is no better time than the present to rectify my bad manners, ja?" I said in the tone dripping with honey.

Roselina's initial expression of arrogance ended and all the blood ran from her face. The usually haughty lady began to shiver. I would've smiled if I could've upon viewing those signs that indicated she'd finally found the fear that there was danger afoot. She approached in silence, gripping the infant prince so tightly he began to softly cry from the discomfort of it.

With the slightest bow I calmly stated, "Prince Christian Axel is begging to be held by his king, ja? Barely a few weeks old and already he's wise. See how eager he is to demonstrate his love and loyalty to his powerful lord and master? Ah, this boy shall go far with such natural gifts as to understand his continued existence depends upon earning the favor of the Mortar Monarch. You will hand him over so that I might grant him the blessings he wishes to receive." I opened my arms before the trembling black collar wife of my Shadow King.

Roselina gulped loudly while casting the anxious eyes upon my disabled hands then said softly, "Forgive me your majesty, but giving possession of the Mortar prince over to you may endanger his safety. Your injuries perhaps will result in the accidental dropping of his most fragile frame. If you would permit me to suggest." I immediately interrupted her in mid-sentence.

"How dare you think to suggest any fucking thing to any Dominant of this house, much less to the Lord and Master of it. Oh I know, you are fearful that this baby will be injured by being dropped on his head, because this is something that has happened to you, ja? This brain injury is why you, the no account nothing black collar without title, believe you can speak without permission to do so. Your memory has become so compromised that you've completely forgotten that while your husband is the Shadow King, you are only the vessel that bore the precious prince for him. You have no blood tie to the Mortar King nor do I recall ever granting you the mercy of elevating you to the level above the house servant. I wonder, is it possible that many of your brother and sister collars have also been afflicted by this disordered thinking that you apparently are doing? Do they see you in the embrace of the Dominant Rolf, who holds the shaky title of third prince of the Silk and incorrectly assume his favor grants you some special privileges they aren't receiving? Hmmm, I suppose that may happen if it hasn't already. Tell me something Roselina, if your Silk prince cares so much for, you his Dark Bonded, why does your neck still sport the black metal?" I growled out while sneering at the now observably frightened woman.

Roselina dropped to the kneel before me and whimpered, "I beg your mercy, your majesty."

I sneered at her as I replied, "Beg all you fucking like, worm. It'll do you no good. Hand over what I've politely requested before I have one of these Russian brutes wrest him from your arms by force and then bash his royal head into the nearest fucking rock."

Tears burst forth from her eyes but she didn't dare to push me any further. She placed the baby into my hands quickly. Her sudden interest in saving her own skin after appearing hell bent to shield her child from harm convinced me of her guilt. Any truly loving mother would have fought tooth and nail to protect her offspring, even to the point of risking her own death.

It took all that I had to prevent the wriggling prince Christian from slipping from my weak grip. I pulled him close to my chest without taking any chances of dropping him. Though I was very interested in getting the good look at him. *You should know Meine Liebe, I absolutely adore the babies.* Roselina was the worst of fools to actually believe I wasn't more than willing to do what she obviously wouldn't. If she hadn't been so full of greed for power that wasn't hers to begin with, she'd have realized that everything I had done, and was going to do, was so that Christian Axel could have a life free of the pain his mother and his King has known.

However, she only thought of the comforts of Roselina. Fuck her best friend and grateful husband Cary. and fuck her terminally ill daughter and helpless little son. She was and is willing to use all of them, and anyone else dumb enough to join up with her, to pave her path to the top.

Anyway, pointing out the truth of her low status in front of the collared people wasn't going to be enough. It hadn't been much more than a month since I last I'd stomped my subjects on their heads, and already there was the serious plotting going on among them While Roselina hadn't been there to witness the things I was willing to do to prove I'm not the monarch to mess with. She was in labor that night and since it was the prince of Mortar she was birthing she was given the pass to be absent, remember? These other faces in the huge crowd I did recognize as my recent guests. They should've known better than to believe Rosalina capable of doing anything for them other than getting them killed.

Therefore I happily continued with my plan to keep the possibility of any more plots coming from the collars against their King from ever happing again. Or at least, for the next few months I had left above ground, ja?

Roselina dropped her tear filled eyes to the ground and mumbled, "I've nothing to say in my defense to your most correct statements, your majesty. Again, I beg your mercy and swear that I'm your most loyal servant."

I nodded while allowing my expression to soften to one of mocked pity as I responded, "Of course you are dearest lady. I know if others put you upon the pedestal of power you never possessed, there's not much you can do. These idiots standing around us have the empty heads and cold hearts, ja? The cruelty of celebrating you as their leader is surely unjustified and unwanted by you."

She nodded rapidly then blubbered out, "You know how the gossiping can take on a life of its own, your majesty. I dare say our beloved Lord and Master has often been the victim to it himself."

That made me chuckle as I replied, "Ah, you refer to the wagging tongues that say the Mortar King is the willing catamite that curses any man that uses him for their pleasures with the violent death? Oh, or maybe you mean that silly rumor about my loving to have cock inside me anyway I can get it? Nein, surely you didn't mean that one. I know. You pointing out the constant whispers about my perverted lust for head. The kind that is housed by the neck and not the one between my lovers' legs, ja?"

Roselina glanced up nervously then returned her gaze to the earth as she said, "Your Majesty, I don't believe anything I hear whispered in the halls. I only say that there isn't anyone among us that hasn't suffered from the harsh effects of the idol gossiping."

I sighed then responded, "While that may be the truth of it, dear lady, I believe servants spreading the lies that you are the woman rising in the ranks of power isn't equal to the humiliation of everyone believing you are the overeager house whore, ja? So, since you and me agree that this tendency for rumor that runs rife among these low born nothings needs to end, you'd be happy to assist me in seeing that it does stop immediately."

She nodded and replied, "Ja. Ja. I'm thrilled to aid his majesty in any capacity, he wisely deems me fit for."

I let out another evil sounding chuckle as I said, "Wonderful. Now, Isoff, tell me something. Do you know the lucky bastards among your rank that were claimed as husbands by these ten silver servants of the house?"

Isoff glanced at the prostrated girls for the moment, then while nodding replied, "I do, your majesty."

With the grimace I clutched the baby Mortar prince more tightly then said, "Do you, Maksim, Grisla, or Petrov call any of them wives?"

He frowned as he shook his head slowly, "Nein, Sire. These women belong to the Guardsmen that are assigned to our canine unit."

Feigning surprise I exclaimed, "You mean the Russians that had been forced to feel only the vicious affections of the Haus dogs managed to capture the hearts of these most beautiful works of art? Ah, but that makes sense. It would require much experience handling the wild heart of the animal to obtain such loyalty from those that should have been loyal to another master, ja?" I turned my infuriated gaze upon the terrified silver hostages at my feet.

Isoff appeared confused as he replied, "I don't understand your meaning, Sire."

I nodded as I said, "Of course you don't Isoff, because you're not fluent in the language of the idiot. Get off your knees and gather up the ten fools that are the other half of these corpses." I motioned toward the female silvers.

Isoff's expression went pale but he offered no argument. I watched him rush toward the Russian Guardsmen standing at attention along the ranks of the loitering dungeon masters. Jonas cleared his throat behind me, several times. I rolled my eyes then called out in the irritated tone, "Either blow your pointed nose bat or I'll feed it to Maksim for his dinner. Your rude noises are getting on my last nerve, dammit."

Jonas scoffed loudly then said, "Your majesty, if these pleasure submissives have offended their king in some way, then I don't question your right to see them amply punished for it."

I turned around and glared at the bat as I growled out, "I'm warning you only this one time. Choose your next words to your Lord and Master carefully, sweetheart. My husband, Elder, or the man with many secret connections to the powerful you may be, but immune to my authority you certainly are not. If you dare try to question the legal actions of the Collar King and Supreme Dungeon Master again, I will finally get the chance to prove to this entire Haus you're not the immortal creature you pretend to be."

The Vampire's expression seemed to contort into that of worry as he responded in the slow deliberate tone, "Your Majesty, I've got information from the sound sources that several of these submissives are carrying their husband's child. There are indications, not that I'm assuming, that you intend to burn down property that you've generously gifted to your Russian brothers. If you seek only to fine them by reclaiming your favor, I will hold my tongue. However, if you were thinking of the punishment that's more permanent, I thought you should recall it's illegal to destroy the innocent along with the guilty."

I snorted then with the feigning of surprise I glanced at the trembling beauties as I said, "Is what the honorable Elder says the truth of it? If so, which of you low dogs are burdened with the seed of Mother Russia?"

Six of the ten silver females lifted the pointer finger on their right hands. *As you know Meine Liebe, this is the proper way to answer ja, when asked the question by your master while in the prostrate kneel before him.*

I tisked loudly, then turned my attention back toward Roselina and said, "And they call me the eager whore. Not even thirty days since they first rode the hairy cocks of these

283

brutes they call mates and already their greedy wombs contain the half breed menaces of the future. Ah, well that's truly too bad for them since that law about sparing the woman in the motherly way only covers the girl that bares the fruit of the Fatherland. I dare say not even that bitch Silk queen will give a fig if I burn all sixteen of them. Do you agree with me, my lady?"

Roselina gasped then looked into my storm filled eyes appearing horrified as she replied, "My Lord. Why would you require my agreement? If you say the Silk Queen doesn't have any interest in the future of her lowest subjects, I must believe this to be the truth of it. However, if I may ask, what have they done to anger their King to deserve the most severe of punishments?"

I leaned down into her face and whispered, "Have you already forgotten our recent discussion, dear lady? Are you no longer interested in aiding me in ending this bad habit the collars have about spreading vicious gossip?"

Roselina shook her head slowly then said, "I've not forgotten, Sire. Yet I wasn't aware that being guilty of speaking false tales carried the death penalty."

Another chuckle broke from my throat as I growled in reply, "It doesn't, but plotting the death of the Mortar King in favor of the Prince does." I squeezed the baby slightly which caused him to cough.

His mother set her anxious eyes on him and whispered out, "Oh my Gott. You've heard the rumor that these people have done such an evil thing, Sire? But maybe they are innocent and like you and me are victims of the cruel gossiping of those that enjoy seeing others injured."

I nodded and glared at her in the deadpan stare as I responded, "That is very possible. That's why I've asked for your wisdom in this sensitive matter, dear lady. You see, if I ask them about these awful things I've been hearing, they will surely claim themselves innocent of such a terrible crime. Especially since admitting there is any truth to the rumor would automatically result in execution, ja? If I attempt to get the truth by sending them to visit with the Torture Master and Mistress Jason and Amanda, they may confess to anything to end their pain. But if I let them go without doing anything, well, even if they are truly innocent and totally loyal to their King, others will see it as weakness. Sooner or later, a plot against me and your husband Cary will play out. Then this youngster I hold in my arms will usurp me from my rightful throne. Ah, now you can see the terrible dilemma that's been caused by the practice of rumors, ja?"

Roselina frowned and quickly averted her eyes as she responded, "I understand, your majesty. You asked for my wisdom in this matter and I say to you. You must do whatever necessary to protect your crown."

I nodded my head and replied, "Do you really? Ah, you are not as stupid as I thought you to be. Well that's good to know. It's truly the curse that you're never going to be anything other than the no account house collar, Roselina. Yet, that is your fate, and it's best you never forget your place ever again. If you wish to live long enough to birth that little bastard I know you're carrying for your lover Rolf that is." I pointed at her belly with the wink.

"However, this little bastard in my arms, does pose the greater threat to my throne than any fucking rumor or plotting by stupid house whores. As long as he lives there will be some assholes seeking to replace me with his diaper clad butt." I stood up to full height with suddenness.

Roselina let out the shrill wail and fell to her face in the prostrate as she screamed wildly, "Oh please my Lord. I beg of you. Don't hurt my baby."

I turned my eyes toward Cary while Rosalina groveled. His eyes had gone wide and his color pale as milk. He shook his head nein, but didn't dare to move the muscle or burden me with the sound of his voice.

Without acknowledging the begging Roselina I returned to my place before the ten silvers. Isoff was approaching with ten of the ugliest, hairiest bastards I'd ever had the displeasure to gaze upon. I glared at the men and they all dropped their eyes to the ground to avoid my own.

Isoff said, "This is all of them, your majesty. I must beg your pardon, Sire, but several of them have stated their vives are verified as pregnant."

I nodded and sighed as I replied, "So I keep hearing. Though I could care less about their nasty spawn since none of them considered it before attempting to betray my good favor."

Isoff frowned then responded, "Your Majesty? I don't understand what's going on, but I don't wish to be involved in the murdering of mothers of unborn babies if that's what you're intending to do."

With a glare I said, "Oh you don't? Ah, so you have scruples that I thought impossible for the Russian to grow. I mean after all, the helpless little babies you and your brothers have raped and murdered over the many years I just assumed you'd be eager to add more to your list."

Isoff lowered his head and nodded as he replied, "Your Majesty knows how to kick the man right in his hodensack. Though this you accuse us of is the truth, I must beg that you release me from this dark work you seem to be ready to enact. I've become the changed man and I don't wish to return to the soulless beast I'd once been." He fell to his knees before me appearing genuinely apologetic.

My eyes turned toward the ten accused Russians and I growled out angrily, "Your brother has offered his life in place of yours and the ones you claim to love. Though I doubt he realizes that he has, I appreciate his courage and accept his offer for atonement. I fear I must reject his request because I'm not in the habit of destroying the loyal in place of the useless. Isoff is hereby forever forgiven for the crimes he has committed against the helpless subjugated of this Haus. I further reward him by granting him the honored place as second in command to your Captain. Rise dear Isoff and take the Prince into your worthy care."

Isoff stood and with the most bewildered expression I'd ever seen absent mindedly accepted my offering of the baby. The moment, Christian Axel was safely deposited in his surer grip I turned back toward the group of my gathered adopted family.

"Matilda, come and join the unworthy black collar mother of our Mortar Prince. I require counsel on this delicate matter that only the fairer sex can offer me. It's the truth that I've become the brutal bastard that often reacts before thinking." I motioned the servant to the Silk Queen forward.

The busty woman quickly took the place next to Rosalina and immediately dropped to the kneel.

I motioned Isoff to herd his captured hounds men to follow me as I returned to my original hostages.

The moment I'd gathered every one of the guilty parties together, I yelled out loudly enough that most of the mass of collars could hear my words clearly.

"So, it's come to my attention that there has been a foul plot to see me deposed in favor of the Prince. This of course if proven the truth of it requires I punish the ones involved by burning at the stake. There are ten pleasure submissives and ten guardsmen that stand accused. Of the ten pleasure submissives, there are six more that have yet to take their first breath. Because the accused carry the children of persons that are not full members of the Haus, they aren't protected by the law that forbids destroying them along with their mothers. This entire situation breaks your Lord and

Master's heart. I've suffered many times already for each and every single one of you ungrateful bastards. Have I not provided you with better treatment? How quickly have you forgotten that my sacrifice has assured a future none of you had before I took the Mortar Throne. This constant worry that my subjects are unsatisfied with the hard labors their Monarch continues to do for their welfare isn't something I'm willing to endure. So, here I stand before you. If the majority of you believe this tiny baby could offer you the better leadership than your current King, than I will hand over the metal crown to him this very minute. Go ahead worms. Speak up if you wish to see me abdicate the Mortar Throne." I stood there casting the most brutal glances at every face I could see in that sea of nothings.

Silence reigned among them. Not even a cough nor sound of fidgeting was heard. After several very uncomfortable moments I scoffed loudly then addressed them again,

"I must assume that for the moment you all understand that I'm the better suited to serve as your voice to those that care nothing for your comforts. That should cause me to rejoice but it does not. This is because I understand none of you have any idea how difficult it is to be your King. You believe I possess power and that equals wealth and a wonderful living. I could waste my breath trying to explain to you that's far from the truth but since I bless you with your favors for free, you'll never realize the price I pay to give it to you. This means I must do more than tell you that my power comes with the harshest of prices. I command each of you to witness this brutal display of one of my many payments that assure you'll live the best life possible given the pathetic circumstances we are slaves to."

I motioned Rosalina, Matilda and all ten silver females to stand. They did this without hesitation. I then approached the female black collars and said softly, "Ladies, I grant each of you q vote. Look upon these worthless servants that are rumored to have betrayed your king. Do you advise I end ten young lives plus six unborn ones. Or do I send the focus of the plot, our Mortar Prince to suffer purification in the flames."

Roselina quickly replied, "Burn the silvers, your Majesty. They are nothings, but the Prince is royalty. If he were to perish then the Mortar Throne will be compromised until your great Majesty is able to produce the rightful heir of the priceless pedigree."

I nodded and did my best to appear serious as I responded, "You do have a valid point. and given that I'm the perverted catamite, who the fuck even knows if I'll ever produce such a mythical heir, ja?"

Rosalina frowned and said, "I'd never dare to believe such an insult, your Majesty."

With the chuckle I replied, "Ah, but you already did or else your son wouldn't be the Prince of the Mortar Throne now would he?"

She dropped her gaze but remained silent. Rosalina knew better than to argue that it was her idea to send her gay husband Cary to seek the Dark Bond with me. She'd assumed, like everyone else had, that I was enjoying being used as the plaything of the Elders.

I quickly turned my attention toward Matilda and asked, "And what of your vote, honorable lady? I must find the proper solution to end this foul plotting to see me replaced by this baby. So, do I burn the sixteen or the one?"

Matilda frowned and her eyes rapidly went from the Prince to the gazes of the frightened silvers as she replied, "Well, those submissives if they are guilty of this crime deserve to be punished severely. Killing them will be a loss of property for the house, and perhaps further cause for bad blood between you and the Guard. It seems to make more sense to destroy the object of these plots. I imagine it would cause your Shadow King much grief but everyone knows he is the loyal heart to his monarch. As you already said his black collar mother is of no consequence. She already carries another baby that isn't of the royal line anyway, ja?"

I nodded and pursed my lips as if deep in thought while enjoying the hateful glare Rosalina was given to her rival Matilda.

"Seems that I've got one vote for sending the Prince to death, and one for sending the plotters to burn. Hmmm, that's not helpful. Alright, Isoff. Go and ask the husbands that claim their accused wives are pregnant and ask them if they would be willing to give up their lives in their place." I motioned the baby laden man to follow my orders.

While Isoff quietly spoke with the ten Russians, Rosalina blurted out, "I beg your mercy, Majesty, but burning the Prince won't end the chance that plots will rise to see you replaced."

I snorted and shot her the look of irritation as I replied, "I should have you whipped for speaking without permission. However, I'm most intrigued to hear your faulty reasoning on why you believe destroying my adoptive heir won't prevent further plotting against me. Beware before you attempt to accuse your husband and the true Prince of the Mortar Throne of thinking to dethrone his King. I happen to know that Cary is not only the loyal heart but he also no longer shares your bed. There will be no more possibility that you'll produce another Prince with him. Plus, he doesn't want the burden. That's because unlike you, my lady, he knows the truth of the position."

Rosalina glared at Matilda as she growled out, "You speaking the truth about my husband neglecting his duty to me, your Majesty. It's also no secret that I carry the Voter Rolf's baby in my womb. However, there can be another problem with plotting because there may soon be yet another contender for the Mortar Throne. Matilda is the sister to the late Mortar Queen and therefore any sons she bares also would be of the royal blood line. She has carefully concealed that she's recently become the expecting mother. If you send the Prince to the stake, you'll need to send her to it with him."

My eyes lit up as I watched Matilda begin to tremble and I replied, "Ah, now there is a thought I'd not considered. It's impossible to predict where the next threat to my crown can come from with so many fertile ladies ready to offer their children to fill my stony throne. It's no secret I don't desire to end the life of any of these innocent babies, born or unborn. They cannot help that those around them are seeking to use them to pave their way to higher levels. It's unfair to the extreme that they should pay for that and the guilty walk away to try again, in more ways than one, ja? So, perhaps there is a way to save the princes but block the plots. Tell me Rosalina, will you offer to burn in the place of your son? Matilda, if you bear a son, you'll need to send him to burn or taken his place instead. Up to you."

Matilda gasped and replied quickly, "I change my vote, your Majesty. Burn the guilty submissives and that will scare everyone enough to put the stop to plotting against the Lord and Master of the House."

I chuckled loudly and glanced at the silver females as I said loud enough for all the collars to hear me, "Do you hear that ladies? These woman are eager to see you burn. However, I noticed neither of them are willing to sacrifice themselves for their sons. I bet each of you are feeling the fool to have ever believed these power mad fiends would have made the better regent for your baby Mortar King than this man you've betrayed has been to you. The mother that would send her son to rot in the Mortar Palace as the plaything of the cruel leaders certainly care less for all you, ja?"

The silver females glared in fury at Matilda and Rosalina as did most of the faces in the crowd that I could easily see.

Suddenly one of the tallest of them blurted out, "They promised us if we found the way to murder our Lord and Master, they'd free us from our silver and paint us black."

I pretended to appear shocked as I replied, "Oh my Gott, they did? Wait, who promised you such a fantasy?"

Another of the silver females shouted out, "Both of them promised us, Sire. Those two women in the black collars. This one that calls the late Mortar Queen and that one that lied and said she was your sister through the Shadow King. They came to us separate and said if we could empty the Mortar Throne, they'd paint us black because as the mother of the Prince of the Mortar they would have the power to do this."

I snapped my head toward Matilda and Rosalina as I growled, "Is that a fact? So, this gossiping that reached my ears wasn't the false rumor after all. It's truly the shame to hear that the ones standing behind my throne are the ones in the best position to stab me in the back."

Matilda shook her head nein, while Rosalina quickly blurted, "They are lying, your Majesty. They are saying these things in the hopes that you will spare them and send us to the stake instead."

Matilda then added, "Rosalina tells the truth of it, Sire. Beware of listening to the condemned. They have every reason to see your kinswoman and the mother of the Prince put to death. Once that happens they will be capable of carrying out their crimes and once they succeed, the Mortar Throne will be no more."

I glared at the women harshly as I replied, "But why the fuck would these submissives wish to do that? Once the Mortar Throne is closed, they have lost their voice and their chances to enjoy the brighter future. Let me give you some good advice, dear ladies. If you insist in telling lies, make sure they make some sense before you dare to speak them."

One of the silvers spoke out loudly, "We are telling the truth, Sire. We love our Mortar King, but the promise of being free of our lives of enforced sex and humiliation was too powerful to ignore. We beg your mercy for being the fools to dare to think only of ourselves and be ungrateful for the few comforts you have provided to us in our harsh existences." All of them fell to their knees in perfect unison as if they'd been practicing that move for years.

I banged my cane tip upon the earth and roar in reply, "You say you love me? Making plans to murder me is the strangest way to demonstrate that affection, isn't it? You know the saddest part of this? That is never occurred to any of you idiots that the promises you say these nothings gave to see you freed was bullshit. Don't you think I would have done that for you already if the Mortar King possessed such power. Well, the jokes are on all of you because I can do many things but free the girls that are already collared above dungeon level that isn't my property is illegal for me, for them, for the Prince, for the Shadow King, for every fucking rat that lives in the Haus. Fools, you've betrayed the King that fights for you, and your forfeited your lives over a promise that you should have known was the bold-faced lie."

Isoff returned as I finished chastising the criminal silvers. He dropped to the bow at my feet and politely waited till I acknowledged him before speaking.

"I've done as you asked, Sire. It pains me to report, none of the girls' men agree to be punished in her place. They say, if their wife has offended their King, they will not argue his right to do as the law demands. They also say they won't suffer for crimes she alone has committed against his royal Highness."

I shook my head then said in the bitter tone, "I ask you once more ladies. Do you offer to take the place of your sons if it's determined the Princes must be destroyed?"

Matilda and Rosalina both shook their heads and replied almost in unison, "Burn the silvers, your Majesty. The Princes are innocent of this crime as are their mothers."

I sighed loudly then called out to Cary, "What says you beloved Shadow King? I beg your wise counsel in this heavy matter."

The Shadow King teared up and replied in the stoic sounding voice, "I will go in the place of my son. If his Majesty requires that blood be drawn, I joyfully volunteer to go without fear to see that his will is satisfied."

I glared at Rosalina with the fires of hell in my eyes as I said loudly, "You owe your husband a great debt my lady. He just saved the lives of you and your son. Matilda, you can also be grateful to the real Prince of the Mortar Throne for doing the same for you and your future son."

Isoff signaled to Maksim to arrest Cary but I halted his actions with the hand gesture.

I glared at the crowd as I said, "Your ears have heard the truth of the cruelty that is rife among your number. These two black collared mothers were unwilling to sacrifice themselves for your Princes. These so called loving husbands are unwilling to protect their wives or children. It would be the darkest of days if not for the true heart of your honest Shadow King. He's the only one among your ranks that demonstrates the proper loyalty to you and to his Monarch. This baby that some are viewing as the Prince is nothing but the helpless bag of flesh and until he's seasoned, is nothing compared to the greatness of his father. If either your Lord and Master or this amazing Prince of the Mortar were to be ended, these heartless harpies would become your voice. The next time any of you are approached by some asshole that makes promises of things I've not already freely given to you in return for ending the lives of the men willing to die for you to see you gain as much comfort as possible. Remember what you've seen and heard here this sad day. I cannot allow these misguided submissives reprieve for daring to conspire against their king no matter how much I wish I could offer them mercy. It's the truth that like painting them black such a luxury isn't within my power. So, I hereby condemn them to death by fire. Isoff, Maksim, and Grisla. Divide them into two groups, march them to the cottages that been prepped with petrol. Force them inside, light the flames and guard the exits so that none of them escape their sentence. Go now."

Isoff handed the baby Prince off to his unworthy mother and with speed ordered several of his Guardsmen to carrying out my orders. He kept his honor by not laying a single hand on any of the women nor doing more than keeping his men in line.

The condemned silver collars began to wail, and weep loudly. Two of them attempted to run, but to my extreme dismay their Russian husbands blocked their escaping.

As I watched the beauties marched off to suffer their horror, the numbness within protected my heart from feeling any pity for them.

Jonas took this moment of chaos as the opportunity to slip up next to me. I felt all the hairs on my back raise as he leaned in close and whispered, "You're the most beautiful creature I've ever seen when you are cruel. I almost wish that I was that cane of yours so that I could feel the firm grip of your hand wrapped around me while you send the wicked to their just deserts."

I didn't taking my eyes off the scene of the Russians stuffing the silvers into the cottages as I replied in the growl, "That's twice today you spoke about my new cane. You've spent far too many years admiring the things that don't belong to you, Jonas. That be as it may, I too wish that you were doing something else right this minute. Such as one of those poor little girls that honestly don't deserve to be executed. In fact, it's my truest desire that I was ordering ten from the top instead of from the bottom into that inferno. I'm sure it's unnecessary to say it, but if you don't get back into line where you belong I might just make your dream of feeling my cane become the harshest of realities."

Jonas let out his breath as if in ecstasy and said, "Bonding with you was the smartest move I ever made. I realize that I'm the luckiest Mann in the world though I've been guilty of not telling you that often enough." Before I could retaliate, as I said I would, he retreated with haste to rejoin the rest of my so-called kinsmen and women.

It didn't take long for the wails of fear coming from within the blazing cottages to become the screams of agony. The mass of collared submissives wore the collective expressions of grief upon hearing their doomed sisters cries for mercy. Their pathetic sounds wafted on the early spring wind like the mournful howling of the banshee.

During this dishonorable act of punishment I kept my eyes on the newly created widowers. I suppose I expected to see some expression of emotion, even if only mild grief. Any man worthy of the love of the woman would have had much difficulty remaining stoic while his wife and unborn baby were burned alive only a few feet away. Or at least I thought they would anyway. Turned out, I understood nothing about the wisdom in that saying, 'easy come, easy go.'

Isoff quietly approached me after the sounds of dying came to the end and whispered, "Your Majesty, though it isn't really my place to ask for you input to completely resolve this situation. However, since the Captain isn't present at this moment I feel it's my duty as his second to bring this up to you. No doubt, he'll wish to know how you desire to see that the men involved in this crime be punished While it's Ruslan's domain to reprimand his men, in this case due to the great damage they've helped cause, he'd agree you have some say in the matter."

I nodded and responded in the bitterest of tones, "You assume correctly Isoff. Since your men intended to aid those girls in killing the Master of the House, I believe I have more power to see that my wishes be taken into account by Ruslan than you realize."

He frowned then said, "Agreed, your Majesty. May I offer his Highness, some advice on how best to hurt these brutes in the way that won't cause too many questions from the higher commanders?"

With the sound of resignation I replied, "Of course you may, and I thank you for the mercy of it Isoff."

Isoff leaned in close and whispered, "There isn't any need for so many men caring for the dogs. That's the job Ivan created to assure no Guardsmen was left without something to do. Petrov hasn't healed well from his injury that he got during the funeral for the Mortar Queen and Prince. Ruslan could assign him to this light duty function and it's no secret that Petrov loves working with the canines."

I shrugged then replied, "Okay, I agree that Petrov should take over their positions if this creates no hardship for your Guardsmen. However, relieving these criminals of the comfortable job playing with cute puppies all day doesn't sound like much of a punishment. Especially given that their better halves have paid the ultimate price for their part in this mess."

Isoff nodded as he responded, "This is the truth of it, your Majesty. Yet sending ten Guardsmen to join their women would cause the high-ranking Russian authorities to investigate with vigor. That's something none of us want, ja?"

With the heavy nodding I replied, "Of course I don't want any of those monsters poking around asking questions. So? Stop stalling and get to you point, dammit."

Isoff grinned with the gleam of mischief in his eyes as he said, "You have an awful lot of fellows down in your dungeon that seem to have the same problem as those ten brutes do now that their women are gone."

My gasp was louder than I intended it to be as I responded, "Brilliant idea Isoff. Wait a moment. Can you assure me that Ruslan will agree to see his men are forced to comply with this type of punishment? I doubt your fellows are going to be eager to attend to the lusty dungeon masters needs on a regular basis without requiring chains and lots of beatings. I cannot have my boys so worn out from trying to get their kicks they are useless in training the new submissives or worse, incapable of carrying out sentences on those ruled criminals by the Haus thrones, you know."

Isoff chuckled low as he said, "There is no reason to be concerned about that. Ruslan can make sure they are softened up before they are sent to entertain your dungeon masters nightly. Once me and the other fellows get done thrashing them, they will be pliable as the kitten."

I glanced at him with the expression of wonder creeping over my face as I replied, "You are willing to beat them into submission nightly? For how long?"

He nodded, "Beating the hell out of each other is our idea of a fun time, your Majesty. And for as long as you wish this to happen, it can and will. Daily Ruslan will put the brutes to hard labors, and nightly they can play mares to your lonely studs. No man is left unaccounted for by the top brass, but all them will regret not taking your offer to grant them the quick release from their punishment, ja?"

I held out one of my hands to offer as the gesture of sealing the deal as I replied, "Perfect, Isoff. You've barely taken your spot as second and already you prove yourself valuable to your Captain and to your King." He gently shook my extended paw with the proud grin spreading across his hairy lips.

After that secret discussion with Isoff, I ordered my dungeon masters to return the collars to the house. I watched the brutes in the leather breeches and harnesses herd the huge mass off like the sheep dog does the flock of nervous lambs. My eyes were drawn to the distant figures approaching from the back exit of the dungeons. I couldn't make out their faces but I knew that Ruslan had finished correcting Noah and Ivan. The three of them were returning with haste too late to witness anything but the smoldering cinders that once had been two fine new cottages.

While my full attention was focused on the return of my loyal bodyguard and sexy lover, Matilda had approached with stealth. I almost trip over her kneeling only a few inches behind me before I realized she was even there.

After rebalancing myself from that near spill I growled out angrily, "What the fuck are you still doing here? Don't you have duties to attend to, my lady?"

She nodded but kept her eyes to the ground as she replied, "I do, your Majesty, but before I return to the Silk palace I wished to speak with you."

I growled out, "Go ahead and speak if you dare."

Matilda took the deep breath then said in the softest tone she could muster, "I pray your Majesty doesn't actually believe that I did the things those criminals accused me of. I wish for you to know I'm forever your most loyal and trustworthy servant."

The cruelest of laughs broke from my throat, "You're not as adorable as Ruslan believes you to be, my lady. Save your manipulation skills for his pleasures and stop attempting to stroking my cock behind his back. I know Gott damned well you are hungry for power, but don't think that worries me. I've dealt with and deal with the greediest souls that ever were spit out of the devil's asshole every second of every day for years longer than you can claim to remember. I've captured that stony throne in the palace of pain that rots in the center of this hell hole. With honesty you're no match for the Priceless, nor are you worthy of breathing the same putrid air as he does. I've generously gifted you with a man of fine character and rising wealth. He has blessed you with budding motherhood and pays for your comfortable apartment that is far above your low station. Be grateful for the wonderful things you done nothing of worth to earn and stop reaching for things that are not within your ability to hold. Or dear lady, I fear that I will be forced to see that you share more in common with your honorable sister than just her pedigree."

Matilda gulped loudly then responded, "I thank you for your wisdom and mercy, your Majesty."

I motioned her to leave my presence just as Ruslan, Noah and Ivan reached our position. The three men glance at each other with questioning expressions while Matilda rose with speed to obey my command.

Ruslan kept an eye on his wife's hasty retreat toward the safety of the house as he said, "Your will has been minded to the letter, your Majesty. I must assume based upon the evidence you've attended to the situation to your satisfaction?"

I shot him the look of humor as I replied, "Ja and nein. I named Isoff your second in command during your absence. He served me well. I request you formally appoint him to this post."

Ivan glowered then blurted out, "You cannot remove Petrov from his post nor do you have the right to demand that Ruslan accept your desired candidate for that position. You may be the King of the Haus, but this Guard isn't subject to your authority."

Without acknowledging Ivan's statement I addressed Isoff, "Please fill your Captain in on the details of the things he missed while attending his more pressing duties. I thank you again for your magnificent services this afternoon. It's too bad there are not more like you. If there were I think I would grow the softer heart for our hairy prison guards."

Isoff laughed then replied, "Forgive me for saying this, Sire. But you'd need to possess that organ to see it become fonder of your Russian brothers, wouldn't you?"

With the chuckle I responded, "Ah, that's the truth of it Isoff. Yet I'm content to boast that my chest is void of such useless baggage. Which reminds me, Jonas dearest. Why the fuck are you still loitering? The show is over. I release you so that you can fly back to whatever dark, bat shit filled cave you normally haunt during the daylight hours. Honestly, I thought your kind couldn't be out in the sun too long or you'd be crispier than those criminal submissives over there. Ah, too bad that is only the myth. It's one of the few I really was hoping was true."

Jonas scoffed loudly then approached the group of us and said, "Your sarcasm is one of your most enduring qualities, your Majesty. Though I do grow tired of your underhanded threats. I wonder is it wise to allow your Shadow King to travel back to his idiot Master Wobben unattended?"

I groaned and replied, "The Elder has made a wise point for a change. Ruslan, can you spare a moment to catch up with Cary and escort him back to Matz's place?"

305

Ruslan responded by nodding, then motioning Isoff to follow him. Silently, Jonas, Noah, Ivan and I watched the two of them rush off to protect their Shadow King. Once they were out of our sight Ivan resumed his furious glare at me.

"Jonas, I must ask that you step in and knock some sense into this boy. I've tolerated as much as I'm willing to. He's already gone too far with his delusions of absolute power. Yet still you and the real leaders of this house sit on your thumbs and spin. What the hell is wrong with all you? Have you all become infected with his madness?"

I started to verbally assault the misguided ex-Captain but Jonas interrupted by yelling at Ivan in the harshest tone, "You are dismissed Ivan."

The Russian's glaring turned to an expression of bewilderment for only the moment. Then to my complete surprise, Ivan turned tail and rushed off toward his Guard shack without offering any further argument.

Jonas shook his head while saying, "The man is brave as the lion but as hardheaded as the mule."

"Well at least he isn't the flea covered rodent with leathery wings." I replied flatly.

The vampire shot me the angry glance then calmly replied, "If you wish to stand here and swap insults, which suits me fine. However, my beloved husband, I think our time together could be more wisely used by discussing the big problem you now have that your Palace is missing it's dungeon mistresses. If I recall correctly, your dungeon also has the important Head Mistress vacancy needing to be filled."

I rolled my eyes and blew out my breath in frustration as I responded, "It's unclear to me how any of that is any business of yours. However, if you must know, I'm working on the problem as quickly as I can."

Jonas shrugged then said, "You're not doing it quickly enough. Every second you leave the new recruit female silvers without a guardian, you risk that the Haus coyotes will take advantage them. Or worse, your brute Dungeon Masters will slip in and damage the entire crop. You are already created a huge deficit of viable pleasure submissives by handing the best off to the Russians. Do you really think you can take your sweet time in replacing the only thing standing between the frustrated Dominants and the fresh flesh in the cells below?"

I growled out angrily, "Noah, did I hallucinate that you and the other masters raised me to wear the buckles of gold?"

The headmaster shook his head, "Nein, your Majesty. You did not."

I sneered at the Vampire as I said, "You hear that Jonas? The headmaster says that I'm the Supreme Dungeon Master and not you. That also means I've been deemed more the expert in these matters than you, puny fur prince. So, keep your opinions to yourself and get the fuck out of my presence." I didn't wait for him to respond.

Instead I limped off fast as I could towards the house. Though I wouldn't allow the Vampire to know it, I realized his concerns were valid. A new headmistress had to be put to work before his words of warning became the truth of it.

The moment I was sure we were out of earshot I called back to Noah, who I knew was following without being instructed to do so.

"Noah, it's going to take some time to assign the important duties of headmistress to the right candidate. I've got the perfect woman in mind for the job but while I go break the good news to her, the silvers below are unprotected. Please go stand watch over them until I bring down Birgit's replacement to relieve you of this important duty."

Noah called back to me sounding anxious, "As you wish Mad Maxx. I will do this happily, but before I leave you, do you wish me to send one of your other worthy dungeon masters to act as your protector in my place?"

I chuckled lightly as I replied, "I send you to be whipped and now you are full of lustful interest in me, ja? Why else would you use the flimsy veil of concern for my safety to mask your obvious jealousy."

The headmaster sounded confused as he answered back, "I don't understand why you jest about this when not more than the few moments ago you had to put ten to death for plotting to murder you. I'm being serious Mad Maxx. You shouldn't be traveling around the house without a loyal pair of eyes guarding your back at all times."

My rapid pace halted until Noah caught up with me. I stared into his pretty eyes and replied, "I know you are worried Noah, but there will be times that I must do things without anyone, not even you, there to witness them. This is for your protection as much as it is for my own. I appreciate that you care but don't assume that I'm the helpless babe unable to defend himself if necessary. You forget I managed to survive a damned long time without you around to fight my battles for me."

Noah sighed and for the briefest moment appeared very sad as he said, "Of course you did, Mad Maxx. Just please be careful. I don't wish to have to say goodbye to anyone else that I love today or ever again. I'll be there waiting in the girls' colony until you arrive with their new dungeon mother. Be assured no man or woman will touching the hairs on their heads as long as I'm there to guard them."

I longed to pull him to me and offer the lippy caresses, but I knew there were eyes everywhere watching us. So, instead I motioned him that he was released. Then I stood there watching his delectable frame shrink into the distance as he rushed off toward the dungeon.

It was time to call in the favor that had long since been owed to me at last. I realized the lady I'd chosen was the perfect match for the job, though I knew getting her to realize that would not be easy. I sucked in my air, took one last look at the outside world, then walked into the Haus front door in the brisk stride.

No one, collared nor Dominant was dumb enough to block my journey to the third floor. Each moved aside with speed the moment they saw me coming their way. My path was completely clear of obstacles which means I arrived at Karstin's apartment door far sooner than I expected or actually wished to. Though I'd known the woman for what seemed like the eternity, she still made me nervous as hell every time I had to speak with her.

She answered my knocking rapidly and appeared mildly irritated upon recognizing the identity of her unexpected visitor. However, she said nothing that gave away her true feelings about my interest to visit with her as she bid me entrance.

Karstin closed the door and turned to me with suddenness and said, "Why are you here Maxximillian? Have you come to gloat over your tarnishing my reputation to completion?"

Her lack of candor in letting me know she was still furious I enforced her blood bonding with the silver collared Nicholas caught me off guard.

"My lady, I'm offended that you'd believe me to be capable of such cruelty as that. Is your handsome husband that much of the disappointment that you'd find no further affection for your one time good friend?"

Karstin crossed her arms and snorted as she replied, "Nicholas is the sweetheart that works hard to please me. With him I find no fault. You however are the brute that rivals any other common scum that lives in this community.

How dare you call yourself my good friend. You snub my public announcement of my true love for you and then pair me with the lowest level in the house. I'm the laughing stock of everyone. I cannot even go have a peaceful meal in the Great Hall without suffering the snickers and whispers of those that are enjoying my loss of status. Do you have any idea the humiliation that I must endure thanks to your callous actions?"

I dropped my gaze to the floor and nodded while I said, "More than you will ever realize, dear lady."

Her hard expression suddenly shifted to one of sadness, "Oh my, I forgot whom I was speaking to. Forgive me Maxx. I mean I'm beyond pissed at you, but no matter what you've done, I've no right to play the victim in front of the one soul that has that honor far more than I ever could. Just please grant me the mercy of explaining why you've done this to me. I knew you were upset that I found solace in the arms of the Elder Malfred. But honestly, I didn't believe you'd care as much as you obviously did. My offer to be your lover in confidence was the honest one. You told me that you didn't want me the way I did you. You never told me that I was forbidden to find another to warm my bed after you refused to do so."

I couldn't life my gaze to meet her own accusatory one, because honestly her beauty was causing me great distraction.

"If you would grant me a second I wish to offer you compensation for the things I've unfairly stolen from you."

Karstin shook her head then replied in the exasperated tone, "What do you plan to do to fix this problem? I know. You believe you can pay me off and then I will just forget that I'm no longer welcome in the Haus's high society? It's not the easy Maxx. These people are the heartless eaters of those they mark as less than them. No matter how wealthy you offer to make me, it cannot buy back my good name."

With the long sigh I softly responded, "Karstin, believe it or not I did want you, and to be brutally honest I love you more than you can imagine. I did my best to explain to you why I couldn't be what you needed me to be. These idiots you speak about may view you as damaged goods but they are blind fools. you're such the wonderful woman, that even the Lord and Master of this house is unworthy of your affections. I have dreamed so many times of the perfect world in which I could have you for all my own. But when I open my eyes, the darkness of reality reminds me that can never be. Instead of knowing the joys of being forever your love slave basking in the glory of your eyes, I am forced to crushing subjugation. Daily I must suffer perversions beyond your imagination. This isn't going to end in this life because I was fated to be the Priceless. I looked upon your beauty in the face of your own misfortune, and I found the sweetest of sanctuary. This boy, Nicholas, he is in possession of everything you desired in me, without the curse that I endure. Though you believe I gave him to you as punishment, the honest truth is I sacrificed my own desires for your happiness. So, I ask you to be honest with me too. Do you really think Nicholas wasn't worth whatever you must sacrifice to have his pure adoration?"

Her voice trembled as she softly replied, "I wanted to be angry with you. Nein, I wanted badly to hate you, and at first I think I may have. But you're correct. Nicholas is my rock. He's everything I ever wanted and so much more. To have his love, I wouldn't hesitate to give up all that I have and everything that I am." I heard her sniff lightly trying hard to kept her hidden emotions under control.

Though I needed to know she was truly content with Nicholas, it still hurt to hear her confess her love for him. The things I'd said to her were true. I was desperately in love with Karstin, and even on that difficult day, the strength of it hadn't faded in the least.

It took everything I had to appear stoic as I said, "I'm pleased that you're pleased. However, I'm not such a cad that I don't appreciate your predicament of losing your status in the name of unconventional love. Karstin, have you not considered what will become of you and your black collar children after I'm incarcerated in the Mortar Palace this summer?"

Her voice sounded strained as she replied, "Nein I hadn't Maxx. I suppose I assumed that you'd continue to look after us by using the vast fortune you have at your disposal down there."

The unintended cackle escaping me before I could halt it. Karstin huffed softly apparently misunderstanding my bitterness for levity.

"Am I to assume you've come by to tell me that pretty soon I'm going to have to figure out the way to support my

313

children without your help? If so then I retract my earlier accusation that you're the cruel bastard. Instead I wish to say you're a far worse monster than that."

With suddenness I raised my eyes to meet her own and quickly replied, "I don't disagree with your assessment Karstin. Yet despite that dishonorable truth, withdrawal of my support for you and our children won't be voluntary. The legendary Mortar Palace treasure is just that, the legend. The only thing down there in that toilet is straw, rats and spiders. You already are aware I'm the Dominant without any fortune. Our lost little Marc told you about my hustling business. You've surely been aware that all this time I've been selling my sexual artistry to support all of us. Well, once the leaders make me their prisoner, I cannot be certain that I'll be capable of providing for you any longer. In fact, if I don't find some way to earn the living wage, my regent will be forced to auction me off to the highest bidders in order to afford my upkeep."

I returned my gaze to the floor but this time because I felt the sudden rush of humiliation to be admitting this undignified future to the woman I desired the most.

Her breathing had become shallow and several moments passed between us in silence before she said very softly, "Oh, my poor sweet Maxx. I don't know what to say. I feel horrible to have been in denial so deeply to have ever thought the worst of you. Like everyone else I merely assumed that snob Lucus was spoiling you with gifts that you generously shared with all of us that rely upon you. Magnus and Valentin did say they continued their jobs as your guardsmen, but I assumed that was for the gambling tables only. I suppose I believed what was easiest for me to so that I never had to face the terrible truth of the lifestyle your kindness was bringing to me and our black collars. I'm so ashamed. Can you ever forgive me for being the shallow lady that I surely am?"

Without moving anything other than my lips to speak I replied, "There is nothing to forgive, Karstin. You've been the savior for so many and the perfect mother to the forgotten and unloved. I thank you for your perfect services to me, and to them. Without you, more would have been lost to feed the greed of this Haus of soul eaters. But I didn't come to see you to bid you the early goodbye. Instead, as I said in the beginning, I've arrived to restore you to your rightful place of dignified power. That is, if you're willing to look beyond the present and place your bets on a glorious future."

Karstin took one step toward me and responded, "If you're guiding the ship Maxx. You must know I am your willing passenger. Take me where ever you believe I'm fated to go and I will serve you until the earth calls me home."

I looked up and gazed longingly into her beautiful face as I said, "Then pack your things Karstin. I officially grant you the high title of Head Dungeon Mistress and declare the Dungeon along with everything in it must answer to you." I fell into the graceful kneel at her feet.

Karstin gasped and approached me to offer her hand for the ritual kiss as she replied, "I thought you stole my chances to be named the Silk Queen one day and blocked any chance

I had to make the advantageous marriage with the honorable Dominant. Nein, you are the wisest of Kings, far more clever a leader than I ever could be. You blessed me with the husband of uncommon beauty and rare loyalty. You repair my tattered reputation by placing me at the top of the bottom thus you put me on the path to one day rule on the Fur throne. Even more than that you've defied mother nature's curse on me by filling my barren womb with a million children. Oh my Gott, I love you more today than I did the first time I saw you through Marc's eyes."

I brushed her pale, soft knuckles with my lips and replied, "I thank you for your tender mercy beloved Mistress. I know you shall serve me well. I will arrange to send the proper messengers to inform Jacob and Jager of their trainee's good fortune. I further assure you that once Nicholas has completed his daily training with them he is to be permitted to reside with his wife when not managing his staff in the Great Hall. Take everything from this apartment with you, including our black collars. They will be of great value to help you look after the young ones when they are not in class themselves, ja?"

Karsten smiled brightly but I could see the storm clouds of sadness in her eyes as she said, "Consider it done, your Majesty. Again, I find that words of thanks aren't strong enough to indicate my honest gratitude for the blessings you grant me today, and every day since first we met."

I stood up slowly still holding her hand as I replied, "Your lips say your joyous over this honor I've granted you, but your heart is troubled. What is it you're keeping from me? Tell me of your dissatisfaction and I will discover the route to see you unhappiness erased."

Karstin pulled me to her lips so quickly I couldn't prevent her from engaging me in the brief but passionate kiss. She withdrew from this overly intimate action as rapidly as she'd begun it and turned her back to me. I stood there shocked to stupid listening to what I was sure was the quiet sounds of her weeping.

She turned around to face me and said, "You are the man of miracles Maxx, but in this case there's nothing you can do to casc my pain. Because as long as you suffer as you do, I always will too. That's the true sacrifice of love. It can make the heart beat with thrill or break it with the knowledge that the one you care for the most is beyond your ability to provide them honest comfort. Please leave me now. Go before I'm no longer strong enough to let you go." With those words she broke down into the heaving weeping.

Then swift as the skittish deer she fled into the back rooms leaving me there with her words echoing in my ears.

I slowly limped to her door and politely let myself out of that apartment for the last time. I knew I'd chosen wisely. In my bones I believed that if Birgit could say it, she'd agree the better Headmistress than Karstin Bose, didn't exist. I hoped that eventually, thanks to Noah blocking the advancement of any Dungeon Master into the position he'd need to claim the Fur throne. Karstin would be the only one qualified to claim it as the Fur Queen. To have that gentle lady command as the joint ruler with the conscientious Noah as her king, almost assured that I'd found the way to finally end the chronic cruelty that'd run unchecked for far too long.

As I stepped into the empty hallway, I briefly allowed the tiny bit of comfort to wash over me. Things that day hadn't gone smoothly, but at that moment, they were looking up.

Ah, and just when I thought it couldn't get any better I saw the delicious candy bar laying there in the middle of the walkway. It must have fallen out of someone's pocket unnoticed because there wasn't anyone around to claim it. My stomach rumbled with eagerness as I picked up the found treasure. I had missed lunch and that breakfast Lucus handed me earlier that day wasn't big enough to sate my hunger.

This bit of pick me up was just what the doctor would have ordered. I took a big bit of that velvety treat just as I recalled Doctor Atilla demanding that I leave found chocolate to the rats.

Chapter 25: Ring A Ding Ding, Bat

"Your Majesty. Your Majesty, can you tell me how many fingers I'm holding up?" a deep voice asked.

It felt as if I were floating in the angry seas as I replied through my dry, cracked lips, "First I need to know what the fuck this thing you call fingers are to be counting them, ja?" Though I tried hard I couldn't lift my heavy eyelids to open.

"Oh my Gott. He must have had the seizure. Go fetch the doctor, dammit. Tell him to hurry." The unknown man demanded sounding quite anxious.

I reached out into the darkness and attempted to snatch at the fellow doing the speaking as I mumbled, "What have you done to me you bastard? Where is Noah? I'm warning you the second I figure out what fingers are I will feed them to you."

"Maxx, wake up," I heard Magnus yell out.

I opened my eyes to find the fuzzy vision of the Wolf Voter staring into them far too close for my comfort, "How'd you get in here? Does Lucus know you're sneaking around in the apartment? Are you in the hurry to be sent to the Pit you fool?"

Magnus frowned then replied, "I've no fear of that Maxx because we are nowhere near that man."

With the sudden startle, upon realizing I was laying on my back in the middle of the third floor hallway, I cried out,

"Shit. What time is it? Oh hell, I'm about to be late." I attempted to sit up but the strangest wooziness overtook me with speed.

Magnas caught me before I flopped harshly back onto the carpeted floor, "Whoa there Maxx. Take it slowly before you injure yourself. It looks like you've already busted yourself up enough as it is."

"What? I asked you to tell me what time it is, and you insist upon babbling nonsense." It was then that I caught the faint scent of fresh blood.

Immediately and clumsily I backhanded Magnus as I yelled out full of fury, "How fucking stupid are you? I can see you executed for daring to strike your monarch, you asshole."

The Wolf Voter reeled slightly from the blow I directed at his face but managed to exclaim, "I'm innocent of this you accuse me of Maxx. Valitin and I found you laying here unconscious. We're attempting to get you medical aid, not causing you to need it."

Suddenly I recalled eating the found chocolate bar. Slowly it began to occur to me that Superman may have left it there as the trap. He'd done this dirty trick to me before, ja? Once more I attempted to sit up. This time, I was successful in the action. I saw the entire front of my shirt was damp. Though the black material masked the true color of the drying liquid, the smell indicated it was likely red. My stinging chest made it clear that cuts or stab wounds were the cause of this leaking I had sprung. Yikes.

Fear overcame my expression as I whispered to Magnus, "Unbutton my blouse. I need you to examine the extent of injury I've suffered before I move another muscle."

He nodded while moving briskly to obey my orders.

I listened with great interest to his breathing pattern hoping to discover if I was in mortal danger or if this was merely the superficial wounds doing the bleeding. To my relief, upon uncovering the situation, his expression seemed to indicate relief.

"Well? How bad is it?" I asked impatiently.

Magnas blew out his breath then replied, "The damage to your royal flesh doesn't seem too serious, your Majesty. There are several fresh cuts here, but none of them appear too deep. Maybe it'd be wise to stitch at least one of them, but the others all seem pretty minor. It's not possible you did this to yourself during the fit. Both because of the location of these marks and when we found you, we saw no sign of the weapon on you other than your cane. The only conclusion I can come to is that you've been attacked. Do you recall seeing or speaking to anyone before you fainted?"

I shook my head and responded, "Nein, no one that would desire to see me dead. Though I do believe you're correct in assuming I've been ambushed. I also have the strong suspicion of the identity of the criminal that had done something this stupid."

Valitin, that had been standing silently behind his brother Wolf gasped then said, "Name the sonofabitch you suspect, your Majesty, and we will make him sorry for being born."

I lifted my aching hand to halt further threating from the well-meaning Voter as I replied softly, "I thank you for offering to fight my battles. Yet, in this case, I must be the one to deal with the issue personally. I would be grateful for the aid in getting off this nasty floor, if you'd be so kind."

I offered my arms for their grip to hoist me back to standing. The Wolves moved quickly to do as I requested. For the first few moments I was too dizzy to stand without using the hallway wall to keep me on my feet. While I waited for this symptom of the drugging to pass, I scanned the area for signs of my new enemy, Superman. I'd been so confused until then, I'd managed to miss that kneeling only inches behind my allied Wolves were their unhappy servants. Hubertus and Almut kept their eyes to the floor in sullen silence while I took notice of dem.

Magnus caught my glancing and with the chuckle said, "Well, if you insist on dealing with this motherfucker that cuts you up like the Christmas goose without our aid, that's your right, your Majesty. It's only important that you know we are willing to do whatever you require to assure to your happiness and to your safety. Both of us are beyond grateful for the many favors you've granted us, though we understand we're unworthy of them."

I nodded then hoarsely replied, "Damned right you aren't worthy. Especially since you make pretty promises to serve me loyally yet still haven't told me what fucking time it is.'

Valitin startled then hastily responded, "Last I checked it was five thirty."

The groan of dismay escaped me as I yelled out, "That's doesn't tell me shit, fool. You may have looked at the clock five hours ago, ja? Gott dammit, one of you better find out what time it is to the letter. Or so help me, I'm gonna give you twice the lashes I'm will receive for being late to the appointment I dare not miss. Why are all my allies such fucking idiots?"

Magnus growled out, "Hubertus, hurry to the platform, look at the house clock and return with haste to provide your king with the answer he demands." The huge ex-torture master took off like the bullet without being told twice.

Then Valitin sheepishly said, "Other than giving you the time, is there anything else we can do for you, Sire? Perhaps, we could send for Doctor Atilla to see that the nasty gash gets sewn shut properly?"

I turned my attention to the exposed flesh of my chest as I replied, "Nein, leave the sawbones to his more important work of embalming the honorable Birgit and Vivianna. There is something more important I need one of you to do. If there is any time left to get it done, that is."

Hubertus returned at that moment, knelt at my feet with grace and mumbled, "Your majesty, it's currently twenty minutes till six o'clock."

323

With the loud sigh of relief I motioned him to return to his original spot next to Almut as I said to Magnus, "Ah, I'm grateful to hear that, and I believe there may be just enough time for you to do that favor for me too."

He nodded with the grin as he replied, "Your will is my own, your majesty."

I motioned him to come forward so that I could tell him of my wishes privately.

He chuckled with much humor as he listened to my request then said, "Valitin and I will go make the arrangements. If it pleases you, I wish to suggest that until we can get back you stay here and regain your strength. Almut and Hubertus will be capable of making sure you're able to do that in peace, ja?"

I nodded then said in the irritated tone, "Ja, which works for me if you motherfuckers can return quick enough. I must head up to the sixth floor before six. Stop wasting time I don't have shooting the breeze and do as I asked you to."

The Wolves hauled ass down the hall in the direction of the staircase without further hesitation. I let the wall hold up my weary bones while glaring hatefully at the two still kneeling failed torture masters.

Though neither stupidly said anything, I could tell I was making them nervous. This was evident by the slight trembling I sensed in their heavy breathing. I allowed the silence to continue between us for a bit then with the humored tone said, "Nice weather we have been having, ja?

It's a bit hotter than normal for the spring, but I suppose that's to be expected. With so many wicked tongues stoking the flames of hell lately I think it's only natural it will be a real barn burner."

Hubertus and Almut both said in unison, "As you say, your Majesty."

My evil giggling filled the air as I replied, "I suppose you boys are getting accustomed to the discomfort of the chronic burning though, ja? I guess you both wish you'd paid closer attention to the rapidly changing environment. If you'd been flexing your skills of watching for signs of storms on the horizons instead of assuming nature the passive mistress, you fellows would still be downstairs enjoying torturing the helpless instead of becoming one of them. Ah, but they say the elderly are often plagued with pains anytime mother nature becomes the fickle bitch in the switching of seasons. Tell me Hubertus, is your family doing all they can to offer comfort in your suffering? Or do you find your marital bed as cold as your asshole is hot?"

He didn't lift his gaze from the floor as he responded, "My wife is grateful to your Majesty that you've shown mercy in sparing my worthless life. She's wouldn't dare to complain about the conditions of it."

That caused me to giggle harder as I replied, "I'd think she wouldn't since she's not the one forced to suck cock daily, ja? Or perhaps I'm incorrect that she isn't. I bet it likely that when you return home you're insistent in teaching her the proper oral skills you've been learning from your lusty Master. Hahaha. How about you Almut? Does Blume still find you the sexy lover now that she and you both familiar with the position of playing the mare?"

Almut responded in the throaty growl, "My wife is the honorable woman. She asks no questions because like Hubertus's frau, she is grateful your Majesty the he spared the life of her Mann."

I nodded and responded with the twinkle of cruel mischief in my eyes as I said, "Then the mistake of accepting the word of men that swore to protect their Lord and Master is truly my own. You see that I'm not such a bastard that I cannot admit when I'm the one in the wrong. It's obvious that if I'd placed my trust in your women instead of either of you, we'd would be in the far better situation at this moment. Well, at least two of us would be, that is. So, now that I've realized my error the only thing left to do is to correct it."

Hubertus and Almut both snapped their heads up at the same time. I glared at them coldly enjoying their frightened expressions for a few sweet moments I dared to spare on such a luxury.

"What's the matter boys? Is that terror I read in your eyes? Ah, ja, I think it is. Whatever in the world could make two big brute bitches like you fellows tremble like the virginal frau on her wedding night? Go ahead, give your King the answer he's asked you for." I said without breaking my accusatory gaze from their own.

Almut snuck the glance at Hubertus then softly replied, "I think my brother agrees with me when I say do with us as you wish, and you'll find us happy to serve your will without hesitation. We don't argue that no matter how harsh or brutal your punishment of our useless flesh. It is what we surely deserve. We beg of your majesty to spare our families from the wrath we alone have earned from our Lord and Master."

I pushed forward away from the wall and walked toward them slowly as I growled out in the low voice, "Do not presume that I'm the same foolish boy that once you could easily persuaded to believe the pretty words of those with no more information than he had. You both misled me into demanding the Mortar Throne that you knew only through gossiping and poisonous rumors. The burden I am cursed to bear thanks to your bad counsel I've accepted. If only to assure none of your people must suffer the same fate as I surely will. Do you find your existence at the end of your Master's cocks the rough situation?"

The men dropped their heads low and nodded.

I scoffed then said sneered as I replied, "Of course you do. This dishonorable truth about my shitty life in this house was never the secret to anyone. Yet, until lately you two turned the blind eye to my pain. You like everyone else assumed I wasn't too bothered by the torture of it, ja? Now you've truly found empathy for the pathetic situation that I've endured so long I cannot recall when I wasn't being violated in one way or another. Too bad you've discovered this important emotion too late to save your asses, literally. However, despite your constant failures to keeping your promises to me, without it coming to needing brutality to keep you honest. As I said, I'm not perfect either. No doubt you wished me to assume my place as your Lord and Master because you believed I was the man that was best fit to do the job. I ask you, have I not demonstrated your instincts were valid? Do you find me the worthy and wise monarch? Have I not been willing to do whatever it takes to make sure your children have the future far greater than your best days?"

The big brutes' shoulders slumped as they both nodded with vigor.

"Ah, you're hearts have finally matured, but also it seems you've managed to increase the growth of your brains. Perhaps it's that new diet high in protein the two of you been on recently, ja? Hahaha. Well, better health is the lucky side effect for you boys, but for the moment, I'm more concerned about the welfare of your lovely families. Soon the full terror of your bad advice is going to assure I can never think of either of you without cursing your names to hell. Once I'm taken down by this, my ability to keep your wives, children and the black collars I've assigned for your guardianship will be compromised. If it were within my power, I'd drag you down to live with the rats alongside me. Then, and only then, would the debt you owe me be truly paid. Since I cannot do such deviltry, nor do I desire to see your loyal kinsfolk suffer for the crimes you've committed. I'm forced to make yet another difficult decision today. Tonight when Magnus and Valitin release you from your duties to them, you'll go with haste to pack up your shit and move it all up to the freshly emptied apartment of the lost mistresses Birgit and

Vivianna. I hereby assign your wives the duty of protecting the recently raised headmaster Noah. Because his level is far above that of any of you or yours, he will be given the finest room in your home. Your most honored houseguest will be treated with the respect his rank demands until his duties below recall him this summer. After that, do as you please. From tomorrow until the end of your lives, that huge palace is yours, courtesy of your daily payments to your dark bonded lovers the Voters Magnus and Valitin."

Hubertus and Almut raised dare head slowly, this time dare expressions of shame was replaced by that of extreme shock.

This sight made me laugh wildly as I said, "You say you have chosen your King wisely, yet still you don't have any faith in your own good judgement. Hahaha. Is it such a surprise to receive the very power that caused you to pluck the strings of fate in the first place? As the head torture masters you held false status but were above no one. But as the fifth-floor mercenary bitches of the Voters and Mortar Kingsman, you boys have elevated your family straight to the top of this house. Your next generation will automatically become Dominants, and your grandchildren will never know the cold metal on their throats. So, the next time you bend over and take it up the tail pipe, smile. you're not really being humiliated, ja? Nein. you're happily sacrificing your comfort for the ones you love the most, just like your king has."

Hubertus's eyes began to fill with rain as he responded in the breaking voice, "You honor us to the extreme. There are no words strong enough to demonstrate our gratitude for the favor you've blessed us and our kinsfolk with, Sire."

Almut nodded and also began to erupt with silent tears as he said, "We thank you for your mercy, your Majesty. You are the Monarch of the legends, and this truth makes our crimes against you far more disgraceful than either of us could ever conceive."

With the snort I replied, "Oh no worries there, Almut. The years of harsh treatment will erode away all the filth of your shortcomings. wipe your eyes brutes. Just because you're being treated like women doesn't mean you should start behaving like the pussies."

Magnus startled me from my bullying of the ex-torture masters, "Your Majesty, here are the things you asked for. Do you need aid in rebuttoning your blouse?"

I turned around and nodded as I replied, "Ja, and hurry the fuck up will you? I'm really cutting this close as it is. Ah, and Valitin, I've given your servants strict instructions to vacate this floor immediately. you'll need to release them early so they can obey my orders."

Magnus began to rapidly close up my shirt as he said with the anxious sounding tone, "You're throwing them out of there house? Shit, Maxx you are the mean bastard. I mean no matter how angry you are at them it seems to me giving them over to us to use as we please is harsher than killing them. Besides, what did their wives and children do to earn homelessness?"

With the bellow of fury I yelled, "I've just about had all I'm going to take of this constant disrespecting. If I wished to bash their babies heads into the wall, I'd do it without any commentary from a dipshit such as yourself. You will remember to address me properly and without the insult of questioning my royal will, dammit. Otherwise I'll see you lowered further than I've raised either of you."

Valitin quickly bowed low then said hastily, "The honorable Magnus is an idiot, your Majesty. I beg you forgive his stupidity. I give my solemn oath that your will is to be obeyed with speed."

I calmed down the bit and replied, "That's bedder. Taken the lessons from your ugly brother Magnus, and you might live to become an old man, jet. As it is, I've given these nothings the gift of setting their families free, after they've finished their service to your worthless asses. The Silk Palace is theirs, and you boys shall be responsible for paying off Amanda and Jaison's offsprings metal debts."

Magnus halted his buttoning task with a gasp, "Huh? What the hell. Are you seriously that pissed that I forgot to call you, your Majesty to punish both of us with poverty, Sire? Do you realize how much it costs to do as you're asking us to do?"

I chuckled and motioned him to finish his dressing service to me as I replied, "It's not the punishment you stupid fool. I merely am forcing you to pay these mercenary men the honest wages for their hard labors to you. I'm aware it costs ten thousand dollars per freed black collar. That's not so much since you have lots of years to rip off enough funds from the house fees you charge the residents to collect what you'll owe them. Besides, maybe Amanda won't be the fertile gal if you're lucky. Plus, I'm releasing you fellas from coming up with rent money for your own apartment down here. By summer, you'll be moving up to the fifth floor where you belong. The Voters don't have to pay for their homes. With no wives or children of your own eating away at your income, you'll still end up rich men before you can grow the full beards."

Magnus's frown return to the sly smiling as he said, "Ah, I understand what this is all about. Why you clever bastard. Oh, uhm, I mean very well, your majesty. As Valitin says, your will be done."

I shot him the cautious glare and replied, "That's better. Now, if you don't mind. Get the fuck out of my way. I'll see you tomorrow afternoon in the chapel. Let your brother Matz know, my sins are piling up and I'm in desperate need of attending confession. However, make sure he recalls that I mustn't engage in rigorous religious practicing. Light prayer will have to suffice, for now, ja?"

He smiled while bowing and backing away, "I will be sure to bring my bible and the holy water, your majesty."

I ignored his attempts to behave the smartass as I pushed past him headed for the staircase. The anxiety of showing up at the Vampire's place late aided in making my still sluggish frame move faster. Jonas was sure to use any excuse to make this new arrangement I'd made with him worse than it already was sure to be.

I saw that Jonas was standing in his doorway with his arms crossed. He seemed to be watching the steps with the expression of anticipation on his pointy face. Though he'd more than once appeared overly eager to have me visit with him, this behavior was more over the top than normal, even for this weirdo.

Before I was completely on the sixth floor landing I called out in the snotty tone, "You waiting for someone Dracula? I know. you're worried Van Helsing is sneaking around with the plan to drill the stake into your black heart, ja?"

Jonas scoffed then replied, "You should be the one concerned as you are about to get drilled, not me."

That caused me to slow down in my approach as I replied in the serious tone, "If you thinking to rape me Jonas, better reconsider it. I've the doctor's note that says I'm on light duty for at least another week or two. If you've forgotten that conversation we had last night, I've got to wonder if your dementia has progress further and faster than usual for the elderly."

He gave me the evil looking smile and said, "My memory is like the steel trap, boy. Come inside, and I'll prove that to you."

My inability to set off his temper with my usual insulting put me at ill ease immediately. I'd known Jonas far too long to not recognize the signs that he was up to no good. For a second, I considered making up some reason to excuse myself from our pre-arranged meeting. In hindsight, it would have been the smart move to make. *But as you've already discovered in our time together, Meine Liebe, I've always been the fucking idiot.*

He pushed open his apartment door and with the overly dramatic bow bid me to enter. I glared at him hatefully while I rushed past him accepting his invite. The moment I was too far inside to easily retreat he closed the door and locked us inside together. I spun around, temporary startled by the clicking sounds of his bolts. Jonas stood there eyeing me with the expression of wantonness that I'd come to fear more than I care to admit. Doing all that was possible to appear unruffled by his creepy leering I stood my ground and gave him notice I was prepared to fight if need be.

Jonas didn't come any closer but instead said in the low tone, "I appreciate that you've kept your word. Now that your here, I'm eager to prove that I'm just as honorable. Please take a seat and visit with me for a while. I'll get us some nice hot tea to refresh us while we speaking. Ah, do you take sugar or cream?"

That made me roll my eyes as I replied, "Are you practicing your comic routine, Jonas? If so, then I must say, better kept your day, uh, I mean, night job cause you're not the funny man. What the fuck is this about? And since when did you begin using good manners? I didn't even know you had any."

The Vampire's weird grin turned stormy immediately, "Obviously my manners are more advanced than yours are, boy. If you wish, I can be vulgar instead of the gentleman during this completion of our contract. Either way I think it's in your best interest to sit down as I've kindly asked you to and to stop running that pretty mouth of yours."

I continued to disobey his request as I replied, "How is it that in all this time you never bothered to notice if I enjoy sugar or cream in my tea?"

His face fell into the expression of confusion, "I suppose I didn't think knowing such trivial information was important. I apologize for that. I'm happy to fix it. Sit down and tell me all about the things that bring you pleasure, Christian Axel." He motioned toward his gothic styled sofa.

I narrowed my eyes into the squint and replied, "You've violated me in every way possible and as often as you could. Yet even knowing me with such deep intimacy, my tastes were not of any concern to you before today. So, what's caused this sudden change of attitude with you, Jonas? I think it's only fair to warn you I don't enjoy playing mind games with you or anybody else for that matter."

The Vampire nodded then after blowing out his breath he responded, "Okay, letting me know what you don't like is the good place to start I suppose. You prefer honesty in our communications and I definitely can respect that. Just remember, that goes both ways."

A sudden bout of dizziness overtook me. This threatened to send me sprawling to the floor. Despite my anxiety over the Vampire's odd behavior, I decided to taken him up on his offer to take the load off. With slow deliberation I limped over and sat down before I ended up falling down.

Jonas seemed overjoyed at the thought that I was surrendering to his silly attempts to play the mannerly host. The moment my bottom hit his sofa cushion he took off to his kitchenette to retrieve that tea he'd been babbling about. While his attention was temporarily distracted, I did my best to clear the fog from my mind. If I was to have any hope of keeping this fiend from taking advantage of me during the finalization of our new agreement I'd need to have all my wits about me.

Though I'm partial to coffee, I wasn't going to turn down his offer again. My throat was parched and at that moment even the water drawn from the bathtub would have sounded good to me. Jonas returned rather quickly carrying the fancy tea service on his expensive silver tray. I recalled this fine china set from my time in his bat collar. He reserved using it for only the most important occasions. Seeing it for the first time since those dark days of my youth, caused the involuntary shiver to crawl up my spine.

The vampire saw that I was staring at this with the expression of nervousness written across my features.

He shot me the sheepish smile and said, "It's not every day that I'm entertaining the Master of this Haus. There should be the extraordinary for the extraordinary, ja? As you realize, I'm demonstrating the honest respect by giving you the best I have to offer. Here, allow me to remove your coat. I wish for you to stay for a while, ja?" I nodded that I was happy to permit him to do this.

The second he pulled the heavy trench coat from me, he let out the loud hissing noises, "What the fuck."

I chuckled heartily as I replied, "Ah, so this myth about the vampire repellent is true. That's good to know. I'll have my tailor get to work on making boxers of it for me."

He rapidly backhanded the comedy out of me. He ripped the bulbs of garlic on the string that I'd had Magnus fetch, then hide under my coat, from my chest while cursing loudly.

"Gott dammit, you're pranks are starting to piss me off, boy. You realize this bullshit you've pulled will foul up my house. I wonder if the black collar maid will find this joke so funny while she figuring out how to get rid of the fucking stink."

I shrugged then replied, "Tell her to use whatever magic she already using to kept the stench of bat shit to the bare minimum. The way I see it, likely she be grateful for the improvement of the air quality in here." He backhanded me again, harder this time.

Jonas was preparing to strike me once more, but to my surprise, halted mid-blow and said, "Return to your seat, Christian. I refuse to allow your childish antics to cause me to lose my temper. I've swore to myself that I'd refrain from using domestic violence to maintain the peace between us. I must apologize for that momentary lapse in judgement. It won't happen again."

He pointed at the place I'd been sitting. I decided it was likely for the best not to push him any further. Without any more smartass commentary, I did as he asked.

He tossed my jacket and the garlic across the room. Then leaned down and placed the delicate cup with the matching saucer and spoon on the coffee table in front of me. I kept the baleful eye on him while he poured the brown liquid into it. Then he grinned as he poured the correct amount of cream for my taste without any input from me.

I sucked in my air and said, "Perhaps I want sugar too?"

Jonas snuck the humored glance at me as he replied, "Since when? You may eat sugary treats to near sickness but when it comes to everything else, you choose to stick with the bitter. Always just enough cream or milk in your coffee or tea to add color but nothing else." He quickly headed to sit down in the love seat across the table from my spot on his sofa.

I raised my eyebrow then responded, "If you assumed you already knew this about me, why the hell did you bother asking me about it earlier?"

Jonas shrugged and chuckled softly, "Ah, well I thought you'd appreciate my attempt to offer the mercy of giving you the illusion of control. You know since after you sign the contract between us that'll be the thing of the past."

With the scoff I growled out, "I told you I don't enjoy the head games Jonas. Stop being the asshole and hand over the written agreement you've created. I wish to read it over to make sure you're not trying to slip something in there other than what we've discussed." I held out one of my mangled hands.

"You're still the paranoid bastard you've always been, Christian. I can assure you that the paper contains nothing shady. It's the sad they when my own husband and son insinuates that I'd be so dishonorable to attempt to double deal. You know there was the time that you'd trust me to be fair without the need to create the signed document between us." He reached into his old-fashioned gothic styled vest and pulled out the item I'd requested.

"Ah, ja you're correct there pops. Thankfully since then I've learned to know better than to take the wooden nickels. You've no idea how many times I've wished the human aged backwards. That way, I'd been the wise old man instead of the innocent fool that was easily mislead by your charms and lies. If it's all the same to you, I'd like to get this over with quickly. Give it to me and have the lancet ready so that I can sign it after I double check it." He grinned widely and placed it in my impatient hold. "My goodness, Christian. I'm impressed. It's not often you surprise me, but I confess this time you have managed it. I assumed you'd do everything possible to stall sealing this deal for long as you could. Are you really in such the hurry to sell yourself back into bondage to me when you've spent so much energy trying to remain free of it?"

Almost absentmindedly, because I was focused on checking that agreement, I replied, "Go ahead and gloat if it brings you pleasure, Jonas. I may have won the battles but in the end I've lost the war. I'm not so stupid as to not realize in another few months I'm your prisoner worse than before I broke my metal. Seems to me you're the idiot in the hurry to pay for what you already owned in the first fucking place. So, I'll place my name on this line, then call you Master just as I did so long ago. My only solace is that at least this time I'm getting something of value for the freedom you're taking from me." I finished checking the document and impatiently motioned for him to cut my finger.

He frowned while he leaned across the table and pricked it deep enough to release the ink required to see our business completed. I didn't hesitate to making my mark. Then I pushed it back toward him so that he could add his own.

Jonas sat there staring at the drying blood as he said, "You could've had much the first time too if you'd have met me half way, you know. All I've ever wanted is for you to love me the way I do you. This time, I'll try harder to make your service to me something you're grateful to do. It's my sincerest desire that one day you say to me your happiness is my pleasure Master, and you truly mean it."

I chuckled bitterly then replied, "And it's my true wish that you die the most horrible death imaginable, Master. If you agree that would bring you honest pleasure also, I think I can finally provide you with perfect service."

Jonas's glared at me full of barely restrained fury, "I hope that getting that off your chest has brought you some peace. Because I'm not going to be putting up with anymore of your lip, Christian. I expect that from this moment forward, you'll use that tongue to excite me and not piss me off. Oh well, I need not threaten the priceless since he's more than aware of the horrible things that happens to the rude submissive, ja?" He rapidly drew his own blood and signed below my own.

I dropped my eyes to my lap and replied, "As you wish, Master."

His head snapped up with suddenness with that strange expression of confusion as he said, "Wait, aren't you going to try to sneak in a final smartass remark? I mean, there is at least another minute or two before the signatures dry."

I shook my head, "Is that what you want me to do, Master?"

The vampire pursed his lips as if deep in thought. "Uhm, not really. I mean, I just assumed given your past behaviors. Ah, never mind. I said this time things are going to be different between us, and I see you are as willing as me to see that's the truth of it. So? What would you like to do now?" He offered the friendly smile at me.

I kept my eyes downcast as I responded, "You're the one in control, Master. I live only to serve your pleasure."

Jonas snorted then leaned back into his loveseat roughly as if irritated, "I've done nothing but dream of this moment since that day you escaped your metal. Yet somehow now that I hear you speaking the words I've longed to hear they sound, hollow and unsatisfying."

I shrugged then replied, "That's because they are, Master."

He shifted in his seat and his brow furrowed, "But I told you I wanted honesty between us. How can I be sure you truly trust me, love me, and enjoy being with me if you're only doing what I tell you to do?"

I shrugged again then responded, "A submissive is the well-trained liar, Master. This you already know. I will tell you that I trust, love and enjoy you all day, because if I don't you'll hurt me till I obey. Yet, no matter what you enforce upon me, all you manage to do is make me hate you more than I already do."

Jonas nodded and blew out his breath, "Ja, I know what you saying is the truth. However, that doesn't answer my question though. What would it take to get you to do what I really want you to do?"

I took the chance and lifted my desperate gaze to meet his frustrated one as I responded, "Help me escape, Master. If you would set me free, I can swear on my honor that I'd love you like I've loved no other. I'd even agree to live with you in the outside world and attend your every desire happily. Can you do that? Would you do that?"

Jonas's expression lit up as he whispered, "Do you really mean that, Christian? You're not just saying this because you think I'm incapable of making it happen?"

My breathing became shallow with barely restrained excitement as I nodded wildly, "Ja, I mean this, Master. Take me away from here, and I'd be your honest lover for the rest of your days. I swear you'd never be sorry because I'd make you the happiest man on earth."

The Vampire leaned forward across the table and said in soft tone, "Why must we leave the Haus for you to love me with honesty? Am I to assume it's not really me that you hate, but what? my taste in interior decorations? Or is it the bother of having to travel up the steps to the sixth floor to visit with me perhaps?"

My heart sunk, "I take back everything I boasted before, Master. It seems I'm still the fool that I told you I wasn't anymore." I dropped my eyes back to my lap feeling truly humiliated that Jonas had bested me yet again.

He laughed with the evil sound as he replied, "Ah, what's the matter, my little pet? You need not be upset. No one can predict the future, you know. Anything is possible for the man that works hard to get what he wants. You say you would give me your heart if I can see freed of the Haus. Maybe if you prove to me that you really can love me, then I'd be more willing to try to see you satisfied too. What do you say? I'm ready to explore this possibility if you are."

I winced and replied, "As you wish, Master."

Jonas growled out, "You're off to a poor start, my pet. Never mind. I suppose if this is to work I'll need to do my part too. So, I told you earlier today that I had the surprise for you. Aren't you curious to know what it is?"

With a groan I replied, "I'm sure I can provide the good guess, Master."

He laughed for the few moments then motioned me to look at him as he said, "I'd be offended if you weren't so damned cute when you behave upset over the idea that I enjoy partaking of your skills. It's also thrilling to me that for the change I've something I think you're going to love. Come with me." He stood up and motioned that I was to follow him.

Though I tried hard I couldn't prevent the moan of dismay from escaping me as I stood to obey his command. Jonas heard my noise of discontent. He turned and shot me the glare of caution but continued to lead me down the hallway toward the red door of his bondage room.

He stopped at the entrance and turned around to face me, "I'm aware of the fragility of your skill sets as of this moment. I spoke with the doctor this morning and he's assured me that by middle of next week if you pass examination he'll reluctantly lift all sanctions. Though I don't wish to wait for the taste of you that I need to retain my youth, I realize the blood coupling cannot be completed correctly without slowing down your healing. Therefore, as agreed, I won't demand full special services yet. Until next week we'll just have to explore other avenues to assure that you don't leave me the unhappy husband every night, ja?"

I nodded my head then glumly replied, "As you wish, Master."

He reached out and grabbed me by the chin to force me to look into his eyes, "You will have to try harder if you wish to convince me that you're capable of honest affection for me, boy. I know the obvious disgust you feeling over your duties in our bedroom are partly my fault. I've not always been the gentle nor kind partner, ja? As I said, today we shall start over, and this time I'll demonstrate that I can be the Mann worthy of your love. Okay?"

There was no attempt by me to veil my fury as I replied through gritted dentures, "As you say, Master."

Jonas smiled sheepishly, "Ah, I suppose I'm also partly to blame for your dental situation too. I realize now that I could've been merciful. If I'd not lost my temper and thought to leave you some back teeth you'd not require fancy dentures to chew your food, ja? I suppose I apologize for not thinking of that. Do you forgive me?"

Meine Liebe, I swear to Gott I nearly lost my shit when he said that. Thankfully the rage within me was so hot that I was literally paralyzed by it. All I could do is stare at him blankly.

The Vampire apparently took my lack of response as the one he desire as he said with the relieved expression, "Wonderful, so that ugly business is settled at last. Now, come with me, my pet. Allow me to wash away the bad blood between us and build the strong bridge that will connect our hearts at last. I've waited a long time to lavish you with all the affections you've more than earned." He pushed open the door with his free hand and pulled me by the chin inside with him.

He was correct in his promise to surprise me. His private room that he'd tortured me in too many times to recount was barely recognizable. If you recall, since the they he'd first tricked me into the blood bond with him, there had only been that awful bondage bed, and the huge black dresser in there. The Spartin furnishing had always added a bit of creepiness to that place.

Well, he'd obviously spent a pretty penny redecorating. On the walls were numerous paintings of peaceful cottages nestled among majestic mountains and green fields. On each flocks of lambs and their shepherds wandered about. That nasty metal bondage bed had been replaced by the luxurious canopy bed. The curtains were of the deep red color with the matching down stuffed comforter and many coordinated throw pillows. On the once barren stoney floor lay many thick, soft elaborately patterned rugs.

All that was pretty stunning to see, but my shocked eyes were drawn to the center pieces to this changed space. There, where the lancet drawers once sat, was the most modern model of television available for that age. Next to this amazing machine was the finest stereo speaker set that money could buy. Of course, not everything I spotted in the room was a pleasure to the senses.

Next to the lavish bed was this ugly black metal table, with many drawers. The top one was open slightly and I could see it contained lancets, handcuffs, and to my dismay many nefarious sexual devices that Jonas tended to enjoy torturing me with. Yikes!

This unsettling sight was made possible thanks to the light provided by the newly installed chandelier. It seemed to be made of crystal and designed in the over the top gothic design to which Vampire is partial.

Jonas had stopped dragging me by the maw and moved aside so that I could have a clear view. For several moments he'd stood next to me in complete silence. I didn't have to look to know his face sported the huge grin of pride over my obvious surprise at the changes he'd made.

Upon deciding he'd given me enough time to survey the territory he said, "What do you think of our new bedroom, husband? Surely you'll find our lovemaking less of a burden now that you'll be surrounded by pleasures and comforts while you service me."

With a wince I rapidly dropped my gaze back to the floor as I shrugged and replied, "As you say, Master. Is that what you desire this minute? That I service you?"

The intense startle overtook me when he suddenly grabbed me by the upper arm and growled out, "Gott dammit, I've spent a fucking fortune trying to provide you with things I was sure would please you. Yet still your responses to me are as cold as the stone throne that sits in your Palace. Tell me what is it that I've not provided you with here that would cause you to thaw if only a tiny bit? Is it the color you dislike? Or maybe the music box isn't fancy enough? Tell me what the hell else do you want in here and I will move the heavens and earth to see that you get it."

By reflex I tried to cover my head while falling to my knees as I yelled out full of the unexpected rush of fear, "Forgive me, Master. I beg your mercy. Please don't."

If this involuntary reaction caught me off guard, the next one nearly blew my mind. I broke down in the crying jag on the floor right there at Jonas's feet. Try as I might I could not end this pathetic display of weakness. Nor could I comprehend what had set it off in the first place.

It was no secret that I could've easily bent Jonas in two, at least beaten him into the blood stain with my cane, now that I was the big fellow. His outburst of fury had long since lost its ability to send me running in terror, or at least I thought it had. There didn't appear to be the reason for my breakdown of the epic level merely because he was pissed I didn't thank him in the way he believed he deserved.

I've considered this situation many times since it happened. The only thing I've come up with to explain it is his gripping me while shouting must have set off some residual trauma. That Stasi had tortured me far beyond what any human should endure and live with the memory of it. If I'd been under less stress or had been permitted more time to heal before that afternoon with Jonas. I doubt I'd been so easily broken. However, time wasn't on my side and I assumed that Jonas wasn't either.

I think at first, Jonas believed I was faking this emotional breakdown. He stood there doing nothing but staring at me while I wailed and writhed. As my internal pain grew more intense, the Vampire finally realized this was no act. His initial stance of indifference became one of deep concern.

He dropped to his knees and attempted to wrap his arms around me. I let out the scream of mindless terror and tried to crawl away before he could embrace me. The Vampire understood at this point I was responding on the auto pilot. There was no doubt I'd lost complete control of myself.

It took all of Jonas's strength to prevent my escape from his clutches. He latched on tight and held me to him. No matter how much I struggled he refused to let me go. I'm ashamed to admit I bit him several times and even attempted to scratch his eyes out.

You may find it interesting that later he told me that I was barking and howling like the wounded dog the entire time. He said the more he tried to assure me that I was safe, the louder my noises of agony got. The Vampire believes to this day, based on the faraway look in my eyes and strange behaviors, this was the violent flash back of severe PTSD he witnessed.

I suppose that his theory is possible. However, I suspect there was more to this embarrassing display then merely his setting off the symptoms of stress that I demonstrate sometimes. That drugged chocolate and whatever that bastard Superman did to me while I was unconscious likely is the true culprit.

Anyway, eventually this weird fit passed. I slowly calmed and offered Jonas the heartfelt apology for that unmanly display. To his credit he didn't try to further humiliate me by teasing about it.

Instead he motioned me to follow him to the fancy new bed. I was a bit anxious that if he insisted in pushing me into special services without giving me at least a few minutes to shake off that experience. I was sure to freak out again.

Yet Jonas once more shocked me by not immediately demanding sexual favor. Once on the bed he pulled me into the spooning cuddle without ordering I disrobe. I lay there in his arms listening to his heavy breathing for what seemed like forever before he said, "I'd forgotten how good you smell, Christian. What cologne does that bitch Lucus give to you to wear these days? I must know the name of it so that after you are home with me for good I can get you a gallon of it."

I rolled my eyes, thankfully he couldn't see that move, as I replied, "I'm not wearing any, Master."

He shook me gently while chuckling as he replied, "Stop lying. I can definitely smell something absolutely delicious on your flesh. Though your beautiful to gaze upon without needing the artificial additions, I dare say your natural smell is as foul as any man's. So, if you wear no perfume then it must be the soap you bathe with."

I tensed up as I felt Jonas's hands begin exploring my chest with interest. He halted his mild groping and sat up with suddenness. The Vampire rolled me to my back and took the straddle across my stomach. I braced for what I assumed was his move to sexually assault me.

He dropped and buried his nose into my chest. I heard him taking in his air with force. Then he lifted and ripped open my blouse with the single violent move. The sharp cry of shock escape me before I was able to stop it. He sat there glaring at my flesh with the expression of complete fury over coming him.

"I thought I knew that magnificent scent. Who the fuck has been sharpening their blade on you, Christian? Did Lucus do this? If so why? I won't tolerate him copycatting my blood letting ritual with my donor, dammit. Tell me, has he forced you to give him the taste of your mystical gifts?"

I shook my head and did my best to not appear as worried as I truly was, "Nein, Master. Lucus's perversions aren't of the blood sucking."

Jonas frowned but didn't take his eyes off the unexplained wounds as he said, "If not him, then who did this to you, Christian? These resemble the marks the vampire leaves when they feed."

My stomach flip flopped with the idea that Superman was possibly another of the vampire people in the house as I replied, "I had a strong seizure only an hour before I arrived, Master. I had the pen knife on me and was checking it for sharpness. You know, to prepare for that contract signing. It seems I injured myself with it when the fit overtook me," I lied.

The Vampire's facial expression soften as he said in the calmer tone, "Ah, okay that makes sense I suppose. Besides, if there were another vampire attempting to steal the gift that belongs to me exclusive, they'd be left wanting. Since at the moment no blood coupling can be completed due to your severe injuries. I apologize for frightening you, Christian. However, I demand until Doctor Atilla gets your epilepsy under control, you stop fooling around with sharp objects. You could've killed yourself, baby."

I nodded and did my best to appear apologetic as I replied, "As you wish, Master. I thank you for the mercy of your wisdom."

He smiled at me, then to my disgust engaged me in the deep kissing. This adoration of my head with his tongue went on for quite a while. That action led him to become the man eager for release. Jonas was beyond being picky about the way he found it. After swearing he wasn't going to break the agreement between us, he removed my clothing. I was still incapable of doing that on my own thanks to my broken hands.

He of course stripped too. I was told to hold still while the nasty bat fondled, caressed and licked at my flesh. This was his best attempt to incite lust in me but as usual my cock isn't the skilled liar my tongue is. The lack of physical response from me didn't appear to bother him like it had in the past. He just kept repeating,

"Patience, Jonas, Patience."

Finally he tired of this game and requested that I prepare to give him the oral service. I didn't offer quarrel over this expected demand from him. To be honest, I was eager to get this gross part of our visit over with. Mostly because I was in the hurry to check out the cool new electronics in the room. Hahaha.

Jonas prevented me from starting the service and leaned over to the retrieve something from that ugly metal table drawer. I grimaced thinking he was getting some nasty sex toy to humiliate me with.

He grabbed the unmarked bottle and leaned back into the fancy pillows as he said, "I'm going to pour this entire bottle onto my schwanz and hodensack. I expect you to clean up the entire mess before it stains these sheets with that talented tongue of yours. If you manage to do as I ask perfectly, I'll give you the reward for being the good boy."

I shot him the glance of irritation and said, "I thank you for the mercy, Master."

That response made him laugh so hard he had some trouble squeezing the contents free of their container.

Then the third surprise he had for me spilled across his pale flesh. The sweet smell of chocolate filled my nostrils. I could hardly believe my eyes but the scene was undeniable. That bottle I thought was nasty lube was filled with my favorite desert. I was drooling so bad as Jonas covered himself with it, I thought my slobber was more likely to ruin the sheets.

Despite the fact that he'd placed this goody in the grossest places possible, I happily followed his command. My eagerness to make sure not a single drop went to waste, sent Jonas into sexual overload. He moaned, pitched, clawed at the sheets and yelled out for the Gotts through the entire kinky blow job. It goes without saying, the Vampire blew his top far sooner than he'd hoped to do.

For the only time I could recall, the salty taste of this forced indignity didn't bother me at all. That's because I was able to quickly dispatch it by swallowing and gratefully wash it down (along with the horrible after taste of it) with the velvety goodness of the delicious chocolate.

Once I was sure I'd exhausted my supply of the sweet treat from every nook and cranny of Jonas's nether region, I ended my searching for it. As I lifted from his lap I was greeted by the sight of him staring at me. His glassy eyed expression was broken by the appearance of the most contented smile I'd ever seen on him.

"If only I'd had this idea sooner, I'd been the most relaxed man in the house, ja? Christian, baby, that was, ah, magnificent. You've truly outdone yourself. I must say you've more than earned your reward." He reached out and caressed my cheek that was sticky with chocolate.

I craned my neck to get another look at the fancy television and stereo system as I said excitedly, "I thank you for the mercy of it, Master. How long do I have to enjoy them?"

Jonas grabbed my mane and pulled until I was forced to look back at him, "You think watching a little television or listening to some of that awful music you seem to love is the reward? Nein. Here, give me your right hand."

The excited feeling left me as I obeyed his command. I tried hard to hide the disappointment over his refusal to release me.

He snatched my paw with enough force to cause me to grimace in pain. He smiled wickedly, then before I could protest, he tore at the linen wrapping. Each time I attempted to pull my hand from his grip he'd jerk it hard till I quit moving. It didn't take him long to expose all the fingers on it. He briefly examined each of my discolored digits.

"The swelling has receded substantially. I believe you're capable of receiving the token of my true affection without fear of it cutting off your blood supply," he said just as he reached under one of the pillows and pulled out a small box.

I sat there stunned to stupid as the Vampire opened it to expose the silver wedding band contained within.

"I realized the other day that our wedding night wasn't the romantic one I'm sure you'd hoped it would be. That is something I cannot change. What is done is done, ja? However, I also shortchanged you on the trappings any bride of worth expects their husband to provide. As you can see,

I'm wearing the match to this one on my own right finger. You will wear this with pride. No one, man nor woman of the Haus, will ever dispute that your happily wedded, and off the market ever again. Now, what do you say, Christian?" He said as he forced the ring onto my second largest digit.

I wanted to tell him I wasn't interested in wearing his damned wedding band. That if this was the reward then hell surely is the place of peace. However, for a change, I wisely kept my complaints to myself. After all with Jonas, his tendency to make me wear the marks of his ownership had in the past been far worse and permanent. Such as cock cages and branding. Yikes.

"It's beautiful Master. I thank you for the mercy of it."

The Vampire's eyes lit up with joy as he said, "Do you really mean that?"

I nodded then replied, "I do, Master."

"Then I'm contented at last. Our first day together and already we've come far to reaching the point of true romance, ja?"

I nodded again and replied, "If you say so, Master."

His smile became less sure and the expression of unease once again cast the shadow across his face as he said, "I suppose you're still interested in checking out the luxuries I've bought for you, ja?"

I brightened up and said with the furious nodding, "Ja, I thank you for the mercy of it, Master." He didn't get another word out of his mouth.

I'd already hauled my naked ass out of that bed. Without any concern for my undignified state, I rushed over to the electronic pleasures. Jonas could have sprouted into a dragon with two heads or threatened to work me over with the pinwheel. I was beyond giving a shit about anything but those wonderful creations.

Once again the Vampire overindulged my simple whims by not disturbing my explorations for the next hour. I didn't even notice if he'd left the room or was still in the bed watching this show of curiosity. It didn't take me long to find the detective show that interested me and the rocking radio station with music that intrigued me. I couldn't decide which I enjoyed more, so I let both of them play at the same time.

It didn't take long before I was whirling about the room dancing to the music. All the while doing my best to see what that clever detective was going to do to figure out who done the crime. This may have gone on for the rest of the night had the deep, throaty laughter of the Vampire not brought me back from this electro heaven I was in.

"Christian, at least let me put some breeches on you. I cannot be sure my lust will remain contained with you shaking that gorgeous bottom in front of my hungry eyes. Ah, and I seem to recall you're due back in Lucus's care at nine. That's only fifteen minutes away, you know."

My wild gyrating halted abruptly, "Oh shit. Can you help me get dressed quickly? If I'm late he'll have the right to see me punished for it. Ah, I mean I thank you for the mercy of your aid, Master."

Jonas didn't give me any trouble about my momentary lapse in proper protocol. He patiently aided me to become presentable once more. Then he forced me to endure more of his nasty deep kissing with fondling, yuck.

The moment I was able to pull free of his octopus arms, I rushed toward the door. To my irritation he was following hot on my heels. There was no choice but to wait for him to undo his locks, while he snuck glances of desire at me.

"Before you go, there is one more surprise I have for you, Christian."

He turned to me and I saw the cane he'd confiscated from me years before in his claws, "I believe you're now legally able to possess this tool. I happen to know you're quite skilled at the proper use of it too. I'm sure Milo would've wished it to be given to the man that'd happily kills, to have it."

I stared at this long lost object unsure if I was hallucinating as I replied, "I thank you for the mercy of it, Master."

Jonas handed it to me and said, "Again, you behave like the puppet only able to repeat the simple sentences or nod in agreement. I fear no matter what I do, you'll find the way to thwart my honest attempts to earn your affections."

I took the cane from him, limped into the hallway, turned to face him and replied, "You know it's impressive that for the Elder, you're growing older without the side effect of getting wiser. I told you in the beginning that I'm incapable of loving you the way you want me to. You didn't listen then, and you're getting harder of hearing every time I see you."

The Vampire glared at me as he replied angrily, "Well looks like my coach turned back into the pumpkin. At least that means I can have the decent conversation with you now that you've dropped that boring submissive speaking. If so, then you can also tell me without fear of retribution why you believe you cannot love me the way I need you to."

I cut the cane through the air just barely missing his pointy nose as I replied flatly, "Exactly."

Then I hoofed it out of there, leaving the Vampire both confused and pissed in my wake.

Though that meeting with Jonas had gone far smoother than I ever could have dreamed, I realized that I now had far worse to worry about than trying not to anger the volatile Elder. His remarks that the strange cuts on my chest looked like vampire feeding marks scared me. I knew Superman was my only real hope of finding the secret way out of the house. So despite his rudely drugging me and taking our agreed upon services without asking. I wasn't willing to alienate him to the point that he'd withdraw from his part of our deal. Though I was sure going to read him the riot act about being more careful not to be break what he was buying.

But it hadn't occurred to me that Superman was one of them blood suckers. This certainly would explain his tendency to take my favors with such brutality. It also made sense that he was escaping detection of the guard and Stasi by using the vampire powers he was getting by sipping my fluids.

However, Jonas had said Superman wouldn't be capable of getting the strength he needed from my veins because he couldn't complete the act with me. I knew of course, Superman had in that first attack. But this time, he'd drained me more heavily but ended it before fucking me. I hurried down to the dungeon to retrieve Noah thinking it likely someone interrupted him before he could finish.

As I stepped into the darkness of the dungeon staircase, the horrific pain ripped up my spine. I nearly went head first down the steps trying to grip at my aching groin. The agony came in the rhythmic waves emanating from my ravaged sphincter muscles.

I found myself unable to do anything but lean into the mortared wall of the staircase and moan. My truest despair was not caused by the recognition that Superman had obviously used drugs to put more than my mind to sleep. Otherwise I'd have recognized sooner I'd been sodomized during my moments of unconsciousness.

While the possibility Superman had seriously injured me, yet again, was bad. Understanding that I was going to have to murder this rapist Vampire motherfucker with haste was far worse. Once he was gone, my last hope of avoiding the palace was going to be dashed.

My pop and click pulled me out of my deepening hell as I heard Jacob call out, "Oh will you look at this? It seems everyone getting so wasteful these days. That's a sure sign there's too much wealth around here, ja? I mean, holy hell they are leaving the perfectly gorgeous hunks laying around everywhere."

I let out my breath then said in the trembling tone, "Thank Gott your here, Jacob. Can you please help me. I cannot stand up."

My eyes strained in the darkness expecting to be greeted by the face I was grateful to see. Yet instead of the skinny Dominant dressed in pink, the disheveled weirdo from the walls approached.

With the gasp of terror, because I was in no condition to defend myself, I whispered, "It's you, Superman. Where is Jacob? You better not have hurt him or I swear I'll kill you, dammit."

Superman's hairy lips took the expression of the huge grin.

He popped his tongue and in the perfect impression of the honorable Jacob replied, "Oh my goodness. This kitty has claws."

To be continued in book four of
The Most Brutal Man in Europe Series

About the Author: Alexandria May Ausman

Alexandria May Ausman in her 16th year was diagnosed with Schizophrenia. She was quickly abandoned by her foster parents. While still only a teen, she was forced to battle this devastating illness alone.

Alexandria has struggled with lack of a support system, numerous psychotic episodes, exploitation, homelessness, and an uncaring mental health system.

Alexandria raised two healthy children. After obtaining her bachelor's degree in psychology she worked as a child abuse investigator and became a diagnostic psychologist while acquiring her Master's in psychology. Alexandria never forgot the experience of 'slipping through the cracks.' Her life's goal is to help people suffering abuse and/or mental illness have access to necessary services. By accident, she became a model of 'gothic attire' and the World Goth Queen.

She began writing a fictionalized account of her life experiences after a catastrophic return of psychotic symptoms. Today, Alexandria is retired, and homebound due to crippling symptoms of Schizophrenia. She currently lives in Tallahassee, Florida, with her loving husband and a loyal support dog.